Sahm'Allah

(The Arrow of Allah)

in

St. Augustine

by

Howard Johnson

senesis word - st. augustine, florida

PHONE: 904-687-1865   **CELL:** 574-265-3386

Website: http://hojowriter.com   (Not up yet)

Email: Senesisword@yahoo.com

SASA-txt-16C25W

The Cover:

The St. Augustine Lighthouse about three in the afternoon in late April 2004. The author and his wife, Barbara were returning home to Indiana from their winter stay in an RV park in Zolfo Springs when they stopped to visit the lighthouse. This unusual photo was taken directly toward the sun which is behind the lighthouse. The bright area of sky showing slightly below the center and behind the lighthouse surrounds and is evidence of the sun. The photo can barely capture the brilliant contrast between the blue sky and white clouds so apparent to the eye of the on-site viewer.

The staircase inside the lighthouse - looking up toward the top.

Books by Howard Johnson - year of publication

Blue Shift - 2002 - An unusual Armageddon type novel about people dealing with a rapidly moving star that will pass through our solar system in thirty years. Its passing and possible annihilation of life on Earth is a menace man can do absolutely nothing to prevent or change. The main characters battle with government agents and others to ensure the danger is portrayed accurately when the information is released to the public.

Energy, Convenient Solutions - 2010 - A non fiction book on energy, its history, sources, uses, and possible future technologies. This is a book written for average Americans, not skilled technicians and scientists—a comprehensive look at everything related to energy production, transport, and use. It gives special attention to the real effects of increased atmospheric CO_2.

Starring - 2012 - An anthology of the author's short stories, mostly Science Fiction, written between 2002 and 2012. There are a variety of fiction stories that take place on Earth, and other planets near and far. Some even involve other universes. Many describe and interact with strange alien life forms.

The Crystal Feather - 2012 - The author's second Sci Fi novel is very different from the first and won an important award. It received first place in the FWA Lighthouse novel contest in 2008. Dr. Draxel Syl enjoys a wild, off-Earth adventure with a drop-dead gorgeous lady named Leura Clauson. He wonders about trying to learn what really happened, who Leura actually is, and what these strange happenings are about. He ends up involved with two different related human species from two universes.

Climate and Much Worse Dangers We Ignore - 2014 - This publication is a collection of Howard Johnson's commentary on Global warming/climate change from 2005 to the present. It includes some commentary from other individuals and remarks about other possible menaces to our planet. Mr. Johnson, says about this book: "This controversial book is quite the opposite of Al Gore's *An Inconvenient Truth*. Al's book had very little truth of any kind in its pages."

Memoirs from the Lakeside II - 2015 - is a collection of memoirs from a long and varied life that replaces several earlier editions. This large book contains more than 90 memoirs, stories from the author's experiences from the early 1930s to the present. It contains a number of essays, letters, poetry and commentary from a wide range of sources of general interest. There are also quotes, mostly one-liners, from 270 famous and not so famous individuals dating as far back as before the Christian era. The author saved these favorites over a lifetime. It makes a terrific coffee table book.

Double Jeopardy - 2016 - The second book of the *Blue Shift* trilogy starts several months before the end of the first book with a slightly different cast of characters. Dr. Charlie Botkin, from Cal Tech, one of the worlds top authorities on high energy physics is asked for help in determining just what the effects of the star's passing so close to the Earth might be. Working with the original group from Gemini, Crazy Charlie helps in their effort to keep the public calm. Armed with increasingly accurate projections of the path and possible effects of the ghost star, Charlie predicts there is a good chance it will pass with little or no effect on the Earth. In the midst of this, a new menace appears as a large asteroid is on a collision course with Earth. International cooperation on an unprecedented scale is organized to try to solve this unexpected new cataclysmic danger. The book ends right after the Ghost passes Bernard's Star, four years before it passes Earth.

Days of the High Morning Moon - 2016 - **This** is an adventure thriller that takes place in Northern Indiana in and around Lake Tippecanoe where the author lived for many years. A retired Chicago homicide detective, Ragan Yoder, moved to a home he bought on the lake where he grew up and spent his formative years. Because of the influence of the son of one of his best friends from high school days, Ragan was soon involved in helping the local law enforcement agencies cope with a small but devastating crime spree. Murder, mayhem, theft and deception plague him as he becomes deeply involved in catching criminals of several different kinds. In the midst of this, he meets and falls in love with a lovely nurse.

The Ghost Passes - Should be released in 2016 or 2017 - The third and final book in the *Blue Shift* trilogy picks up the story just before the end of Double Jeopardy and follows the next generation of the original Gemini group as they deal with increasing international tension and unrest as the Ghost gets closer to Earth with completely unknown consequences. The situation is complicated by the differing opinions and predictions of a number of scientists and others. The media simply goes wild making things even more hectic.

CONTENTS

CONTENTS

✳ *Calder Voss* ✳

Chapter 1 - Attack on Geothermal Well #2
✳ Saturday, March. 2, 2013 ✳

A coyote lifts his muzzle and howls. He stands on a rocky Nevada hill named Elephant Head sprinkled with sage brush and mesquite. The night sky is cloudless, moonless, and star peppered. Light pollution from the town of Battle Mountain to the northeast and the brightly lighted well site to the west hides all but the brightest stars. Headlight beams of cars and trucks traveling I-80 pierce the darkness as they ramble east and west. "Voted the Armpit of America" according to one huge sign west of town by the interstate, Battle Mountain is a desolate, treeless human presence in the high desert.

At four in the morning, the sound of the starting of a powerful diesel engine breaks the silence. The truck engine from the tractor of the drilling rig at the center of the fence-protected well compound is running and should not be.

✳   ✳   ✳

The pleasure of spending several cold Nevada nights in the equipment warehouse running 48 hours of tests on one of the new countercurrent heat exchangers for the planned power plant is not much fun. This equipment will use the heat from Geothermal Wells number two (GTW2) to generate steam to drive the turbines of the power plant. On the hour for two days I record temperature and flow readings. In between night readings I catch some Zs on a cot in the warehouse office. Calculations based on those readings are done by computer back at the main office of Berne and Associates near Roswell, New Mexico. I'm Calder Voss, chief engineer for the drilling of GTW2.

Designed to tap into a geological hot spot deep in the earth, the well will become the heat source for a geothermal power plant connected to the grid. My engineering responsibilities will continue through the construction of the power plant. Well number 1, about a hundred miles east of Elko, had to be abandoned. Fault problems discovered shortly after drilling started proved the well to be economically impractical.

✳   ✳   ✳

The unmistakable sound of a large diesel engine morphs into my dream. In the dream I am operating the drilling rig's big diesel engine. The sudden absence of the sound takes me out of my dream and causes me to sit up startled and wide awake. The dead silence woke me. My watch shows a quarter to five, about ten minutes before my hourly alarm will go off.

Did I dream the diesel sound or did I hear it? No diesel should be running at this time. An uneasy feeling grips my insides. A sixth sense warns me something is amiss. I climb out of my sleeping bag, stand up and stretch. Starting to shiver in the cold warehouse I slip into my denim work pants and flannel shirt, and put on my shoes. The time for the five o'clock instrument readings and operations check is near at hand.

A single step on the cold floor and BANG . . . THUD. A deafening explosion and following concussion shakes the building. A sharp jolt bounces the concrete floor and almost knocks me off my feet. I stagger for the outside door through air fouled by showers of dust shaken from the bar joists in the ceiling. I reach the door and step into the clean, cold early morning air, coughing, choking and unable to see much from the dust in my eyes. When my eyes clear, I observe the compound bathed in the pinkish orange light of the cesium vapor lighting that keeps the site near daylight bright. The quarter mile wide clearing around the well is empty. The drilling rig is nowhere in sight. The sound heard while dreaming was the engine of the rig. The flat pad of crushed rock where the rig stood for a month is now a low mound of broken rocks and soil about twenty feet across. Clouds of steam rise from the entire mound. GTW2 has been blown up by a large charge exploded deep underground.

While standing and looking across the empty compound, I wonder who, why, and how. Two small flashes from the far side of the well clearing are followed by the thunk, thunk of two bullets piercing the wall within a foot of my head. Instinct drops me to the ground. Then the *crack, crack* of gun shots reaches my ears. *What the hell is going on?* I struggle to decide what to do. Some sort of attack is in progress, *who and why?*

My deer rifle is in the trunk of my car on the other side of the warehouse. My mind clicks in place as old Army Ranger training kicks in. *Gotta get that rifle.* The distance to my car is about five hundred feet, almost all in the open. I take off at a weaving run and put the warehouse between me and the shooter. The sound of three bullets hitting the wall before I reach cover around the corner of the building spurs me on. I dive for the ground and peer back around the corner to find from where the shots are coming. No luck! The firing stopped. I pick myself up and cross behind the warehouse. My car is about three hundred feet away, out in the open. The intervening space is partially shielded by the warehouse. Two of our trucks are parked between me and my car. I back up a few feet, make a running start, and dash for the closest truck. The truck provides momentary cover. Then I charge for the next one.

The bright flash of an RPG headed for the second truck catches my attention. The truck is my obvious destination for cover. A quick detour from my original path keeps me a good eighty feet from the truck when the rocket hits. The truck explodes in a white-hot blast, somersaults and lands upside down. The explosion and fire shield me from the shooter's sight. The remaining open space between me and my car is about a hundred feet. With few choices, I zigzag across the space and reach my car which fortunately faces the shooter's position. I open the trunk and grab my rifle and a case of cartridge clips.

My eyes scan the area for cover. Two figures are running for a service truck about a quarter mile across the clearing near the guard shack. *They must think the explosion of the truck got me.*

About eighty feet in front of my car and off to the right are several stacks of steel drilling pipe strapped together, a relatively good spot of cover for a sniper. I run to it, slipping a cartridge clip into the rifle as I move. As I near the stacks of pipes, the delivery van starts across the open space toward the warehouse. I'm thinking the truck is loaded with explosives to blow up the warehouse and everything in it. *I must stop the truck.* I reach the pipes, position myself, adjust the scope, and tighten the sling on my rifle. The truck is half way across the clearing, heading for the warehouse.

My first and second shots kick up dust right in front of the left front wheel. My third shot blows the tire and the truck careens left, close to rolling over. Somehow the driver regains control and starts again for the warehouse. I pour the rest of the clip into the engine compartment hoping to damage something vital and stop it—no luck.

I slip another clip into the rifle. A fusillade of automatic weapon fire spatters the stacks of pipe. The sound is of dull bells ringing in rapid succession. None of them comes close. I concentrate firing the next clip into the driver's seat. The truck slows and turns to the left. The driver's door flies open and a body tumbles to the ground. Again, the truck starts toward the warehouse under the control of its new driver. I concentrate the third clip on the front brakes. My bullets hit and shatter the rotor. The wheel locks and the truck shudders to a stop.

Two figures jump out and run away from the truck. I try to pick off one and miss before a white fireball erupts vaporizing the truck. *Thank you!* I mutter, knowing the explosion was intended to destroy the warehouse and all the vital equipment inside along with yours truly. Concussion from the explosion breaks the straps holding the pipes together. They roll and bounce toward me. I scramble away from the cascading pipes in time to keep from being crushed. The end of the nearest pipe catches the calf of my left leg, rips the entire pant leg off and gashes the back of my calf. The wound is a nasty one, but no blood is spurting so no artery is cut.

Keeping low and hoping to be unseen, I rip up the torn off pant leg and tie several lengths around my calf to hold the skin on my leg together and stop most of the bleeding. I can worry about properly dressing my wound if and when I am out of this battle alive. My hiding place now a flat jumble of steel pipes, I am back out in the open. I need a new sniper spot ASAP.

The explosion ripped the front of the cab and hood off the truck and dropped them in a mangled pile in a small gully about half way between the truck and my position. I take a few moments to hobble over and dig in behind the remains of the cab. The flattened hood is a near-perfect sniper's blind providing a wide field of view and hiding the flash of the rifle. The gully only offers a degree of cover, but wanders off down the slope on the north side of the compound opposite from where the shooters are. This wash will provide a likely escape route if needed.

For the first time since that big bang, things are quiet. With the rifle scope I survey the area across the field, the location of the source of the shots. Four men in uniform are in front of six or eight men in black coveralls and hoods. A truck is moving behind the men in black. This truck, like the one blown up, has "Orwell's Well Service" in blue letters on the side of the van body. My guess is they will use this truck for another attempt at blowing up the warehouse. They will need to hurry since the bus carrying the day crew will arrive in an hour. In the eastern sky is the faint glow of the coming dawn. I realize the four men in dark blue uniforms are the guards from the gate, two from each of the shifts. The gate is the only possible entrance or exit for vehicles into or out of the compound.

Chuck! What the hell happened to Chuck? Chuck Long, the future chief of operations at Geothermal Wells Number 2 power plant, is a hands-on guy who wants practical knowledge of each piece of equipment to be used at GTW2. I expected him to meet me in the warehouse as my test on the heat exchanger finished. I planned to go through its operation with him as I shut down the test. Chuck, a close friend I met in Ranger training, was to arrive at the warehouse about the time of the big bang. I hope he hasn't walked in on the guys in black or he will be dead or captured like the four guards.

The truck moves into the well clearing and heads for the warehouse, the four uniformed guards walking in front of it. Plainly, the attackers are using the guards as human shields protecting the truck.

Chapter 2 - The Tide of Battle Turns

A new sound startles me, the sound of a vehicle laboring up the steep hill behind my position. Someone is coming up the gully toward me. My back against the truck cab, I bring my rifle around to bear on this new threat. The vehicle is hidden from view in the gully below me. My finger gently on the trigger, I wait, prepared to fire. *Those gooks aren't going to catch me unaware.* There's time for me to dispatch this new threat and turn and stop the second truck loaded with explosives.

A jeep with two occupants rounds a rock outcrop and comes into view. I take careful aim and tighten my finger on the trigger as the vehicle climbs toward me through the gully. I hesitate and hold off firing. In the early dawn light, the bright orange of Chuck's jeep comes into view. *The cavalry to the rescue* I think and smile, lowering my rifle. After a moment torn between staying at my position or slipping down the gully to meet Chuck, I choose the latter.

"Where the hell did you come from and how did you get inside the compound?"

Chuck grins and replies, "Heard several loud explosions and saw flashes coming from the site. This spelled trouble so I lit out in my jeep. We cut a hole in the chain link fence where it crosses the gully and drove up the gully. Aren't you even glad we're here?"

"Damned right I am! I'm glad you're safe. I thought you may have walked in on our friends in black and were dead or captured."

"By the way, Calder, this is Emory Boozer, a neighbor I grabbed on the way. He happens to be an ex Navy Seal."

"Nice to meet you, Emory, and I won't hold the Navy bit against you."

Emory, a large man well over six feet with straight, long, brown hair, grins and replies, "If you Rangers can do half of what we do, things are about to go our way. Incidentally, what is the situation any way? Chuck here shows up at my door in the middle of the night and tells me to grab my fighting gear and come with him. Here I am. What happened to your leg?"

I explain the injury and what I think is about to happen. They grab several satchels of what I assume to be firepower out of the back of the jeep. We head up the gully for my sniper den keeping low and hidden till we are under the truck hood. A quick look through the scope brings me up to date on what's happening.

"The truck and the guards walking in front are starting across the clearing toward the warehouse," I shout.

"I think old Betsy here is the first thing we'll need," Emory remarks as he opens a heavy case and begins assembling his sniper rifle. "One shot of these depleted uranium rounds in a truck engine will stop it dead."

Concerned about the guards I ask, "Did you happen to bring an automatic rifle? We should use all the firepower we can and all at once. Otherwise, they will kill the guards."

"How about this?" Emory pulls out an assault rifle with barrel cooling fins and a huge magazine. "It's an NDAR, the Navy's new combination of the M16 and what the old BAR tried to be, but lighter and more accurate."

Urgency pushes me. "We had better hurry. The truck is half way to their target and the men in black are spreading out. Emory, hit the truck first. Fire when you are set. Your first shot will be our signal to fire. Chuck, take the men in black starting from the left. I'll take out the driver and anyone left standing when you are both through."

We spread out flat on the ground in the gully and behind the remains of the truck and aim our weapons.

"Okay!" Emory says, and **BLAM!** His rifle goes off like a cannon. The engine of the truck disintegrates, and the NDAR chews up several of the men in black. On the first shot, the guards hit the deck. They can't run or get away from each other. Their legs are tied together loosely enough so that they can shuffle, but not walk or run. I pour a full clip into the driver's seat of the truck, slam in a new clip and start firing at the men in black. The remaining men and the two in the truck move fast, putting the truck between us as they run for the guard shack and cover.

In the sudden silence Chuck hollers, "Grab your knife, Calder. Let's cut those guards loose before the truck blows up. Emory, cover us."

Emory picks off one of the men running for cover when he turns and tries to shoot at the guards.

"Are any of you hurt?" I ask the guards when we reach them.

"We had the hell scared out of us and thought we were done for, but I'm okay. Are any of the rest of you hurt?"

"My pride's a bit injured by them foolin' us like they did, but otherwise I'm okay" another reports.

The other two echo similar thoughts.

"Can any of you run a dozer?" Chuck asks.

Raleigh, one of the guards answers, "I can. Why?"

"Go start the one in the equipment shed. Lift the blade and use the dozer like a tank to go across the compound. We'll be close behind you to clear out any of these goons who are still alive. Okay? The key's in the ignition. Go!"

"Okay! Boss!" Raleigh calls out, as he sprints toward the shed.

A rumble and a puff of black smoke tell us Raleigh is on his mission. We grab our weapons and follow the dozer closely across the compound and toward the office and entrance gate.

A gray SUV takes off from behind the office and heads for the gate.

"He's mine!" Emory shouts as he drops to the ground, sets his rifle in firing position and spreads out prone.

A single loud report and the SUV shudders to a halt, spilling its occupants. All of them wave their arms over their heads in surrender and shout, "Don't shoot! Don't shoot!"

"So much for dying for your cause," Emory says.

A cursory examination of the area and Chuck says, "Those four are the only ones left of the attacking force unless some sneaked off before the dozer started."

"Let's round them up and try getting some answers before the locals get here," I suggest. "We'll have no chance for a real interrogation once they are in the custody of the local police and their lawyers arrive."

"We can lock them up in the back room of the guard shack. There are no windows and only one strong door," Raleigh says.

Chuck takes charge. "Thanks Raleigh. Lock the prisoners up in that room. We must do something about these *souvenir* weapons. We don't want them around when the locals get here."

The guards secure the prisoners' hands behind their backs with plastic Tywraps for handcuffs, herd the four into the back room and lock the heavy door. We enjoy the first quiet moment since the well explosion. I carefully examine Emory's rifle, a strange gun with a large breech and bolt.

Curious about the sniper rifle I ask. "Emory, before you go, tell me about that riffle of yours. What the hell is it? Never even heard of anything like it."

Emory grins. "It's a World War II long range sniper rifle called a squirt gun. Few of them were made, about a hundred I believe. They came out late in the war in 1944. They fire rounds starting off in a 20-mm barrel which narrows down to 13 mm for the final six inches. The soft lead compresses in the barrel and the resulting acceleration greatly increases the gun's muzzle velocity and range. A good sniper can pick a man out of a tree from as far away as two miles."

"I wondered how one shot from your rifle destroyed that truck engine. Hell, it's almost an anti tank weapon."

Emory hands me a huge and oddly shaped cartridge. "Funny you say that. The design is based on a Russian 37 mm light antitank gun. The Russians punched lots of holes in German tanks with the original. Those soft lead fins on the front hold the shell in the center of the barrel. They compress going out the narrowing bore. The lead skirt at the rear of the shell seals the barrel and compresses the same way. The increasing pressure behind the shell coming out through a barrel reducing in size kicks the shell up to unbelievable muzzle velocity, presto, a squirt gun."

"How in the devil did you manage to own that, and where do you obtain the shells? They must be rare."

Emory laughs. "My dad shipped aboard one of the ships carrying arms and ammunition to Europe at the time the war there ended. They were ordered to turn around and dump their entire load of arms into the Atlantic. Everyone aboard thought that to be a stupid waste. They hid everything small enough in duffle bags and every other conceivable container they could find. He thinks the officers turned a blind eye to what went on. He broke the gun down and stuck the parts in a huge duffle bag. None of the hand guns went into the ocean. No one searched anyone as they left the ship. In addition to the rifle, he took about fifty rounds of ammunition, two 45s and a Sten gun. He made three trips to take everything from the ship. By the time I inherited his weaponry there were about twenty rounds left plus thirty shell casings. My dad never threw any of them away so I make my own rounds reusing the shell casings."

Chuck says, "You told me about your gun, but I never thought I would see it in action. I am impressed. You must take both guns out of here before the local authorities arrive. They would frown on those weapons being in civilian hands."

Emory breaks down the rifle and stores the parts in the case. He then searches for and picks up the two big shell casings from the sniper rifle. "Don't want anyone finding these," he says as he stuffs them in the bag along with the gun case. "Let's pick up those casings from the NDAR. They're different from the ones from your deer rifle."

"Right away," Chuck replies.

Emory puts the weapons into the jeep and prepares to head down the gully toward home.

Before he drives away, I say, "Emory, thanks for the help! Why don't you act like none of this ever happened? No need for your name or information about those weapons to be brought up. That will save lots of explanations for all of us."

"Good idea, but how you gonna explain the holes old Betsy put in the truck engine, and in the SUV? Those holes are bound be noticed."

"Over by the shack, those rocket propelled grenade launchers our friends left behind will do the job." I reply grinning. "Need I say more?"

"Right you are. A truck loaded with explosives will obliterate them and a blown up SUV may only be examined casually."

"You got it!"

"Thanks for the invite to your party, Chuck. If you ever need me again, gimme a call,"

"You bet!" Chuck says. "Wouldn't be a party without you. I'll stop over to pick up my jeep later today."

They all grin at the exchange. Emory heads the jeep toward the gully and away from the upcoming investigation and reports.

Emory drives away as Chuck says to me, "After the authorities are finished and things quiet down, remind me to tell you the sad story about Emory."

"Oh? He appeared to be a with-it guy. One you could depend on in times of troubles."

"That he is—sometimes. I'll explain once we are not under such pressure. Right now we had better prepare for the coming storm of investigators. We have lots to do, and little time. You should take care of that leg right away."

Chapter 3 - Mopping Up

Back at the guard shack, Raleigh says. "We should retrieve our own hand guns. The last I knew, those goons were dumping them in the trash container by the door when they surprised and disarmed us."

In a few minutes the guards retrieve their weapons,

"Now we've got some cleanup to do," I say to Chuck.

We start picking up the shell casings from the NDAR. After we recover all the casings we can find, we head for the RPG launchers. One more huge explosion and our vehicle obliteration is complete. We head for the guard shack hoping to find some answers.

I say, "Let's talk to the prisoners before anyone else does."

"Do you think there's much of a chance we can wring any worthwhile info out of those goons?" Chuck asks as we approach the shack.

"Not likely! I take them to be from the Middle East, al-Qaeda hiring out as mercenary terrorists for someone with lots of money who doesn't want any new American energy sources."

"It ticks me off that our government provides such tight security for nuclear power plants but absolutely none for any other type. Why is that I wonder?"

"I can think of many reasons including a few scary ones I don't like to talk about in public."

"Oh? And what would those be?"

"Let's have that conversation another time," I say as we walk to the shack. "Be ready to question some nasties. Should we do the good cop—bad cop thing?"

"Sounds like a plan. Can I be the bad cop?" Chuck asks with a grin.

"Of course! Must stay in character you know."

"Aw! You say the nicest things!"

We enter the shack and Raleigh asks me, "Did you notify the authorities? Our phone lines must be cut and we're out of range of any cell phone tower."

"How could either of us contact anyone? We use the same phone system as you. Do you have any idea where the break in the line is?"

"It must be up the road a bit. The line at the shack is in place. I wager they cut our main line somewhere near the connection into the trunk out by the highway."

"Could one of you drive out and check? I assume those cars in back belong to several of you. I hope they didn't disable them."

Roy, one of the guards, says, "They paid them no attention. They drove up in those two trucks and the SUV. I was on the gate during our shift change. Two guys in business suits got out of the SUV and walked to the shack. They at first appeared American to me. I thought they would give us papers to explain what they wanted . . . like an equipment delivery. They pulled out automatics and tied and hobbled us. None of us even had a chance to draw a weapon. Damn! I felt stupid. I'm a retired peace officer. Should have been more suspicious. Incidentally, two from the SUV are among the prisoners."

I reassure Roy. "No one will fault you, Roy, or any of you. This was a coordinated attack masterminded by someone who knew a lot about GTW2. They even knew I would be in the warehouse building and started shooting at me the minute I exited the door. Thank God they were lousy shots. Let's take care of the immediate business at hand."

"Okay, chief! You or Mr. Long tell us what to do next and we'll do it," Raleigh says.

"First off, find the cut phone line and fix it if possible."

Another of the guards speaks. "I'm Elrod Shoop. I retired from the phone company about six years ago. With a few basic tools, I can fix those lines. My guess is they were cut at a pole. The break should be easy to spot now in the daylight. We can drive down the line to find it. There are ladders and tools around here somewhere."

"Okay! Take your car and find the break. Meanwhile, we must begin questioning our prisoners."

With Raleigh dispatched to find the line break and Roy needed to assist in the questioning, Elrod and Vincente are assigned to find the ladder and needed tools.

Before we can bring out the first man to question, Raleigh pops in the door and says, "Found the break! I glanced down the line from behind the shack and about two hundred yards away there's a ladder leaning against a pole. Must be their ladder where they cut the wires."

"Terrific!" Chuck comments. "Now find Elrod and tell him to tackle the break. All he needs are the tools."

With the phone line problem under control we can question the prisoners.

We start with a big man in a grey business suit. From all appearances he could be an executive, salesman, or a Mafia hit man. He doesn't look like a terrorist. We sit him on an office chair, secure his hands behind his back and fasten his ankles to the chair using duct tape. We remove everything from his pockets and pull a few wraps of duct tape around his arms, chest and the chair back. He isn't going anywhere. Chuck places several objects on a small table in front of the chair. These include a battery operated drill with a small bit, a hammer and a roll of fine steel wire, all of which came from the tool shed. Included was a bottle of ammonia from the cleaning stores.

As the *good cop*, I start the questioning. "What's your name?"

"I won't tell you anything," he snarls.

"Come on, no secrets will be given away if you tell us your name, or should we call you shit head?"

"I don't give a damn what you call me. I won't tell you a thing."

"In addition to being stupid, you're uncooperative eh?"

"I'm not stupid."

"You came here with the intention of blowing up the well, the warehouse, all the equipment, and everything else of importance, and meant to kill all of us in the bargain. You got the well and that's all. We can re drill that in a few days. You blew up your own vehicles, and those killed were about a half dozen of your own men. The rest of you were captured. That sounds stupid to me."

"Your drilling rig is gone."

"I'll wager our rig is down the road a bit and you didn't get the chance to blow that up either. You screwed up. I wonder what your masters will do to your families because of your failure?"

"You'll get no information from me."

"Such being the case, I'll turn you over to Chuck here. His methods are nastier than mine. You'll wish you answered my questions. Do you understand how painful drilling various parts of your body can feel? Such pain will be excruciating."

"We're trained to endure pain."

"Have you ever had your fingernails drilled and ammonia poured into the hole, or had several parts of your body drilled, strung together on wire and hung on a hook?"

The big man glances at the items on the table and squirms a bit. "Okay, I'm Alonzo. I'll give you that. You don't scare me. You guys can't torture us. Our attorneys and the media will be all over you if you do."

"What makes you think your attorneys or the media will ever learn about it?"

"We'll tell them."

"What makes you think you'll be alive to tell them?"

"Well—our bodies will show we've been tortured."

"Oh Alonzo, you don't get the entire picture here. There's a whole lot of wild, rocky land back east of the plant. By the time your body is found, if ever, your bones will be picked clean by coyotes, wild pigs and vultures. There will be no evidence of torture in your gnawed and scattered bones."

"You can't do that. The law will punish you."

"Alonzo, Alonzo," I say, laughing. "You still are not getting the picture."

I continue in a voice loud enough for the other prisoners to hear, "I don't think you're getting our message yet. Right now we are the law here and we will abuse you and keep you alive and awake until you tell us what we want to know. When we're done, we'll cart you out in the wilderness and leave you. Rot and the critters will do the rest for us, wild pigs for example. They're known to start eating people while they are still alive. They tear open your stomach and rip out your soft innards as you watch, a nasty sight. When we finish with you, we'll do the others, one at a time."

Alonzo's eyes grow wide. His face blanches as he speaks. "I will answer a few questions."

"Okay Alonzo, you're getting smart. What are the names of the other three?"

He provides the names of the men in the storeroom and several of the dead. There's little chance of verifying the names and he balks at providing details about the overall plan and others who are involved. He is stalling.

"You're being uncooperative," I comment. "You think supplying us with non confirmable and insignificant information will do you any good? I'll turn you over to Chuck here. Alonzo, he's much better at extracting information than I could ever be."

Chuck picks up the drill and pulls the trigger a few times. He can change in an instant from friendly to fiendishly evil. He is the ideal *bad cop* for this type of situation.

The sounds of a scuffle draw our attention to the store room. We open the door. Two men are struggling on the floor. One managed to knock the other man down and is trying to kill him by biting his throat. We pull him off, slam him face first against the wall and tell the fallen man to go out into the office. He leaves a trail of blood as he rolls onto his knees and crawls out of the room. When he clears the door, we step inside, close the door, and hobble the prisoners so they will be unable to kick at anyone or even walk fast. We lock in the remaining two.

"Freaks!" the man shouts at the others as he sits on the floor, blood oozing from a bite on the back of his neck. "That bastard tried to kill me."

Chuck winks at me. "Should we put this one back in there and let the other guy finish what he started?"

"Please, no! I'll tell you what you want to know. I'm not one of them."

"Shut up!" Alonzo hollers. "Don't tell them anything. They're going to kill us all anyway."

"Not if you help us out we won't," I say. "Who knows, you might even earn a reward if you cooperate. We can't promise a horde of virgins, but cash and a new identity could be in the offing."

The wounded man speaks up. "I'm Shaukat Rehman from Pakistan. They're holding my family and forcing me to work with them."

"Your entire family will be killed because of your actions," Alonzo shouts angrily.

"I understand how these animals operate. I've not heard from them in a year and I'm convinced they already tortured my family and probably killed them. They have most likely been dead for some time. With hope for my family gone, I can't do this any longer."

I felt sorry for the poor soul. "Perhaps we can do something to help them. Your friend Alonzo here gave me an idea."

"The others will find a way to kill them no matter what we do," Shaukat replies through growing tears. "His real name is Shahzad Rehman and he's my brother."

I can't believe it. "Your brother? How'd you two grow to be so different?"

"He's the stupid one," Shahzad shouts. "Refused to attend the training camps with me and went to a university in India—damned Hindus. They brainwashed him."

Chuck can't let his remark go unanswered. "Brainwashed? You're full of pig crap! You're the one who's been brainwashed, brainwashed with such intense hate you would kill anyone your slave masters tell you to including your own brother and his family. You're nothing but a mindless tool of those you feel compelled to serve, too stupid to think or act on your own."

Shahzad starts shouting a string of canned propaganda and nonsense that stops only when I grab a roll of duct tape from the supply cabinet and shut his mouth with it. He even tries to bite my hand as I apply the tape.

"Let's take him outside. We don't want blood all over the guard shack," I tell the others in a voice loud enough for the men in the locked room to hear.

He struggles violently against all the duct tape and plastic Tywraps which hold him securely as we lift him, chair and all, and carry him outdoors. I motion Shaukat to come near me as we put his brother down.

In a quiet voice I say to him, "If you help us out here we will try to save your family. We've done this before, quietly and successfully. A few years back I joined an extraction team that brought two entire families out of a similar situation in Afghanistan. They were in an area the Taliban controlled. You might be surprised at what can be done in isolated hostage instances, done with few losses."

Shaukat was teary eyed. "These fanatics are completely heartless. I'm certain my family is lost. I decided to help you, what can I do?"

I explain my plan. "I am going to remove the tape from your brother's mouth," I say quietly, so Shahzad cannot hear. "I want you to scream as if in pain and as loudly as you can when I muzzle him again. Will you do it?"

"Yes, of course, but why?"

"Come with me and I'll explain," I answer, motioning him away from the shackled prisoner to where we can talk without him hearing.

"What's up?" Chuck asks.

"Just a little ruse that might loosen those lips in the back room. Divide and conquer you might say. Shaukat here says he wants to help and you all heard me promise to try to arrange for his family to be rescued."

Chuck glances at Shaukat. "You're not going to trust him are you? You cannot be so stupid."

"We don't need to trust him for our actions to work. If he doesn't do precisely what we ask he will show us he can't be trusted and we can deal with him then. Here's what we do . . ."

I explain my plans. Chuck heads inside the shack and noisily retrieves the drill, shouting, "You want the drill, hammer and wire too?"

"Of course . . . everything! Don't forget the ammonia, and bring the duct tape. We can use the tape to cover his eyes and mouth, and the Tywraps," I shout in reply. "I don't trust this other one. We will shackle him before we start."

We position Shahzad, his back to the open shack door. Chuck brings the drill, inserts a small bit, and turns the switch on. He waves the spinning bit menacingly a few inches from his nose. I rip the tape from his mouth.

"Dogs!" he shouts. "I'll never tell you anything. We're trained to resist torture."

"I doubt you ever had your knees drilled and ammonia poured into the bloody holes. Should we start with your fingers?"

"You wouldn't dare."

"No?" Chuck says with a snarl. "Just watch me."

I slap the duct tape back over Shahzad's mouth. Chuck turns on the drill. At the same moment, Shaukat screams loudly. A few seconds of terrible screams and he shouts, "Stop! Stop! I'll tell you. Stop!" in a convincing half scream, half voice.

"So much for their training," Chuck comments. "I didn't even run the drill half way through his knee and he's ready to blab everything he knows."

"Let's take him over to the office where we can record what he says," I say, loudly. "Grab his feet."

Chuck, Roy and I start to carry Shahzad, chair and all, across the clearing to the office in the warehouse. Shaukat walks with us, moaning loudly. We pass the smoldering remains of the two trucks and trudge the three hundred yards from the guard shack. Shahzad is no lightweight and his constant struggling doesn't make the task any easier. After walking about a hundred feet on the loose, crushed rock spread where the concrete for the generator building will be poured, we stop to rest for a while,

"This is a bitch," Chuck comments. "Why don't we hook him up to one of the guard's pickups and drag him over? Throw a rope around one of his ankles and tie the rope off on the hitch. Dragging him a mile or two might even loosen his tongue a bit."

"You're joking."

"After what they did to some of our guys they captured in Afghanistan it would be a small payback. No! Of course I'm joking. If we did, we'd be as bad as they are. Feeding them to the wild pigs while they're conscious is bad enough," Chuck adds with a grin and a wink.

Shaukat doesn't appear happy with that comment and steps toward me. "Don't do that, please. Death is nothing, but the idea of being eaten by . . . pigs . . . would be beyond cruelty for a Muslim."

"If you two provide us enough accurate information we'll forego that indignity," I'm sure they do not understand that such an action on our part would be impossible. I choose to tell them otherwise, a little added insurance of cooperation.

Roy motions me aside and asks in a quiet voice, "You are joking aren't you?"

"Come on, Roy, of course. You know and I know and Chuck knows, but they don't, and let's not share our secret."

"Gotcha!" Roy comments, grinning.

"Okay, Shaukat, give us a hand with your brother. If the four of us work together, carrying him will be a bit easier."

✳   ✳   ✳

It takes about an hour for us to finish writing down everything Shaukat relates about the al-Qaeda cell and how they work and report to their cell leader.

"My brother knows a lot more, but I doubt he would tell you."

"Okay," I assure him. "There are two more to interrogate and from what you say, they may be more informed than Shahzad. We will do our little kill and dump routine for the benefit of those two remaining in the shack."

We step out of the office and Raleigh and Vincente show up in Vincente's pickup.

"Elrod says the phone line will be up and running in about an hour," Raleigh reports. "Says he doesn't need us and we should come back and help you."

"Great!" Chuck comments. "Help us load the mummy here into the back of the truck and we can pull off another little act for the two prisoners in the shack."

We load him into the pickup, chair and all.

Chapter 4 - A Useful Ruse

From the viewpoint of the two prisoners in the shack, the following sequence of events takes place. First a pickup drives up to the shack and then they hear voices. The first is Chuck's.

"We're not going get anything else outta him. He keeps passing out from the pain."

"Right you are. Let's get rid of both of them."

"You gonna leave them out where the pigs can reach them?"

"Of course, why?"

"We did get some information from them. Why make them suffer any more?"

"Why don't we put the little one out of his misery? He did cooperate as much as he knew how. I vote the pigs get the big one, alive."

"Okay, hand me your gun," *(Sound of two shots.)* "Now go dump them where the pigs can reach them. I'll go in and select another, How about Abdur. Shaukat indicated he might be the most cooperative. Go, now," *(Sound of pickup driving away.)*

✳   ✳   ✳

I open the storeroom door to two confused and apprehensive terrorists lying on the floor.

"Abdur? Which one of you is Abdur?"

Silence!

"Whichever of you is not Abdur might earn a reprieve by telling me which one is."

Silence!

"Okay! You, come with me," I say pointing to one of the men who immediately points to the other.

"He's Abdur! Him!"

The accused man points back at his accuser and shouts, "He's Abdur. I'm not Abdur. He is."

"Okay Mr. Abdur, you're coming with me."

"I thought you wanted Abdur."

"I want you, whoever you are. I'll help you to your feet. Those hobbles keep you from moving up or down."

"I'm not Abdur," he pleads as he stumbles across the concrete floor.

"And I'm the man in the moon. Whoever you are, you're next. Raleigh! Give me a hand with this gook."

Raleigh and I help him outside and sit him on a chair, search him, and truss him up with duct tape like we did Shahzad.

I lift his billfold and remove a plastic card. "According to this illegal New York State driver's license—it is illegal is it not—you are, Abdur Zaman. Funny how you deny being Abdur and you show me his driver's license with your picture on it."

Chuck comments, "Aren't you stupid for carrying your driver's license with you on a terrorist raid in Nevada?"

"I drove the SUV and had my driver's license in case we were stopped. It is a legal license."

"Is this your real address?"

"Yes."

"Man, you are one stupid gook."

"We were assured there would be no resistance and we would be long gone before anyone discovered the damage."

"You didn't count on my friend, Calder being an ex special forces guy and making war did you?"

"We were told there were no weapons on the site except the handguns the guards were carrying."

"Surprised you didn't they?" I say.

"Very much surprised. May I ask a question?"

"Shoot!"

"What kind of weapon did you use to stop the truck and the SUV?"

"Why, my trusty old big game hunting rifle. Most Americans own hunting rifles?"

"I lived in America for quite a few years and had friends who hunted. None of my friends had a rifle so loud that could do so much damage."

"My rifle is a powerful big game rifle, an elephant gun. Let's change the subject to how you are going to help us."

"I'll tell you all I know, but that's not much."

"We'll be the ones to judge and decide when and how we use the drill on you. What we wondered about is why hit a geothermal plant under construction?"

"We were told GTW2 was a cover for a nuclear silo with a nuke aimed at Iran. I decided that was not true when I spotted the drilling rig in the middle of an area of crushed rock. I was sure this was no hardened missile silo because there's no concrete. By this time I was trapped. Escape was too dangerous. A few members of the group knew the truth but I wasn't one of them."

"You are quite savvy to be in a terrorist cell. You're not like the others we questioned."

"I'm working on my PhD in mathematics at the University of New Mexico. I plan on staying in the US and becoming a citizen. This changed when I joined a group called *The Muslim Brothers* about two years ago. One of their members approached me about helping Islamic refugees. Sounded kind of positive, like I'd be doing good work for others. By the end of the first year things started changing. We started hearing from militant members about fighting injustices. Then about disarming nuclear weapons aimed at Islamic countries in the Middle East."

"You must have been suspicious of their real motives? You don't seem to be the fanatical type."

"Most of the others are illegal immigrants or are on expired student visas. They're fanatics. Once I became involved and was told of some of their plans, I found out I would be killed if I left the group. The thought of having your head hacked off by a dull sword is a powerful motivator."

"So you're a peace-loving regular guy, right?"

"It sounds like a convenient excuse, but by the time I realized the true nature of the group, I knew too much. The original group may have been a terrorist cell or possibly terrorists came in and took over a legitimate organization for their own purposes."

"No matter. Can you give us any information about other activities, contacts, meeting places, anything that might help us prevent or thwart another attack?"

"This activity is all I was told about. I can tell you of one contact, a strange man for an up level al-Qaeda member. His name is Mao zu Chin and I think he is Chinese. How he came to be our up level contact is a mystery. We were told he laid out the entire strategy for the attack on GTW2. He provided the vehicles, the explosives, the weapons and all the information about GTW2. He knew about your installation even if he did describe it as a hidden missile silo."

"Interesting, if true. Were you aware al-Qaeda has been committing terrorist acts for hire recently? In many instances they are merely hired bombers or killers working for others and getting paid by them for those actions?"

Abdur is puzzled. "No, I never heard of such a thing."

"My guess is this was that kind of operation. What I wonder is, who's behind it? Who's paying to destroy GTW2? I can think of a number of reasons, but what's the real one and who is pulling the strings? And don't use the convenient Chinaman."

"I can't help you there. Mao is the one person I know about. Shahzad is the one who was aware of other contacts and plans. He's the leader of our cell and a real fanatic. His brother, Shaukat, is a decent guy. My guess is he got caught up in the group in the same way I did. His brother could have been a factor. Shaukat cowered around his brother, feared him. Too bad they're gone. They're the only ones who knew about anything outside the cell."

I have no intention of letting Abdur find out the other two are alive. This leads me to an idea of what to do before the authorities arrive. We pull the same torture act on Abdur we used on Shahzad. Vincente provides the screams. We bring the other man out of the storeroom and tape him to a chair. He tries putting up a brave front but the signs of intense fear are written all over his face.

In the nastiest voice I can muster, I ask, "Who the hell are you, ass hole?"

"Najeeb Awan. Look! Here on my drivers license, Najeeb Awan. I will tell you what I know. Please don't feed my body to those pigs."

"One of your guys told us you are the big cheese of this operation. Are you?"

He squirms against the tape. "He lied. I'm a little fish. I do what I am told."

"Oh? Who tells you what to do?"

"Shahzad. He ran the cell. He's the one who knew everything about our operation."

"You expect us to believe you? Now that he's conveniently dead, you expect us to take your word he was the head honcho, right?"

"He was, as you say, the head honcho."

I lean down and stare directly in his face from a few inches away. "Abdur told us otherwise. Under considerable duress, he said you were the boss, the head man."

After lots of the same kind of evasive nonsense, we realize we will gain little useful information from him.

"Let's put a bullet in his head and dump him for the pigs," Chuck says as he pulls out the handgun one of the guards had given him and chambers a shell.

"I'll tell you about the man Shahzad reports to, a Chinese named Mao zu Chin," Najeeb says out of the blue.

That gets our attention, big time. "What about Mr. Mao? We might let you live if you give us some good information."

"He works for the American government, in the Department of Commerce, but he is a member of the Chinese Communist party."

"Are you sure about that? You're not joshing us to save your sorry ass, are you? We need confirmation," I say, acting with shocked disbelief.

"Yes I am. You could check with the US government for confirmation."

I drew Chuck aside so Najeeb couldn't hear. "That must be another ruse. He knows there is no way we can check it out from here. We can only after they're gone. They are lying and trying to confuse us."

"Yeah, you may be right. Anyway, Elrod should soon repair the phone line so there is little time before the local authorities arrive. What should we do before they arrive here?"

"I'm thinking—first, let's hide Abdur and Shaukat, keep them away from the authorities. My guess is if they are taken into custody they'll be dead in a matter of days if not hours, murdered by other terrorists. They understand, so I'm betting they will cooperate."

"What about the other two? They're certain to tell everyone what they think happened here, and about the missing two hiding at Emory's?"

"We'll convince them they are dead and their bodies are out in the desert feeding the pigs."

"Shahzad will tell them his brother is alive and hiding somewhere. How can we counter that?"

"Easy, both bad guys will tell different stories of what happened. We'll suggest to the authorities that they keep the two apart so they cannot compare notes. We will easily convince the cops their stories don't jibe and are mostly lies. We provide a cohesive story about what happened including that the two missing men were blown up when the trucks exploded. There are enough bodies and body parts lying around to confirm our story for the present. They won't be able to positively identify them unless they use DNA records and analysis for confirmation. Whom will they believe?"

"The cops may take our story as gospel, but what about the inevitable federal agents? They may doubt our story."

"Hell, by then our stories will be down pat, all backed by the four guards. They will certainly help us. We saved their lives, didn't we?"

"It's worth a try. I'll take Abdur over behind the hill and fake shooting him. Then we load the two 'bodies' in Elrod's pickup and drive out in the desert, out of sight. We stay there dumping their bodies for the pigs and then return. To make things realistic, we can load Abdur's 'body' into the pickup within sight of Najeeb. That will provide the clincher."

"What happens if the cops search for the bodies and find nothing?"

"You cops believe those terrorists? You've got to be kidding. They're messing with you. That's what we tell them. We say so and stick to our story even if they start to search. We can tell them to search all they want to."

"Got it. Whom are they going to believe, those lying bastards, or we good American citizens? Go ahead take Abdur behind the hill and shoot him."

After we return from the act of dumping two bodies in the desert, Elrod shows up. "The phone lines are working so you can call and report what happened."

Chuck goes to call the authorities, while I load Abdur and Shaukat into Elrod's pickup. We head down the gully, through Chuck's hole in the fence and off to Emory's place in the desert. We drive about six miles down an old desert road in fair condition. Emory's wife, Shellie, accepts the two impromptu guests we are leaving in her care. She is not happy.

"Wait till Emory returns," she says. "He should be back in about half an hour."

About fifteen minutes later, he returns.

After a quick confab, Emory says, "Shellie, our moral duty is to give sanctuary to these two who will be dead if we don't. There are some bad guys after them and there is no way they could discover they are here."

Shellie scowls. "If you okay it, I'll go along with it. Who's going pick up the tab for their food?"

I volunteer, "My company will gladly reimburse you, Shellie, I promise. You might even earn a bonus for your help."

"Thank you, Calder. I'll take care of them the best I can. This little house has no room. They'll sleep in the equipment shed out in the back. There are two old bunks against the back wall. We use them occasionally for hired help."

"They will be fine. I must go back ASAP. I'm expecting a visit from lots of police. Emory can fill you in. Bye!"

Chapter 5 - The Authorities Arrive

I pull up and park just as the bus with the day crew arrives right on time at 7:45. Within ten minutes two police cars roar up the road, lights flashing. The sight of all the carnage gives testimony to the morning's gruesome events. The sight of Chuck and me in one piece relieves the crew. The fusillade of questions from them is soon followed by another from the local and state cops who arrive simultaneously. The two terrorists, bound in chairs, are left as they are while the cops ply them with questions. They are told they will remain taped to the chairs until a proper vehicle comes to take them in. The police treat them as extremely dangerous. Shahzad's constant ranting strengthens that opinion.

State Police Lieutenant Gleason takes charge of the site from the start. The locals are happy to let the state take control. They gladly step aside and let the state troopers handle things. All the carnage tells the story. Obviously there was quite as battle. There are eight dead bodies, some in pieces, two terrorists taped in chairs, two substantial craters, and pieces of vehicles scattered all over. We are told to stay put until they can question us. Within an hour there are six state police cars on the site and a special team of investigators are on their way. The obvious terrorist connection ensures a Homeland Security team from Washington will be here, possibly before nightfall.

Then of course, the TV news cameras will be here as well, once the authorities let them.

Around ten o'clock, two military helicopters land and disgorge an armed security force. The military are here to take over. The first TV helicopter arrives and is followed by military helicopters that fly up and herd the TV crew away from the site. The military declare the area within five miles of the well off limits to everyone, news people included. The remoteness and inaccessibility of the area make this easy.

Shortly after the military arrive, the State Police complete the first part of their investigation and questioning. They ignore the ravings of the two terrorists and take our enhanced version of what happened as the truth.

We are looking forward to a long day of sitting around and waiting. No one is allowed to leave. Fortunately for Chuck and me, our fridge in the warehouse is well-stocked, filled with the stuff Chuck and I eat and drink when we are stranded here and can't go into town. This happens quite often. There is such a long drive to the nearest place to eat, we keep plenty of food, beer, and pop on hand—at least for the two of us.

✳   ✳   ✳

The Homeland Security team arrives late in the afternoon. They speak with State Police Lieutenant Gleason for about an hour and then head for us. We are sitting on chairs outside the warehouse door, enjoying a cold beer as they approach.

The HS team is coming our way in their government standard dark blue suits. "Don't look now but methinks we are about to be grilled by our government. My bet is they will keep us separated so we can't hear what the other is saying."

Chuck grins. "Well, old buddy, we practiced the routine, what to say and how to say it. I plan on being friendly and cooperative to a point."

"Here goes nothing," I say before they are within earshot.

"Would you gentlemen please accompany us into the office in the warehouse?" the tall, black man says, and keeps walking without another word.

Chuck and I arise from our chairs and fall in behind the two of them. Everything in the office is covered with dust brought down by the nearby explosions. Several minutes are needed to clear the dust off of the desk and chairs so we can use them. Once things are cleaned up enough, the smaller man, an obvious New Englander with almost white, wavy hair, breaks the silence. He is all business.

"I am Roger Bean and this gentleman is Lutoch Mandan. We are investigators from Homeland Security in Washington. We would like you to tell us in your own words what happened here. Charles Long, you will tell your version to me, and Calder Voss, you will speak to Mr. Mandan. Tell us your versions and we will ask you some questions. Is that clear?"

Not to be out done in sparse speech, we each answer, "Yes."

Mandan is stiff, almost automated. "Tell me what happened, please."

We each explain our edited versions with my hunting rifle and without Emory's cannon and NDAR. The spent uranium rounds are unlikely to be found and the 30 caliber rounds from the NDAR are almost identical with those from my hunting rifle or from the weapons of the terrorists. In any event it would take quite awhile for even experts to retrieve many rounds to study. Earlier we picked up all of the shell casings from the NDAR. The only casings that remained came from my rifle or from the attacker's weapons. We hoped they wouldn't count the ones from our positions.

"All right gentlemen," Bean announces when we finished telling our stories. "There are a few questions we need answered."

There is no effort to separate us and they proceed to ask a number of technical questions about our actions, those of the attackers, and what we experienced during the attack.

Then Bean asks, "How did one man, armed only with a simple deer rifle, defeat a dozen attackers with automatic weapons, and destroy three vehicles in the process? Impossible!"

"He's an ex Ranger and one hell of a good shot," Chuck answers.

Mandan frowns. "That may be, but I seriously doubt the possibility under the circumstances. Things are missing from your explanations, important things. Weapons were used here other than a deer rifle. What weapons and where are they?"

A little bluster is in order. "I am an expert shot, a ranger sniper in fact. Yes, there were other weapons used. You'll find the attackers left a few RPGs near the guard shack. I used them to blow up the SUV. The trucks blew up on their own—probably had timers on their explosives. They were lousy shots. You can tell by the wide spread of bullet holes in the warehouse, right over there."

Neither of them is convinced. Bean smirks as he says, "A dozen men armed with automatic weapons surprise a single man whose hunting rifle is 500 feet away in the trunk of his car? He kills how many? Ten? And doesn't receive a scratch? Unlikely."

I corrected him. "There were ten of them, not a dozen. Six were killed in the truck explosions, There are two prisoners alive, that means two were shot by my rifle. I would call my leg wound more than a scratch. Seems quite reasonable to me."

"One of the prisoners told the State Police you had a loud gun that stopped one of the trucks and the SUV. How do you explain that?"

"My deer rifle with maximum loads in the cartridges is loud, much louder than their automatic weapons."

"Even if you shot out the tires on those trucks, they would continue on their course and hit this warehouse. How do you explain that?"

"A shattered disk brake rotor locks the wheel and stops the vehicle. A locked wheel is more effective at stopping a truck than shooting out the tires and works on any vehicle."

Chuck says, "What the hell difference does it make anyway? All they managed to do was blow up the well. They didn't accomplish any of their other obvious objectives and all thanks to Calder here, who by the way received a nasty wound to his leg while protecting the well by putting his life on the line. That leg wound should be getting treatment. He needs to be in a hospital."

Bean did not like this. "We are quite certain a lot went on here that you are keeping from us. Your stories are different from what the prisoners are saying, or what our investigation indicates. We will keep digging until we find out, and we will find the truth. We will find out why you are not telling us the truth."

Chuck explodes. "We spoke a lot more truth than you lying bastards in Washington ever do. If not for Calder's quick and decisive action in spite of overwhelming odds, this entire complex, all its people, and all its equipment would be blown to pieces. He effectively did the government's job. A job they are supposed to do themselves, protecting citizens and their property. Instead of being nasty, you should be thanking him and giving him a medal."

Bean says, "There is no need for hostility. We're merely doing our job. I think we are through for now, but once the investigation of the site is over we will be back with more questions. Think about the answers you will give us."

That said, he and Mandan stand up and leave the office without another word.

Chuck rolls his eyes, slams his fist down on the table and says with disgust, "Bureaucrats, I despise those anal retentive leaches. Wait until we learn what they decide to do with their investigation. No matter what, I think we should stick to our guns."

"I agree completely. The big mess we must clean up is a lot bigger problem than some meddling government official. We should start drilling as soon as we can, the day after tomorrow if possible. Raleigh said he found the drilling rig out by the highway, intact. I'll bet they meant to blow it up when they left."

"Do you suppose the government will even let us clean up? They may treat this as a crime scene and stop any cleanup."

"The day crew is out there. Let's have them start cleaning up and observe what happens."

Chapter 6 - Clean up and Back Drilling

The EMT ambulance Chuck called arrives to treat my leg. The medics put me on a Gurney and slide me into the ambulance. They do not like the mess they find on my leg. Chuck starts the day crew on clean up while they are treating me.

"That's a nasty gash," one Medic says. "We must take you to the hospital for proper surgery."

"Come on, can't you fix it here? We have a huge mess to clean up."

"You need to be in the hospital so surgeons can properly treat your leg."

"If I go, how long before I can be back?"

"That will be up to the doctors at the hospital."

"How far away is the hospital and how long will it take us to go there?"

"It took us 45 minutes to drive here from the hospital so that's about how long."

It will take at least four hours to clean the place up and move the drilling rig in so I call Chuck over.

"How's the leg?" He asks when he pokes his head in the ambulance.

"They want me to go to the hospital right now."

"Well, what are you waiting for? Go so you can return soon."

"They can't give me an idea how long the doctors will keep me. I can't be away for long."

"Damn it, Calder, get that leg taken care of proper no matter how long it takes. Doc, tell me what you think."

"Frankly, I can't tell if he will need surgery or not without cleaning up that wound. The injury is bad enough and should be treated in the hospital rather than here. If he needs no surgery, just stitching it back together, he could be back in four or five hours. Of course, that's if all goes well."

"Calder, you have a top notch experienced crew you can count on. I'll be here to help so go, now!"

"Okay, but keep me posted by phone. Call Glenn over. I want to speak with him before I leave."

Glenn, my sometimes assistant when he isn't working as a driller, is soon with me in the ambulance. A weathered outdoor type who worked on drilling rigs for many years, he is a bit shorter than I am, but weighs a bit more. He is one I can count on.

"Glenn, do what must be done. You'll be the boss till I'm back. Your crew is quite capable. Do things the way you know. I'll expect you to keep things moving so we can be back on schedule."

"Okay, Calder. Our crew will do their best while you're gone, but be back as soon as you can. And take good care of that leg. We don't need you hobbling around the well."

The police wave us through the gate when we head out with the ambulance lights flashing

✳   ✳   ✳

Getting the drilling rig back and setting it up will require removing the remains of the trucks strewn all over the site. Glenn sends Pedro, our drilling rig supervisor, and several of his crew to bring the rig back to the well. He asks Jake, our dozer operator, to use the dozer to start clearing the site. Right after noon Jake fires up the dozer and starts to clear the site. Lieutenant Gleason comes storming over.

"What the hell do you think you're doing? This is a crime scene and nothing is to be touched until we finish."

Chuck is pissed. "Damn it Lieutenant, we have a deadline to put this plant in operation and this shenanigan put us a week or more behind schedule. You picked up all of the bodies and had all morning to look over the wreckage. Can't we push all the junk off to the side so we can move our drilling rig in and go to work?"

The lieutenant is an unhappy man. "You can start when I okay it, but not until," he snaps angrily.

Glenn asks, "How many hours will you need? Your men quit poking around the wreckage hours ago. Come on Lieutenant, don't add to the damage those gooks did."

The Lieutenant softens a bit. "I understand, but we have a job to do. Let me check with my forensic team and the Homeland Security guys to find out if the wreckage can be moved."

"Damn!" says Chuck. "Those government clowns will hold us up to show they can. They love to show their power."

Pedro drives up to the gate with the drilling rig. He parks it where the police cars are blocking the road and walks over to Glenn.

Pedro explains, "The rigs okay. I checked it out. There's no obvious damage to anything but the lift. They didn't clamp that down when they drove away. A couple of hours will be needed for repairs. Everything needed to do the repair is in the warehouse."

"We were lucky they didn't blow it up," Glenn says. "Ask the cops to let you drive the rig over to the equipment shed by the warehouse. You can do the repairs there."

"Okay, boss."

After about ten minutes of animated persuasion, Pedro waves and drives the rig around the wreckage and into the shed. "He must have been convincing," Glenn tells Chuck.

"Now, if only they will let us clear the site," Chuck says.

One of the state cops walks toward them. "Lieutenant Gleason okayed clearing the wreckage," he shouts as he nears us. He points toward the access road. "He asks you to put it all in one place right over there where it will be easy to load on trucks."

"Tell him thanks a lot, and I mean it," Chuck tells the officer. "Thank God. I wonder why those Homeland Security boys let us clear? Surprised me. Now we've work to do."

The day crew got busy stacking the pipes strewn about by the explosions and cleaning up the small pieces the dozer left behind. By sundown the drilling rig stood in place ready to start drilling. Calder returned with his leg in a hard plastic cover over the dressing.

"Okay, Calder, what did they do to your leg?" Glenn asks.

"They told me I was lucky, no damage to my calf muscle, just badly ripped up skin. The doctor took nearly four hours to stitch, clamp, and glue things back together."

Chuck was incredulous. "Glue? They used glue?"

"Yeah, tissue glue. After it was glued, they packed my leg with some gooey stuff, wrapped it with special material and encased it in this plastic cover," he said, tapping the cover with his finger. "They want me to wear this armor for ten days. Told me the cover would protect my skin while healing proceeds."

"Can you get around?" Glenn asked. "Are you going to be able to climb up on the rig?"

"Not till my skin heals. I'm supposed to keep from stressing my calf muscle for the next three weeks. The most strenuous exercise I'm to do is walk on level ground. They want to see me in ten days to check on the healing. That's when they will tell me what else I can do. There could be some real problems if the skin doesn't heal properly so I plan on behaving myself. They want to prevent any infection."

Chuck grins at me. "I'm glad you will still be able to work. Prepare to do a lot of checking on your crew. They'll do everything they can to take up any slack."

"They sure will. They're a capable bunch we can count on."

✳   ✳   ✳

The crew got the drill and some oversized casing down through all the rubble from the explosion. If the blown part isn't too deep, we can clean out the debris from the hole and begin drilling fairly soon. What the actual conditions are will be a mystery until the crew clears the rubble and begins operating the drill.

✳   ✳   ✳

About midnight, Pedro comes into the office. "We inspected what's left of the well. The explosion pulverized at least the top fifty feet or more. We don't think the hole collapsed below that level. The rock below fifty feet is quite solid. Fortunately we hadn't set the casing. All we need to do is run an oversized casing down through the pulverized rock and soil. Part of the well will be plugged with loose debris. We'll drill and pump the rubble out before we can continue drilling the bottom part. The job will be messy, but at least doable."

"Thanks, Pedro. Your news is better than I expected. Thank God we did not start drilling the return well yet."

"We're at least a month away from reaching 700 degree rock" Chuck says. "Think we can drill both holes and case them in the time we have?"

"It will be close," I say. "What do you think, Pedro?"

"You're the engineer, Calder. You tell me. Conventional oil wells are my meat, but this is a different animal. The job of connecting and casing both holes a mile deep at the bottom of the wells is something the likes of which I never even imagined. I don't know how much time will be required."

"Pedro's right. We've both studied your drawings and the procedures you developed, but making the connection is going be another matter," Chuck says.

"We did fine in the mock up trial. Working a mile below the surface will be much harder. And then there's Murphy's law."

"You may work out the details on paper, but we must do what has never been done before. Thank God we've got such a great crew. If anyone can do the job, our crew can." Pedro is proud of his crew.

"Now I need some sleep," Pedro says as he moves toward the door. "Tomorrow will be a long day."

"Go! Calder and I will be right behind you. Till morning."

✹ Sunday, March 3, 2013 ✹

The next morning the Homeland Security boys call us into the warehouse office. Neither Chuck nor I are happy about that.

"Okay, G-men, let's hurry this up. We are quite busy."

Bean smiles. "Tell us what really happened and we're out of here. You can go about your business."

Chuck takes the offensive. "Okay, what did your scavengers find that doesn't jibe with what we told you?"

"Several things refute the story you told us. The prisoners said two of their members are missing and not among the dead. Said they thought you shot them in cold blood after the fight was over. They said they were bound, you took them behind the guard shack and shot both of them. Where are their bodies?"

Chuck shrugs his shoulders, looks at me and says, "Possibly a couple of them ran away during the fight. We did not shoot anyone who was bound. Why would we? You didn't shoot anyone who was bound, did you Calder?"

"Of course not. Those devils are messing with your mind, Bean."

"Another thing, our team found the engine of the SUV blown apart. They don't think an RPG could possibly do that. The brake rotors were not shattered as you claimed. Those we found were all intact but one. That blows your story of shooting out the rotors. Why don't you tell us what really happened out there?"

"I only told you I shot out the brake rotor on the first truck, just the one. Where did you learn that I said any of the others were shot out? Not from my words."

Chuck had enough. "Gentlemen, this interview is over. We must get back to work now. No charges were mentioned about any illegal activity on our part. Either charge us with something or let us go back to work. How you react will determine what we say and how we speak to the inevitable news media reporters who I'm sure are salivating over the prospect of interviewing us on camera."

The two of them fold up their notebooks, and head for the door. Mandan says, "We're through for now. We'll be back, possibly with charges."

"Screw you," I say loud enough they can hear.

"Is that a nice thing to say to our friendly government officials? They are only doing their job, or so they said," Chuck grins as he says it. "Apparently their job is to delay getting this place up and operating as long as they can. Oh, and how about those two over at Emory's? What are we going to do about them? We can't keep them where they are for long."

"I'm sorry, Chuck. I didn't tell you, but I confirmed it. I called a guy named Tim Sutherland from Rescuers Anonymous. They're the international group who helps relocate guys like those two. They worked with us when we had a number of Iraqis we rescued and pulled out of Afghanistan. They would have all been killed if they returned home. Tim told us they are living a new life in a safe place, wouldn't even hint at where."

"When are you supposed to hear from them?"

"He said he had some details to work out, and would be back to me within a week. He hoped to arrange to pick them up in a week or two."

"That's good news. Emory's wife will be happy," Chuck says. "I understand Shellie's unhappy with them staying there. Oh yes, I hired the company that installed the security fence to fix the hole we cut and beef up the gate. I don't want any reporters getting in and sneaking around. I granted the media a press conference day after tomorrow to shut them up. I told them the press briefing would be held outside the gate at ten in the morning."

✷ Tuesday, Mar 5. 2013 ✷

The press briefing started promptly at ten. There are many reporters and things start off badly. Chuck manages to calm them down. He takes our bull horn and tells them we will stop taking questions if they don't stand back, stop shouting, and stop waving their hands.

"I will decide who gets to ask a question and will select by pointing. I will not choose you if you are shouting or making any slight commotion. I will stop if there is any kind of disturbance. I hope I make myself clear."

After that things proceed smoothly. There are a lot of great questions and a few foolish ones. Chuck does a terrific job. He responds to several questions about weapons by referring the questioner to the police reports. Several times he says simply, "I do not know," or "I choose not to answer the question as asked." At the end he says, "This is a privately owned and financed operation. The government is here because of criminal and possibly terrorist activities. We appreciate and applaud their effort and compliment the local and state police, their crime scene investigators, and the members of the federal government for the thorough and courteous way they conducted their investigations. We also want to thank you for the orderly fashion you responded to our rules for the questions. If any of your questions were not answered, submit them in written form and we will try to answer them as soon as we can. Now, folks, we are about two weeks behind and I must go back to my job."

With those words he turns and goes back through the gate and to work. The media seemed pleased with our response to their questions because the resulting news reports were quite complimentary. They painted Chuck and me as some sort of combat heroes saving GTW2 from enemy terrorists.

✳   ✳   ✳

I wore that hard plastic around my leg for two weeks. The doctor is pleased with how the leg is healing when the dressing came off and he examines the stitches. I must now wear a loose covering on my leg for two more weeks until the skin is completely healed. I am not to climb up on the drill platform till then. After that I should be back to normal. I push a little and am back working on the platform two days early. No harm results.

Chuck and I are part of the work crew except for the time we are doing necessary paper work, or handling our managerial and engineering duties. We are *hands on* people, and easily change hats and become *one of the boys*.

Chuck often says, "If I don't work as hard as or harder than my crew, how can I expect them to work hard."

He does that and I choose to be right in there with him when I can. Three weeks after the attack we are finally able to resume drilling at the bottom of the well. No one is happy about the delay.

Chapter 7 - Another Visit from Our Government
✶ Monday, July 29, 2013 ✶

Several months after the bombing, the second well is nearing completion. Through a herculean effort by all 24-7, the GTW2 crew gained back to a week behind schedule. Chuck and I are pleased. Early Monday morning they are finishing some of yesterday's paperwork when the phone rings. Chuck answers. After a short conversation, he hangs up, a broad smile on his face.

"They are delivering the rest of the special casing pieces today," Chuck yells to Calder. "We'll be ready to set the casings in place Wednesday, two days ahead of our original date. All we need to do is finish the second well and flush it out. We will break through in the morning."

"That crew is amazing. I never thought they would be able to regain so much ground," I say to Chuck.

The door bursts open and one of the guards hands Chuck a large envelope. "This came from the U. S. Government, Department of Commerce, boss, addressed to you. Must be something important. A messenger hand delivered the package to the guard shack. We had to sign for it."

"Thanks Gene," Chuck says as Gene walks out the door. "I wonder what the Department of Commerce wants with me?"

"Well, open the damned thing and find out."

"Some guy named, Mao zu Chin is coming to visit GTW2," Chuck reads to Calder. "That's all we need, another nosy VIP getting in our way."

"Sounds like he should be in the Chinese government, not ours. Wait a sec. Isn't that the name those two Arabs described as their up-level al-Qaeda contact? Something's wrong here."

"It says here he's a subhead of the Department of Alternative Energy in the Commerce Department. Wonder what kind of a title 'subhead' is? Must be a high-ranking official. Sounds pretty high up to be visiting our lowly installation, and before we're near being finished. There is a large packet of forms we are supposed to fill out before he gets here. I wonder what this is about."

"I don't like it one bit, Chuck. I am suspicious of any government official asking questions. I don't trust the bastards and what they told us about Mao makes things a lot worse. Does the note say when he is coming?"

"Shit! The day after tomorrow. That's the day we'll most likely be setting the casing connection. I can't take time to fill out all this crap. I won't have the time to squire him around either. Nobody will."

"What will we do with him?"

"Whatever we do, let's not tell him what our Arab friends told us about him. I still wonder if they weren't messing with our heads."

"Were they simply trying to send us off on a wild goose chase? I think they would be extremely unlikely to switch loyalties and be on our side. They're Muslims and you cannot trust them."

"Yeah, we should keep this information to ourselves."

I grin and say, "We can save it to use should we ever need an edge on Mao in the future. In the mean time, why the devil would the US Department of Commerce be interested in our little well? That makes absolutely no sense at all."

Chuck is getting upset. "This is a private installation. There is no government involvement other than the usual regulations and reporting requirements. Even the environmentalists left us alone and that surprises me. I'll figure out what to do with him when he comes. Think about it. We've only 36 hours to come up with something. Oh, regarding your last comment, he's a subhead of the Department of Alternative Energy. That is what we are all about, alternative energy. So he does fit."

"I missed that bit. I will tell you if I do think of anything."

✳ Tuesday, July 30, 2013 ✳

At seven o'clock Tuesday morning, Chuck, Pedro, Glenn, and I are meeting for cereal and coffee in the office. I am excited and animated when I enter.

"Guys! I think I found an answer to our problem."

"Which one? We've got a ton of them."

"The government guy, Mao. The problem you asked me to work on yesterday, Chuck."

"Oh, that problem. I assumed you had forgotten all about it."

"I'll ignore that. Anyway, I talked to Raleigh, the guard. He has Wednesday off."

"How is that going to help if he's not here?" Chuck is sarcastic.

"I asked him if he'd be willing to work a different job, be a guide on his day off. I explained we had this guest coming and we were busy. He said he'd gladly do it—for time and a half."

"Don't tell him, but I'll gladly pay him double to take this guy off our hands." Chuck is happy with my idea.

I tell them about him. "Raleigh is a sharp cookie. He started here as a guard the same time we started and knows the place quite well. I have no idea what he did before he retired, but he's no dummy, and he can talk your arm off once he gets started."

Pedro asks, "Supposing Mao balks and won't accept anyone but you, Chuck?"

"I'll tell him I'm busy, right to his face if necessary. It'll be our luck to be mating those two casings at the bottom of the wells when he gets here. That's a whole lot more important than answering dumb questions from some stupid government official. Great idea, Calder. Will you take care of setting that up with Raleigh?"

"It's done. I told him to be ready and at the gate in the morning. When is Mao getting here? Does his pack of papers say?"

"Nine tomorrow morning. He's staying in town tonight and coming out in the morning." Chuck shifts mental gears. "Okay gang, let's go to work. This is going be a long, busy day."

✳ Wednesday, July 31, 2013 ✳

Wednesday morning at nine, Mr. Mao's driver drops him off at the gate. Raleigh goes to meet him and do his thing. Mao, a tall man with an athletic build and wearing a typical government dark blue suit, was not amused.

"Where's Mr. Long? I must speak with him. We need to talk."

"I can take you to him."

"Do so, and now."

"Okay, but he may not be able to talk. He'll be up on the rig, working the drill pipes at the turntable. They will be trying to couple the casings at the bottom of the well. He'll be covered with drilling mud. They're doing a messy job today."

"I can't understand that. Isn't he the manager?"

"Yes," Raleigh explains as they walk toward the drilling rig. "He's a working manager, and because of the attack several months ago, we're behind schedule and trying to catch up. Everyone's been working hard and for long hours."

"How about the engineer, Mr. Voss, is he available?"

"Calder will be up there on the rig with Chuck. They're both working many hours trying to help the crew catch up to the original schedule. What they are doing now is important, difficult, and has never been done before."

Mao calls out when they are near the rig, "Mr. Long. I must speak with you."

"I doubt he can hear you for the noise on the rig."

Mao shouts. "Mr. Long. Come down from there. I must speak with you, now."

A loud "Go to Hell!" is his answer.

"He swore at me. That's uncivil."

Now, Raleigh is getting angry. "Mr. Mao, I suggest we move back from the platform now because when the next connection is made, drilling mud will splatter all over. Careful! You're standing in it."

"He swore at me, a visiting, high ranking Federal government official. He swore at me."

"He'll do it again if you bother him again. What he is doing requires great concentration and is perilous work. Please, sir, move back."

Mao moved back and away from the platform. "This is upsetting. I came all the way here from Washington to talk to Mr. Long about this project and learn about its operation. I expect to be treated in a much more professional manner."

"Pardon me, sir, but I believe you gave them only two days notice of your visit. You should be more practical and call ahead for an appointment, schedule a time when he is not so terribly busy?"

"My schedule is quite full. The opportunity to be here today came up two days ago."

"Do you know anything about field drilling a well, sir, any kind of a well?"

"No, but what's the difference? He should have been able to rearrange his schedule to meet with me as I requested."

"Sir, the drilling of an oil or heat well like GTW2 is an operation where some incidents cannot be scheduled. Demands can come at any time midday or midnight. I'm sorry, but you came at a bad time for a visit. Perhaps you should arrange another visit at a better time."

"My driver will pick me up at precisely noon or about two and a half hours from now. My trip will be a total waste if neither Mr. Long nor Mr. Voss is able to clean up and meet me during that time. My trip will be expensive but a total waste."

"I'm afraid that will be impossible, sir. They told me they will be working until at least seven this evening. There are about two and a half hours left. I will be glad to show you around the site and answer most of your questions. I am quite knowledgeable about GTW2 and I am the one who is available. We don't keep a large crew here, and each person has a job. Most are quite critical to the operation."

Mao looked defeated. "I might as well let you show me around if that's the best you can do. Who's your boss?"

"Why, Mr. Long, sir. At least he hired me and everyone else who works at GTW2."

"Tell him he will receive a letter from me in a few days which will report my displeasure at the treatment I received at his hands and that the purpose of my visit was not served."

"Sir, what is that purpose if I may ask?"

"No, you may not ask. The purpose is between Mr. Long and myself. Now, show me around, please."

✳ Wednesday, July 31, 2013 ✳

The job of mating the two separate pieces of the well casing a mile and a quarter below the surface is a difficult task. The crew including Chuck and me took until ten at night to finish this part of the job. Once the casings are pressure tested, the liquid sodium heat exchanger is lowered into place and cemented in. Then both of the in and out pipes are put in place and connected. The final steps are taken in order. The empty space in the bottom 100 feet of the two connected wells occupied by the heat exchanger and connecting pipes is filled with heat conducting materiel. The space around the casing of the down pipe is filled with dense concrete and the space around the thick-walled up casing is filled with light weight concrete insulating material. Spacers hold the rising pipe containing the sodium in the center of the casing. The air between the pipe and the casing provides the needed insulation. Installing all of this and connecting the various parts to the surface heat exchanger and steam turbine takes another six weeks.

The entire GTW2 power plant grows inside the sizeable building being erected around the well while work on the well progresses. Chuck and I oversee the construction of the power plant when we aren't involved in the drilling. The contractor built two nuclear power plants much larger than GTW2 before this project started.

"This plant will be a piece of cake compared with those nuclear plants," he tells us when we all first meet. "There's no problem complicated by radioactivity and all the crap that entails including AEC security getting in our way every time we turn around. Yep, building GTW2 will be a real pleasure." After the bombing occurs, he isn't so happy, even though this does not affect his work.

The plant is nearly completed when we finish the heat pipes and connect the surface heat exchanger. Three months are required to complete the building and mate the well systems with the steam turbines. Once the cooling tower becomes operational, we are ready for the first tests of the overall system. This leads to a number of startups, tests, and shut downs to fix problems and adjust the control systems.

✳ Monday, March 3, 2014 ✳

At last GTW2 is up and running, generating power for Battle Mountain and nearby cities. The power plant is also connected to the electrical grid. Everyone cheers as the power plant is officially turned over to the power company during a gathering in the brand-new offices of the plant. The ceremony takes place on the exact date the original hand over was scheduled.

We smile as I say to Chuck, "Now your power plant is on line, and on schedule. Everyone is happy, except Mr. Mao and the two Homeland Security guys. Of course, they're off bothering others so who cares? I don't miss them one bit."

"What's your next project?" Chuck asks me as everyone disperses to their various responsibilities.

"Some idiot wants us to drill a geothermal well near Kansas City."

"Isn't ground heat a bit deep there? I think a GT well would not be practical anywhere around KC. Adequate heat must be far too deep."

"This guy claims there is a hot spot where he wants to drill. He says the well depth should be only a hundred feet or so deeper than this one."

"How'd he get that idea? I examined the USES map of hot spots and don't remember any within several hundred miles of KC."

"He's a geologist who specializes in geothermal sources and should be knowledgeable in what he's saying. I hope he's right."

"Why there anyway? I would think there are many more practical places."

"Not necessarily, KC Power and Light scrapped the nuclear plant planned for the area several years ago and the local environmentalists joined the national group in opposing a coal power plant. We're to drill eight wells for the new plant, ten times the capacity of this one. Once completed it will fill a fair sized void in the grid. KC Plant 7 will be a combination plant, part liquified natural gas and part geothermal."

"An interesting concept. Who came up with that idea?"

"The investment group at KC Power and Light. The LNG part of the plant will be used if and when load requirements exceed the maximum output of the geothermal section. They are interested in GTW2 and the final okay for contracting to drill the wells just came through. After we had our first successful test run at GTW2, one of their people came here to visit at least five times."

"He's the guy from KC you oked to let on our site, right?"

"Yeah, that's the guy."

"His name . . . let me think . . . Peckinpaugh, Rick Peckinpaugh."

"He's the guy. I thought him quite young to be doing an investigation for investors, but what do I know."

"I thought he asked a lot of questions. He was courteous and considerate, but a bit of a pest with all his questions."

"Now you understand why."

✳ *Carol Mitchell* ✳

Chapter 8 - A Walk on the Beach - Meet Jack Chandler
✳ Wednesday, April 3, 2013 ✳

A smartly dressed young woman prances down the beach, her bare feet dance in and out of the far reaches of the surf which barely sloshes over her toes. The bubbling surf never reaches the hem on the skirt of her business suit. The only sounds are of those of the breaking waves, the wind in the beach grass, and seabirds calling. In the west, beyond the beach homes, the sun is about to complete its plunge below the horizon. A narrow, bright orange bank of clouds hangs above the setting sun. In the clear sky above the cloud bank several short white contrails with arrowheads of tiny swept wing jets identify air travelers heading both north and south. An osprey glides west, searching for its evening meal. Several black vultures soar toward their roost.

In the east a thin bank of dark clouds hangs just above the horizon, almost blending with the dark water of the Atlantic. No planets or other celestial objects are visible in the eastern sky.

Just beginning to be visible, low in the western sky is the planet Mercury. Pale pink and barely visible, Mercury is knowingly observed by few people. Far above Mercury, Saturn is the evening star, the only bright object yet visible. No other visible planets grace the clear, darkening sky as they are elsewhere in their orbits. At this time, the moon, Venus, Mars, and Jupiter are only visible in the dawn sky. The sky is still too bright for any stars to be out. Everything appears peaceful and serene.

✳　　✳　　✳

After the usual harried drive home from my office, I head straight for the beach and my daily exercise. I walk south toward a rocky outcropping about a mile from my apartment. To the west the sun is dropping behind the forest beyond the Intercoastal Waterway. Kicking off my heels, I step onto the sand, enjoying the warm, dry grains oozing through from beneath my toes. Savoring the flow of sand at each step, I prance toward the water, dodging the edges of the waves as they bubble and dance up the sand and then sink into it. I enjoy this little game of tag with the ocean most evenings as I take my treasured daily dose of outside exercise. This walk is my one daily private moment when I loosen the bonds of business cares and worries and revel in just being alive. I reverse course at the rocky marker and retrace my footprints northward. The breeze flows through my hair and assails my nostrils with the delicious smells of the salt water shore.

Carol Mitchell, you are a most fortunate woman, twenty-eight and owner of a successful travel arrangement company that practically runs itself, I think as I sidestep a piece of kelp on the wet sand.

An old man walking down the beach toward the water interrupts my thoughts. At the pace we are moving we will meet at the water's edge. I resent anyone invading my private space. The temporary intrusion irritates me. The prospect of looking eye to eye at another person, let alone an old man, brings uncomfortable feelings. I find little in common with older people, avoiding contact whenever possible. Nedra, my capable assistant, directs all of our older clients to one of our associates. I handle 'special' clients: celebrities and the wealthy, important people. I'm a bit snobbish about my business, but I worked hard to earn it.

Before reaching the wet sand, the man drops to his left knee, leans on his right knee, and rests his bearded chin in his right hand. White hair flows out from beneath a faded blue cap with an ancient military insignia. He stares intently at the sand a few feet in front of him, a forlorn figure in wrinkled khaki shorts and shirt. He huddles as if cold, even in the warmth of late afternoon. He continues staring at the sand as I pass a few feet in front of him. I am grateful he doesn't acknowledge my presence; I can continue my private thoughts as I walk on uninterrupted.

Then my thoughts startle me. *That old goat's gonna walk into the water and end it,* pops into my mind. A knee-jerk reaction causes me to whirl about and head back to the huddled figure.

"Are you all right?" I ask, stopping in front of him. He looks up at me trying to focus on this intrusion into his private world.

"Why - uh - yes," he replies. "I'm okay. Just doing a bit of reminiscing."

He seems forlorn, on the brink of tears.

"Are you sure? I was worried. You were staring at the sand, oblivious to everything. I thought you might . . . I mean . . ."

His eyes change from dull to clear blue with a bright twinkle and look right through me.

"Gonna throw myself in the ocean and end it all? Is that what you thought?" His lined face broke into a friendly grin. The accuracy of his words surprised me.

"It has happened."

"No chance. I'm not the kind to do stupid things like that. Life's too precious. I am quite sad though. I guess it showed."

"I'm glad you're okay. You are all right, aren't you? I'm not nosy; concerned, yes, nosy, no. You seemed so . . . defeated as I passed you. I try to avoid older people because they usually tell some sad story, or complain about the insensitivity of young people."

He pauses, wistful for a moment. "I am a bit sad at the moment. I found out my wife died last week. Brought back many memories . . . ghosts from my past you could say."

"I'm sorry. Was she ill?" I am right, another sad story. I decide to walk away from him shortly.

"She had several strokes a few years ago, then she had one big one last week that did her in."

"It must have been hard on you, taking care of her I mean."

I wonder how I can end this and leave without being cruel?

He shakes his head. "It wasn't that way. We divorced more than thirty years ago. I was only with her a few times since then. She lived with one of our daughters. The news of her death brought back a flood of memories. I guess I am sort of revisiting the past and feeling sad that past was so long ago."

I start to go, but something about the sparkle in those clear blue eyes stops me and turns me back. Surprised by my interest in this old man, I am at a loss as to what to do. Normally I would avoid him like jellyfish poison on the wet sand.

"I'm sorry. I didn't mean to pry."

"No need to apologize. Old memories die hard. But making new ones, there's the real joy in life."

"That's quite profound. Makes good sense."

He no longer seems so forlorn and uninteresting.

"Take right now for instance. Here I am, an old coot, moonin' about things that happened so long ago they're hard to remember and along comes a beautiful young woman to bring me out of the past and back into a pleasant present. I'll remember this for a long time."

"Thank you. You made a good day even better for me. I too will remember it."

My curiosity is suddenly and unexpectedly aroused. I want to learn more from him.

"Do you mind if I sit here on the sand with you and talk for a while?"

"Mind? I love it. A current reality beats a long past memory every time."

His transformation from the somber to the merry, even mischievous surprises me. No longer does he seem huddled, but strong and full of life.

"I'm glad I returned to talk to you and I did worry about what you might do."

He shifts his position, sits on the sand and leans back on his hands. "See how wrong first impressions can be? You're a bright young lady and from the clothes, you must be quite successful, at least financially. Or do you have a sugar daddy?"

"A sugar daddy? What's that?"

Mischief again crinkles the skin around those blue eyes. "Sorry, I forgot about the multiple generation gaps. That's a word from the dark ages, a name for a man, usually wealthy, who keeps a young woman in clothes, cars and apartments so she will grace his arm when he goes out and please him in bed when he doesn't, all without the commitment of marriage."

I feel almost insulted. "Not in this life! I make my own way. I'm proud to say I own a travel arrangement company, Travels by Carol, right in downtown St. Augustine. My business is not called a travel agency because we do so much more. Our main business is arranging guided tours to exotic places. The business keeps me so busy I have no time for anything else in my life, men in particular."

"So your first name is Carol and you're a fancy tour guide with a positive professional attitude and no time for fun or men. What's your full name?" His question rolls pleasantly with a broad smile.

"Mitchell, Carol Ann Mitchell, and I don't dislike men. It's just that most of the ones I meet are either immature or sickeningly macho. At least they act that way and I deplore wrestling matches. Real men seem quite rare these days. And what is your name?"

"Jack, Jack Chandler. And I agree with you about real men."

"Where are you from, Jack Chandler, and how come you are on this beach?"

"I'm certain you don't want my life story," he says.

A merry chuckle follows his comment. "I built the little house behind us about six years ago. I came here to relax, walk the beach, fish a little, read a little, find interesting conversations and write whatever comes into my mind."

"You're a writer?"

"I write strictly for my own enjoyment or as an outlet for anger about all I find wrong about people. Sometimes I write about the things I find are right, my own opinions of course. I even had a few op-ed pieces published in the newspapers. I'd rather fish most of the time. I find few people to talk to, mostly small people and small talk, few interesting conversations."

"I hope I don't fall into that category."

"No way of knowing yet. We 've had no real conversation and might never have one. Most young people lack the patience and intellect for real conversation. A verbal wham-bam-thank-you-ma'am is all they ever take time for. That's why they like to text. Most older folks' conversations center on kids, grand-kids, the weather, their aches and pains and, on rare occasions, a social or political subject. Once those are dispensed with, there's not much they ever say except how bad things are."

"Interesting. I never quite thought about it that way. I agree with you. That's a fair brief description of the conversations of my friends. The young ones I mean. I rarely speak to the older generations, except those in my family."

"Most of you young people seem to think folks more than fifty are out of the loop: no feelings, no emotions, no zest for life, no dreams, no drive, no hopes for the future. Things changed in that direction since the sixties. I view the growing youth culture as an effort to avoid or at least ignore the inevitable. I think one should lie back and enjoy it, to paraphrase an old saying."

"I sort of understand what you say. You lived a good part of your life before the boomers came along, like my grand parents."

"You don't need to remind me."

"I didn't mean it that way. My parents are boomers. That makes me a generation Xer. Those labels are gross generalities. Boomers are quite different from both you and me. Your generation and mine are much more in sync than either of us are with boomers."

"Never thought about generations that way, but you may be right. That's a rather astute observation."

"People like my parents think so differently from my generation, and from yours. I understand my grand parents better than my parents. We are close, but there are many subjects we don't communicate about. People over forty—boomers especially—I avoid them when I can."

He cocks his head like a dog twists its head at a strange sound. "If that's true, why did you stop and talk to me?"

"Honestly, when you headed down the beach, I dreaded coming face-to-face with you. I was relieved when you stopped and ignored me as I walked by."

His eyes laugh. "You came back to keep me from doing myself in. Right?"

"True, I'm afraid. Then something about your eyes triggered my interest. I surprised myself when I sat down beside you, but it—it seemed the thing to do."

Jack laughs hard at that. He intrigues me even more. This is an unusually different me. I have no idea where I am headed, but fascinated to find out.

"Possibly there's a real person inside the cover-girl shell. I watched you come down the beach. You switched from a little girl to a sophisticate and back in rapid succession. You dodged the waves and then walked like a clothes model on a runway. The dichotomy of your actions fascinated me. I admire the little girl. She is real. She belongs in the scene. The other one—a plastic caricature."

"That may be why I enjoy my daily walk on the beach. Walking in the surf makes me feel so—free—one of the few things that does."

"You're afraid to let go except when you're alone on the beach. You ought to let that little girl out more often, and in other places. You might be surprised at what happens."

"I can't spend the time. My business keeps me too busy."

"Big mistake. I remember another young woman who was like that. No time for anything but work. How long have you been in business? Can't be too long. You're not old enough."

"Four years. The bank and the ex-owner own more than I do, but that's changing rapidly. My debt to them will be paid off in seven or eight years and the business will be all mine. The 'all mine' sounds positively delicious."

"Then, what will your plans be?"

"I'll probably open several branch offices by then."

"Why?"

"So I can make more money."

"Odds are you'll be borrowed to the hilt and having little real fun. What will you do when your work isn't fun anymore, keep on pushing?"

"I enjoy my work. I meet lots of usually interesting people and travel to many exotic places to check them out for clients."

"So everything you do centers on your business?"

"That's right."

"What do you want for your life? Build a mountain of debt and own a whole lot of things?"

"With any luck, I'll be able to retire at forty and do whatever I please. You know, a home near the ocean, time to do what I want, not what I'm compelled to do."

"No husband? No kids? You all by yourself?"

"No interferences. No compromises. No arguments. Things I don't need. Yes, I rather like that."

"How about family? How do they fit in?"

"My family are fantastic. Two older sisters, Renee and Andrea, and my father is a retired Marine whom we three adore. Renee has two kids, a boy about five and a baby girl who's four months. I visit them fairly often in the highlands of the state near Mt Dora. Nice thing about being a visitor is if the kids get to me, I can leave. Renee can't. Dirty diapers and snotty noses are not my favorite things."

Jack laughs again. His face crinkles and dances with life. "Don't you think she is happy with her life and family?"

"Deliriously so. Mack, her husband, manages a large herd of beef cattle in the cattle country where they live. Started off as an accountant for a rancher, a bookkeeper to be correct. In two years he took over running the place. They hope some day they will own a ranch of their own. Renee's a legal secretary. Had a great job in town which she gave up when Terry came along. Since then she's been a stay-at-home mom. She helps out with the ranch. Keeps track of all kinds of things using her computer right from home where she can care for the kids. Their finances are tight, but they manage each month to save a little toward their dream ranch. I hope they make it. They're both good people and hard workers."

"Sounds like quite a different way to live from your own. I take it you don't care for the lifestyle?"

"Occasionally I wonder how I could find a man like Mack. He's a kindhearted gentleman and devoted to his family. They're a great couple. Men like Mack are few and far between."

"I'll bet the little girl in you could find one if you let her."

"She's tired of searching."

"Looking in all the wrong places is my guess. What about Andrea? Where is she and what is she doing?"

"Andrea is an engineer, has a great job working for KC Power in Kansas City, Missouri. She owns a lovely home in Raytown, a KC suburb. Like me she is into her career big time and doesn't need a man in her life. She's a classy lady and a bit too accomplished and independent for most men. We manage to get together at least once each year, usually here in St. Augustine or at Renee's. I visited her place in Raytown twice, a lovely home with a huge pool and lots of art she collects. We're a lot alike and close."

"You remind me a lot of my ex when I first met her."

"Oh? Tell me about her. Let's talk about you for a while."

"You don't think an old man's story will bore you to death?"

"I suppose I had that coming. No, I don't think so. Anyway, how did your ex fit into this picture?"

He was wistful and removed for a moment, then he came back. "---Cheryl? A year after returning from Nam, I ended up in Austin, Texas hunting for a job in May 1972. I walked into a pilot training school to discover if I could become a real pilot. For that I would need a multi engine rating and flying those beautiful Northrop F-5As in combat wasn't enough."

"What do you mean, a real pilot?"

"Commercial pilot I should say. I loved flying, thought to be a pilot a great way to make a living. Flying those F-5s from Carriers in Nam was exhilarating. We had great pilots in our combat group. We learned not to form friendships, but to keep everything light and impersonal. You never knew who wouldn't be coming back from a mission."

I turned twenty-seven the day before I was shot down. We were guarding a flight of B52s on their way back from a run when a large flight of MIGs jumped us. One of my engines caught a piece of flak from ground fire or broke something about the time the MIGs broke off combat. My group saw me losing altitudes and slowing down so two of them broke formation and headed back to follow me. Before they reached my position, a couple of MIGs jumped me from above, and put me in the drink. I ejected and landed in the water uninjured but a bit too close to shore. My buddies got both MIGs before they could come around and machine gun me in the water. I found out later they radioed my position for rescue. Before our rescue craft could reach me, a North Vietnamese patrol boat picked me up. They banged me around before they deposited me in a tiny prison at their base."

"You were in the Viet Nam war? I never met anyone who fought in the war and talked about it. A lot of those who were in the war don't like to talk about it."

"I can understand why, but I don't mind talking. Not much to tell, but Sherman said it, 'War is Hell.' I was soon transferred to Moa Lo prison, the Hanoi Hilton, where life was pure hell. I was finally released as part of a prisoner exchange in 1972. The most significant thing I remember about prison is the visit by Hanoi Jane and the lies she told afterwards about prisoner treatment. I can't say for certain, but she was possibly responsible for many of my friends being severely beaten. You probably heard the story."

"Didn't she gather notes sneaked to her by a number of the prisoners and then hand them to the guards? And weren't the ones who wrote the notes severely beaten?"

"That's the story we heard which sounded reasonable. I wasn't in the group used in that propaganda piece so I had no first hand knowledge. The story could have been cooked up. They never did use any of us that had recently been beaten, only the ones who looked healthy. There wasn't a man there who wouldn't have given a lot to get his hands on that traitor. I'm surprised none of those men ever got to her. I don't want to start talking about those people. Thinking back makes my blood boil."

"Sorry about that. How about getting back to the flight school?"

"Okay. The school trained jet fighter jockeys to fly heavy, multi engine aircraft, quite different from flying those nimble jet fighters."

"I sort of understand. How did your ex fit into this picture?"

"This multi engine school was a private company that trained military pilots to fly multi engine jets and become certified to fly commercially. I finished their entrance exam and went in for my interview. She was the interviewer. Here's this gorgeous female staring at me like she's my drill instructor and firing questions at me about my record. She was all business. By the time I left she had convinced me she was hard as nails and I would have great difficulty graduating. That was one of the toughest interrogations I ever endured. A week passed before I received my acceptance.

"About three weeks into my training I ran into her at lunch in the school cafeteria which was a stark room, a place to satisfy the basic needs for food. Everyone sat at long tables, ate, and left. The place wasn't conducive to conversation. I had started on my usual dry sandwich and carton of milk when she sat down next to me in the one open seat at the table. She glared at me like I had no right to be there. She made some comment on how the school must have dropped their standards to let me in. I replied something to the effect that she could chew up the spoon propped in her coffee cup and spit out bullets, an inauspicious occasion. My fellow students described her as a drill instructor in babe's clothing and referred to her as miss B with the obvious meaning. We wondered if she slept on a bed of nails and ate nuts, hull and all among other nastier ideas."

"She was merely protecting herself from the horde of horny young guys back from who knows where who came through the school. I'll bet most of them wanted to bed her. You men are so predictable."

"You're right on that, I found out. I had taken a small room in a private residence where seven other guys stayed. I became friendly with Carla, the lady who owned it. She was a sharp old gal who took a special liking to me. Quite a few times she invited me for dinner with her and her husband, Armano, in their private section of the rooming house. One night Carla told me she had a special surprise for me at dinner and I should dress in my best uniform. I walked into their dining room and there sat miss B at the table. In complete innocence, Carla introduced her friend's niece to me. Cheryl gave me a look that would freeze a firecracker. When she greeted me with an icy, 'We've met,' I started expecting an uncomfortable evening filled with tension. Carla gave me a look of complete surprise at Cheryl's cold response."

"I can imagine. Why did she try to put you two together?"

"I doubt she knew anything about Cheryl's cold relationship with the students. She liked us both and wanted us to meet. A few moments of tension and Cheryl got up and rushed into the living room, crying. Carla ran to her and I could hear their conversation clearly. Things were just as you called them, a protective device. I felt uncomfortable and wanted to leave, but Armano told me to hang on. Apparently, he knew what was happening."

"So, miss B wasn't hard at all. Of course, otherwise you would never have married her."

"Right again. She came back to the table red eyed and apologized. A totally different Cheryl sat down at the table next to me. Much later she confessed she treated me hard because she was attracted to me and wanted to avoid any entanglement. To make a long story short, we were married a month after I graduated from school. I stayed on as a trainer at the school and Cheryl continued interrogating prospects and putting the fear of God into them although less convincingly than before. She had a little gold band for protection and me around the corner. She was no longer referred to as miss B, but as Mrs. Chandler, a more complimentary name."

"I'll bet you two were quite a pair. You mentioned a daughter before. When did she come along and were there any others?"

"Sandra was a bit of a surprise, unplanned, but welcomed and loved once we got over the initial shock of realization. Three years later we had twins, a boy and girl, Jack with a different middle name from mine and Rebecca."

"Sandra and Rebecca are pretty names, but couldn't you come up with something other than Jack? Or did you want a namesake?"

"Cheryl wanted to name him Jack. We had a major disagreement over that and you see who won. The skirmish was between two strong-willed people. We had some donnybrooks over the years, but they were fair, clean, verbal battles, no nastiness. Neither of us ever wanted to back down, but one of us always did. We enjoyed the making up. I used to accuse her of starting fights so we could make up."

"So you think people can fight and be in love."

"If you don't fight once in a while, you can't be in love. They're both strong emotions and I think one can lead to the other. Of course brutal fights are out of the question. We had strong disagreements over some things and our battles were to decide those disagreements. Our love was never in doubt in spite of those highly charged emotional conflicts."

"That's a strange philosophy about love. I don't think everyone could be that way. Emotional scars can be hard to heal."

"Have you ever been in love? I mean so much it hurt when you disagreed?"

"That's a strange question. I thought I was in love several times, but things faded away when I found out the guy wasn't the man I thought he was in the first place. I had one good experience with a super guy I lived with for two years. Ted was wonderful, treated me royally. We got on well for about a year and a half. I was trying to buy the travel business at the time. We argued about the increasing amount of time I spent with my job. I told him things would be that way until I had the business, was on my feet, and with the previous owner gone. A few months later I found a goodbye note on the fridge. He said he loved me and most likely always would. He left me money to pay his half of the remaining lease on our apartment and took a job in San Diego.

He's never contacted me since. I cried for two days. He was a wonderful man, but couldn't take second place to my work. Now I'm quite wary of relationships."

"He put up with second place longer than I would have. He must have cared a great deal for the little girl in you. A woman married to her work is a bad bet for marriage or any relationship."

"Sounds like you speak from experience."

"It's what happened to Cheryl and me. I couldn't handle being a minor part of her life compared with her job. Our priorities grew to be different."

I shuddered at the familiar feelings. "Ted and I had some of the same kind of problems. What did you do when you separated? What happened to Cheryl?"

"She went back to work full time when the twins started school. Then she took over much of the administrative work I had been doing, and I spent most of my time flying and training. She was much better at running things than I was. Anyway, all I wanted to do was fly. Things went okay for the first few years, but then she was promoted several times. The year the twins started junior high school, she was named general manager. Shortly after that we pooled our resources and bought the flight school when the aging owners made us an offer we couldn't refuse. That took over her life. She turned into a full time executive. I left a few days after the twins graduated from high school.

"For a year I raced those midget aircraft. I had some success so I decided to turn professional and race the circuit. That meant I would be traveling all over the country. I used racing to forget about Cheryl. The other guys said I had a death wish, flying close to the edge. I was soon winning most of the time, garnered a great sponsor and began making lots of money. For the next eight years I spent each week in a different place. Raced all over the world, Europe, Canada, the US, Mexico and even some in Brazil. One day in the pre race meeting I found myself examining the other pilots. Most were about the same age as my kids and the next oldest to me in age was twelve years younger. That scared the hell out of me. I was way overdue to hit the ground. I heard those kids referring to me as 'dead man flying' and decided the time had come to quit. In spite of the fact I was points leader at the time, I packed it in. My sponsor hit the roof, but I didn't care. I was fifty three years old and thinking I would like to live a long time. I walked away from racing as the oldest three-time international points winner in history. In spite of missing the last two races I came in third in the points standing, the only pilot ever with five consecutive seasons at third in the points or better."

"You were a natural at racing. I rode a Harley and once a guy I dated took me around a road course in a sports car, but I never even drive fast. I watched a few of those tiny plane races on TV, but never went to one. What did you do after you quit racing?"

"A friend of mine, Roy, ran a charter fishing boat out of Boca Raton. He showed me the ropes for six months and then I bought a boat like his. We started working together. When the fishing wasn't good, we took sight seers on whale watching trips. I thought I would lose money, but running the boat became fairly lucrative. Between this income, money from the sale of my part of the flight school and my investments from racing, I no longer had to work for a living. I stayed fishing and whale watching with Roy for nearly ten years."

"Did you ever try to get back together with Cheryl?"

"I thought about it several times, but decided against any return to those days. The kids made a few attempts to put us back together, but she was still running the flight school and I didn't want to chance it. In case you didn't notice, the sun is now below the horizon, darkness will soon be upon us, and the brightest star in the sky, Sirius, will appear right about there." He points low in the southeastern sky. "There's no moon tonight, so it will be quite dark on the beach. I'm getting hungry and will go home to cook dinner when I take my butt off the sand."

"You're trying to get rid of me," I kidded, standing up. I reached down and took his hand to help him up and looked into those clear blue eyes again.

"Not a chance," he replied as he straightened up and stretched muscles that had been sitting too long. "I did enjoy talking with you. Where do you live?"

"In the grey apartment—the two-toned one with white awnings?" I pointed north.

"We're practically neighbors. There are only five houses between my house and your apartment. If you'd like, you can join me for dinner. I made a green salad and there are plenty of fresh fish and shrimp. All I need to do is zap 'em in the microwave. They'll be ready to savor in five minutes."

"I don't know. I wouldn't want to put you to any trouble."

"No more than what I'll be doing for myself, and I'm a terrific cook. Why don't you run home and change into jeans or the like, eatin' clothes for finger food? Uh, you do own jeans don't you?"

I laugh. "Of course, silly, and I would like to get out of this suit. I've worn it since six-thirty this morning. It's a bit restrictive, for eating I mean."

"By the time you return everything will be ready except the sea food. I don't want to start that until we're ready to eat. They take just a couple of minutes."

He heads for his house, and I start for my apartment.

"With you in a few," I call out as we walk away from each other.

The air will be cooling after dark. I put on jeans, walking shoes and a sweater and head down the walk toward his house. I can hardly believe I am so pleased to be having dinner with a white-haired man older than my grandmother.

Chapter 9 - Dinner and More in St. Augustine

I am overwhelmed. "That was fabulous," I say quite truthfully as I down the last morsel of fish. "The dinner was excellent and the Pinot Grigio perfect. You ought to open a restaurant."

"Thank you kindly, but I prefer to cook for myself and a few select friends. Would you like a small glass of brandy with me?"

"Sure! Might as well. I don't feel like doing any work tonight."

"You mean you were going to work tonight?" he comments as he pours the clear tan liquid. "You **are** married to your business. How about taking a look at some spectacular astronomical objects for a major change? Do something wild."

"You're kidding me."

"Not one bit," he says walking out onto his deck and motioning me to follow. He slides a white plastic cover off a man-sized object revealing a rather substantial telescope attached to a 30-inch flat screen TV set at eye level. "This baby is pointed at Orion's sword right now. Let's find out what the great nebula in Orion looks like."

In a short time a spectacular picture of the nebula appears on the screen in full color. I can only say, "Beautiful, absolutely breathtaking. How do you get the colors so . . . brilliant? I remember seeing photos of that object, but never so clear or colorful."

He replies with a knowing grin, "That is because this telescope views the object through three different colored filters of special wavelengths. Those three images are enhanced for color separation and combined to provide the color enhanced image—quite simple."

"Simple for you, but I'm no scientist. Your description sounds complicated to me, complicated, but beautiful, positively gorgeous. Orion, the dippers and Cassiopeia are about the only constellations I can recognize. Incidentally, where is the Orion nebula right now."

"Right overhead almost, right there," he replies, pointing. "Look for the three stars that are his belt?"

"Yes, I've seen them often."

"Below the belt are three fainter stars pointing down. They represent his sword. The middle object of the three is the Great Nebula of Orion. The view stays fixed on the display since my telescope uses a computer controlled motorized mechanism that moves to follow whatever object I focus on. I punch in the coordinates of any object in the heavens and the scope will move to display what I selected."

"Can you show me, please?"

"Anything in particular you would like to view?"

"Just pick something pretty. I'm not very knowledgeable about the stars."

"Okay, let's view the Andromeda galaxy, our nearest galactic neighbor," With that he enters several keystrokes on the keyboard. A list pops up in the lower corner of the screen. He selects from the list and steps back. "It'll take a few minutes to find those new coordinates."

The motor on the telescope hums and swings around and up. There are several short bursts of humming and then silence. A new picture emerges on the display. Jack makes a few adjustments and the shimmering spiral of the Andromeda galaxy fills the center of the screen. "Again, the pictures I remember seeing of that before, were in black and white. Your display is dazzling and beautiful in color."

"It enhanced the color exactly the same way as the nebula. The eye can't view it that way unless we intensify the colors. They're the real colors, all right, but greatly enhanced. Makes it easier to separate subtle differences, details that would be invisible otherwise."

"You are a fascinating man, Jack Chandler. A great cook, an astronomer, an airplane racer, and you were in the war. I'll bet there are many other interesting things about you."

"When you've knocked around this old world as much and for as long as I, you can't help but have had some interesting experiences. Some of those I was lucky to live through. There are so many things I enjoy doing and knowledge I make a practice of pursuing, I never experience a dull moment. As long as this old body keeps on working I'll continue. Of course, some of my abuses are paying me back with pains and stiffness. My doc says I'm wearing out. I don't surf anymore . . . bad knees . . . and I can't take the stairs two at a time like I used to, but my reactions remain quick and my mind and memory seem to be holding up."

"You seem to be in good physical shape, for a man your age . . . If you were in the Viet Nam War you were at least seventeen. That makes you . . . My God, you must be more than seventy. I find that hard to believe."

"Seventy-two to be exact. I'll be seventy-three in June. I said I was an old coot. Physically, I'm carrying about twenty extra pounds I'd like to shed, but with my knees limiting my exercise and my love of good food, I'm having a hard time losing any."

"You certainly don't act like seventy-two. My grand father is seventy and he seems much older."

"Some folks try to act like their age, or at least how they think people their age should act. I try to live up to no one's expectations but my own. I earn a lot of freedom by doing so. Incidentally, I want to thank you for leaving that stuffy cover girl at home. I much prefer the mature little girl in jeans and sneakers."

"Oh, I'll bet you say that to all the girls."

When I say it, we both burst into hearty laughter. We walk around his main room, viewing pictures of his plane, his fishing boat and lots of his family. The following quote is framed and hanging on one wall:

Perception, ah yes, perception, it is what drives our decisions, controls our emotions of love, anger, joy, disappointment, friendship, hatred, virtually everything we think or react to. Perception overrules facts, logic, and reality. Whether from love, avarice, or foolishness, and no matter how removed perception is from truth, it rules us and determines our life decisions. We do not live in a real world, but live totally in a world created by and subject to our perceptions.

— 1995

"Quite profound," I say when I read it. "Is that a quote from someone famous?"

"Nope just a little something that popped into my head during a discussion about reality I was having with an old friend. I polished it up several times and saved the result back in 1995. It's one of my favorite ideas."

"A philosopher no less."

"Not a philosopher, a realist. I keep a book of quotes and other things over on the coffee table, a collection of writings I saved over the last fifty or so years. My book includes quotes from at least 270 different people mixed in with about a hundred of my own. They are a bunch of ideas I like and admire, a never-ending collection I add to whenever I find a new one I like."

"Love to read it. Could I borrow it some time?"

"You can take the book with you if you like. Of course, I want it back sometime."

"Or I'll read when I visit."

"Whatever is your pleasure. Would you like a tour of my humble abode?"

"Love one."

He took me for a tour. The house is much larger inside than it appears from the beach. His home is different. One huge room spans the entire front opening onto a deck. Steps lead down from the deck to the upper reach of the beach. Huge glass doors slide smoothly open on each side, matching the windows which completed the entire front of the room. The doors hang on rollers and ride above the wooden floor. When they are closed and latched, a seal moves down and closes the half inch space between the bottom of the doors and the floor. Otherwise, they move easily with the lightest touch. The well-equipped kitchen fills most of the rear of the main room. Sunken deep into the back wall, the sink counter is flush with the rest of the back wall cabinets. An island across from the sink holds a cook top, a broiler, an oven, and a hidden microwave. A section dropped to table height runs across the entire front of the island. There are four chairs for casual dining at this counter top. The table where we had dinner is near the island toward the front.

The single bedroom is offset to the north of the main room. The east end of the room is all glass facing the ocean. A wide utility/storage room runs across the back of the house providing an open passage to the rear door and a small guest room on the south side. Between the kitchen and the utility room are two bathrooms, one for each bedroom. The guest bath opens into both the hall and the guest room.

"I designed the house myself," he explains, "Couldn't find any design to suit me. The doors and floor are designed together to ensure sand from the beach causes no problems. Those thin openings between each board on the deck and inside are the key. Any sand that is blown in or carried in will eventually slip through the cracks and end up beneath the house. A quick sweep with a broom and presto, all gone."

"Don't the cracks plug up? And how about windy days, doesn't sand seep inside through those cracks? I think that would be a problem."

"Not at all. In windy weather I keep the doors shut. By maintaining a positive air pressure inside with my HVAC unit, air is always going out through the cracks and not a single grain of sand comes in. Another thing, if I spill say, a cup of coffee, it goes through the crack in an instant. Makes cleanup easy. Even the bathrooms use this floor."

"And I suppose you designed that too."

"Guilty! Several contractors came by to examine my floor and he operation of my doors. Many then use the design in homes they build. I'll bet there are thirty or forty homes in the area with those floors and doors. I feel greatly complimented."

"And you let them do it, copy your designs, free?"

"Sure! They were all decent guys. I met a number of nice people showing them this floor. Been in many homes for dinner as a result. In the six years here, I met many new friends that way.

Money can't buy that—sharing freely surely does. Read the little phrase on the brass plaque there on the wall, one of Jack Chandler's rules about life."

I read aloud, "Givers are given. Takers are taken," I think for a moment . . . "That's not always true though."

"Don't be so cynical. Few sayings are true all the time. I'll bet it's true more often than false. At least, that is my experience."

"You could be right. I never quite thought that way, but I will say one thing. Most of the real takers live miserable little lives, even the wealthy ones. They make lousy friends."

"Sounds like you have had first hand experience."

"More than one."

"You too?"

"That little girl in me was taken in a few times."

"I'll bet you prefer being you rather than like the ones who took advantage of you. The little girl in you can't see some things coming, but she can see things the other you can't. Here's a suggestion for you."

"Oh?"

"Take one day each month and let that little girl run your day. Do and act the way she wants to act. Be crazy, no matter what. Go to work in the clothes you are now wearing, smile at everybody, but don't tell them what you are doing."

"That's insane."

"You'll be amazed at what happens. I guarantee it."

"What about my customers, my people? They might not care for the new look. I hate to lose a good client or mess up my employees."

"Aren't you the boss? If you must tell them something, tell them it's your . . . 'free-to-be-me' day, the one day each month you're going to hang loose. See what happens."

"They may want to do the same thing. Our dress and conduct rules are quite strict. I couldn't break those."

"And why not?"

"There would be chaos."

"A little good clean chaos never hurt a soul and might be good for you, all of you."

"No way. I couldn't take the chance. There could be a revolution on my hands. Some of my people have been in this professional mode at work for ten, even twenty years. They would be shocked out of their skulls."

"If you're afraid, or worried about image, blame it on me. Tell them some crazy old coot who holds a minority interest in the business gets legal control of your company for one day every month and insists you dress and act like this for that one day. Tell them they are free to dress how they like for one day, but conduct normal business. I'll come down in my shorts, sandals, T-shirt and cap to confirm your story."

"You are crazy. I can't believe I'm even considering doing this. Let me sleep on it."

"Call me and tell me when you're going to do it. Here's my card with my TC number. The call will reach me wherever I am - - even in the shower."

"How did you get such a low TC number? I never heard of one so low. You must have some real pull to get that low number."

"I worked for TelComm for a couple of years, flying their executives around in their private jet even before they put their satellites in orbit. That number is one of the perks. The 1001 series is available only for high-ranking TelComm executives to this day. Their president gave me number thirteen for life long before they started using the series for their own people exclusively. I'll be 1001-1000-1013 'til the day I die."

"How about leaving me that number in your will? Having that low a number on my business card would be certain to impress people."

"There's a waiting list of about twenty ahead of you," Jack grins broadly as he speaks. "I couldn't resist a little jab," I wasn't getting ahead of him.

"Me either. You're difficult to get ahead of, aren't you?"

"I try to stay on my toes, even if they are a bit shaky."

"Speaking of staying on toes, I should head home. Six o'clock comes early and tomorrow will be a big day for me. I want to thank you for a great evening. The food and the company were great. You must come to my place for dinner."

"Gladly! Can you cook?"

"I'll ignore that remark. How about Friday evening, say six-thirty? You can tell me about your life, and about the war from someone who was in it."

"Sure my war stories won't bore you?"

"I am quite certain they won't. I've heard nothing boring from you yet."

"Friday . . . dinner . . . six-thirty . . . I'll be there."

"Until Friday."

"Nope! I'm going to walk you home."

"There's no need. It's quite safe around here at night."

"My mother taught me a gentleman always takes a lady to her door after dark and I do what my mother taught me."

"Yeah, right."

"I'll also remember where I'm going on Friday."

"Okay, but it's not necessary."

We walk down the walkway and I show him my apartment door. When he is about to leave, I take his head in my hands and plant a big kiss smack in the middle of his forehead.

"That's about the most uninspiring kiss good night I ever received from a lady. All things considered though, it was rather pleasant. Till Friday."

As he walks toward his house, my eyes follow him. "What a fascinating man," I think out loud before I step back into my apartment. But the thought of a *free-to-be-me* day frightens me terribly. No way can I manage that.

Chapter 10 - Business as Usual, and Dinner
✳ Friday, April 5, 2013 ✳

Late Friday afternoon I find myself involved with one of our better clients who is planning a tour of the Riviera with about twenty people. When five o'clock rolls around, my irritation starts growing. I can't believe dinner with an old man seems so important, more important than taking care of one of my special clients. What's gotten into me?

I ask my client, Dan Quinn, "Could Nedra take over for me? She's fully capable of covering all we must cover and I have an important personal appointment at six. I didn't think this would take nearly so long."

Dan Quinn, a man who feels important, is not pleased. He always deals with the top people of any company he works with. He expresses his displeasure. "Couldn't I work this out with you? Call and postpone your appointment."

I am inwardly furious. Obviously the fragile ego of this pompous ass drives him. He knows that Nedra can handle things from this point out, and that I will turn it over to her when he leaves. He wants me to change my appointment to feed his need for control. With measured determination I insist.

"I made a promise and it's important that I keep it. You understand the importance of keeping promises of course. You wouldn't be here if I didn't always keep my promises, would you?" I cornered him and he understands.

"You're certain she'll handle things the way you would?"

"If I were taking this trip myself, Nedra would handle it for me."

Without giving him a chance to change his mind, I call Nedra in and ask her to take over. "Give Mr. Quinn here the full treatment," I tell her, say my goodbyes, and leave. I can't remember being so upset with a client, and such a high profile one. I am almost forty minutes behind schedule. I hurry to my car, and tap Jack's number into my TC phone.

"I'm running a bit late. Can you give me another half hour before you come over?"

"No problem. I can mosey over and give you a hand if you like."

"That would spoil everything. Dinner is all planned and I want to surprise you. If you came over early, the surprise would be ruined."

"Okay sweetheart, have it your way," he replies in a fake voice, obviously imitating someone.

I reply with, "I'll expect you at seven."

✳   ✳   ✳

Jack finishes dessert, sits back in his chair, stares up at the chandelier and says, "On a scale of one to ten I would give the ambiance a nine, the service a nine, the wine a nine, the food a solid ten and the company at least a twelve, all together a most memorable meal. And I must admit, from the candles on the table to the great brandy, quite an impressive surprise."

"Wow! That's enough to turn a girl's head."

My reaction surprises me. I am strongly attracted to this man my grandparents' age. I am giddy as a young girl with a crush on her teacher.

"You're quite accomplished for a woman your age, or a man your age for that matter," he comments, his eyes wide in amazement that morphs into a look of mischief. "You are quite gorgeous, bright, a terrific cook, an excellent conversationalist on many subjects, and a successful business woman. In a nutshell, you are a class act, a real rarity these days when most women your age are totally self-absorbed and wouldn't be able to boil pasta fit to eat."

"I can thank my grandmother for that. She was an active socialite hostess back in the forties and before the war, before the big cultural shift of the sixties rearranged our society. She tried hard to teach me how to be a traditional lady, even how to prepare and serve elegant dishes, told me innumerable stories of life before the war. I resisted of course, but some of her efforts sank in. I do enjoy preparing a dinner like ours this evening, especially when appreciated."

"Your grandmother did a masterful job. There's much more to you than a snazzy business woman. I'm quite impressed by the new parts I'm discovering. There's a warm, creative, giver behind that hard cover. Must be the influence of that little girl."

"Thank you kind sir. I love all the compliments. Now, you were going to tell me some things about the Viet Nam War, at least, I asked you to. Why don't you start while I'm clearing this up?"

"Can I help?"

"Sure, if you want. Hand me the things and I'll drop them in the dishwasher."

It took a few minutes to clear the table and walk into my studio room facing the ocean. "It's not as big as yours and there is no patio up here, but the view's just as great." I pointed at the couch for Jack to sit and plopped down beside him. "Now I want you to tell me about Viet Nam. I'm fascinated hearing about it from someone who was there."

"Do you realize that's more than forty years ago? It's hard for me to believe it's been so long."

"What were you doing when the war started?"

"I was in high school, graduated in '60. At seventeen I enlisted in the Marines. I wanted to fly more than anything. The next thing I'm on an aircraft carrier in the South China Sea providing fighter escort and ground support when the war was just starting. I told you about that the night we met on the beach, and also about my being shot down and captured."

"That was before my parents were born. My grandmother told me about the wars. She described the Pacific war from Pearl Harbor to Hiroshima. Her brother died in the Pacific, his ship sunk by the Japanese. She told me much about the Viet Nam War and all the protests. She thought it quite stupid for us to be in that war and she was right on. She disagreed with the ways young people were protesting. According to her, dividing our nation and creating such discord was terrible. That goes on even today."

"Yeah, and we were in the military doing what those politicians in Washington decided we must do. I think things would have been quite different if those politicians had to fight themselves. Throughout most of history, leaders were out leading their soldiers in combat. Many kings and military leaders were slain in battle leading their troops. Now the leaders sit back in their easy chairs, drinking booze and eating caviar while their young men are being slaughtered far away from home and coming back devastated in mind and body. That's another subject I would rather not think about, but must. It's why I do what I do, including writing those articles that receive so much flak."

"Oh? What do you write about?"

"I told you nothing about my research and writing, did I?"

"Now my curiosity is on high alert. What do you write about that gets so much flak as you call it?"

"I received only a few threats so far, most recently, while doing research and writing articles about Wahhabi Muslims. Al-Qaeda and Osama bin Laden first appeared on the scene thirty years ago. I was working in Africa as a private security consultant for a consortium of American oil companies when I first ran into the beginnings of al-Qaeda. From Pakistan they established their first African cell in Liberia to sabotage the oil industry there. Shortly after I published my first detailed reports, our government wanted to recruit me to spy on al-Qaeda."

"So you were a spy in Africa?"

"No, I turned them down and continued with the oil group. I feared the government would restrict my activities, my research and my writing. I was right. They tried to restrict my activities even though they had no authority do so. The government of Liberia both authorized and supported my work. That was a big help. I'll give you access to what I wrote about. Most all was ignored by both our government and our media."

"That figures. What did you end up doing?"

"I spent the next three years writing reports for the oil group and doing research on al-Qaeda, almost all on my own. Everything is included in the manuscript of the book I'm writing on the Wahhabi Muslim threat to the rest of the world. I'll let you read my manuscript. It's easier than talking about it."

We talk about his experiences in the war and research on al-Qaeda until quite late. As he walks away, I watch him for a long time until he disappears into the darkness.

Chapter 11 - Getting to know Each Other and Wow!
✳ Friday, May 17, 2013 ✳

Some six weeks later, we are relaxing after dinner at my apartment. I find myself examining my new friend. He is quite an attractive man, even at his age. We sit in silence for a few moments while surprising thoughts flow through my head. "How about some music?"

"Fine if it's real music. I don't care much for all that modern social/political crap. To me it's not even music," Jack answers in a clear voice.

"I'm sure you'll like my selection. It's music to relax with. I'm not keen on any of that social/political stuff myself. In fact, you won't find one recording in my entire collection. There are some older recordings that are great and some new stuff by Karamunda that is wonderful to slow dance to."

"I'd love to listen. I rather like Karamunda myself. It's good music to relax with."

I tap several selections into my sound system and pleasant music permeates the room. "Do you like Karamunda? He's old African, but that's about all I know," I ask, quite certain he would know.

"His parents were part of the small group of South Africans who had political ties with both sides during the time of apartheid. He was one of the first to be born in Africa after apartheid was demolished and Nelson Mandela became prime minister. He studied music in New York including the classics. He studied the recordings of old African music while performing lots of modern political stuff. I think Bakay, or something like that was the name of his group."

"I never got into that kind of music. I remember Bakay, but didn't connect them with him. Interesting."

"Then he switched direction, started his new group and they took off in popularity. His marriage of old African sounds and rhythm with the classics was a new and unique sound. Numerous others picked up his style, but they're all relatively poor imitations of the real Karamunda. Almost single handedly he's been bringing soft melodic music, even romantic music, back into popularity. The piece playing, 'Dreamwalker,' has old native American origins."

I am surprised. "Really? Are you sure? That seems quite a stretch to me."

"Positive! He spoke of researching Native American themes quite often. That brings up some interesting thoughts about the changes in many racial, ethnic and cultural groups in America over the last fifty years."

"I feel another serious observation coming on."

"You don't like serious observations?"

"Not usually. Actually I do, but few people make serious observations and most don't know how to talk about them. Small talk is their entire conversational world."

I feel some strange emotions about where this is going. I am absolutely enchanted by his memory, knowledge and willingness to talk about anything. He makes everything so interesting and real.

A devilish grin graces his expression. "I take it you want me to continue?"

"Please!"

"I was thinking, how ironic. Europeans come over and take America away from the natives; treat them terribly, steal their land, infect them with their diseases, banish them to reservations, and forget they even exist. They were treated even worse than the Africans who were brought here as slaves.

"Then there came that startling revelation by a huge, ten-year DNA study of Americans by a group from several respected universities. The study revealed virtually all Latinos are primarily native American while more than half of the other two major American racial groups are at least part native American. Also, at least 40 percent of those of European ancestry are part African. The study claimed around 80 percent of African Americans are part Caucasian. The massive DNA study that revealed this was controversial since it dealt with race. Do you remember the ruckus it created?"

"Absolutely! The study was denounced by virtually every public figure, politician, media personality, religious figure, the entire politically correct crowd—you name it. They all jumped on the anti study bandwagon, condemning the study, its results, the researchers who conducted the study, and the universities that organized the study. The people involved in the study were denounced as racists and called every nasty name in the book. I guess that's human nature. 'When you don't like the message, kill the messenger.' We are so strongly sensitized to anything associated with race. The PC crowd especially goes berserk over anything racial. It's the third rail to them no matter how positive or innocent the discussion."

"Right on! I detest bandwagons and most people who jump onto them. They're sheep playing follow the follower."

He is expressing what I had thought many times. "I can identify with that."

"I believe the entire protest was orchestrated by the PC crowd to further their own agenda."

"You may be right, but I never considered that. When that study was released it even caused some problems for my business. Several of our favorite tourist spots were shut down. We had to find new destinations for at least a dozen clients. Most were unhappy about that, but of course, there was nothing we could do about it."

"I thought the results were quite revealing and all those idiots who condemned the study were brainless, driven by unthinking emotional mob reaction. I was rather impressed and quite pleased with what the report said about the native American genetic invasion."

"Oh?"

"I'm part Algonquin myself. My great great-grandmother was a full-blooded Algonquin and my family has always been proud of that."

"You're part native American?"

"Positively! I had my DNA tested to check on my granddad's story about our Indian ancestry, and it partially confirmed what he told me."

"I am part native American as well. My grandmother told me my native American ancestry is Potawatami. They were driven from their homes in Indiana in the 1830s and forced to march all the way to Missouri and Iowa in the winter. Many of them died during that cruel march and after being driven from their homeland at that."

"What a coincidence. My parents had a summer home on lake Tippecanoe in Kosciusko county in northern Indiana. I do believe that's near where several Potawatami villages stood before they were driven out in the 1830s. As a kid, I found many Indian artifacts near the cottage where an Indian trail existed. That trail came down to a point jutting out into the lake. That point made a narrow place in the lake where the Indians swam across to a trail on the other side. Next time we're at my place I'll show you one particularly unusual piece I found when my friends and I were digging a hole near the trail."

"How amazing! My grandmother used to tell me tales about our Indian ancestors. Stories she learned from her grandfather or even her great-grandfather. I did a little research on the Potawatami Indians when I was in college to learn about 'my people.' They were supposedly descendants of Algonkians who were driven west out of New York and Quebec and into what was then the Northwest Territory including what is now Indiana, Ohio, Michigan and Illinois. White men did not drive them out, the Iroquois did. They were a powerful Indian nation who wanted the territory and trade with Europeans for themselves. They drove all of the Algonkians out of the east to west of the Appalachians."

"We could even be related," he comments, laughing. "Stranger things have happened. We could be long lost cousins," he adds with a grin.

Karamunda's *Dreamwalker* finishes playing.

"The next number is more conventional."

He looks at me with that impish grin as it starts playing. "As I remember the album, it's less native American and more African. I can't recall the name, but it's quite melodic with an underlying beat that is pure African."

Once more I am surprised at the breadth of his knowledge. Inspired, I stand up. "Dance with me."

"You want to dance with this old body?" he comments as he stands and gathers me into his arms. "It's been such a long time, I may not remember how."

"Yes, I do and I'll bet your comment is an out and out lie."

We dance for a long time, at least half an hour, with a tiny bit of conversation here and there. I can hardly believe how thrilled I am. We stop dancing facing the window, stand there in each other's arms gazing at the night over the ocean and listening to the tumbling waves. All kinds of feelings stir my body while crazy, romantic thoughts run through my mind. It's been a long time since I experienced those.

"I hate to break a magical moment, but I think I had better head for home," Jack says as we slowly and reluctantly untwine. "It's way past my bedtime and I must head out early in the morning."

"Oh?"

"As much I hate to leave such wonderful company, I need to be sharp tomorrow when I interview some people for an article I'm writing."

I couldn't believe the disappointment I felt at the prospect of his leaving. "You're writing an article? About what?"

"Remember me telling you about my work in Liberia for those oil companies?"

"Yes."

"It's about what I learned then and since, about the early efforts of Osama bin Laden to develop the al-Qaeda network to promote Wahhabi Islam in Africa and several Islamic lands long before they became the dedicated terrorist organization they are now. They presently range all over Africa and the middle east, in fact, the whole world. Wahhabi cells are even active in the US. I had several run ins with them over the years. Because of my experience with them in Africa while they were organizing, America Now Magazine commissioned me to write a series of articles about them."

"America Now? I'm impressed. I never heard of Wahhabi Muslims before."

"They're a nasty bunch. They were for many years before 9-11 when few Americans had ever heard of them."

"I never heard of them until you mentioned them."

"They are extremely dangerous. Unfortunately, few people in the intelligence community or military are the least concerned about them. They ignored all the warnings from my small group and others who were aware of them. By the time 9-11 happened, many of us had become disgusted because our well-based warnings were being ignored and even put down. Were you aware we even supplied them scads of weapons to help drive the USSR out of Afghanistan?"

"Those weapons were supposed to be supplied to friendly Afghan freedom fighters?"

"Supposedly, but lots of those weapons including many stinger missiles were stashed in their camps high in the Afghan mountains. They were being stockpiled to be used against the west. Sadly, few people would even listen to our warnings."

"Did you know about 9-11 before it happened?"

"No, but remember the first attempt to blow up the World Trade Center?"

"Yes, but wasn't it a failure?"

"Not completely, the blind sheik who masterminded the first attempt is a Wahhabi with ties to bin Laden. While in jail, he said they would destroy the WTC. I don't believe that was ever investigated thoroughly. If it had been, or if we had taken his threats seriously, those towers would still be standing and 3,000 horrible deaths would have been prevented."

"You must be furious about that. I mean all the snafus that let it happen."

"I got over it. Trouble is those same idiots whose policies led to disaster are back at it again. I never cease to be amazed how blind the public can be to real, dangerous menaces, dangers as obvious as a blotch of black on a yellow wall. The media mostly ignores so many menaces. I find it hard to believe it's not deliberate."

"Deliberately ignoring such a serious menace? You can't be serious?"

"I believe Islamic fundamentalists and Wahhabi Muslims in particular, possess the determination and the ability to destroy Western civilization. They're a much greater danger than most people think. They have been at it for a long time, destroying and devouring any civilization that didn't bow to the supremacy of their beliefs. All you need do is read the history of Islamic invasions of other lands since the eighth century. They took a step backward when the Ottoman Empire collapsed and they were driven out of Spain. Other than that setback, they have never taken a step backward. No land that came under Islam ever threw off the Islamic shackles. They are in it for the long haul, something few Westerners comprehend, Americans in particular. All the considerable experience I had with those Wahhabi fanatics confirms what I said. If we don't stop them soon, we're done for."

"Why isn't there more about this problem in the news? Until recently the federal government treated them as though they were a relatively small group of minor troublemakers. The media then affirms that position."

"I'll give you a copy of my research and my published articles when I get back. You can decide for yourself how big a threat they pose. Right now I should go home. Five o'clock will roll around quickly so I'll need to sleep fast."

"Please, let's get together when you return. I want to learn more about your writing and I do enjoy your company."

"No more than this old coot enjoys yours. How about Sunday? I'll be back late Saturday night. Come over about noon. I'll be fixing dinner. You can help me finish."

"I like that."

"Now, how about a real goodnight kiss?"

I never wanted more to kiss a man in my life. I look into his eyes and slip my arms around his neck. "How about it?"

After he walks down the steps, I watch him until he is out of sight, thinking, *Carol, you're falling for a man three times your age. Are you out of your mind?*

Chapter 12 - Anticipation
✳ Sunday, May 19, 2013, Noon ✳

I decide to let this take its course and follow where it leads. The chances of it being anything but a momentary infatuation must be small. Surely the huge difference in our ages will prove insurmountable before long. I am anxious all day Saturday and by Sunday noon I am practically a basket case from the waiting. This is unusual for me. By the time I walk up the path to his house I am literally shaking with excitement. I cannot believe my feelings.

"Greetings, milady, please enter," he exaggerates formally with a sweeping bow and extended hand toward the main room. Mock seriousness controls his face.

Not to be out done, I curtsey, take his hand and prance inside. "Thank you kind sir."

Next thing, we are entwined, right back where we left off on Friday. After a long kiss we stop and our eyes meet and hold. My heart is jumping out of my chest.

"Yup! I'm right," These words of his come with a broad smile to fit the moment perfectly.

"What's that supposed to mean?"

"I decided Friday you were the best kisser I had ever kissed and this one proved I'm right."

"Well, sir, you say the nicest things. It's enough to sweep a poor girl off her feet," I reply in my best fragile female voice.

"Methinks I hear words from the distant past, distant even for me."

We both break into laughter and head into the kitchen.

"I'll saute these shrimp and dinner will be served. If I can catch my breath, that is. Young lady, you can't know how you charged up my life. I'm not at all sure where we're going, but I'm on board for the entire trip. Tell me if and when you feel any different."

"It shows every sign of being a long trip and I wouldn't think of quitting until we reach wherever we're going," I walk over and put my arms around him. "It's quite unlikely, but I'm falling for you big time. This is no little girl crush."

"I love this, but it's dinner or smoochin', not both. Shrimp are touchy and I can't cook and handle serious kissin' at the same time. What'll it be?"

I put on my best pout for the answer. "Oh, all right, but when dinner is over, look out."

We sit down to relax after everything is cleaned and put away. I feel warm and cuddly. I want this man more than I ever wanted another. I stick my lips in his ear and whisper, "Make love to me."

"What? You're likely to get me in serious trouble saying that."

"I do hope so."

"Are you sure I'm not too old? I mean . . ."

"Let's find out," I interrupt, take his hand and pull him toward the bedroom.

Chapter 13 - Reality Check
* Sunday, May 19, 2013, 4:30 pm *

Late Sunday afternoon Jack shakes me awake. He is quite serious. "Carol. We've got to talk. I don't want anything to interfere with what's happening to us, but we need to face some realities, talk about them I mean."

"Right . . . Can't we wait and just enjoy things for a while?"

"Sooner or later we must deal with a few necessary things and I'd like doing it sooner rather than later, before we're in so deep neither of us can back out gracefully."

"I hate being practical at times like these."

"I do too, but my mind keeps waving red flags and I'd like to rid us of them right away."

"I don't want any of those, 'I'm old enough be your father' routines."

He smiles his impish little boy smile. "That wouldn't work because I'm actually older than your grandfather."

"Oops. I did tell you about him didn't I?"

"At our first dinner."

"Oh, all right. Give me your best shot."

Jack rolls his eyes knowing I am having a hard time being serious. "At best, we are an unlikely pair. That doesn't mean we can't make it. I'm not one for short term relationships. If either of our hearts is to be broken, so be it. I may be an old man, but my heart feels the same way my entire adult life. That's the real problem for me."

"Okay, I've been giving this some serious thought since I first realized how my feelings for you were growing. Like you, I am not big on short term relationships. How long could we last? Ten years would be longer than most relationships, even marriages, last any more. By then you'll be eighty-five and I'll be thirty-eight. You look like one of those ageless people to me. You might make it to a hundred in relatively good health. At least, we could hope."

"My concern is you would be giving up the chance for children. I'm not about to become a father for many reasons, primarily the kids. It wouldn't be fair to them."

"Truthfully, I'm not cut out for children anyway. I love my nieces and nephews, even like taking care of them occasionally, but I don't long for that as a full time responsibility. What about you? How long have you been living alone? A relationship might put a crimp in your lifestyle."

"Answers, in order: first, you may one day wake up and regret not having children, second, I lived alone, but not by choice. I never found anyone crazy enough to put up with me. I rather like the prospect of a pleasant companion."

"You mean you tried?"

"Sure. Even had one lady move in for a short time about six years ago, a bad mistake which took me six months to correct."

"Tell me about it."

"Evelyn was a widow, fifty, pretty, talkative and searching for a husband. A friend put us together and for a short time it worked out. We were not in love, but she was a decent sort, you know, comfortable. After several months she moved in with me. Within a week of her moving into the house I realized I had made a terrible mistake. We argued over little things, totally insignificant things. I was as much to blame as she, even more. We were a poor match. When we parted, we agreed we had waited too long. She was at least intelligent enough to realize it was the fault of neither of us. Afterwards, I quit even thinking about the opposite sex."

"Now I understand why you want to put things in order. You were burnt once and think it could happen again. I made my decisions about children long before I met you. I hope you're clear on that. And I don't find any tie-in with your previous experience. I hesitate asking, but I wonder about one thing."

"What's that?"

"Did you two enjoy making love?"

"Never made love."

I am incredulous, "You lived with a woman for six months and never had sex?"

"It sounds weird when you put it like that. I thought about it, but it never seemed . . . appropriate."

"I feel sorry for her. She missed out on a fantastic lover. No wonder it didn't work. That's one problem we needn't worry about."

"And we're not living together either. That helps keep conflict to a minimum."

I nearly choke on what I am thinking, but decide to ask anyway, "How'd you like to try it for a while? Living together I mean. We could discover if there would be any terminal conflicts."

"You're serious?"

"Never more serious in my life."

"You want to find out how soon we would be at each other's throats?"

"No, how often we would make love if we slept together every night."

"Touché."

"Of course, you will throw out all your masculine furniture and move mine in."

"You're full of it."

"Just wondered if you were paying attention."

"What would your family think?"

"That I am crazy, but they are already sure of that. I think my sisters would like you, lots. You and my father would get along well. You two are alike in so many ways."

"I just realized another strange thing. You're younger than my grandson, Eric."

I chuckle. "Follow me on this, I'm younger than your grandson and you're older than my grandfather. That makes us about even."

Jack wrinkles his face. "You exhibit strange reasoning . . . sound, but quite strange."

I feel warm and tender. "There is a poem Ted gave me when we were together, an old one by George Ethridge. I read it over and over many times during the pain-filled weeks after he left. Let me think and I'll repeat it for you.

'It is not, Celia, within our power to say how long our love will last.

It may be within this hour may lose those joys we now do taste.

The blessed that immortal be, from change in love are only free.

Then since we mortal lovers are, ask not how long our love will last,

But while it does, let us take care each minute be with pleasure passed:

Were it not madness to deny to live because we're sure to die?'"

Jack shakes his head. "That's like hitting below the belt. I'll admit you got me with that. It's quite beautifully true."

I face him expectantly. "What do you say we give it a try? Neither of us has anything to lose."

His eyes widen. "A commitment?"

I reorient my mind. "Uh . . . yes. A commitment. Definitely a commitment . . . for both of us."

He seems a bit worried. "Just what kind of a commitment are you speaking of?"

"We already made a serious commitment. We both admitted we love each other. When you say you love someone and mean it, it's a big commitment. You did mean it, didn't you?"

"Absolutely! I never said those words without meaning them and meaning them for a long time into the future. I never said, 'I love you.' to anyone I didn't love. At least not since I was in my teens."

"I can't believe you said that. I used those same exact words myself several times to explain my feelings on the same subject. No wonder we hit it off so well."

He grins and puts his arms around me. "Well, little girl, you got yourself a man, at least a commitment from one. I fell in love with you about our third dinner, but never dreamed you would ever feel the same way. I'll remain committed until I am committed to the looney bin."

His worried face returns. "You didn't mean any kind of legal commitment did you?"

"Not at all. We can think about that later if we don't kill each other first."

His worried look morphs into a gentle smile. "Well said. I was checking to make sure we were on the same wavelength."

The little girl in me is impish. "Now, why don't I go home and pick up a few things for tonight and tomorrow. Tonight we can play old married folks and I can go to work from here after I fix your breakfast."

"Absolutely not," he says firmly while crossing his arms. It shocks me till he adds, grinning, "I'll do the cooking in my house while you are making yourself beautiful for work."

Chapter 14 - Together in Two Homes
✳ Sunday, June 9, 2013 ✳

Within a few weeks we settle into a routine. Friday evenings I go directly to his house from work. After dinner I stay the weekend. Sunday dinner is at my apartment and Jack stays with me until I leave for work Monday morning. Sunday, June 9 I surprise Jack with a birthday party dinner.

"I never told you today is my birthday," He responds when I plop a birthday cake down in front of him.

"You didn't. You did tell me the month is June. Remember giving me your card with your TC number?"

"Sure, but my birthday's not on it."

I grin slyly. "You'd be surprised at the information one can gain in a credit report if you use a person's name and TC number."

Jack is disturbed. "You ran a credit check on me?"

"Don't be upset. I did it only to find your birth date."

A bit ruffled, he asks, "What other information did you glean from that report?"

I laugh. "I do believe the man is a bit peeved."

"Wouldn't you be if you found I was secretly prying into your credit history?"

"Don't be a jerk. I wanted to surprise you for your birthday and that was the only way I could find the date without asking you."

Jack is apologetic. "I'm sorry, Hon. I was being a real jerk wasn't I?"

I put on a stern face. "Yes you were."

He pleads, "Can we go back to where you surprised me with the cake and start over?"

I smile pleasantly. "Of course."

"Okay! What a wonderful surprise. I love surprises and I love you. How thoughtful. I didn't even think you knew my birthday."

"A bit of overkill, but you did redeem yourself."

"I learned my lesson and promise to behave in the future."

"In that case, I have a big present for you."

"Oh? You didn't need to get me anything."

"I know, but I wanted to. I need to finish wrapping it back in the bedroom. I'll call you when I'm ready and you can come back and unwrap it."

"Sounds like a plan," he replies as his bright eyes sparkle in a full face smile.

I tie a huge red bow to the package and call for him. He opens the door and finds me standing by the bed wearing a huge red bow tied around my waist and nothing else. To my surprise he doubles over laughing.

"I didn't expect you to laugh."

He grabs me in his arms, grinning. "I imagined many things while I waited, but this wasn't one of them. It's much better than anything I imagined."

Some time later he whispers in my ear. "That's the best birthday present I ever received."

✳ Sunday, July 7, 2013 ✳

During the next month I move a number of things into his house and we are together each night. Sunday and Monday we are in my apartment and the rest of the week we are in his house. We maintain this routine for the next two months. During this time increasing numbers of my belongings find their way into his house.

During an evening meal Jack surprises me by asking, "How long is the lease on your apartment?"

"My annual lease will be coming up for renewal in a few months. Why do you ask . . . as if I didn't know?"

"You're hardly ever there except to retrieve something and bring it here, and we're now a fairly permanent thing. Why don't you drop your lease and put your furniture in storage?"

"And be dependent on your good will for the roof over my head? That'll be the day," I throw at him with a big grin.

Not to be out maneuvered he says, "Then you should move back over there . . . today."

"And miss out on all this great food? Not on your life," We both chuckled at that exchange. "Seriously, I wondered about that ever since moving in, but decided to put off bringing it up until the end of the lease was a bit closer."

"What are you going to do when and if we have a big fight?"

"Throw you out of course," I say emphatically. "No, this is what I plan to do should we get into a fight." I stand up, drop my dress to the floor, reach over and grab him and drag him off to the bedroom.

Afterwards, as we lay snuggling in the warm bed he says softly, "I guess we should fight often."

When all my belongings are moved into his place, stored, or disposed of, I turn my keys over to my ex-landlord without hesitation.

Chapter 15 - A Little Remodeling

✳ Wednesday, August 21, 2013 ✳

One day I come home and find a huge stack of new lumber in the back yard. "What's all the lumber for?" I ask as I walk in.

"Just a little remodeling."

"A little? That pile of lumber contains enough wood to build another house and you act like the proverbial cat that swallowed the pet bird. What's going on?"

He grins, kisses me and asks, "Would you like to pick out the fixtures for our new bath room?"

"New bathroom? What's wrong with the old one it works fine for me."

"I decided it's much too small for the two of us. I'm having it enlarged. We'll use the guest room and bath until the work is finished."

"And how long will the renovations take?"

"My contractor friend says about six weeks, but I'm betting eight or ten. How about picking out the fixtures?"

"Who decorated the rest of your house?"

"I did, Why?"

"I think you should stick with the same decorator. I'm a lousy one to pick colors or decorating so I let others to do my decorating for me. Everything comes out better that way. I like to think I'm smart enough to realize my talents and my limitations. Decorating is not among my talents."

"I thought all women liked to decorate."

"Not this one. All I can guarantee is a disaster."

"So be it. We'll live in the guest room until the project is finished. Why don't you stay out of the master bedroom until it's ready? Then it will be a surprise."

"I doubt my curiosity can handle that, but I'll try."

Staying out of the master bedroom while the remodeling proceeds is difficult, but I manage. Living in the guest room is a bit crowded, but we keep conflicts to a minimum. My being away at work while all the stuff goes in and out the hall is a blessing. I am amazed at how clean things are each evening when I come home. Several times they start work before I leave, but they are always gone by the time I arrive home. After two months Jack announces we are about a week away from the grand opening.

Chapter 16 - Revelations
✳ Wednesday, September 11, 2013 ✳

Brooks McKibben, child prodigy, expert in several fields including communications and digital security, was generally recognized as the top man in the world in manipulating digital information and communications even before he graduated from the University of Florida at eighteen. The year before he graduated, he founded BMK Systems, which soon was the top information security company in the world. He became wealthy when BMK Systems expanded and then grew to several hundred employees.

Brooks was also thought be part of the group responsible for the creation and introduction of the weaponized malware worm called Stuxtnet. That's the name of the cyberworm designed to attack and disable the nuclear centrifuges in Iran. No one admitted creating or releasing this dangerous cyber weapon that appeared in 2009. It did considerable damage to Iran's nuclear program, and spread to computers throughout the world, lying hidden waiting to be activated. If its replications are manipulated maliciously, it's anyone's guess what kind and how much damage Stuxtnet could do. All efforts to eliminate it and stop its spread proved futile.

During the growth of BMK, his involvement in spread spectrum communications grew rapidly. Spread spectrum communications use rapidly changing or "jumping" frequencies to mask all kinds of transmissions and make them indistinguishable from normal background noise or static. This technology, developed early in World War II, was used by the military. The glamorous movie actress, Hedy Lamarr, was the co-inventor of the first system to use spread spectrum radio, and together with George Antheil, was issued the first patent on this technology.

One accomplished computer scientist, asked him, "Do you think anyone will ever be able to find and decode spread spectrum communications?"

"Are you kidding?" Brooks said. "That probability is remote. The ability to do so will likely be developed in the distant future, but not in the foreseeable. We don't have that kind of computing power yet."

Brooks had already done it and didn't want anyone to know. The exception was Lydia d'Ober, another free and independent spirit. He met Lydia when she applied for a high level job at BMK. During the second interview she so charmed him he asked her to go to dinner. This led to such an intense relationship that he didn't hire her. He feared if he did, it would negatively affect their growing relationship. Lydia agreed and continued the free lance computer consulting she had been doing while getting her Masters degree.

While working together decoding the first few spread spectrum communication, SSC messages, I lead Lydia into the hidden computer lab beneath my house, revealing its existence to the first and only person I ever told of it.

As we go down the stairs, walk through the library and into the lab she asks, "Wow! Who would ever suspect this hidden place under your house? How did you manage to build this underground lab and library without anyone knowing about it? Obviously it was in place long before we met."

Brooks laughs. "It's a complicated story. When I bought the house, I discovered the original builder had been a survivalist who built an underground bomb shelter. He did so in secret, hiding it from his friends and neighbors. He built the shelter in the fifties when everyone expected the Russians were going to hit us with atom bombs. A later owner bricked up the entrance for some reason, sealing it off and hiding it. When I bought the house, I became curious about the unusual brick wall at the end of the laundry room. I wondered about the wall for about two months until I couldn't stand it any more. I started with a sledge hammer and busted the bricks out. Boy, was I surprised at what I found, a ten foot long passageway and a flight of stairs going down eighteen feet to a twenty by twelve room, all in concrete. It was a mess of course, two feet of water, spider webs, and small critters everywhere."

"When did you decide to turn it into a secret library and lab?"

"That came a bit later. My first thought was to hire a crew to clean it up and drain the water. I thought I could use it for something. Then it dawned on me. Nobody knew about this. It would make for a secret room if I ever needed one. I decided to do all the work myself. I found wiring for lights and outlets, none of which was connected. There was a sump in the back corner I used to pump the water out. There was even an air vent, a four-inch copper pipe that went somewhere from the ceiling in the same corner as the sump. The pipe ended in a drain in the yard above. That was how the water and all the spiders, insects, and other critters had gotten in."

"Yuk! It must have been a mess."

"It was, but it cleaned up surprisingly easily. The wiring was all in conduit connected to a main box beside the entrance. They disconnected it by removing the connections at the main electric box in the house. I hooked those wires back up and everything worked. I bought a sump pump, hooked it up to the drain pipe coming out of the wall, and plugged it in. The sump pump worked perfectly.

"It took me more than a year of spare time work to turn that dungeon into a useable room. Several years later I added the powered cabinet/door and replaced the electric service with the generator that is now built into the back wall. I did that when I started working on SSC systems. It morphed into the present form over the years since then."

"Wow! What fascinating information may lie hidden right beneath your feet." Lydia says with a broad smile.

I begin to tell her what I discovered. "Speaking of hidden things, you won't believe the people in our government who are in league with the Chinese, at least they seem to be."

Lydia is incredulous. "People in our government, in league with Chinese officials. I find that hard to believe. Surely you are mistaken."

"Not a chance. In my records are copies of communications, bank transfers, numbered and coded accounts. People holding the highest positions in our federal government are playing Footsie with their counterparts in the Chinese government. They are planning some kind of a coup involving our currency most likely. The final step was planned for about ten years from now, but they unexpectedly changed their timetable. They have not given the actual date yet, and that date may not be set. It could happen in a few months, right before the next election I'm guessing."

"My God, Brooks, can't you tell anyone? Surely someone could do something with that information."

"Right now my cousin Ralph is the one person connected with the government who knows anything about this. He works for Homeland Security, but is not very high in their hierarchy. There is no one else in any position of power I am certain is not involved in the conspiracy. It sounds paranoid, but that's the only way I can describe it, a conspiracy. I can't trust anyone. Hopefully I can change that before too long. I need time to do so, lots of time."

"How are you going to do that, find someone you can trust I mean?"

"How about we move upstairs, out of this dungeon. We can fix some coffee to sip while we relax and talk?"

As we walk up stairs and into my kitchen, Lydia continues talking.

"That's unbelievable. What can we do? Can't you go to the news media? They would at least warn people of what's going on."

"Several of the messages I intercepted recently revealed our news media are partly controlled by those consorting with the Chinese. They are the last ones I would tell. One peep to them and my life wouldn't be worth a plugged nickel."

"Could they have figured out what you are doing—about their messages I mean?"

"I don't think so. Should any of this leak out, they might think their confidential means of communication had been compromised. Then my sources of information would dry up. I wouldn't be able to access any knowledge of what they are planning to do, or who is involved with them. So far that has not happened, thank God."

"Surely they know of your work on spread spectrum communications. Wouldn't they be spying on you, tapping your phone line, intercepting your communications? This room might be bugged. Did you ever think of that? Damn! Now I'm becoming paranoid."

"I realized that several years ago, but fear not. After I decoded the first few messages, I shrouded the lab in grounded metal. No electronic transmission can get out of the lab and no probe can get in. Wiring is the only way information can move in or out. I made sure of secrecy by removing every bit of wiring connected to anything outside the lab, even the electricity. That's why I use a generator, so I am not connected to the electric grid, a little extra security. You know, don't you, the electric grid is the perfect way to spy on anyone in a room with an electric outlet."

"How can that be? Surely some sophisticated equipment must be plugged into the outlet for that to be possible."

"Come on, Lydia, this is the twenty-first century. Electronic technology is in every product. Code requirements put special specifications on every duplex outlet sold or installed in America for a number of years. There is a little safety device in each one of those outlets, required by law. What no one is telling is there is also a chip in each of those devices that converts sound into digital and transmits it into the grid. Listening devices sort this by key words, store those deemed suspicious, and can identify the location of the source. It's a huge source of billions of bits of information from millions of locations, all hidden from the public."

"My God, the power grid is a perfect surveillance system. Big Brother is listening. But isn't that too much data to handle? How can they make any sense of it?"

"Fast computers can process billions of bits of information in seconds. I'm not sure, but they must employ algorithms that discard all but the most significant messages. A tiny portion are retained and those go through another level of algorithms. Most of those are discarded. A tiny portion of the data gathered, those few that survive several levels of algorithmic examination, are examined by people for significance. The few of those selected by individuals are all that prompt further examination. My guess is there are significant numbers of valid concerns of the state found and acted on. In addition, certain outlets can be monitored individually. That means those who can access the system can listen in 24/7 to any of the locations with those outlets. The entire electric grid is now one giant information gathering system and few individuals know of its existence."

"Then they might be hearing what we are saying right here in your kitchen."

"No way. I put a little signal scrambler on my main box. It turns the signal from those chips into what amounts to static."

"Wouldn't that make them suspicious?"

"Not a bit. Their algorithms search for specific words and phrases. If no key words or phrases are read, the data is discarded. The grid could work both ways. For me it could be another huge source of data in addition to their SSC messages. As long as I can use their SSC messages to find out what they're up to that matters, I don't need the grid. It would take a great deal more effort for me to use the grid than SSC. I would need to set up and monitor a complex set of computers, just to confirm the information by using the SSC messages. It would not be worth the effort. If their SSC messages ever stopped, then I could use the grid. I keep searching and hoping I can uncover what they intend doing, so far with little luck."

"Did you think of any thing we could do, anything that might be able to stop whatever evil they are planning?"

"That knowledge would be a powerful tool in the right hands and I intend it to reach only the right hands. The big problem is, who can I trust? *Who has the right hands?* From what I learned by finding and decoding government SSC messages, there are a great many people in our government involved in some extremely dangerous conspiratorial communications, dangerous for Americans that is. And, it's not just the Chinese."

"No? Who else?"

"The major players in the world of Islam, including our friends in Saudi Arabia. All of the Wahhabi operatives and activists are involved as well. It's quite complicated. I must learn about whom all the players are and whom they are working with. They don't trust each other at all and each of them has their own hidden agendas they want no one to learn about. For that reason, each faction uses their own SSC codes to communicate internally and with each other while keeping their communications secret, or so they think."

"Typical political intrigue complicated by religious fervor whipped into a frenzy by fanatics. Why do people follow those ridiculous Pied Pipers anyway?"

"Most humans are too lazy to think for themselves. They prefer to let others do their thinking for them. Eric Hoffer wrote extensively about them in his book, *The True Believer*. One of my favorites of his comments is:

'Passionate hatred can give meaning and purpose to an empty life. Thus people haunted by the purposelessness of their lives try to find a new content not only by dedicating themselves to a holy cause but also by nursing a fanatical grievance. A mass movement offers them unlimited opportunities for both.'

"Hoffer is still one of my favorite philosophers."

"Wow. He was right on the money."

"Unthinking people will take the path of least effort. They eagerly believe the truth of that which they want be true or commit as true since that path requires little effort. Each time an unproven or untrue statement is made and claimed as fact, commitment cements the belief stronger in the mind of the one making the statement. It takes diligent and often painful effort to search out real truth. Such effort is far more than most are willing to spend. This is especially true if the answers found go against one's previously stated positions or committed beliefs. Humans often follow leaders who espouse those beliefs, even to their own detriment. I think it's human nature, or maybe overwhelming primate nature. Apes and monkeys do the exact same things on a different scale."

"My goodness, such a philosophical statement. That sounds quite profound. We're not so different from our primate relatives, to our own detriment and even demise."

"Those words are my own version of what Julius Caesar said two thousand years ago. To return to the present, the last significant message I decoded is confusing. It stressed the importance of the original date for their action, yet avoided mentioning the new action date. I believe it is not as yet set and won't be until the last minute. The Saudis and Chinese are playing a little game of financial chicken and our people, those in the US government, are being deliberately mislead and kept out of the loop. That's my own conclusion based on many of their messages. No, I do not know for certain that this is true. Vague hints are popping up occasionally in some of their messages. Of course, each nation and group has its own hidden SSC network including the big three, US, China, and the Saudis. All three of those were significantly silent in recent weeks. They may even have developed a new type of SSC system completely unknown to me. That would put an end to my spying on them."

"It certainly would. Could they be using high level encryption in their SSC messages?"

"Not yet, or the presence of such technology would reveal itself. It would stick out like a searchlight on a dark night. No, they remain confident their SSC messages are secure. They are all much more worried about moles within their organizations. That is the biggest concern of each of them. They are all paranoid about it. It's what I'm counting on to enable me to create dissension within their ranks."

"You told me about messing with them. Divide and conquer, you said. Who first said that?"

"I think Julius Caesar said that referring to Gaul."

"You talk a lot about Caesar."

"You might be surprised at what he wrote about. I was."

Chapter 17 - A Vicious Attack

✳ Thursday, April 17, 2014 ✳

Light rain falls steadily through a thin fog. The night is a cold and unpleasant, a nasty one to be outside. Brooks's rambling house, nestled on an isolated hilltop in the forest north of Cummins, Georgia is the only break in the wild, forested hills within its view. The house is on a narrow road that winds through the North Georgia mountains.

A pair of headlights moves slowly through the fog past the house. This alarms Lydia who is having dinner with Brooks.

Lydia says, "I may be succumbing to paranoia, but with all that's been going on lately those headlights scare me. Your house is the only one on this road, isn't it?"

"Yes, my nearest neighbor is at least a mile away. The driver most likely got lost in the fog, but you're right to be concerned. The research we've been writing about stirred up some nasty people. Where I live is public knowledge."

"I worry about the threats you've been getting. Those on the Internet were bad enough, but the recent phone calls . . . how did they find your unlisted number?"

"The enemies I garnered since I first started writing about the discoveries found by my SSC work at BMK are some nasty people. Many of them are in places in our government where they can access private information about anyone. I never had the need to hide my actions or whereabouts before now. It's all new to me."

"All the more reason to protect yourself out here so isolated. There are no nearby neighbors to report anything suspicious or come to your aid if need be."

"My doors are sturdy and locked. It would take some time for anyone to break in. We could retreat to the hidden room below the basement if anything like that happens. They could never find us there so don't worry."

✳   ✳   ✳

The headlights disappear into the fog and darkness. A short way down the road and out of sight of the house, the car stops and the headlights turn off. Two figures emerge and start walking back up the road.

✳   ✳   ✳

Lydia and I finally sit down to dinner ten months after I revealed my underground lab to her. She's the only person that knows it exists. We are discussing progress on the new advanced SSC project. We both laugh at what is not a laughing matter. My cell phone vibrates. My cousin Ralph is calling.

"I'm worried, Brooks," are the first words out of his mouth.

"Oh? You sound worried. What about?"

"Your name is on my computer 'pick' list. This morning there were a number of low level communications with your name in the subject. Before I had the chance to check them out, they disappeared—wiped out. That is most unusual. The few I did read were coded and most of their code is a mystery to me, but what I did learn is you are on Homeland Security's list of those exhibiting suspicious activities. That is not good."

"What does it mean?"

"Nearly everyone on that list is suspected of terrorist or subversive activities reported by someone in the government. What have you been doing? This is serious, so serious I went outside the agency to make this phone call. Since I'm related to you, my name will be on the list along with yours sooner or later. They'll be watching me carefully for the foreseeable future. Who else might be on the list is a mystery to me. They changed my clearance and I can no longer access that information. That's another thing that makes me nervous."

"I do not know what activities of mine landed me on the list. It couldn't be because of my suspicions, the ones I told you about. You're the only one to whom I mentioned that and you certainly did not spill the beans. When I can, I'll try to find out."

"I don't want to talk any longer. Who knows who might be listening? You can be marked for the most innocent of communications if they fall into the wrong hands. Particularly if some official dislikes you personally for any reason."

"Okay, Ralph. I'll talk with you soon. Bye"

Lydia notices my concern. "What's that all about? From what I heard it sounded ominous."

"That was Ralph. He hung up recognizing our old signal. 'Talk with you soon.' That means as soon as we can be together in person, not on any phone. We are meeting for lunch tomorrow and if that's not soon enough, he'll be showing up at my door this evening."

I proceed to relate Ralph's conversation to Lydia.

"Do you know how serious this is?"

"It could be quite bad, or nothing. I won't know how bad until I check things out in the SSC world which I am going to do as soon as we finish dinner."

"Aren't we about finished adapting those iphones to the new system? Yesterday you said you had worked out the last few changes."

"Yes, Lydia, we will do it tonight. I built another uplink converter so we can each use our iphones from anywhere we are in line of sight with the satellites. I worked out the details of the changes to our SSC converter and will rely on your skillful hands to make them. You're much better at fine work than I am. I doubt I would be this close to converting those iphones if not for your skills."

"Oh, Brooks, you say the nicest things," she says coyly. "Seriously though, maybe you should wait until they work properly before you pat me on the back."

"They'll work. I'm certain they will. I realized the slight positioning error I made last time. That must be the reason they didn't work then."

"It would be a hell of a lot easier and quicker if we could do this at BMK during normal hours. Yeah! I know. It would be impossible because of all the prying eyes. I was just wishing."

"It shouldn't take you . . ."

Automatic weapons fire and bullets ripping through the house cut Lydia short.

"Down! Down on the floor, now," I shout as I dive for the floor. "Quick! Into the laundry chute and keep low. You first."

We crawl as rapidly as we can. As Lydia dives into the chute, something strikes my arm, tearing the skin.

"Damn!" I shout in pain as I dive into the chute.

We end up sprawled on the floor of the laundry below ground in the basement, out of the range of the bullets flying through the house. I grab a towel and wrap it around my bleeding arm.

"I don't want to leave any signs of blood. See if there is any in the chute. I'll check the floor."

"There's none in the chute, but there's quite a bit on the floor where you landed."

"Wet that towel and wipe the blood up thoroughly please. I'll open the door to the passage. Oh, and bring the towel with you."

I open a cabinet door on the wall of cabinets at the end of the laundry room, reach in and hold my iphone against the back wall. The entire cabinet swings out revealing the narrow passage leading to the flight of stairs downward.

Lydia says, "Listen . . . the firing stopped."

"Yeah. Now they'll try to come in and finish the job. That attack surprised me. I did not anticipate them trying to kill me by shooting up my house. They probably were in the car you worried about. Your instincts were right on."

"That must have shown you they mean business. Shouldn't you close those cabinets? You don't want them to find this place."

"I don't hear anything else . . . wait . . . that sounds like a car racing away. Do you suppose they left? I wonder why?"

"They must think they got you. They fired an awful lot of rounds into the house."

"I'll go upstairs and check things out. You stay here in case."

"Let me tend to that wound in your arm."

"It will be okay."

"Baloney. I don't want you to die of infection. Don't you keep antibiotics and bandages upstairs in your bathroom? I'll go up with you and dress your wound."

As we walk up the stairs Lydia asks, "I wonder if anyone heard all that gunfire. Your house may be far from any other, but that gunfire was awfully loud. I expect to hear police sirens any minute."

"Don't hold your breath. It's a mile to my nearest neighbor. Homes are few and far between out here in the hills."

We walk up to the second floor bathroom where Lydia pulls a large splinter, the cause of the wound, out of my upper arm.

"Ouch! Damn, that hurt."

It continued hurting as she cleans my wound, applies antibiotic lotion, and wraps my arm in a length of gauze.

"That should do for a while," she says. "The wound is not deep and the wood came out cleanly. It missed any significant blood vessels and is only oozing blood. Still, blood will be coming through the dressing before long."

"They're gone now, but I think we should go away from here ASAP. It's not healthy for us to stay. We may not be able to come back here for a long time so there are a number of things we should take with us. Our entire advanced SSC project for one. We can talk about what we need to take with us down stairs. Let's go."

"You may be right, but where will you take it. You can't go to BMK, not during business hours."

"I have just the place. We will need quite some time to get there, about 24 hours if we drive straight through, and we must hide our tracks carefully."

"I'm game, but how will we hide our tracks?"

"Your RV."

"My RV?"

"Sure. We can load everything we need from here into my SUV and take it to where you store your RV. It's in a campground near Cummins, right? Isn't the campground just a few miles from where my road joins the main highway?"

"Yes, about seven."

"There are a few things we'll need from here, but most of them are in the lab or at BMK where we won't be able to go. Let's start packing—now!"

✸   ✸   ✸

We go down to the lab and start packing what we will need, talking as we pack.

"We will transfer all our stuff into your RV and drive to the Everglades, a trip of about 800 miles. It will take us eleven or twelve hours if we drive straight through. I have a fishing cabin on a small hammock about thirty miles northwest of Flamingo. There are no roads within miles. The only way to get there is by boat. The trip will take all day, at least ten to twelve hours if we don't lose our way."

"That sounds risky. What about your SUV? Won't it be a give away? Where will you get a boat?"

"We can stash my SUV near the airport where it's unlikely to be found and it won't matter if it is. I also keep a boat down there at the marina. Didn't you tell me you had a lot of survival stuff in your RV?"

"Great thought, I have survival food that would feed us for a long time, hand tools, batteries, a hand crank radio, lots of stuff besides staple foods, even a bunch of MREs."

"We will pick up your RV, then I'll drive my SUV to Atlanta and park in a shopping center while you drive your RV. From there we will head for Flamingo in your RV. If we time things right, we should arrive there before dark. We will avoid all toll roads and pay for everything with cash so we leave no trail to follow."

"Sounds like you had this all planned out."

"My dad and I made that trip many times over the years. We built the cabin for us to use when we went wild fishing as he called it. I was ten the first time we went there and helped him build the original cabin. We went every year for two weeks or more until I finished college. Each time we would take stuff to add to the cabin until it became a well-furnished place for a fishing camp. After I graduated, we missed a few years, then went every year until he died. That last trip was eight years ago. I can think of many fond memories of those free days with my Dad."

"You must have had a great relationship with your dad."

"He was a prince, the best dad ever. We lost him much too soon."

"You say we will require a trip in a boat to get there. Did I understand you to say you own a boat? Where is it and how will we get it?"

"There's a john boat with a ten horse Johnson outboard in storage in Flamingo. Been there for years, since about our third trip. Before we got the john boat, we trailered a fair sized utility boat each time we went. With that big boat we had to go twelve miles farther and needed three hours longer than with the john boat. We went up the canal from Flamingo in the dark before dawn so we could reach the cabin before dark. We had to use the bigger boat to haul all the lumber and building materials to the site. We used the big outboard one more time when we made a major addition. Even with that big boat we had to make several round trips to haul all the lumber and supplies we needed for the construction. I was a high school senior when we made that trip."

"What if the outboard won't start, and how long will we need to get to the cabin in the john boat?"

"The trip will take eight or ten hours, and don't worry about the motor. Like always, I will call and tell the marina folks to prepare the boat and put it in the water for us. We will find the boat tied up at the dock and ready go when we get there, like always."

"What else do you want to take? The entire project is already in those two boxes."

"My tools, my computers, I'm taking a small portable printer and five reams of paper in case. If it is too much for the john boat, I'll leave all but one ream in the RV. We might end up leaving quite a bit of stuff in the RV. That john boat will safely handle no more than 500 pounds plus the two of us. Any more than that and we could be swamped if Whitewater Bay kicks up. We will need to make a two-day round trip to pick up anything we must bring from the RV."

"Let's hope we won't be there too long and won't need to make the trip."

"We'd better be prepared for as much time as possible. We'll tow a boat-shaped 100 gallon plastic drum of gasoline behind us. The tank is sitting in the boat empty right now."

"Why so much? And won't it slow us down a lot?"

"That's why the boat-shaped tank. Once we are moving fast enough for it to plane, towing will hardly slow us down at all. We'll need lots of gas for the generator which I hope we will be able to start. It's been sitting unused for eight years and always started before, but that's a long time sitting idle. We treated it for long term storage before we left like always, but eight years is a lot longer than it ever sat before without being used. With fresh spark plugs and gas it should start. I guess we'll find out when we arrive there."

"What if it won't start?"

"Then I'll have to fix it. There are plenty of spare parts and it is a fairly simple machine. Don't worry. I can fix it. Then we need to pack clothes for six months. We can head for your place and pack your stuff."

✳   ✳   ✳

By eight-thirty everything is loaded in my SUV. We close up and secure the house, back out of the garage, and head down to the main highway. When I turn onto the highway from my road, a car in a small parking lot turns headlights on and pulls out behind us.

"We just picked up a tail, Lydia. Just like I told you. They are following us."

"What are you going to do?"

"Lose them."

I drive to the nearest freeway entrance and pull on southbound. I quickly cross three lanes, pull onto the median, stop and turn off my lights. As soon as I think they passed, I drive across the median, head north and exit at the place we entered going south. I pull into the first parking place I find, a small office building, and turn off my lights.

"Watch that exit for any car in a hurry. They may have seen that maneuver. If so, they should be charging up that ramp any minute. They should blast right past us."

We wait five minutes and when no car exits I say, "That was almost too easy, but we definitely lost them. Now we can drive leisurely to your place."

Chapter 18 - Off to Flamingo

The transfer from my SUV to Lydia's RV goes without a hitch. We stop at my bank in Cummins and use the ATM to withdraw the maximum amount. While I am getting my money, I explain several other things we need to finance our trip.

"Now, if you'll do the same at your bank, there will be enough cash for the trip. They will find my photo showing I was here, but that won't show them where I went. They will realize I'm running, but not where to. I don't think we need to worry about you at the ATM. Still, we can't use any ATM while on our way. I exchanged about ten grand into bitcoin. We can convert that back into dollars should we need it. You understand that is an untraceable transaction, right?"

"Of course. You told me about bitcoin some time back."

✳　　　✳　　　✳

We drive to northern Atlanta and pull into a small shopping center. I step out and walk back to Lydia in the RV. "Short detour. I want to stop at Ralph's and talk with him. He lives a short distance from here. Wait here till I return."

I stop at Ralph's, but no one answers my ring. I drive back to where Lydia waits and walk to her RV.

"Ralph doesn't appear to be at home. That worries me a bit, but there's not much I can do. Calling him is too dangerous so let's go. I'll try to contact him later."

I walk back to my SUV, and we leave together driving both vehicles. We drive south through Atlanta to a large shopping center near Hartsfield-Jackson Airport. There I park the SUV in an unobtrusive spot, backing in so the license plate is not easily seen. I hop into the RV and Lydia heads south on I-75. We leave the mall parking lot at ten-thirty that night.

"You okay to drive for a while?" I ask Lydia.

"I'm good."

"Then I will get some sleep. Wake me when you need me. Oh yes, when you reach I-10, go east toward Jacksonville and take I-95 south. That will take us it a bit farther, but we must avoid the Florida turnpike. I don't want to travel any toll roads where they use cameras. Around Stuart we'll head inland and go south past Okeechobie. We take 15, 27 and 997 all the way to Homestead. That will take us away from those East Coast Cities and several toll roads. The route goes through mostly farmland. There's not much traffic and the roads are good. My dad and I drove that way every time we went to the cabin. I've driven those highways enough I could probably find my way blindfolded. I'll be awake and driving by then."

"What? You don't trust me to be able to follow directions? I'm devastated."

"Ha!"

✳   Friday, April 18, 2014   ✳

Those are our last words before I fall soundly asleep. I wake up at about four o'clock and we are past Jacksonville.

"Why didn't you wake me? You've been driving steadily for six hours."

"You didn't wake up even when I stopped to fill the tank. You needed sleep."

"Let me drive for a while so you can sleep."

"Gladly. There's a rest stop coming up. I'll pull in there. I need a pit stop anyway."

"It will be good to walk about a bit and stretch."

✳   ✳   ✳

About ten in the morning we pull into the Pilot Travel Center where the Tamiami Trail crosses Florida 997. We are 68 miles from Flamingo. While we eat a late, leisurely breakfast, I explain a few things to Lydia.

"I don't think I told you, but I kept all I learned—all the significant messages I intercepted—in encrypted files on two tiny, high density USB drives. One I keep on my person. The other was hidden inside one of my books, the one on spread spectrum radio in the 1940s in fact. Fortunately I remembered and took the time to retrieve the book from the shelves of my library before we left."

"Does anyone else know about those hidden rooms in your house, anyone at all? You can be honest with me. I won't mind."

"I'll ignore that remark. I never told a soul my secret but you."

"It took you a long time before you trusted me enough to show me."

"Come on, Lydia. It was only a few days after we realized there was something between us, something magic and wonderful."

"Okay, so you took a long time to recognize what I did much earlier. You men are so slow."

"Caution, pure caution."

"No, poor perception."

"Must you rub it in? Can I change the subject back to my secret rooms? Unless they take my house apart with a bulldozer and know where to look, they'll never find the lab or my library. In fact, the room is even isolated from fire. The house could burn to the ground and those rooms would not be exposed. Now I think we should go. We've relaxed enough and still have a lot to do. I'm hoping to be able to leave in the john boat at first light in the morning. We can continue this conversation on the road."

"Yes boss."

"You enjoy saying that, don't you?"

"Yes, because you always react," she says with a little laugh, knowing I can't be angry with her.

We pay cash, fill the tank, and hit the road at eleven o'clock. We were stopped and relaxed for an hour. Once on our way, Lydia picks up our conversation right where we left off.

"You have been concerned, right? All the complicated secrecy would be considered high level paranoia by many people."

"Probably, but I think there's a good sound basis for my concerns. My big worry is what to do with the information. The other thing is the advanced SSC project the two of us were working on. We were about to test it when those assassins attacked us and shot up my house."

"I wonder why they attacked when they did. You had no hint of such an attack from any of the communications you intercepted. We were fortunate we were able to go down into your hidden lab and library with only a wound to your arm. Why did they break off and leave? You would think they would make certain of their goal before leaving."

"I realized why they left when they did when I noticed we were being followed."

"When you told me we were being followed I was scared."

"Obviously they wanted to let me leave so they could follow and learn to whom I might lead them. They must think I am a small cog in a much larger organization."

"No, I don't think so. That attack was deadly. They meant to kill you."

"Could be, but I doubt it. I checked the walls when we went back upstairs. The bullet holes were all above head height. If they intended to kill me, those holes would have been much lower. They wanted me to run."

"You never told me that."

"We were so busy loading all my stuff from the lab and losing their tail before heading for your place, I never had the chance tell you about the bullet holes or what I suspected. They must not have known you were with me."

"That little maneuver on the freeway was clever. Where did you ever learn that?"

"Believe it or not on a crime story on TV. The detective realizes he is being followed so he drives onto a freeway, crosses through traffic fast as he can and pulls off into the median. The guys following him pass him before they realize what he did. After they go by, he crosses over the median and drives off the freeway going the other way before they can turn around. The maneuver was easier and worked even better than I thought possible. Caught them flat footed."

"I would have loved to see their faces when they realized what happened."

"I wonder why they didn't look for us at your place? Surely the two of us being together is evident to everyone."

"Not necessarily. We never made a big deal and it never hit the news. As far as the public is concerned, we are boss and possible employee."

"Could be. I recognize the sly little grin on your face. All is not lost. You figured out a way to mess with them I'll bet. You hinted at that some time ago."

I cannot deny the obvious. "I think so. Here's what we can do. You will help me design a series of cleverly worded messages some underlings will send out to protect their family and friends from the coming disaster. These messages will be sent via SS communications to several of the news media. They will appear to come from those we select. There are a few weak links among their people. The media talking heads will think the messages are real and will include them in their broadcasts. Since their high poobahs will be the only ones who are sure the messages are fake, it will shake them up. They will think their planned actions are unreliable because of the selfishness and greed of some of their lower level members. All of a sudden they will be suspicious of everyone in their organization. We'll let good old human suspicion foil their plot."

"They wouldn't be able trace the source of those messages, would they?"

"I hope they do. The messages will actually be sent from the computers in the offices of the ones who supposedly originated them. Our SS communications that do that are absolutely untraceable. Their traceable signatures will be of the computers on their desks. A clever check by experts will tell them they were a keyboard entry. That should ruffle a few feathers."

"Wow! That's ingenious. Do you think your trickery will work?"

"All totalitarian and authoritarian systems are peopled with those who are suspicious of everyone. Cultivate a little minor suspicion and no one trusts anyone. Distrust grows and divides until a major purge takes place. The meanest SOB around will be the only one left standing. Think Stalin's murderous purges or Mao's cultural revolution. We may be able to precipitate a similar devastating purge in this organization."

"My God, Brooks, you need some help, lots of help."

"Yes, but how can I get any. I have no idea how to learn if a person is trustworthy or not. I didn't even tell my cousin Ralph. He doesn't know much. He understands some of my work in SSC, and my suspicions about the Chinese and Saudis, but not that I solved the SSC code problem. You're the only one I told about that."

"You remember that and treat me right," Lydia says with a wicked grin.

"You know, of course, if I ever suspect you might let the cat out of the bag I will be forced to kill you," I reply with an equally wicked grin.

✳   ✳   ✳

We are past Homestead and on Florida 9336 headed for Flamingo when flashing red lights appear in the rear view mirror. The Florida State Police are stopping us. I feel a moment of panic and glance at Lydia who looks like she is about to freak out.

"Prepare for anything," I say as I pull over and stop. "If he asks for my drivers license, all of our plans are for naught."

"Yes officer?" I say in my most polite manner when he reaches my open window.

"Retract your RV door steps. You forgot to retract them the last time you used them. You could hit a curb and tear them up."

With a great inner sigh of relief I thank him and go back to press the button and pull them in.

"Drive safely," he says as he leaves to get back into his car.

"I will officer. And thanks again for stopping us."

"Scared the hell out of both of us, didn't it?" Lydia says with a shaky grin as I pull away from the curb.

"Absolutely! My heart's still racing. I thought we were done for, all our clever planning shot."

We drive without conversation for a long time, still recovering from shock.

✳   ✳   ✳

Shortly past one we pull up to the marina in Flamingo. I point to the john boat tied up at the dock. "There's our boat. The gas tank tow is filled and tied alongside. I told you these folks are great."

"Should we load the boat now or after we are settled?"

"There are a few hours of daylight left so we should load the boat first. Let's get at it."

We spend the next two hours putting as much as we can into the boat. We carefully balance the load, getting into the boat to make sure it will handle all the weight.

"I think we've loaded all we can safely carry. Winds are supposed to be light tomorrow. I hope the weatherman is right. Charley from the marina told me the motor is in great shape. 'Just needs some exercise.' He said."

We hook up the RV on a spot back near the middle of the main RV park. Quite a bit of Lydia's stash is still in the storage bins.

"What's all that?" I ask pointing to several unopened boxes.

"More food, mostly MREs," she replies. "If we need them, we'll make a round trip to the RV park."

Chapter 19 - A Cabin in the Everglades
✳ Saturday, April 19, 2014 ✳

Light is beginning to show in the east as we pull out of the marina and head north in the canal.

"Damn!" I say as the boat accelerates slowly and finally breaks onto a plane. "We may have loaded too much. A few big waves and we could be swamped."

"Do you want to go back and take some things out?"

"As long as Whitewater Bay doesn't kick up we'll be okay. Our tow settled down and we're moving fast enough. Check for gators in front. Warn me if you see one. With this load I don't want to hit a big one which might turn us over."

"How do you expect me to be able to warn you in the dark?"

"It'll soon be light. We'll chance it till then. As long as we don't slow down, we'll be okay unless we hit a big one. They're mostly near the banks this time of day."

✳   ✳   ✳

We stay at full speed through the canal, across Coot Pond, and through the short channel into Whitewater Bay. By then the sun is up and I set my heading by compass as I have done many times before. By about ten the wind picks up and we are driving against a light chop. We are lucky the wind doesn't seem to slow us down.

"I hope this wind doesn't get any stronger," I say. "Then I'll need to head directly into it for some time. That will lengthen the time to reach the shore. Changing direction will also make it difficult to find the cut that we must take back into where the cabin is. This shallow water kicks up quickly. We're getting some water in the boat from the spray."

"Do I need to bail?"

"No. The spray seems be drying."

A half hour later the chop increased to where I must turn the boat west into the wind. "I was afraid we might have to head into the wind. We must change our route some and that will add close to an hour to our trip. Our timing will be close, but we must be there before dark. We should have started out an hour earlier. My fault."

✳   ✳   ✳

We reach the first patches of mangroves about a mile north of where I want to be. I can find no familiar markers, in fact, no markers at all. I will rely on our GPS to guide us and it only tells us where we are. Finding a navigable path through this maze of mangroves and small islands will be no easy task. I decide to head southeast until I recognize familiar landmarks. We use most of an hour to find the familiar channel marker.

"At last!" I say as we round the marker. "Now I can head northeast again. I can tell exactly where we are."

An hour later I see a familiar stand of trees and point. "Those trees on the horizon are where we're headed. It's a good two miles away and will take us most of two hours to get there. We can use the motor part of the way. We'll pull it up and pole the last half mile or so. In the mean time, grab the pump and bail most of the water out of the boat."

"My gosh, I didn't realize how much there was. The water must be three or four inches deep."

"We'll need to bail out all of the water in order to pole the last few hundred feet. We sit low enough in the water as is."

✳   ✳   ✳

The sun is on the horizon when I shut off and tip up the motor to clear all the water plants. "From now on we use manpower. You can hear the bottom of the boat scraping the vegetation. If you'll pole from the back, I'll take the front and guide us. Be careful. Lose your balance and over we will go. That we do not need. Have you ever poled a boat before?"

"Never."

"Let me give you a few hints."

It doesn't take her long to catch on. Soon we are poling along about as fast as the boat can be poled.

"I am pleasantly surprised. You are a quick learner."

We pole the john boat northeast in a familiar passage through the mangrove and sawgrass-covered islands. Memories of my dad and me doing the same thing flood my mind. The bandage on my left arm is soaked in blood.

"Brooks, your arm's bleeding again. Let's stop now so I can change it."

"Not until we are in the cabin."

"Are you sure? I will only need a minute or two to change it."

"I'll be okay until we reach the cabin. The sun will soon go down and we must get there while it is still light. If we don't, it may be impossible to find our way in the dark. I don't want us to spend the night in this john boat. The cabin is about half a mile away."

I hope the shack is still there and habitable, I think as we continue poling the boat as fast as we can.

"It's been eight years since the last time Dad and I stayed there. It was our last fishing trip together."

"How long will we be holed up, do you suppose?"

"A lot longer than my last stay, maybe much longer. Thanks to you we have enough supplies to last for six months or more. As long we catch plenty of fish that is."

"My Gawd, I hope we aren't isolated out here for that long."

"Lydia, we escaped from a group of assassins a few hours ago. The situation will not change much in the near future, not until a lot of people catch onto what's going on. I hope we can figure a way to change that, and soon. We're stuck here until we solve that little problem."

"Is that why you brought the arsenal? To protect us here?"

"Our only hope is they don't find us. If they do, no amount of weapons and ammo will keep us alive. The arsenal, as you called my hunting rifle and automatic, is for our use when we leave here and go on the offensive. Automatic weapons and a lot more ammo were available if we had lots of time before we had to leave to save our skins."

The sun is below the horizon when we reach the narrow water passage that leads to the cabin.

"The narrow opening ahead is where we're going. Damn, I do not remember so many weeds and so much sawgrass. We will need a hard push to pole the boat through to the pond on the other side. The cabin is right across from where the opening enters the pond. I hope we can pole through to the pond."

"With the two of us poling it shouldn't be too difficult."

"I was thinking of all the weight in the boat. All this stuff must weigh close to four hundred pounds. That makes the boat low in the water and much harder to pole."

"Well daddy-o, lets get at it."

We struggle, making less than a foot with each push. In frustration, Lydia jumps into the water in front of the boat.

I hollered, "You crazy woman. That's not going to help."

"Yes it will," Lydia says as she pops her head up over the front of the boat. "It's a lot easier for me to move these plants out of the way in the water."

"Just be careful of the grass. Those sharp blades will cut you to pieces."

"I know, but my jeans are tough and should protect me. Hand me those leather work gloves. They will keep my hands from being cut."

After we move several feet in a rather short time, I say. "As usual, you are right. We are moving a lot faster with you breaking trail."

I am relieved when she struggles through the final few feet of vegetation and into the pond. She climbs back into the boat and we pole smoothly across the small pond in front of the cabin. We are both exhausted when we pull the boat up on the island.

"Great! We will have enough time and light to unload. The cabin seems to be in good condition from outside. I hope it's in as good a shape inside."

The cabin is amidst a small stand of trees on the only hammock that has trees for miles around. That is one drawback. The hammock sticks out of a sea of sawgrass dotted with mangroves. Mangroves are thickest toward the shoreline a few miles away. The cabin is on the highest spot anywhere around. Fortunately, the building is hidden by trees and bushes that grew completely over it. The growth makes the cabin invisible from any distance, or from the air.

I unlock and remove the padlock from the door. "The door is still locked. Here goes. Pray it hasn't been broken into."

We step inside. "Other than lots of cobwebs and dust, everything is okay," Lydia says.

"Sure is, just like when Dad and I left after our last fishing trip eight years ago. Grab your suitcase out of the boat, dry off and put on some dry clothes as quickly as you can. Then let's take the rest of our stuff inside while there is still enough light."

Once Lydia is in dry clothes, she changes the dressing on my wounded arm. We then pull the john boat ashore and move everything inside the cabin. Next, we muscle the heavy gasoline tank out of the water and drag it up by the cabin. By the time housekeeping chores are finished and our stores are organized and in the cabinets, it is pitch black outside, a moonless night. We spread the sleeping bag on the bottom bunk and sit down together to relax for the first time since early morning.

I put my arm around her. "Sorry to drag you into this, but if I left you behind, they would use you to get to me. We would both end up dead."

"No need to feel sorry. I'm quite attached to you, or haven't you noticed. No way are you going away without me. And besides, what would you have done without me and my survival stash?"

"Most likely the morgue would be my resting place. I could never have gotten away from those assassins without your help. I hope we did a good job of hiding our trail. Transferring everything from my SUV into your RV and hooking it up in a space in Flamingo RV park was the way to go. They may eventually find it, but if they do they still won't have a clue where we went or how."

"Suppose they question the people at the marina?"

"Don't worry. I told Charley there could be some nasties after us. He's known me for more than thirty years. He won't tell them about the boat or where we went. He'll plead ignorance and tell them he doesn't nose into camper's business."

"They can be persuasive, even violent."

"Charley has no idea where we are going—never has. Even if he tells them we left in a boat headed north in the canal they won't be able to find where we went."

"You're right. The Everglades is a huge area of wild land and water with no roads. If we're careful, they'll never find us. You are familiar with this part of the park and our pursuers aren't. Right now I am beat. Let's hit the sleeping bag. We can't do much until morning but snuggle."

I rather like that prospect. I am quite certain the killers won't find the cabin. No one can. Dad and I kept things that way for many reasons.

✳ Sunday, April 20, 2014 ✳

We are up at first light pulling the john boat up to the cabin and leaning it against the side. "There, that should keep it hidden from anyone behind all those bushes," I say.

Lydia agrees. Hidden by trees, dense shrubs, and bushes, nothing is visible from above. I checked all around to make sure the hammock is uninhabited. Satisfied, I go back inside to organize and plan our next effort. Lydia is fixing breakfast.

"Do you need my help?"

"I think you had better try to start the generator. There is not much we will be able to do until there's some juice."

"Right you are babe. I'll start right now."

I clean the carburetor, fuel the generator, and have it ready to go. Starting it is another matter. After a dozen or so pulls on the starter rope, Lydia calls me for breakfast.

"Be there in a minute," I shout as I yank the rope one more time. The engine coughs and fires a couple of times. That is encouraging. A few more yanks and it coughs a few times, catches, and runs roughly. A few small adjustments to the mixture and it is running smoothly. I run into the cabin.

"Surprise! The power is up and running. Turn on the light."

"Hooray!" Lydia shouts when the lights go on. "We'll be able to see our mouths to eat. Sit. Your breakfast is getting cold."

About five minutes after I sit down, the generator sputters a few times but catches and runs smoothly. The lights flicker and stay steady. Then the generator simply quits.

"So much for electricity. My work is cut out for me. I cleaned the carburetor, so that's not the problem. I'll replace ignition parts one at a time and find out what works. I have lots of spare parts available, mostly ignition."

"Eat your breakfast. You can worry about that afterwards."

While eating, we discuss what the order of the day should be. First, fix the generator. Next, set up a lab of sorts somewhere in the cabin. There is not much room, but somehow we will manage.

As I clear the dishes. Lydia starts washing them in the sink. Suddenly she stops, listening.

"What is it?"

"Shhh! Listen!"

All I can hear is my own breathing. Then I hear it, a faint and distant throbbing sound.

"Damn!" Lydia says. "That's a helicopter coming our way and fast. What can we do?"

I run outside in the bright sunlight and hunt for any telltale signs we left. The sound is coming from the east so I look in that direction. I can't see a thing. The sky is empty, at least the part of the sky I can see from under the trees and bushes. I grab and toss an old camouflage tarp from behind the cabin door over the bright red gasoline tank. They can't see anything else so I run inside and close the door. The sound grows louder.

"I hope that's not our friends," I say.

"They couldn't figure things out that quickly. There's nothing with a GPS turned on, is there?"

"Absolutely not. I disconnected the batteries from everything."

"How about the crank radio? Doesn't that use batteries too? Could they be homing in on that?"

"Come on, Lydia. That's impossible. Maybe they will just pass by."

"You hope!"

"My God, they're passing directly overhead . . . and keeping on to the west."

I open the door as the chopper moves steadily west away from us. Then it banks sharply and heads back toward us. I shut the door.

"I don't like that one bit. It's an Everglades chopper with pontoons and can land anywhere out here, even on the water."

We hold our breath when the chopper comes overhead and starts to hover. The downdraft from the rotating blades shakes the trees and even the bushes around the cabin.

I turn to Lydia and say, "Pray."

✳ *Carol Mitchell* ✳

Chapter 20 - Horror and Grief
✳ Thursday, October 24, 2013 ✳

Thursday, when I arrive home a bit later than usual, I am surprised the contractor's truck is still parked behind the house. The remodeling is nearly complete and the back of the house has grown by about twelve feet. My curiosity becomes painful, but I am determined to wait and not look until the project is finished. When I start up the stairway to the door, splatters of red on the steps send a sudden chill of fear through me. My first thought is of a construction injury. I called out for Jack as I open the door.

A silent scream of fear and unimaginable horror explodes in my head when I find a mutilated body lying in a pool of blood in the hall. I can tell the contractor by his clothes. Both walls beside his body are splashed with blood.

I scream "Jack!" rush past the body and down the hall into the main room.

Blood, broken furniture and bodies are strewn around the room. Jack is not among them. My heart nearly bursts in anguish as I run frantically through the house screaming, "Jack! Jack!"

Then, back in the main room, a bloody hand desperately held onto the rail at the top of the stairs down to the beach. I realize the bloody heap on the stairs and attached to the hand is Jack. He was hacked and mauled by the long curved knives lying on the floor near the four bodies. I cradle his bloody head for a long time while unimaginable emotional pain racks my body and crazed fury builds within me.

"I— love—you—" he whispers as I hold him, knowing he is going. "Call—OSI. —Number in pocket—" are the last words he utters before he dies. I hold him for what seems to be hours before reaching for his pocket.

In retrieving the number, I let go of Jack and his hand slips off the rail as his lifeless body collapses on the steps.

The four bodies are quite obviously Islamic terrorists. Each had been shot by the automatic lying on the stairs near Jack's hand. They have not been dead for long. Images of the battle course through my head. I try desperately to reverse time and prevent the horror from happening.

I finally rein in the overwhelming mixture of deep sorrow, pain, terror and rage long enough to punch in the OSI number. I struggle to remain coherent as I describe the scene of horror. When

I finish the call, waves of unthinkable raw primal emotion take over and I explode in passionate anger. I lose control, curse and kick the bodies of the dead invaders. Primal fury grips me. I pick up one of the long curved knives and start furiously hacking away at one of the bodies.

✳   ✳   ✳

When the OSI operatives arrive, a screaming maniacal woman wielding a dangerous knife greets them. The words, "Ma'am! Ma'am! Please put down the knife," snaps back my sanity and I collapse on the floor in uncontrollable sobs. My mind screams in primal hatred. My heart and soul are rent by waves of intense grief. I lie there on the floor, unable to move.

My mind, a jumble of raw emotions, compresses time into jagged, but separate pieces like shards of broken glass. Suddenly I realize there are a lot of people in the house. A kind woman guides me into the bathroom and helps me wash the blood from my face and hands.

"You should get out of those clothes and into the shower," She says.

"Who are you?" I ask, apprehensive.

"I'm Jeanne Long, a grief psychologist with OSI. I'm called on to help people like yourself in difficult or tragic situations."

I babble something about needing a gun and someone to shoot, not a shrink. Somehow, her words, "You're bound to be angry," calm me down and bring some sense of reality to my bizarre state of mind.

Jeanne starts to help me out of my bloody clothes. "Let's get you into the shower. We can talk after." I have no will to resist.

The warm water has a soothing effect on my mind and my body. I stay in the shower for a long time. Jeanne checks on me periodically. I step out of the shower and into the towel Jeanne holds for me. My clothes are gone and not a trace of blood remains in the room. A small syringe lies on the counter next to the sink.

"You've been busy," I remark as I survey the spotless bathroom.

"And you seem to have regained coherence. I thought the shower would help."

I'm still in a mixed state of shock and anger, but I feel like control is beginning to return. The sight of the syringe sends a twinge of fear through my body. "What's that for?" I ask pointing to the syringe with apprehension.

"A fairly strong sedative, it won't put you to sleep, but it will calm your nerves and prevent a panic attack."

"Must I take it?"

"Absolutely not! We won't do anything without your permission. I do recommend it though. The shot will help you through some difficult moments for the next few hours."

"That shower helped . . . I feel limp as a wet towel."

Jeanne stands with arms crossed, stern and motherly. "The tension and anger may be gone but will return if you don't take any calming medication."

She laid out underwear, slippers and my terry robe. "You found my clothes. Thank you."

"You can pick out what you want to wear when we go into the bedroom. There are half a dozen OSI people going over the scene for any evidence. They'll want to speak to you when you are ready. I won't let them until you're okay to answer questions. How about that shot? It won't hurt and it will help."

I am still apprehensive. "I truly appreciate your concern, but let me consider for a moment."

I slip into my underwear, robe and slippers and go into the guest room, A folding screen stands in the room shielding the view of the hall door. Men's muted voices come from the great room as they pursue their examination. Obviously they are being considerate of me. Once in the guest room, I plop down on the bed I will never again share with Jack.

"He's a wonderful man," comes out of my mouth as my eyes meet Jeanne's.

"I'm sure he was," she replies. "Would you like to tell me about him?"

"Okay, mother superior, give me that shot. I'm not thinking clearly and I'm sure I can trust you."

The needle in my shoulder stings a bit.

"I think this will help a lot," Jeanne comments as she removes and trashes the empty syringe. "Now, how about telling me about you and Jack."

Somehow, midst many teary pauses, I blurt out the story of our meeting and how I fell terribly in love with a man my grandfather's age. Jeanne is understanding and reassuring, not once questioning or judging.

"I think the shot is taking effect. I feel a bit woozy."

"We call it a three martini shot for obvious reasons. Don't take any alcohol for the next twenty-four hours or you will become quite drunk."

Jeanne is an attractive woman, about ten years my senior and a bit stouter with reddish blonde hair and a warm, motherly manner.

"You're a wonderful listener," I commented. "So kind and understanding."

"That's my job you know."

"Maybe so, but your kind compassion and understanding must be real or they wouldn't work."

"My mom was a sincere and caring person. I guess some of it rubbed off on me. During my training I was cautioned about becoming involved with clients. The line between true compassion and involvement is a nebulous thing I must deal with."

"You seem be doing so quite well."

"Thanks for the kind words, but let's get back to you. There are several investigators out in the other room who want desperately to question you. My job is to be a buffer between you and them. I'll not let any of them get a moment with you until I okay it."

Her words were reassuring. "I'm beginning to settle down some, but I'm not ready to be interrogated."

"You're doing well at the present, but you will experience periods of uncontrollable grief and bits of extreme anger, sometimes striking unexpectedly. Right now I must explain some things to you, things you don't know. Are you up to listening for a while?"

I am surprised at how calm I feel. The warm shower, the shot and Jeanne's company are powerful tonics. "Right now I feel more in control so go ahead."

"First of all, we have a great deal more information about both you and Jack than you could guess. Don't panic. All we learned is good. About the time Jack built this house we recruited him as a consultant to OSI. He knew more about Muslim extremists and terrorists than anyone. He goes way back with them, nearly thirty years."

"He told me he was writing a series of articles about them for a magazine and that their current leaders were part of a group he fought against in Africa. He never mentioned his working with any government people."

"We asked him not to divulge his connection with OSI to you, primarily for your own protection. He objected strongly telling us you could handle it. Incidentally, he had a high opinion of both your abilities and integrity."

A bit ruffled, I demanded, "Just how much do you know about us."

"Don't worry! All of our knowledge about you and Jack came from him. It was all positive. Jack was a wise man deeply in love. He assured us our concerns about you were unfounded. Of course, he was quite concerned about your safety."

"That's my Jack."

As those words come out in a flip manner, I am shocked by waves of grief that submerge me in a sea of anguish and tears. I shake as a quake of violent sobs courses through my body. Jeanne grabs and holds me without saying a word. Several minutes later the attack subsides. She says nothing, but continues to hold me.

My mind clears a bit and I say, "I'm okay."

"Are you sure?"

"I never sensed that coming. Right now I'm not sure of anything."

"That makes perfect reasoning to me, a good sign," she says smiling as she releases me and our eyes meet.

"Why so?" I ask, after I calm down.

"It's normal to be unsure under these circumstances. Many different experiences and situations will trigger moments of extreme grief. As time passes their frequency and severity will diminish, but they will remain with you, beneath the surface, ready to erupt. This may never disappear completely. That's perfectly normal, but when they're denied or hidden they cause problems, so try not to do so."

"I can't believe how quickly I was overcome."

"That too is normal. If you can, just let fly and don't hold back. That's the healthiest way to deal with it."

"That might be difficult in some situations."

"Grief and expressions of grief are understood by all but the most callus and evil people. Most people will try to comfort the grief stricken. Some haven't the slightest idea how, but do mean well. You can be sure of that."

"How do you understand these things?"

"Much of that comes from my instincts which usually dominate in stressful situations. You possess the honed instincts of a successful business person. That is all about sensing another person's situation and dealing properly with it. I'll wager you are quite good at it."

"Right now I want to learn how you know so much about us."

"Jack has a long history with the military. He was a consultant of sorts to the military, government, and police off and on for many years. His kind of experience and knowledge is hard to come by and is quite valuable. He was especially helpful in our efforts with al-Qaeda. Osama bin Laden's al-Qaeda network."

"He told me about them and gave me some of his articles to read. He mentioned he had been threatened, but didn't seem concerned."

"He didn't share our concern for his safety. He wouldn't join OSI, preferring to remain free of the restraints we would place on him. We tried to get him to stop publishing his articles on Islamic terrorists considering his writing brought many threats. He stubbornly refused believing the public had a right to learn about the danger they posed. He wouldn't let us protect him in any way with security personnel. If we had, he would still be with us. He did let us put you under guard once you and he became involved. He feared they might kidnap you and use you for a bargaining chip."

"You mean I have body guards? I never notice anyone. How long has this been going on?"

"At Jack's request, we've been guarding you since shortly after you two met. We didn't worry about you because your name never appeared in any of our intelligence reports on the numerous Islamic terrorist groups we have on record. Jack became quite upset when your name did appear on a recent report. The report said you were a frequent companion. Apparently they noted you were often with him, nothing more. His own activities were noted in those reports and in detail. In spite of Jack's instructions, we were secretly guarding him at night. A daytime raid like this had never before been staged by any terrorist group, al-Qaeda included. Until now, no assassination attempts were carried out in the US. We thought he was safe. That was a costly mistake. We should have ignored his request for no guards."

"That's Jack's independent streak. He thought he could handle his own security."

"He did put up quite a fight. In addition to the four dead in the house they found another one outside. There were probably a dozen of them. They were only able to disarm him when he ran out of ammunition. I'll wager several of the ones who survived are carrying bullet wounds."

The thought of Jack battling those men brings on another grief attack. Again, Jeanne holds and comforts me until the attack is over.

"I should have seen that coming," I sob when I begin to feel better.

"Not for quite a while. You'll be blind sided the same way numerous times, maybe for years. An occasional grief attack about my dad still hits me, and he was killed in a plane crash thirty years ago. The severity and frequency both decrease, but they never go away completely, not for most people with normal feelings."

"I thought you were supposed to provide me comfort?"

"Knowledge, understanding and acceptance of reality are the best solutions for your distress. My job is to help you gain these, and as painlessly as possible. Sometimes that is not easy to do."

I chuckled cynically. "Just grin and bear it. Is that what you mean?"

Jeanne is a bit perturbed. "That's not at all what I meant. Anger will be the toughest thing to handle and will eat at you unbearably if you don't control it, even take over your life. If that happens you'll become bitter and take your anger out on everyone, even those who care for you. I'm certain you don't want that to happen."

"Right now I'm seething and bouncing back and forth between extreme anger and terrible grief."

"There is a specific direction for your anger and that's good. Still, you are caught between anger and grief, two strong competing emotions. Let's stop all this analysis and resume answering your questions. I was explaining how we knew about you and Jack. Since we had a long history with him, Obviously we knew him quite well. When you came on the scene, we ran a routine check. The results agreed with Jack's information so you were given a clean bill of health."

"I feel a bit violated, but I can understand the reasons."

Jeanne grasps my hand and stands. "Why don't we go for some coffee or tea? A break—getting away will do you good. There must be a spot nearby."

The thought of leaving brought on a minor panic attack. "I - I don't think I'm ready to talk to anyone."

Jeanne was reassuring. "I passed a small restaurant about ten miles south on the beach road. Would that be a good place?"

"You must mean Reggio's. I drove by many times, but I never stopped. The coffee should be okay."

"Let's go," Jeanne said smiling and releasing my hand. "I'll go tell the others where we're going."

As she stepped out and closed the door, a momentary bout of anguish washes over me. The prospect of stepping past the body in the hall triggers another which is all over by the time she returns.

"Everything is all right with Reynard and his men so let's head out. The hallway is all clear. They did that soon after we came back here."

A wave of appreciative feelings flow through me. "Thank God! I didn't like the idea of stepping over a body on the way out."

Once outside I feel relaxed as the sea breeze fluffs my hair. In addition to Jack's pickup and the contractor's truck, there are three cars, a small van and a rather large truck parked along the driveway next to the small pile of lumber remaining from the remodeling. Jeanne guides me to a small BMW coupe. Once in her car, we travel in relative silence down the beach road to Reggio's. She must sense my need for quiet and says nothing as we ride along.

"It seems a bit more run down than I remember," I comment as we walk up a wooden ramp that could have been rescued from the surf.

The porch with its open bar, doesn't look much better. The two men talking and drinking at the bar follow us with their eyes in silence till we are inside. We select a booth at the end of the room away from the bar and near a window. The view is out to the beach road and the darkening sky beyond. This room is clean and bright, with Formica tops, and chrome and plastic chairs, empty except for a couple with a young child finishing their late dinner.

The lone waitress, oriental, came to our booth. "I'm afraid there's not much left on our dinner menu. Sandwiches and salads are all our kitchen can serve after eight."

Jeanne spoke. "A cup of hot tea, please. Carol, what would you like?"

"Decaf please. I don't think I need any caffeine."

While we sit and talk, the outside bar grows busier as the evening progresses and the drinking crowd drifts in sporadically. Far enough from the noisy bar to be relatively quiet, we continue talking. I cathartically pour out my recent life story. Jeanne listens attentively, guiding my conversation when I wander off track. We are off in our own world, not part of Reggio's scene.

We are interrupted by one of the men who eyed us when we walked in. He comes over with obvious intent. "How are you girls tonight?"

Jeanne turns slightly toward him and replies coldly, "We're fine and would like not to be bothered, please."

"Oh, a couple of snooty ones," is his slightly drunken reply as he leans on the table with rough and callused hands. "Wouldn't you girls like to spend the evening with ole Rusty and his buddy? We're fun guys."

"No, we wouldn't!" Jeanne spat out. "Please take your hands off our table and leave us alone."

"And what is miss snooty goin' to do if I don't?"

In a single sudden motion Jeanne slams her elbow down on his hand, grabs his arm and puts him on the floor, face down. She twists his arm behind him to keep him pinned. In the next moment, a man in a dark blue shirt and pants shoots through the door, grabs and swiftly cuffs Rusty. By this time, Rusty's buddy runs over to help his friend, definitely a wrong move. Jeanne and the man in blue soon pin him to the floor next to Rusty and cuff him. No one else moves.

Jeanne looks at my astonished face and introduces the man in blue. "This is Tony Rawls, another member of OSI. He's been outside watching over us in case there were any problems."

"What about these two?" I ask pointing to the pair moaning on the floor.

"Don't worry," Tony said smiling. "They'll spend the night in the local pokey to sober up and be freed in the morning. My guess is they've been in the drunk tank before."

By this time the bartender comes over, astonished at what happened. "Is everything all right officer? I was about to throw these two troublemakers out anyway." Obviously the handcuffs were enough ID to satisfy the man that Tony is an officer of the law.

Tony laughs. "They'll spend the night in the drunk tank. No harm done." He heads out the door towing the two miscreants. "Tad will pick these two up from me in a few minutes," he says as he steps outside. "Till tomorrow, Jeanne."

Clearly awed by the happening, the bartender says, "I'm sorry about those bums bothering you. Please! Anything you want from the menu is on the house."

Jeanne is quite stern with her reply. "Just a little peace and quiet are all we want. Think you can arrange that?"

"Surely! No one will bother you," he answers, almost bowing. "I have one question if you don't mind."

"What's that?"

"How'd you manage to put Rusty down like that? You're a slip of a girl and he's a rather big and ornery guy. No one ever got the better of him here before, but you sure did."

"Martial art is a passion of mine. The bigger they are, the harder they fall you know," Jeanne smiles slyly when she answers.

"I'm baffled. Never saw anything like that in fifteen years tendin' bar. You sure got my respect."

He shakes his head as he walks back to the bar. He and his patrons will talk about this evening's happenings for a long time.

I am curious. "How did you do that? He must outweigh you by a hundred pounds and you handled him like he was a toy."

"The key is all in using an opponent's weight and strength to defeat him quickly. All martial arts use the same principal and we are thoroughly trained in using it."

"You described yourself as a grief counselor. Why would you need martial arts training?"

"No matter what their job or status, all members of OSI receive a great deal of physical training including the latest in martial arts which might be needed at almost any time, tonight for instance."

"I'm impressed. How did you ever become involved with OSI? That's not your average everyday job. I never even heard of OSI until today."

"I hadn't heard of them either when I was contacted. I was on the staff at Flagler College in St. Augustine for nearly five years. One day my boss called me into his office and introduced me to two people who wanted to talk to me. First they explained I was the kind of person they need and asked if I might be interested in a more challenging job. After that intro we talked for about an hour. I agreed to consider their proposal. They were quite mysterious and wouldn't tell me exactly who they were, what the job entailed, or what I would be paid. They said I would be doing important work for the government."

"You applied without knowing what you were getting into?"

"No, not really. They provided me with a packet of information about their indoctrination course. Then my boss assured me they were all on the up and up and it was a great opportunity. He explained how I would be keeping my position as Psychologist at the university, but with a more flexible schedule. During nearly a month of mental, psychological and physical tests and numerous interviews, they explained exactly who they were and what my job would be. That was nearly seven years ago and I have loved every day since. At first I disliked the strenuous physical training, but by the time I became well conditioned, PT was a welcome diversion from the frequent emotional strain. Dealing with people under terrible emotional stress can be draining. Walking the line between detachment and involvement is both difficult and stressful."

"You seem to be handling the stress quite well and doing your job too. I'm more relaxed than at any time since this all happened."

"You are easy to deal with. You are recovering quickly from a terrible trauma. That's a rarity, in my experience You must have a strong will. Many people in your circumstance would be babbling incoherently for several days."

"I never dealt with anything like this before in my life. I'll probably babble a few times before it's all over."

We talked until nearly eleven thirty when Jeanne said. "I think you need a good night's sleep. I doubt I can hold off those interrogators beyond tomorrow morning with you doing so well. Would you like to spend the night at my place in Palm Coast or go to a hotel? I don't think you want to go back to the house yet and my place is a short drive south from here."

"I certainly don't want to stay in a hotel. You're place would be fine. I would appreciate it."

"While you were in the shower, I packed some of your clothes and a few personal items in a small suitcase I found in your closet."

"You think of everything, don't you?"

"Just doing my job, ma'am. Just doing my job," she replies in a stilted voice and with a big grin. We both laugh.

"There's one thing I'm troubled about, something I must do."

"What's that?"

"I'm part of a close family including two sisters and a father. I wonder how soon I will be able to handle the calls to them that I must make."

"We can talk about that in the morning. I can help you, but first, you need some sleep. It's much too late to contact them now."

Chapter 21 - Hangover
✳ Friday, October 25, 2013 ✳

The next morning I awaken in the unfamiliar environment of Jeanne's apartment. This brings on the momentary confusion of waking in a strange place after an upsetting experience. I realize yesterday was not just a bad dream and scream. Jeanne is immediately bending over me and holding my hand.

"Relax! You're okay. I'm right here."

She gave me a pill to help me sleep, but the effect disoriented me. When I awoke the whole bad dream of yesterday played out in my head and I found myself sobbing uncontrollably once more. Jeanne's reassuring hands on my forehead help me regain control.

"That was a bad one," I comment as I sit up on the edge of the bed. Visions of bloody bodies are coursing through my head.

"How about a warm shower? That should help"

Numb with grief I stumble into her bathroom, strip, and step into the shower. The warm rush of water relaxes taut muscles and I begin to think and act rationally.

"Thanks Jeanne!" I shout over the sound of the water. "I'm okay now."

I must contact my family as soon as possible. As I am dressing I tell Jeanne, "First thing I must call my dad and sisters before I do anything else."

The calls took almost an hour of tearful sharing. Renee said she would be here tomorrow and bring her RV with her. My dad said he too is coming. He will call me when he knows his flight arrangements. Andrea said she might need a day or two to organize her work so she can leave and will plan to stay for several days after the funeral.

When we sit down for breakfast, I am completely drained after the phone calls and totally without any appetite.

"I'm glad your family is coming. I know they will provide great support. Now try to eat some toast and drink some juice," Jeanne suggests. "You're going to need some energy today. The interrogation team is waiting in the lobby of my apartment building. I won't let them in until you're okay."

I struggle to down two pieces of toast, but enjoy the OJ and coffee. As I sip my coffee, I glance around at Jeanne's place for the first time.

"You have a delightful apartment. A large living room, a full kitchen with space for a table—nicely decorated I might add."

"Thanks! My place is the right size for my purposes—small and compact, yet the clever design and use of space makes the place feel much larger. Two bedrooms and an office with a view serve me nicely."

Jeanne sets her coffee down and turns to me, a question obvious. "The interrogation team is still waiting anxiously. Are you ready to face them?"

"I think I'm ready. Are they going to talk to me here?"

"Right here in my living room and I'll be with you all the time. They will make an effort not to upset you, but they must ask some hard questions. Try to stay calm and think clearly as your answers could be significant. After asking the questions they will want you to return with them to the house. They need you to tell them if anything is missing. This is absolutely crucial and you are the only one who can do that. . . . Ready?"

I hesitate for a moment, gather my wits and tell her okay. Jeanne calls the men up from the lobby. Their questions are not as harsh as I imagined. After about an hour the repetition gets to me and I become quite upset.

"Why are you asking the questions over and over? I answered the same ones many times before."

Reynard Kronus, a dark-skinned man of obvious multi racial background, is the lead questioner and obvious top authority. He apologizes. "I'm sorry, Miss Mitchell. Repeated questions often bring up details missed in earlier answers. Why don't we take a break for a while?"

"I'm sorry. I didn't understand. I'm not used to being questioned so thoroughly, over and over again. A break now would be welcome."

Jeanne stands and heads for the kitchen. "There's a fresh pot of coffee ready. Why don't we go to the kitchen for a coffee break?"

We all sit and relax around the kitchen table. The two men express their deep concern for my emotional stress.

"One of the most troublesome parts of our job is questioning people in situations like yours," Jeffrey, the second OSI questioner comments. "As hard as we try to be considerate, some of our questions and the way we must ask them are difficult to deal with. They are necessary, but sometimes brutal for us to ask. I hope you understand."

"You have been kind in your questions. I'm certain they are necessary, but answering the same question over and over again got to me. I hope **you** understand."

The two men turn toward each other. Their unison, "touche" makes me smile. We all laugh heartily over that before heading back into the living room. The next series of questions are a bit softer and repeated less often. I appreciate this and tell them so.

The third time Jeffrey asks if I remembered anything unusual about the scene a picture flashes before my eyes, one I had not recalled until then.

"Jack's computer. It wasn't there. It always stays on the table near the telescope, but it was missing when I came into the room."

Jeff scans through a notebook page by page. "There is no computer on our inventory list. They must have taken it."

"Not good," Reynard remarks. "I hope Jack kept a backup somewhere and I hope there was no sensitive data on the hard drive."

I am glad to report, "He backed up each time he used his PC. There are two USB drives with his last two data backups in the glove compartment of his pickup. He kept them there in case his house burned. He never left sensitive data on the computer hard drive. He always worked from a USB drive plugged into his PC."

The OSI men are pleased. Jeffrey is on the radio immediately with the men at the house telling them to remove the USB drives from the pickup.

"There's one thing that may be significant," I comment. "Jack gave me a notebook with paper copies of his most recent work and another USB drive. He asked me to keep them at the office for him. Periodically he asked me to bring them home to be updated. He said he kept this information off his PC in case someone stole it. He didn't want it falling in the wrong hands. Now I understand why."

"Jack was a sly old fox," Jeffrey remarks. "We should go to your office right away and retrieve those records. I don't want to take the chance of them falling into the wrong hands."

As OSI makes arrangements to pick up the notebook I realize I hadn't even thought of my office and how they would be wondering why I hadn't shown up. I thought about the news and nearly panicked. "With this all on TV and in the papers my people will be terribly concerned. I never thought about that until now."

"Don't worry about that." Reynard said kindly. "None of this will make the news. A quiet notification of Jack's tragic death will be the only public announcement. It will not be ballyhooed in the papers or make the national TV news. We try to keep all OSI activities at a low profile. The police will keep this under wraps as well or they might have some serious jurisdictional problems they don't want. For your benefit, we called your office and told them you would not be in today and would not be able talk to them until tomorrow because of an unexpected out-of-town trip on a personal matter. Your gal, Nedra, grilled me for quite a while before agreeing to accept my word. I told her Jack was unavailable as well. She said she would hold down the fort until you return."

I sigh in relief. "So she grilled you did she? That's Nedra, my right hand at Travels with Carol. You're not going to get much past her. She's capable of handling the business while I'm away. She is extremely important to my company."

Chapter 22 - The Funeral
✳ Thursday, October 31, 2013 ✳

The memorial gathering before Jack's funeral is a blur of tears and introductions: the new faces of Jack's family, mind fogging conversations of explanations, anger and disbelief. My introduction to Eric, Jack's grandson, is a heart-stopping experience for me. We stand staring at each other in silence for a minute, a magical minute after Jack's daughter, Sandra, introduces us. Eric is a young clone of his grandfather with his easy manner, smile, and blue eyes.

He even sounds like Jack when he says, "So you are my grandfather's special lady. I must say he had exquisite taste in women."

Somehow I recognized this as a genuine compliment, not a come on. Suddenly the tears burst forth once more. Eric says nothing as he put his arms around me. I continue to sob into his shoulder for a few minutes, regain my composure and step back. When I do, I see the tears on Eric's face. All I can manage to say is, "He was some kind of a special man." I struggle for a tissue and pass one to Eric.

We both dab the tears as Eric struggles to say, "He certainly was special and close to my heart."

We stand for several minutes in the unspoken comradeship of overwhelming grief. The silence is from deep understanding, far better than words can express. Eric takes my hand and leads me to join two men about fifty and an elderly man I guessed to be about eighty. They all wore the weatherbeaten faces of men who spent their time at sea.

"Carol, this is Roy Weatherly and his two sons, Jeremiah and Jebulum. He and my granddad ran fishing boats together for years."

"Oh yes," I say as we shake hands. "Jack spoke quite highly of you. I take it your sons are in the fishing business with you."

"Actually, my boys run the boats now. I help out on occasion when the weather's good," Roy says proudly, gazing at his two sons. "Jack and I go way back, met him when he raced those little planes. He was a wild man back then. This is a real shame . . . a tragedy that never should have happened. Jack was a true and loyal friend, the best friend I ever had."

I hand Roy one of my tissues as his sons put their arms around him to comfort him. There is another silent moment of shared grief. The five of us talk about Jack for about fifteen minutes before drifting off to talk to others.

There are about sixty people at the funeral. Besides Jack's family, there are my sisters, Andrea and Renee and our dad, and Renee's husband, Mack. They are a wonderful, caring support group. My family stayed with me since a day or two after the tragedy sharing both tears and happy memories. Nedra and several others from my office are there. I assume the rest are friends of Jack's from the area. The funeral is quite simple. Each of Jack's three children spoke about their father. Eric is the only grandchild to speak, but his words were a revelation. Until that moment I hadn't realized how close Eric and Jack were. Eric made it quite clear how much he adored his grandfather and spoke of the many things they had done together from his earliest years, adventures he called them. He surprised me when he came over to me, took my hand and led me up to where everyone spoke.

"I want all of you to meet a special lady in my grandfather's life. This is Carol Mitchell. According to my grandfather, she is the only woman he ever loved other than my grandmother. She declined when asked by my mother to speak, but since meeting her and talking with her, I feel fairly safe in asking her to say something. Carol?"

I am terrified. "I am at a complete loss as to where to start," I stammer, trying to find the words. "So many faces of those I do not know." I pause, then continue. "I suppose you would all wonder what attracted me to a man older than my own grandfather." I proceed to tell them briefly how we met and recount the development of our love. "I make no apologies. I simply fell in love with a wonderful man. I will miss him terribly."

As tears stream down my cheeks, I turn and walk to my seat in a room silent but for soft sobs and sniffles. After I sit down, I relive mentally the six months we were together.

Chapter 23 - Fast Forward a Month
✳ Friday, November 22, 2013 ✳

I find it hard to believe a month has passed since Jack was killed. I don't think I'll ever be over it. I assumed I would lose him some day, but not so soon or so violently. Anger mixed with grief is not a recipe for a peaceful life and I had lots of both. My frustration at being unable to do anything about my anger is about to be changed. Jeanne Long asked me to come to her apartment for a visit saying she wanted to discuss something of importance. As I walk into her place, memories of my first visit bring on a flood of tears.

"I'm sorry," I say when she greets me. "As I walked in your door, tortured memories of my last visit hit me."

Jeanne gives me a long hug. "It won't be long before they're gone," she assures me. "The tears I mean. Grief is often associated with a place, several places in fact, and people. For months after Dad died, I burst into tears each time my mother's eyes met mine. Then suddenly it quit. Mom talked with me about the wonderful memories she had of Dad and all they did together and soon we would be laughing, remembering and talking about something funny. That will come to you with time."

"I know. It happened a few times already. I'll remember something and laugh out loud. There are many good memories."

"Good for you. Let's go into the dining room. There are some things laid out on the table I want to show you."

I glance over the large sheet of posterboard sitting next to several looseleaf notebooks. "That could be an organization chart for a business, a rather large business I might add."

"Close! It's an organization chart of al-Qaeda. Jack finished putting the chart together for us about three months ago. He understood more about their organization than anyone. He received much of his information from his own little intelligence operation going on right inside al-Qaeda. He claimed he could do things we couldn't and I think he was right. Some of his people operated outside of the law and there is no way they would cooperate with us."

"His people?"

"Well, no. We called them *his people* merely because he had productive contact with them, something we could not have."

In examining the chart a name caught my eye. "What's Billy Joe Kellerman's name doing there? A Christian TV evangelist? I don't care much for him from what I heard of him. He's such a farce, but he seems out of place with al-Qaeda."

"He's quite high up in the organization, four tiers from the top. He's been with them for years, secretly of course, but he's one of Jack's sources."

"He's a snake oil salesman. He'd be a joke but for all those followers of his. How could a person be a Christian and be promoting the Muslim religion? They're not in the least compatible."

"I doubt anyone in his church knows he's involved with al-Qaeda. Jack never trusted him, but did use him for information. There's a whole notebook filled with information Jack gleaned from him. We never use any unless confirmed by another independent source of course."

"I find several names I recognize."

"You must realize that this chart represents their entire organization down to the leaders of individual cells. There are nearly a thousand names. A few of those names are of some important people. Some of them are our own people undercover."

"What are the notebooks?"

"Those are hard copies of most of what Jack found out about al-Qaeda. We removed them from a safe storage bin hidden in a large pile of sand under his house. The CD from his truck had instructions on where to find them along with a box of CDs with more records."

"Goodness, he was thorough with his records, and secretive too."

"He had to be. In addition to the series of articles, he was working on a book about al-Qaeda and the Wahhabi Muslims. That's one of the reasons I wanted to talk to you."

"Oh?"

"OSI would like you to finish and publish his book."

"Me? I'm no writer."

"I believe you graduated with a degree in journalism."

"Yes, but I never wrote anything."

"How long ago was that? Six years? I doubt you lost many of those skills in such a short time and you have the talent. Your professors told me about that. Read Jack's manuscript and his notes on the subject. Then tell me you don't want to finish it. I'll believe you then."

"You researched me a lot, didn't you? My college professors? What other juicy things about me do you keep on record."

"Come on, Carol. I told you we did that. It's what we do and is not personal. We had another good reason to examine your life closely."

"Oh, what's that?"

"OSI would like to recruit you to be an operative, to do what I do."

"Me? OSI wants me?"

"Very much."

"That's impossible, Jeanne. I have a business to run that is more than a full time job."

"Your business is also a nearly perfect cover for an OSI operative. I don't want you to reject it without hearing what we can offer you. I wasn't interested at first, but then I learned of the challenges, and that I could continue my profession. So, here I am."

"What is your profession? What do you mean you continued your profession?"

"I'm a psychologist, a college psychologist and student counselor. My OSI title is grief psychologist. You understand what that means."

"You gave up your job at the college?"

"Absolutely not. I am still the senior psychologist at Flagler College in St. Augustine, a full time job with a great deal of flexibility. That's the cover for the occasional undercover work I do for OSI. I love both jobs, OSI and at the college."

"Wow, I would never suspect that. Now that you told me, it makes good sense and is quite intriguing. How long have you been living this double life?"

"Seven years going on eight and I love it. Should you want to learn about OSI, we offer an indoctrination course, six weeks of intensive training in the basics of being an operative. No commitment is required and the course will give you a substantial taste of what OSI is and does. No propaganda at all, but actual training. If nothing else, you will gain some valuable skills. I urge you to take it. It's strenuous, exhilarating, and enlightening. You will learn some valuable things about yourself as well."

"How can I take six weeks away from my business? This tragedy took me away for more than a week away already."

"And what happened to your business while you were gone?"

"Okay, so there are some terrific people in my organization."

"Who hired and trained those people? Don't you think you could train them to handle a varied and flexible work schedule for their boss?"

"That's not fair. It was an unusual circumstance."

"That was fair, accurate, and true. The next indoctrination course won't be for two months. There'll be plenty of time to prepare and arrange for your absence."

"Where does the course take place?"

"At a training center near Bakersfield, California, a place that was once a dude ranch. I took all of my training there. Every OSI prospect must take the indoctrination course which is quite strenuous both physically and mentally. Both men and women take the same course. About a third of those who start the course drop out. The experience separates the men and women from the boys and girls so to speak."

"That sounds a bit intimidating—scary."

"I'm certain you can handle it."

"I'll think about it. I truly will."

"Call me when and if you decide. The course is usually filled by three weeks before the start. That is about eight weeks from right now."

"Okay, I'll think about it. Now, I'd better go."

"Please take the manuscript and Jack's notes. Read them and think about finishing his book. I won't make any of the obvious persuasive comments. Read and decide for yourself. In any event, keep in touch."

We share a warm hug before I leave. I have a lot of new ideas to consider. It will take some time. As I drive home on A1A, A dark SUV seems to be following me far behind. When I turn onto a side street and drive through a development and back onto A1A, it makes the same turns I do. I wonder, is it paranoia or real. I decide to find out. I make a left turn in Palm Coast and drive directly to the police station. The SUV pulls up right behind me when I stop and the driver gets out. I recognize him as Tony Rawls, the OSI guy from the incident at Reggio's.

"I did not mean to upset you by following you, miss Mitchell, but apparently I have. You are quite perceptive to realize I was following you. Few people would notice."

"I am experiencing a touch of paranoia, that's all. Glad you are the one following me, but why?"

"Two reasons. One, Jeanne wanted me to make sure you reached home safe and sound. The second? Recently and for the first time your name popped up in an intercepted communication of the local al-Qaeda cell."

"What does that mean?"

"Probably nothing. Your name appeared on a list of about a hundred local business people. Could be a list for charity organization donation calls. We don't know. They list some local charities they use to solicit funds. They use all kinds of sympathetic sounding names, none of which are legitimate. Many people actually donate to these bogus charities. We'll keep tracking them and tell you if anything turns up."

"How about warning me the next time? You did startle me."

"I apologize for that, and I will certainly tell you in the future. I will follow you home and make sure you are inside safely."

"I doubt it's necessary, but thanks anyway," I say as I hop into my car and head for home.

It is comforting knowing Tony is behind me. He beeps and drives off when I enter the house. I wonder if he's lurking around the corner prepared to fend off any would be attackers. It wouldn't surprise me. I go to bed, but can't sleep—too much on my mind. I read for a while, but can't concentrate on what I'm reading. All I can think about is Jeanne's suggestion about OSI. Should I consider it? How might it affect my business? And what about Jack's manuscript? Do I want to take on his project? The minute I think about Jack I think of Eric. Should I go out with him?

Eric's simple question, "Would you go out with me, Carol? I want to know you better," carried a lot of important questions. We obviously are attracted to each other, but is it wise at this point? Maybe after a few months—no, I want to be with him soon. Being with him could help me in my decisions, or confuse me even more.

I go fix myself a cup of warm chocolate milk, and sit down on my couch with Jack's manuscript. After about two hours I run across a phrase that startles me. "These fanatics have but a single purpose. That purpose is the total destruction of the United States, economically, politically, religiously, socially, and culturally. There is no compromise."

I read those words of Jack's several times. It helps make my mind up for me. I will call Jeanne in the morning and ask her to sign me up for the OSI indoctrination course. One decision made, I go to bed and drop off to sleep within a few minutes.

✳   ✳   ✳

Jeanne is pleased with my call. "No matter what you decide to do, you will gain a lot taking the course. I'll reserve you a place today and send you a package of instructions along with several forms to fill out. When you have read the instructions and filled out the forms, I'll come over to talk to you. I want to tell you a few things about OSI that are not in the instructions, some important things."

"Sounds mysterious."

"Not at all mysterious. There are a few important things about OSI you will be pleased to learn. I certainly was. They are best explained in person."

"Now you piqued my curiosity. I'll be anxious until you are able tell me."

"Don't worry, these are all good things you will be glad to learn."

"I'll take your word for that. Incidentally, I have been giving some of my people training in my duties. I told them it was in case I must be away for a while. The three I picked have been with me since I took over the place. There's Nedra who can run things while I'm away. She's helping me with the training. George Yang and Marci Melrose are the other two. George is ambitious and a fast learner and Marci is Miss Reliable. Among the three of them everything should run smoothly and with little or no conflict. All are terrific team workers."

Jeanne says, "You are demonstrating the traits and instincts of an excellent manager, Carol. That's just what we need at OSI and why we wanted you."

"I'll decide where to go after I take the indoctrination course which should finalize my decision. Now I had better get ready for work. I'm still catching up on what went on while I was away. George convinced a major Jacksonville company to try our services for a month. I tried unsuccessfully to break into them for the last two years. He and I will be developing their program presentation together. If we can acquire them as a permanent client it will improve our bottom line and may even help us with a few of the bigger travel and convention venues."

"I had a thought. May I stop by this evening about seven? I can drop off the instruction package and fill you in. Then you won't need to read the instructions first."

"That would be great. I will be able to learn what you are going to tell me about OSI right now instead of waiting."

Jeanne laughed. "Don't be concerned about it, and yes, we will talk about it."

"See you at seven. Oh, would you like to join me for a light dinner? I usually eat around then and dinner for two takes no more to prepare than for one."

"I'm delighted. Sounds like a great idea."

"How does a caesar salad with shrimp sound?"

"Delicious!"

"Bye now."

✳   ✳   ✳

Jeanne arrives promptly at seven and we are soon eating our shrimp and caesar salads and sipping some dry German wine. Dinner finished, our conversation turns from light subjects to OSI.

"Okay, Jeanne, what's all this about OSI? My curiosity is in hyper drive."

"First of all, OSI is an agency of the federal government, an investigative agency."

"That is fairly obvious."

"What you haven't learned and what few people understand is that OSI is a combined federal and private sector group, about half and half."

"That is interesting. How does it work?"

"It came about soon after 9-11 when a group of corporate officers, independent businessmen, asked the CIA what they could do to protect their interests from attack by al-Qaeda and other terrorists, including cyber attacks. The CIA directed them to the new office of Homeland Security who at first turned them away. These were some of the most powerful and influential men in the country, many of whom have their own security systems. In many ways, their systems in place are better and more efficient than their federal counterparts, particularly in cyber security. Industrial espionage is a big deal and earlier they had combined forces and shared information to fight it.

"Some of their friends in Congress called a meeting with the government investigative agencies including the CIA, the FBI, the Secret Service, and Homeland Security. It was a hard sell, but when the private sector people offered to foot half the bill, Congress and the agencies listened. OSI was created in principle at the meeting. A year of hard work, mostly by members of the private sector, and OSI became a reality. The private sector members set up and staffed the resulting organization."

"How on earth did that happen? Who ended up in charge and who made the decisions? Handling such a group must be like herding cats."

"Nothing remotely resembling OSI had ever existed before so a whole new set of rules had to be created. They agreed on a three-man executive group to run the organization, two from the private sector and one from government. The private sector decided on the method of selection of their two and the President selected the government representative which the Senate had to approve. A simple majority of the three ruled decision making. The private sector could always override the government. To counter that, a list of the most important types of decisions was created which required the unanimous consent of all three. This gave the government effective veto power over the two private sector members on important matters. This worked out quite well, even better than expected. The whole organization is run on a cooperative basis. All employees must pass a civil service examination as well as meet the criteria of the private sector group. This brought on the most serious organizational problem we have experienced."

"Oh? And what was that?"

"The private sector insisted all agents not only be natural born Americans, but born of two parents who were also citizens. This goes against the federal employment guidelines used by the CIA, the FBI, and the Secret Service. The private sector people insisted and would not back down. This in spite of a suit that might have scuttled the whole idea. The court ruled OSI as a partially private sector agency was not subject to federal hiring guidelines for security personnel. That solved the problem."

"So OSI is a unique agency, half federal, half private. Do they only deal in private sector security and anti terrorism?"

"No. Sometimes they work outside of their usual realm. They are given police powers and all government agencies must treat them as equal to the other enforcement agencies. Only in matters of utmost secrecy are they excluded, but they must share all their information with any federal officer of the three investigating agencies who asks for it, all under existing federal rules, of course. We've experienced wonderful cooperation from all federal agencies we deal with. Even local police and other law enforcement organizations are quite cooperative. The entire system worked well once staffing was fairly complete, trained, and the organization up and running. We're still growing, adding agents and other staff as you know. While doing this, we are keeping as low a profile as possible."

"That is a fascinating story. I had no idea about OSI. Never heard about them until I met Jack. I am quite excited about joining."

We spend the rest of the evening going through the papers she brought and making my flight arrangements to Bakersfield. I will be picked up at the airport by a bus from the training camp.

"You will be receiving a confirmation along with your trip itinerary and boarding passes in about a week. There is no doubt in my mind you will be accepted. It is merely a formality. Welcome aboard, Carol," Jeanne says with a broad smile and a hug.

"Thank you for coming here this evening. I became enthusiastic about this new and different adventure. I hope I can handle it."

"There's no doubt about that. Once assigned, you will be in my local group. You met several of them already. There are about a dozen of us in the Jacksonville office. We're a small group with varied talents. You'll meet the entire group at your orientation after you complete the course at Bakersfield. You'll like them. They're a close-knit bunch and you will fit right in."

"I'll trust your opinion. I liked the OSI people I've met thus far so I'm positive the others will be much the same."

"Now I need to head for home. Tomorrow is going to be a long day."

I walk her to her car. "Good night, Jeanne,"

"Good night, Carol."

I sit down on my couch to think about what I have committed to. I watch TV until I drop off. About two I wake up and go to bed.

✳ Monday, January 6, 2014 ✳

The course is quite strenuous and after a week I am considering dropping out. I might have done so if not for Thelma Marchant, my room mate in the dorm where we all stay. Thelma is a tiny woman barely five feet tall, tough and wiry. She hails from Minot, North Dakota and grew up on a farm in an area where farming is difficult and chancy. A year younger than I, she has the fresh, weathered appearance of a frontier woman, and determination to match. She will not let me quit. When I tell her I am considering dropping out, she grabs me, stands me up like a drill sergeant with a recruit, right in my face.

"Grow up you wimpy, no guts city girl. I'll beat the piss outta you if you ever again talk of quittin'. We're both gonna make it in spades," she says. "There is an endurance contest as part of the final exam. That contest requires a team of two, and you and I are gonna win it, the female part anyway. I sure as hell won't let you drag me down."

"What can I say?"

"Just say you're not quittin' no matter what. Say it, "

"Okay! I'm not quitting, no matter what."

"Now say we're gonna win the endurance contest."

"We're going to win the endurance contest."

I don't think I have ever been pushed as hard as Thelma pushes me in my life. I don't think I have ever been as aware of the workings of my body. She shows no mercy when we are paired combatants in the martial arts training. My proudest day is the day I finally take her down. Every night we collapse, exhausted. I don't think I have ever slept so soundly. Each morning we are out on the drill field at six. The physical part runs all morning. Classrooms lectures and discussions take up all afternoon. I learn to pleasantly anticipate the daily physical exertion. By the end of the six weeks I am in the best physical condition ever. We won the endurance contest, barely. As we neared the finish line, worn out and muddy, Thelma grabs me, picks me up, and carries me the last six yards and across the finish line even though she knows I will make it. I can't believe anyone so small can be so strong. The indoctrination over, we unwind during the graduation celebration.

It is a teary parting from the many new friends we gained during the training. Something about the intensity transfers to those friendships. They will last a long time.

Quite a different me returns to St. Augustine. I can hardly wait to talk with Jeanne and the others in our section.

Chapter 24 - A Chopper Scares Them to Death
✳ Sunday, April 20, 2014 ✳

The downdraft and shaking slows, then stops. The chopper landed on the water close to the hammock and the blades are idling.

I grab my automatic. "Grab the rifle and prepare for the worst. I'm going to crack open the door to listen to what they are saying."

I open the door slightly and listen. They are at the part of the hammock farthest away from the cabin. I can hear them talking, but can understand only a few words of what they are saying.

"It sounds like Charley from the marina. I heard him say 'a big snake.' They're probably out hunting pythons or boas. They may have found one on our hammock."

"Out here, so far away from everything? I heard those non native snakes were becoming a problem. Is that what they're doing about them, hunting them?"

"I don't know. Anyway they are not out after us so we can put the guns away."

"That's a relief."

"I'm going to put on my camouflage outfit and go where they are within eyesight. If they come onto the hammock, they will find the cabin. I want to be prepared for that. Please stay inside until I come back."

"Okay, boss."

"I'll ignore that."

In about ten minutes I move to the south end of the hammock near where they landed. I peer through the bushes. They are getting into a small boat unfastened from one of the pontoons. I can clearly hear their conversation.

"Is he still there or did our landing scare him away?"

"He's right where we spotted him as we flew over. I don't think he's moved a bit. I'll move the boat to where you can put the net under him."

"Yeah, he's not moving. Something is strange. His eyes are hazy."

"We're in luck. That means he's about to shed his skin. Don't touch the net against anything until you are close enough to catch him."

"I think he's dead, Pete."

"Play it as if he's alive. Slip the net under his position then raise it up sharply. He'll coil backward and fall into the net."

"I got him, but he's dead, no struggle. Damn, he's really dead. He smells putrid. What a stench."

"We'll bag him in plastic and tie it closed. Then he won't smell so bad."

They dump the snake into a plastic bag, put the bag into the boat and rinse out the net. Charley from the marina is one of them. The other man, Pete, wears a ranger's uniform. When Charley turns directly toward me, I freeze.

Pete says, "They are sometimes found together, male and female. The breeding season is year 'round for Burmese pythons like this one. Maybe we should check out the rest of the hammock for another one."

Damn, I thought. *Please don't.*

"That one's been dead for a long time. I doubt any mate would stick around, and don't make any sick jokes."

"I still think we should check out the rest of the hammock."

"All right, if you insist, but I think it will be a waste of time. We'll play hell getting ashore through all those mangroves."

"Let's paddle down the pond. There may be a place we can land around on the side of the hammock."

"Shit," I say to myself in a whisper. "They'll find the cabin and all our efforts at secrecy will be blown when we explain ourselves."

While the two of them paddle around the mangroves toward the cabin, I walk back, keeping out of their line of sight. I take a quick sprint to the cabin and slip inside before they round the last mangrove.

"We're getting company," I call to Lydia. "Charley and a ranger named Pete will soon be pulling up near the cabin. They stopped to catch a python so they are not searching for us. I still don't like it."

"What can we do?"

"Charley will realize it's my cabin when he sees it. He's known we had one out here for years, but not its location. For the time being, stay out of sight. Charley is aware you're with me but Pete isn't. I'll try getting him to not mention you to Pete. A guy alone out here is one thing. The same guy in a cabin with a gorgeous female is a whole nuther thing that might be hard for the ranger to keep from blabbing about to everyone he knows."

"Okay, I'll hide in the storage room in case they come in."

"I'll try to prevent that from happening. I'm going out to greet our visitors."

I walk down to the shore just as the boat comes into view.

"Hey, Brooks. You got out here okay."

"Yeah, Charley, I was finishing breakfast when your chopper flew over and scared the hell out of me."

They pull the boat up and step out. "Brooks, this is Pete Evans, one of our local rangers. I'm helping him look for invasive critters, snakes mostly."

"Pleased," I say as we shake hands.

"Likewise. I never expected to run into anyone out here. This is a big surprise. Charley didn't warn me."

"Hell, I had no idea where your cabin was until now—never was here before. I realized it was your cabin the minute I set eyes on it though."

"My dad and I built this place about thirty years ago. I came out here alone to be away from my work for a while and maybe do some fishing." I look straight at Charley when I say alone. He gets the message. "This is the first time I returned here since my dad died eight years ago."

Pete grins. "You certainly will be alone out here. There's nothing and nobody for about twenty-five miles in any direction."

"Correction. Two uninvited guests are right in front of me and I've not been here a full day yet."

"Sorry about that. A big python lay out at the south end of the hammock and that's what we're hunting for. The snake was dead so it wasn't hard to catch."

"So that's what you were doing on the hammock."

"Yeah, seen any snakes since you got here?" Pete asks.

"Not a single one. If I find one should I call you or catch it myself?"

"You got a gun?" Charley asks.

"Yep."

"Shoot it."

"The ASPCA won't like that," Pete says with a grin.

"The ASPCA will never hear about it," Charley says.

"Let's go," Pete says. "I need to take the snake to our lab as soon as we can. They'll try to find out what killed it. That could be a disease we could use to destroy other pythons, you never know."

"Interesting," I comment.

Charley grimaces. "I wouldn't want to deal with that smelly mess. I'll be glad when we're rid of it. We'll leave the bagged snake in the boat tied to the pontoons. I don't want it in the chopper with me."

"OK guys, I need to go back to work on my fishing gear so don't let me hold you up. Oh, and Pete, I would appreciate it if you said nothing to anyone about me or this cabin. My dad and I kept the place secret for many years and I like keeping it that way, less bother and less worry. You understand of course?"

Pete spins around. "What cabin and what guy? All I found was a dead snake."

"Thanks my friend. I truly appreciate it."

Chapter 25 - The Snake Strikes Back

✳ Sunday, April 20, 2014 ✳

As soon as the boat is out of sight, I return to the cabin.

"You can come out now. They're gone."

Silence.

"Okay, Lydia."

More silence.

"This is not funny," I say as I grab the door to the storage room and open it.

"Lydia!" I scream! She is doubled up on the floor, a python wrapped around her neck and upper body. Her face is blue-white and she is not moving. I grab the machete hanging on the back of the door. The snake tries to bite my left hand as I reach to grab it. I instantly strike the machete down on its head. Two blows killed the snake, or so I thought. Even dead the snake held a powerful grip on Lydia so I had to struggle to free her. She is limp and not breathing. I think about going outside and screaming for the two men to come back and help, but decide instead to work on Lydia. She has a pulse, weak, but steady. I stretch her out on the floor and start mouth to mouth resuscitation. Fortunately, I'm qualified in CPR. After about ten minutes she is still not breathing on her own. I pray as I work on her. Tears run down my face and fall on hers. More minutes go by with me her source of air.

"Come on, damn it, breathe," I keep muttering under my breath each time I pause for her to exhale. I must start her breathing. I hear the chopper engine start, run for a few minutes, and stop. Possible rescue Lydia needs is about to fly away. I check her pulse which is now weaker than the first time, but is still there. Then the goddamn snake rolls over on its belly and moves. I couldn't believe my eyes. Its head is a bloody mess, but the damned thing is still very much alive, or maybe having a reflex action. I can't stop working on Lydia to find out. The next time I release her, I jump up, grab my handgun off the table and pump five shots into the damned snake which quits moving. I resume my effort with Lydia.

After working for another ten minutes the door bursts open.

"We heard shots!" is all Charley says before his eyes tell him what is going on. "My God, Brooks. Let us help. Pete's an expert at CPR. You must be about whipped out."

I realize how beat I am from half an hour of mouth to mouth, not to mention the emotional stress. "She still had a pulse the last time I checked."

Pete drops down on the floor beside me. "Let me take over, Brooks. You are beat."

"Take good care of her. She's my . . . Hell! We can't let her die," I say through a flood of tears.

"Pete's a medic," Charley says. "Pete, don't you carry a medical kit in the chopper?"

"Behind the passenger seat. A big black case. Grab the case and bring it here," Pete says between breaths.

"Brooks, help me with the boat. You don't want to leave her, but she's in expert hands and the two of us can move a lot quicker than one."

I can 't speak, but head for the door. In fifteen minutes we find the kit and bring it into the cabin. When we open the door, Lydia is sitting up and gasping for air. Her eyes are wide open. I burst into tears again.

Pete shouts, "Bring the kit over here and open it. She's not out of the woods yet. The snake could have crushed her trachea. She started breathing on her own about the time you went out the door. I may need to put a tube down her throat because she is having so much difficulty breathing. We must take her to a hospital as fast as possible. There's only so much I can do out here."

"The nearest hospital is in Homestead," Charley says. "Once we put her in the chopper the trip will take about forty minutes."

"Can the chopper hold all of us?" I ask.

"Sure, if we leave the boat behind. Our chopper is a small one without a big payload, but without the boat it's a piece of cake. With her on a backboard we will be a tight fit, but doable."

Pete gives her several shots, a tube so she can breathe easier, and an IV, just in case. We take two round trips with a few scary moments in the small boat getting her and the three of us into the chopper. Nearly two hours after Lydia had been attacked, we lift off and head for Homestead.

Chapter 26 - A Mercy Flight in the Chopper

✳ Sunday, April 20, 2014 ✳

O nce on our way I talk with them. "Guys, Lydia and I have another problem that may be even deadlier than the snake attack."

Charley turns toward me. "My God, Brooks, what could possibly be so dangerous?"

"There are some determined and resourceful people who want the two of us dead. They tried back in Atlanta, about shot my house to pieces. If any public authorities find out where we are, these people will find out as well and come to kill us. It's a simple fact. We did a lot to hide our tracks coming down here and getting out to my cabin. I thought we would be safe there. That's all blown now."

I proceed to explain everything we did after the house was shot up and made up a story about why. I left out all the technical stuff, the SSC, the government's involvement, and some of the classified information. I told them enough that my story would check out with the available information.

"You are in it up to your necks, aren't you?" Charley says.

Pete says, "Right now I am the only law enforcement that knows anything about any of this so listen carefully. I am concocting a plan. You are now Charles and Ruby Detmire from Cleveland. You flew to Miami and rented a boat from Gallagher's Marina in Miami. You were cruising off of Flamingo when you were hit by a freak wave that overturned your boat. You lost all of your belongings and your wife was almost strangled by the anchor rope when it became twisted around her neck as the boat went over. Charley and I happened by in the chopper, and rescued the two of you from the water. Ruby was almost dead, but was given CPR that saved her. What do you think?"

I said, "Great idea, but won't somebody check out the Detmires and find they don't exist?"

Pete smiled. "Not a chance, the Detmires are close friends of my sister, Sue. They live in Cleveland, but are currently on an extended vacation, guess where, on a rented boat headed for the Dry Tortugas. They left yesterday. I helped them set up the trip."

I am worried. "Won't the hospital want confirmation? Surely they will be checking many things. What about radio? Doesn't their boat have a radio? Someone's bound to check that."

"Leave the hospital information to me," Pete says with a grin. "I did lots of favors for the folks at the hospital. They will be quite discrete when I explain to them you would like to keep this quiet so your family won't be all worried and upset. In particular you don't want any of them to endure the expense of a trip here and back. That will be the clincher."

I think about the real Detmires. "What about the real Detmires? Won't they eventually have to deal with some fallout? There'll be accident reports and insurance and . . . and what about the marina? How will they deal with a lost boat that doesn't exist? And you . . . what about all the reports you'll be filling out. Won't others be checking on those? I don't want to cause you any trouble, especially since all of the help you provided. Also, any thing that doesn't check out could be a red flag for those people who want us dead. The bad thing about them is they will not hesitate to kill anyone they even suspect might stand in their way. And they have access to lots of information. I told you all the hoops we jumped through to be down here. I guarantee they are still actively searching for us."

"Will you stop the predictions of doom? This is no big deal. I'm the reporting officer. It will just be one more small accident among thousands like it. We'll have your lady made good as new and put you back on your little island hammock and no one will be the wiser. You do remember we will need to go back there to pick up our boat, don't you? Not a word of this will ever hit the media. They won't consider the story worth their effort. The only thing we will be hiding is your names. With everything else out in the open, no one will pay any attention. Believe me."

"I hope you're right, Pete. I guess there are no other options. Charley, what do you think?"

"I think I'll salvage the boat, put it back in running order and let the Detmires return it to the marina. That's what I think. I salvaged quite a few swamped boats in the water near Flamingo over the years. Piece of cake," Charley says with a Chessie Cat grin.

✳   ✳   ✳

Emergency room personnel grab the board with Lydia and take her in as soon as the chopper lands on the hospital helipad. Pete and I go with them. Three hours after arriving Lydia is wheeled out of the operating room. The surgeon joins me in a small conference room.

"Your wife was lucky," he says. "Her trachea is bruised but not crushed. She will be quite sore for several days and unable to speak. The muscles in her neck have been stretched and even torn in a few places, but not enough to require surgery. This will cause her some pain but will heal in time. I doubt she will be able to speak for at least a week and her speech will be affected for at least a month. You will be given a packet of instructions for her care when you leave."

"And when will she be able leave?" I ask.

"We want to keep her here for at least one day, two if things don't go well. She's a healthy young lady and responded well to treatment. Please don't encourage her to speak for at least a week. Those torn muscles will take that long to heal, maybe longer. She will tell you when she is able comfortably to speak. Right now talking will cause considerable pain which will lessen as the healing process goes on. She should have a pad and pen handy at all times."

"What about care while she heals? What kind of restrictions? What can I do?"

"Everything is described in the information packet you will receive. A couple of days of rest and she will show much improvement. Then she will only be limited by what she feels able to do. There are some exercises she should start after three days. Those will help her neck muscles heal properly. They may be painful at first, but make sure she does them. They are described in the instructions and are easily understood. The nurse who checks her out at discharge will go through the packet with you to make sure everything is understood."

We talk for at least half an hour more. I ask questions, and he provides answers.

"She'll be sleeping and completely out for several hours so if there are things you must do, now is the time. I doubt she'll be awake until at least six or seven this evening. If we don't meet again, have a safe trip home to Cleveland and be careful on your next boat trip," he says as I leave.

Pete and Charley are waiting when I walk out into the lobby.

"How is she?" they ask, in unison.

"She came through better than I expected. Doc says she will be 100% in about a month."

We stand there talking for about twenty minutes about all of the events since they landed their chopper at the hammock.

"Don't you guys have something to do," I ask, "somewhere to go with your bird? I'm stuck here for a few days until Lydia gets out. I plan to walk around and find a motel, a place to stay."

Pete says, "You won't need a motel. I called my wife and she's on her way over to pick you up. We live here in Homestead. We even have a couple of empty rooms when our kids aren't visiting, and they're not around this week."

"That's nice of you. You're positive it won't be a lot of trouble?"

"Not at all. You can even use my car to travel about. You can work things out with Cindy. She's a teacher who rides her bike to work so the car is available all day. Of course, if it's raining, you'll be driving her to work."

An ancient and battered Ford pickup drives up and a tall redhead in jeans steps out.

"I forgot. Cindy's Toyota is in for service. She's driving my car today."

After introductions and some explaining by Pete, I ask, "How are we going to get back to the cabin when she's able travel? I can't ask you to take us back there."

"You don't have to ask," Pete says. "The chopper is usually parked at our station about five blocks from here. I must schedule a trip to pick up our boat. I'll do that when your lady is ready to travel. We can take you along then. No problem and no extra expense for me to report. Until then, you and Lydia will be our guests. Cindy loves guests. She'll be happy as a clam in mud."

"Of course," Cindy says. "It's been quiet around our house since the boys left for college. I'll love having someone other than Pete to talk to. We'll have a grand time."

Cindy's broad, friendly smile emphasizes the sincerity of her words.

We say our goodbyes to Pete and Charley who head for the chopper. I hop into the pickup and we head for their home. We will be unable to leave for ten days, doctor's orders.

Chapter 27 - Back to the Cabin

✳ Wednesday, April 30, 2014 ✳

Ten days later, Lydia's voice is beginning to be useful so we start making arrangements to leave. She still has pain speaking, and her voice is little more than a whisper. Her voice gets stronger and clearer as the days pass. Her prescribed neck exercises are far less painful than when she started. She is much better and finally able to speak and relate her experience in our storage room. Hearing her story for the first time is chilling. Pete, Cindy, Lydia and I are seated around their dining room table enjoying coffee when Lydia is finally able to tell her story.

"When I went into that small store room to hide, I only expected to spend a short time so I made no preparations. I sat down to wait on one of the packing boxes. The space was so tight my knees were against the door. The room was pitch black. Right after I closed the door I heard sounds coming from the shelves above me. Immediately something heavy and cold landed on my shoulder. I reached up to remove it and realized it was a huge snake. It twisted rapidly around my neck and shoulders while I fought to get away. The snake was tremendously strong and soon my arms were pinned to my chest and I could not move. Then came the crushing pressure. The breath was being squeezed out of me. I could not breathe. That's the last thing I remember until I saw Pete's face.

"I was quite fearful. I found it almost impossible to breathe, and an unknown male face stared at me from close range. I struggled to sit up trying to better be able to breathe. Pete helped me sit up and the next thing I remember seeing was Brooks coming in the door. I was gasping for breath, but greatly relieved when he came through the door. Everything after that was a jumble of activities. I must have been going in and out of consciousness. I remember being placed on the back board and I remember the shaky trip in the little boat. I do not remember being put into the helicopter or any part of the trip to the hospital. My next memory is of the ER operating room and all the faces above me. I remember being terribly frustrated because I could not speak. I was groggy."

"Wow," Cindy says. "What a horrible experience. I'm surprised you never panicked."

"I was probably too groggy to panic. All the memories I related are fuzzy, disconnected pieces. My memory of the snake attack until I passed out is quite vivid. Everything after that and until the ER is quite fuzzy—more like recalling a bad dream. I'm grateful for all you did for me. You are wonderful people. I owe you my life—literally. I will be eternally grateful."

"You would do the same thing for us if the situation were reversed," Cindy said as she took and held Lydia's hand.

"It's wonderful to have found such trusted new friends," Lydia whispers. "After all our crazy business is over, we'll be back in touch with you."

"Should you need our help, whatever your *crazy business* is, you can call us."

I say, "Don't worry. We can count on you for sure. I think we had better start. It's going to be a long day. I had a thought. Pete, would you be able to make a stop at the Flamingo Marina, or is it too far out of our way?"

"It's about a mile or so more. That's no problem, why?"

"There are a number of things there that we would take a two-day boat trip to pick up. If we could load them in the chopper, it would be a big help."

"How heavy?"

"Around three hundred pounds, no more, maybe less."

"Without Charley and the boat we could handle close to 500 pounds. We'll stop and pick up your things. The chopper can land in the parking lot at the marina. Will you be able to move your stuff?"

"No problem. We can borrow one of Charley's little motorized mules for that."

We all climb into Cindy's Toyota and head for the chopper.

✳   ✳   ✳

The flight is uneventful. We pick up all the stuff from Lydia's RV and head for the cabin. As we start to land, I realize the mess facing me in the cabin.

"First thing I'll do is drag that stinking snake out of the cabin and clean things up. It's a very unpleasant prospect. I imagine we'll deal with a nasty smell for some time."

"Not so, my friend. Charley took care of that problem while you and I were taking Lydia to the chopper. Didn't he tell you?"

"Nope!"

"He told me he dragged the snake out to the water. 'Good gator food,' he said. He took one of your buckets and washed down all the blood—even scrubbed the floor with a push broom he found. The place should smell fine."

"Will you please tell him how grateful we are? I've been thinking about the snake rotting there since soon after we left—not a pretty picture. I can hardly believe it's all cleaned up."

"I'll tell him. Charley's one of my best friends. He's been so for thirty years. We've been through a lot of fun times and a few hells together. This experience was a good one. Unfortunately we won't be able to tell anyone about it. We will be able talk between ourselves. You will tell us when and if your little problem goes away, won't you?"

"Absolutely."

Pete puts the chopper down gently right beside their boat.

"Now let's load your lady and your stuff in the boat and then into your cabin. Don't worry. You won't need to wade through all that stuff to shore. After we've taken you and your stuff in, I can put the boat onto the pontoon myself. Did so many times."

It takes the better part of an hour to move everything ashore. Lydia is still far from 100% so we insist she stay in the cabin while we bring the rest of our stuff ashore, MREs and printer paper. When we walk into the cabin with the last load, we are greeted by the smell of fresh coffee and some hot soup. Lydia has been doing her thing.

"I thought you could use a little lunch before shoving off, Pete."

"Thanks a lot, Lydia. I appreciate it."

After lunch we walk down to Pete's boat. As he gets into his boat he asks, "Do you have a short wave radio?"

"Yes we do," I answer, "but we only use it to listen. Transmitting might give our position away and you never can tell who's listening."

"Listen on our band. I'll holler if anything shows up that might interest you. I'll use the call sign *Samson* for you and hope you hear me. If it's anything serious I'll broadcast it exactly on the odd hours."

"Thanks, Pete. We will be listening. If anything drastic comes up, we can contact you."

"I take it I shouldn't ask so I won't. I'll accept that as fact. Oh, and if I'm ever in the neighborhood, I may stop to check on you. I can set 'er down in the pond in front of your beach. You can come out and wave to show me you're okay."

Amidst good byes Pete shoves off. My first order of business is to fix and start the generator. All of our equipment that requires electricity will be useless until then. Next I have nearly two weeks of work on our iphones and the SSC setup to catch up on. Hopefully, a recovering Lydia will soon be up to helping me.

Chapter 28 - SSC Reveals a Surprising Scenario

✳ Tuesday, May 13, 2014 ✳

The generator took half a day to repair and run properly. Once we have electricity another two weeks passes before we have the SSC up and working. Locking onto the satellites is the biggest problem because of the trees overhead. I built a tower to place the antenna above the tops of the trees where they will not interfere. Three medium sized pine trees growing along side the cabin provide the legs and do the job. A sturdy flat platform holds the antenna solidly and without swaying. I can climb up the ladder and cover the antenna with branches to hide it if necessary.

Lydia is healing faster than predicted and her voice is nearly back to normal. Our first search for SSC transmissions containing our names is a surprise. There is no mention of either of our names or of the code that is used in some transmissions to identify me.

Lydia is quite pleased. "You must be off the radar, as far as your enemies in the government are concerned anyway."

"I'm not at all sure of that. It could also mean a few other unpleasant possibilities. One, they are convinced I solved the SSC coding problem and are using other means of communication about my activities. Two, they succeeded in developing a new coding system I am not aware of and are communicating using the new system. Three, they are sure of where we are and are waiting for the best time and method to eliminate us."

"How about four? They don't care about you or your activities and you have a bad case of paranoia."

"Come on, Lydia, the automatic weapon attack on my house was damn real. Why don't you check the Internet for Atlanta news at the time of the attack? See if there is any mention of it. Of course, my house is so far from anyone else, maybe no one reported the attack or damage. While you're at it, check for any news involving BMK. Check the BMK website as well. They might be wondering where I am."

"Okay, boss. While I'm checking, why don't you find out if BMK is mentioned in any of those SSC communications? Just a thought."

"That's a damned good idea. I'll check on that right now."

About an hour later Lydia shouts, "Bingo!"

I drop what I am doing to find out what she is shouting about.

She says, "There is no mention of any problems at your house, but there are several news articles about a break-in at BMK. Someone told the police the only thing taken was the laptop from your desk. Isn't that the one you are using right now?"

"That's strange. Everyone knows I take my laptop with me. I never leave it in my office."

"What I hollered Bingo at is an article on the BMK website saying you took a trip to Europe and will not be back for several months."

"That is strange. Someone made that up from thin air. I wonder who and why. No one there has any idea where I am or what I'm doing. Someone took the opportunity of my absence to fabricate a big lie. I wonder why your name was never mentioned. Do you suppose BMK has been infiltrated? We do a thorough background check on anyone hired, but a clever individual with lots of resources might pass through that. We should check out the BMK databanks and find out who issued those lies."

"Can you do so without revealing where we are?"

"Piece of cake. I will need some time, a couple of hours. What to do first?"

"We must quickly modify our iphones to use the satellites. I think that should be the next thing on our agenda. Then we will be able to communicate with your cousin and others without revealing our whereabouts."

"That reminds me, I'm worried about Ralph. He has no way to contact us directly. All he can do is send us a coded message via satellite link and hope we pick it up. We left before we could talk with him and he did want to talk to me about something."

"Won't you be able to contact him when the iphones are linked to the satellites?"

"Yes, but carefully. I could contact him at Homeland Security. He gets lots of calls there. If they are tracking his calls, all they would find is a phone call from a concerned citizen in Atlanta. I can make it appear to be that way. You can be the one to make the call. A woman's voice will be less suspicious. I can tell you what to say in a coded message Ralph will understand."

"Sounds like a plan. Let's modify those iphones ASAP."

✳   ✳   ✳

The iphones take the rest of the day. We try several times before we have a link we can use consistently. Around ten I link with the BMK database and receive a real shock.

"Lydia, someone at BMK changed the pass code to my private database. I can't open it."

"Does that mean they can access your data? If so, we could have a major catastrophe."

"No, and Carla could have done this to prevent hackers from gaining access while I'm gone. I won't be certain until I can talk with her. I'll bet she's responsible for the European trip story too. I don't often keep her in the dark about my activities and she's surely concerned at being unable to reach me. Now that we can use satellite communications, I can call her. She has SSC communication on her PC at home so if I can get her to open a link, we would have a secure means of talking. I'll try right now."

＊ Friday, May 16, 2014 ＊

It is near midnight when Carla answers my call. "Damn, Brooks, I'm relieved to hear from you. Where in hell are you? All kinds of clients and even some government types have been asking me how they can make contact with you. I told them you were on a do-not-disturb vacation somewhere in Europe. I'm certain none of them believed me."

"Thank you, Carla. As you can tell, our satellite uplinks are up and working. We are now able to communicate on this secure system. I'll not disclose where I am so you can honestly say you don't know."

"That will help a lot and ease my mind, Ralph's too. He called me and said he was worried when you didn't reply to his request or try to meet him. We are both concerned for his safety. I drove to your house to find if you were holed up there. What I found scared the hell out of me. I'm sure you are aware someone shot up your house?"

"Lydia and I were there when the shooting took place. Luckily we both escaped unharmed. That attack is what precipitated our going into hiding."

"You did an impressive job. I tried tracking your bank withdrawals and credit cards. One max withdrawal at your local bank, no credit card use, and it's been how long since then, three weeks? Ralph and I were afraid something terrible had happened to you. He's scared to death someone at Homeland will tie him in with you, now that you are on the federal terrorist list. He said there have been some unusual accidents and strange disappearances among the HS staff. Several were people he knew and trusted."

"I'd like to find out how and why I'm on that list. I wonder if I can? I stopped to visit Ralph when we were leaving town, but he was not home. Damn! Let me think . . . I'll try to find a way to come back there in secret."

"Would you like me to arrange for your house to be repaired and cleaned up? If nothing else it might confuse whoever is after you. You gave me a key and I can have it done quietly."

"Not a bad idea. Hire George Young. He's the contractor who most recently worked on my house and he can be trusted. He should tell anyone who asks he's doing some remodeling and not to mention repairing bullet holes. Oh, and ask him to install armor in the outside walls while he's at it. I don't want bullets flying through my house again. Ask him to be quiet about the armor, as quiet as possible. He has the routine."

"Okay, boss. Then what should I do?"

"Continue exactly as you have been. I'll be extremely busy, but will keep you informed. I'll also tell you when I find a way to come back there safely. By the way, did you change the password for my database?"

"I did. Would you like me to change it back?"

"Absolutely, and I'm going to end this call and go back to work."

"Before you leave, How can I securely contact you?"

"Use my cell number from any secure SSC system location. It will recognize your number and make a secure connection. Ralph won't have that capability until we modify his iphone. Bring him to your place and tell him to use your system to call me."

"Okay, Bye."

Lydia frowned. "Did you say you are going back there? I hope you know what you're doing."

"I'm formulating a plan for a trip like the one that got us down here. We'll both go and drive straight through, up and back. My plan will depend on a little help from Charley. Didn't we leave some changes of clothes in your RV?"

"You aren't planning on using my RV to go back there, are you? That would be inviting disaster. Our friends must be searching for it by now."

"Of course not. I plan on asking Charley to buy us an old but reliable vehicle, like a pickup. We'll give him some cash and use a fictitious name."

"Can you actually do that?"

"I think we can in Florida anyway. We'll search to find out. We had better wrap things up here since there will be no computer access to our SSC sources until we return."

"Wouldn't you be able to use the PCs at BMK?"

"The capability, yes, but I don't think it would be a good idea. There are some unfriendlies monitoring all radio communications from BMK and any sudden flurry of SSC activity might give us away. They wouldn't be able to unscramble the signal, but the fact of the signal's existence could tell them I'm back. We don't want them to suspect that."

"Understandable. When do you think we will be ready to go?"

"I'll need at least three full days here before we can leave, if nothing drastic shows up during our scans of SSC from the Middle East or North Korea. We should be able to wrap things up on Friday and leave here about dawn on Saturday. With any luck and if Charley can find us a ride in a hurry, we could be at BMK by Tuesday morning."

"Never a dull moment around you, is there?"

"I hope not."

Chapter 29 - A Fast Trip to Atlanta

✳ Saturday, May 17, 2014 - 6:00 am ✳

We are up about six and soon packed. By the time light is showing in the east, everything is loaded into the john boat. Poling through the reeds is much easier with 400 fewer pounds in the boat and no fuel tank in tow. The trip to the marina is smooth and much quicker than the trip out. Around noon we chase Charley down in the boat storage building.

"Charley, There's a big favor I must ask you."

"Ask away, Brooks," he says when he climbs down from his tractor.

"We must take a run back to Atlanta and can't chance using Lydia's RV. Could you buy me a vehicle like a pickup, reliable, but not new? Something people wouldn't pay attention to. I'll gladly pay for your services."

"Let me think where I might find what you need. . . . Wait a minute. Would a ten-year-old Ford F150 crew cab do?"

"Exactly what we need. You know of one for sale?"

"No, but I do have one you can use. The marina bought a new pickup to use for towing boats a few months ago."

"What's that got to do with what we need?"

"We kept the old pickup which was not worth much, just in case . . . you know, a spare vehicle. That pickup is sitting right over there," he says pointing. "You can use it for your trip and save your money."

The vehicle is a slightly battered, red and grey pickup. "Do you think it is able to make the trip of a couple thousand miles?"

"The odometer shows 250 thousand miles, but it's solid as a rock. We replaced the engine and transmission about a year ago, and it's been used little since. The tires are quite worn and need to be replaced. I wouldn't take a trip of such a distance on those old ones."

"I'll gladly pay for its use, whatever you say."

"I tell you what. Put on a new set of tires, service the truck and we'll call it a deal. A lube and oil change are due, but it runs like a top, smooth and reliable. We take good care of our vehicles as we depend on them for our business."

"Are you positive you can do without it? We wouldn't want to inconvenience you."

"Sometimes that truck sits for weeks on end without being used. Someone here drives it at least once a week to keep the running gear exercised and the battery charged. Take it. I guarantee it's reliable. Your trip at highway speeds will burn out any carbon build up. You will have plenty of power with the big 440 V8, but the gas mileage is not good."

"If you're certain it's not an inconvenience. It's perfect for our needs, and we won't be delayed finding one to buy. Charley, thank you so much."

"The keys are in it, but it may need gas. Better check. The tires will last you to Homestead okay, but I would buy new ones before taking a long trip and don't forget to service it. It's due for an oil change and lube."

"Don't worry, I will, and thanks a million. We should be back in a week, two at the most."

"Use it as long as you like. We will be fine without it. The tire store in Homestead will be open until seven, so be on your way soon to get those new tires. Want me to pull your boat out on your trailer? No point in leaving it in the water."

"Sure, that's a good idea."

"Call me when you're on your way back and I'll put your boat back in the water before you are here."

"Charley, you're a gem. Thank you so much."

"Thank you for being such a good customer and friend for all those years. And have a safe trip. Now you should go."

We load all of our things into the back seat, stop at the marina pump for a fill up, and head for Homestead. We are at the tire store in time, to a service station for a lube and oil change, and then head north. At seven thirty we leave Homestead. I call Carla and tell her we will be there at BMK in the morning.

✳ Sunday, May 18, 2014 ✳

The trip is a reprise of our trip down. We trade driving and sleeping. The sun is coming up when we reach Atlanta and Lydia awakens.

"Where are we going first, BMK?"

"Yes. I want to talk to Carla. I'll park in the employee lot and we'll walk to my private entrance. We can go to my office without anyone seeing us."

"Won't this truck draw attention? There's no employee sticker."

"How about this?" I say as I pull one out of my billfold and stick it on the windshield. "I carry one of these in my wallet, in case I need it."

Carla is waiting in my office when we walk in.

"Am I ever glad to see you two."

"We're both glad as well. You didn't tell anyone we were coming, did you?"

"Only Ralph who is getting more fearful every day. He wants to talk to you ASAP. Is he always this way? I mean so paranoid?"

"No, this is quite unusual. He wanted desperately to talk with me before we left. We even stopped at his place while we were on our way, but he wasn't home."

"When I told him you were coming back he was greatly relieved, but fearful for your safety. He was afraid to tell me why over the phone. He said he doesn't want to do anything that might take him away from his job or deviate from his routine. Apparently that would raise a red flag at HS. He wants to meet you at a safe place after work."

"I'll try to meet him this evening. Change of subject, what about those names I gave you, the ones I wanted fired. What happened?"

"Most of them went quietly, but the two Muslims kicked up quite a fuss, and filed complaints with the labor relations board claiming religious discrimination."

"What a farce. They lied about their citizenship and we're guilty of religious discrimination because we called them on their lies? I suppose they didn't think we would check out their applications and background information. And they were applying for a sensitive security job?"

"That's not all."

"No?"

"Four of the others were found to be illegal aliens using stolen identities. Didn't I warn you your nice gesture to those anti discrimination pressure groups was a serious mistake? Pardon my candor, but your experimental open door employment policy was a disaster, an open invitation for all kinds of evil doers. Fortunately none of them ever got near having any access to sensitive files or information, at least none I am aware of. Who knows what they did when no one was around."

"That was certainly an organized attempt to infiltrate BMK and crack our security systems. Some foreign enemies of the US were probably the ones behind it. Did our tracking systems detect any attempts to access any sensitive files?"

"There were a decided increase in cyber attacks in recent months, unsuccessful of course. Our customer data has never been close to being accessed. Your security systems worked perfectly. None of those attacks ever got past the third level. The increase came mostly from nearby, some from within our own government. Attacks from China and India stayed at about the same level. I added a sixth level of internal security using SSC conversion the same as in level five, just in case. There's a full listing of what we found in the latest security report along with the details of the new level of protection."

"So you've been quite busy during my absence. I assume you terminated the program."

"Yes and yes. I followed your instructions and things stayed secure. I became more concerned each day I did not hear from you. When that satellite call from you came in I heaved a monster sigh of relief."

"We may need to tighten our procedures for investigating prospective employees. Are there any of our employees with Hawaiian birth certificates?"

"I'm quite certain there are not. Why did you ask?"

"Surely you know that for a number of years anyone who wanted a Hawaiian birth certificate could buy one. They were mostly Japanese buying them for their infants. One of the local crime families ran the entire operation. Now I learn the Chinese added a new twist to the racket which was never actually stopped. I would never consider a Hawaiian birth certificate a valid document as proof of citizenship for employment, particularly for any security job."

"Isn't that the reason for the paragraph in our security system about checking all birth certificates against other confirming records?"

"The lady gets an A for accuracy. In light of this, maybe we should go through all of our security investigative procedures and check for possible loopholes, areas where fraudulent data could creep in. Our enemies, foreign and domestic are constantly searching for ways to break our security."

"The new sixth level systems should take care of that. To date, no one from outside has yet broken past the third level."

"None you found you mean. Our internal test attacks got through to the fourth level several times and left no trace of being there. Lots of clever and experienced hackers from all over the world are testing our systems, and often."

"Come on, Brooks, you designed our security protocols yourself and the encryption methods. You tell me if anyone ever got past level four."

I had to laugh. "Gotcha! I wandered if you were on your toes."

Carla and I then concentrate on a complete review of our security including the new sixth level. Meanwhile, Lydia is in the BMK communications center using the BMK SSC system to search through the internal communications of America's worst enemies for anything of interest she can find. No queries of course. We can't risk any transmissions. All she can do is listen. We quit about ten in the evening.

"Carla, Lydia and I are leaving with you. I need to go to my house and retrieve a few things. We will stay there and come in about ten in the morning."

"Is that wise? Suppose they are watching it?"

"I think that is unlikely since we've been gone for so long. Has George started on the house yet?"

"He started on Friday, the day after I called him, said I caught him at a good time when he had about a week between jobs."

"Good, we'll be just one more work pickup at the job site. We can hide in plain sight. I also want to talk to him about the armor."

"Should you reveal yourself to him?"

"George is an ex marine. I can trust him with my life."

"Okay, boss. I'll expect you about ten, right?"

"Give or take an hour or so. I'll call when we are on our way."

About eleven we pull up to my house. I had planned on pulling into the basement garage but a large construction trailer blocks the way.

"We'll park next to the trailer and go in through the garage."

Lydia scowls. "The Florida license is a give away. Why don't you turn the truck around and back in so the license does not show."

"Okay, boss."

Once inside, we notice all the debris from the attack has been cleared.

I say, "George did a thorough job cleaning up the mess, broken glass and all."

"Yes and the entire front wall is gone, replaced by new two-by-fours and Visqueen. He has already done a lot of work."

"Lydia, I'm beat. Let's go to bed. We desperately need a good night's sleep. Tomorrow's likely to be a busy day."

Lydia sighs and says, "I couldn't agree more."

Chapter 30 - Dodging the Bad Guys in Atlanta

At quarter past seven we are awakened by the sound of pneumatic nailers and other tools. The construction crew is at work. We take leisurely showers and put on clean clothes before venturing down stairs.

As I walk into the room where the men are working, I am greeted with, "Who are you and where did you come from?" by one of the workmen.

"I'm Charles Detmire, a friend of Mr. McKibben the owner of this house. My wife and I drove in last night from Atlanta. We came to check on the house for Brooks. Is George Young here?"

"He's outside. Wait here. I'll find him for you."

"Thank you."

When he walks in, I hold my finger to my lips hoping he won't say my name. He catches on and follows me into the kitchen. He speaks quietly as I shut the door.

"What's this all about, Brooks? I did not expect you to be here. Your gal from BMK said you were in Europe for an extended vacation trip. And who the hell shot your house up? They did a thorough job of it."

"It's a long and complicated story, George. I have made some major enemies among some terrorists, mainly by exposing some of their hidden cells. The details are irrelevant, but Lydia and I are in hiding until it gets resolved, which may take quite a bit of time."

"Damn it Brooks, That sounds serious. Is there anything I can do to help?"

"Mainly, don't tell anyone I'm here or have been here."

"You can count on it. My guy said your name was Charles Detmire. Is that the alias you are using?"

"Only for the last ten minutes. When he asked, I used the first name I could think of. What I want from you is information about the armor I requested. I figured you would find the best way to armor the house and keep the installation confidential, right?"

"Armoring a house is something new for me requiring a lot of research. Since working up the design, I am now somewhat of an expert on armoring a building."

"Oh? Explain."

"We are using five-sixteenth-inch, high-impact steel, six-feet high and welding the vertical seams. Nothing short of an armor piercing shell will go through that. I had one of my men specially trained to weld those seams. We are using inch and a half T bars mounted vertically to hold the end of each panel. The plates will be welded to those from the inside. We are fabricating those plates in our shop and will glue standard half-inch foam sheathing insulation to the outside. Once we mount those panels they will appear to be ordinary sheathing. No one will suspect it's armor. We'll use a power lift to put them in place and hold them until they are welded. No way around that. Those panels weigh about a thousand pounds each. Hopefully, no one will realize what we are doing. Your big picture window will be gone. In its place the new windows will be three feet high above the armor. No way around that if you want full armor. Luckily your downstairs ceilings are nine and a half feet high or your windows would be much smaller."

"George, I was sure I could count on you to come up with a solution. That's why I told Carla to contact you to fix the place up."

"Hey, Carla's a big time negotiator. She had me jumping through hoops to satisfy your requirements. She did so without being one bit nasty or demeaning. Your gal has special talent. Most people in her position would not have been so friendly. I dealt with many middle managers and most are a pain in the ass. Hang onto her. She's a good one."

"Don't worry, I will, and you are right on the money. She's sharp, loyal, and dependable, a terrific assistant."

"I hope you tell her that, and prove it, often."

"She's one of BMK's best assets. I not only tell her so, but I reward her with pay and benefits accordingly."

"My dad often said to me, 'Find good people, pay them well, tell them how much you appreciate them, and keep them happy. Do so and your business can't help but succeed.' He was right on the money."

"I'll not argue with you about that."

"He also told me to take good care of any job, so unless you need more from me, I'll go back to work."

I laughed. "Okay, George. I'll be here for an hour or two. If you think of any questions, catch me before I leave."

"I will. Bye."

I walk back upstairs and relate my conversation to Lydia.

"Your contractor sounds like a rare breed. What do we do now?"

"There's a box of hardware I may need down in the dungeon. I'll go after that now. While I'm gone would you pack a few pieces of foul weather gear from the back of my closet. We're a bit short of such gear at the cabin. Somewhere in my chest of drawers, in the bottom drawer there is a box of shells for my automatic. Dig those shells out for me please. Then I think we will be ready to go. If there's anything you need from home, we can stop and pick it up."

"Okay, boss. Consider it done. I'll try to think if there's anything I need."

In half an hour everything is ready and we head for the pickup. When we walk out the side door, a man flashing a badge which was a poor imitation of an official badge meets us.

He asks, "Are you the owner of this house?"

"Who wants to know?"

"I'm the county building inspector and I need to speak to the owner."

"Show me some ID? You could be anyone, an insurance salesman for instance."

He takes out a flimsy badge. "Check my badge."

"That badge could be from a novelty shop with no photo, and no real information. I'll need more than that."

"Now see here Mr. . . I didn't catch your name."

"I didn't throw it. Lydia, call George, and ask him to come here quickly. Mister, unless you can show me some valid ID, I must ask you to leave this property, pronto."

"Then you are the owner."

"I'm the owner's lawyer and hold a power of attorney to act on his behalf. If you don't leave, you'll be arrested and charged with trespassing."

"Mr. whoever you are, you don't know with whom you are dealing."

"Not only do I not know, I don't give a damn."

Just then George came around the corner. I grabbed the man's arm and took him to the ground. George rushed in to help. Together we held him down while Lydia went through the pockets of his coat.

"George, have you ever seen this guy before? He claims to be a county building inspector. He has a fake badge and will produce no ID."

"Mister, I am friends with all the county people around here and you're not one of them. What are you trying to pull?"

By this time Lydia opens his wallet and removes his ID. "It says here his name is Chandra, Melia Chandra. He's from Ft Lauderdale, Florida and his work ID says he's from the department of Homeland Security. I'll wager it is fake as well."

"You are detaining an officer of the Federal Government. There will be serious consequences if you do not return my wallet and release me immediately."

"Before we let him up, check if he is carrying a weapon. I don't trust anything about this bastard. Call the State Police. Let's let them check him out. I wonder why an officer of Homeland Security is nosing around this property and refusing to properly identify himself."

Lydia pulls out a Glock 40 from a holster strapped around his thigh.

On seeing the gun, George says, "Maybe we should plug him with his own gun and toss his body over the cliff back there. No one will ever find him."

Melia is noticeably disturbed when Lydia phones the Georgia State Police. "You'll not get away with this. You'll all go to prison."

"Not without witnesses, asshole. Do you see anyone who might testify against us? I sure as hell don't, only trees and the three of us. There are about a dozen men who work for me on the other side of the house. If you think any of them would testify against us you're stupid as a log. Let's take him around the house and introduce him to my men. They'll gladly hold him for us until the police arrive."

As he marches Melia around the house, George motions for us to stay where we are. About ten minutes later he returns.

"I don't imagine you want to be here when the cops arrive. My guys will keep him where the driveway is out of his sight. Why don't you grab your stuff and skedaddle? We can handle the rest from here. The cop who will show up will most likely be one of two friends of mine. They'll put him in the pokey until someone from Homeland Security comes to rescue him. The cops will have no quick way of knowing if he is the genuine thing or an imposter. They will insist on positive, in person identification. It's a little back woods post without any of those newfangled ways of confirming a person's true identity."

"George, you're a genius. Thanks so much for your help. All of our stuff is right here so we will be gone in a few minutes."

"Safe travels, both of you. When you come back this way again, call me. I can tell you what happened to Mr. Chandra over a beer. It should be hilarious."

"Will do. Good bye."

About five miles down the road we pass a State Police cruiser coming up the hill.

✳   ✳   ✳

Today during the day we will not be able to access any part of BMK outside of my office because we cannot reveal our presence to any employee. The inside of my office is not visible from the main office and Carla has the only keys. We will be quite secure as long as we don't go out into the main office.

Around four in the afternoon, Carla receives a phone call from Ralph.

"Carla, I have a new prospect for your security services. His name is Harold Courtney and he's a long time friend of the family. He's the president of Courtney toys and is concerned about security for their new line of computer games."

"Wonderful, and thanks. We appreciate your help."

"I spoke with him last night, but I'm so busy today I just now found the time to call you. He'll be calling you about five today. Is that okay?"

"Our security systems manager will be with me when he calls. They'll want to talk and set up a meeting at his office."

"Great, now I had better go back to work."

"Thanks again for the endorsement, Ralph."

"You're welcome. Bye."

Carla turns to me. "Ralph's in trouble. He needs to be picked up at five. He'll be leaving via the loading dock and walking down the alley behind HS."

"What exactly did he say?"

"He mentioned the name, Harold Courtney. That's our code meaning he needs to be rescued. He wants to avoid going to his car at all costs. It's a good thing we set up the codes for his message and a plan for picking him up where he normally does not go."

"I'll pick him up."

"Are you positive you don't want me to do that?"

"We set this up months ago after he first became afraid they might tie him to me. We planned for such an emergency and decided how to how to handle it including where to go. The pickup will draw no one's suspicions. Tell Lydia I'll be back after I talk to Ralph."

"They may be watching him closely and following him. If they do, they'll find out it's you in the truck. That's not a good idea. Let me pick him up."

"You're right. Okay, but be careful. I'll be right behind you in the pickup. That way I'll discover if he's being followed. We'd better hurry. You must be there when he comes down the alley."

✳   ✳   ✳

Everything goes like clockwork. No one follows him. After rounding two corners, they stop, Ralph gets out and motions me to pick him up.

"Drive around the block and go past our parking lot, slowly," he asks. "I want to try something. I will crouch down so I can't be seen. Tell me when we are close to the lot."

"What's that?" I ask, noticing a small object in Ralph's hand.

"This is the key and remote starter for my car. I want to start the engine and learn what happens."

"Okay," I say as I head for the street with the parking lot. In about ten minutes we reach the lot.

"We're starting past the lot," I say.

Ralph raises the key and presses the start button. We continue past the lot.

"Pull over in the next block and wait a few minutes," he says.

"Okay, Ralph. Nothing. What did you expect?"

"I thought—"

BLAM!

A loud explosion in the parking lot interrupts him. A huge flame of burning fuel blossoms into the air where his car had been.

"I hope your friends think you were in your car when the bomb went off, and they don't check for body parts."

"I thought that's what would happen. It's why I had a remote starting system installed in my car. This is the first time it's blown, of course."

"Smart move. Thank God you fooled them. That bomb was supposed to kill you. I wonder what they'll think when the police don't find any remains?"

"Wait and learn how the media handles this. They'll soft pedal it, call it a mysterious fuel explosion or something like that. If they even report on it, they won't say whose car blew up or if anyone was in it. My name will never be mentioned."

"You think it's that bad?"

"It is, definitely. Most of my friends at HS, those I could trust, either quit, moved to other agencies, or disappeared. There is no longer anyone at HS in Atlanta I can trust. I firmly believe enemies of America took over Homeland Security, at least the Atlanta division."

"Have you tried to report any of this?"

"Come on, Brooks, to whom could I safely make a report? Those bastards are everywhere, and especially in the Federal Government. They must have been infiltrating our government for years, including some high offices. I even tried searching the Internet for information on government employees that disappeared or died under unusual circumstances. I ran into a message, 'Access to this information requires a written request under the Freedom of Information Act.' You think I am going to sign my name to any such request? Not on your life. That would be like signing a death warrant."

"My God, Ralph, is it that bad? I had no idea. I did run into one of your HS people today. At least he posed as Homeland Security."

I proceed to relate what happened at my house earlier in the day.

"I told you your name is on their list of suspected terrorist connections. I think it means you are on their list of important enemies of the enemies of America. You're one of the important good guys they plan to eliminate one way or another. I'll bet that's what the guy was doing at your house. You say he was from the Ft. Lauderdale office of Homeland Security?"

"Yes, the Ft. Lauderdale office."

"There is no Ft. Lauderdale office of Homeland Security. Everyone in that area works out of the Miami office."

"So even his HS papers are fake. I wonder how he made out with the Georgia State Police? I'll ask George. I am on someone's enemies list since they shot up my house. I have no idea who's. I'll do some serious research into Homeland Security for what I can discover."

"Be careful you don't reveal who is doing the searching or they'll be all over you. Their eyes and ears are everywhere."

"Don't worry. I use methods of gathering info that leave no trace."

"I figured as much. Right now I need a place where I can hide? I certainly can't go to my apartment."

"Ralph, since I'm responsible for your problem, I will provide the solution. You'll be hiding out with Lydia and me where no one will find us."

"Oh? Where's that?"

I explain everything to Ralph as we head back to BMK. We are all about to experience a busy few days.

✳   ✳   ✳

The first thing we do after the employees clear out is goto the BMK lab and fix Ralph a secure SSC satellite iphone. We merely make the same modifications to his existing iphone we did to ours. His phone will use his old number.

I tell him, "Use your iphone as you always do. When you call any of our iphones, the new circuitry will automatically use SSC technology and will be completely secure. On all calls to regular phones of any other kind, it is an ordinary iphone, and not secure at all. Don't ever forget that."

While Ralph is checking out his modified iphone, Lydia and I set up a search of SSC transmissions of US government departments including Homeland Security. What should we run across but a coded transmission from Cumming, Georgia to the Ft., Lauderdale Office of Homeland Security. How are they communicating with a non existent office of HS? A close examination of the address reveals both a period and a comma after the Ft in the address. To electronic mail of any kind, an address with Ft., is a completely different address from one with Ft, or Ft. or even Ft and would therefore not show up in any search except for Ft with a comma and period. That's pretty slick, hiding right there in plain sight.

I send off an untraceable message coded for Homeland Security in Washington. I provide the details of how Ft., Lauderdale is being used as a fake HS office and there is a fraudulent HS officer named Melia Chandra sitting in the Cumming, Georgia jail. I have no idea what will happen to him, if anything. I did my duty. Others will step in and finish the job. I can check with the Cumming post of the Georgia State police, or possibly George can find out for me if anything happens.

Next we start searching SSC messages from Muslim countries. Using my basic knowledge of Arabic and Pashto, I find sensitive messages between or about different Muslim groups, many of whom hate each other. Most of the content of those message is bluster, but once in a while I find something significant.

On more rare occasions I find something important. When I find something I can act on, I usually find ways to change the message so the real intent is masked or reversed. That takes a lot of time and effort and I must be careful so no one suspects the message has been changed. The work is tedious, and I often miss getting it right. One valuable thing is that I am more and more understanding the minds of these fanatics and how they motivate their followers. Perhaps some day I will be able to use this knowledge against them.

The Chinese are the most difficult, mostly due to the language. Neither Lydia nor I can translate any of the several Chinese dialects so we must rely on computer conversion of the languages which is far from ideal. Korean seems much easier for our computers to convert to English. The North Koreans are so primitive in computer use their codes are easy to break. Unfortunately, North Korean messages are so riddled with propaganda it is difficult to make much sense of their rambling. I once thought it might be a clever code, but realized it couldn't be and quit trying to decode them. Usually it is ideological gibberish, but once in a while something worthwhile comes along so I can't stop. About once every two or three months I find something worth my attention. There is lots of chaff, few grains of wheat.

There is one computer set up to record any message my search algorithms single out as significant. This PC usually records several dozen messages a day which I must examine. Most are false alarms, but several times I found important ones. The most significant, damning one is from the French in Mali warning of the planned attack on our consulate in Benghazi. I tried to warn our consulate, but my warnings were ignored, even the ones I sent through Germany and England. There is no doubt in my mind that someone high in our government had all of those messages blocked or destroyed, deliberately.

After a full day checking SSC messages we are exhausted, even with Ralph's considerable help. By ten thirty we are all sound asleep on the office couches.

Tuesday and Wednesday are reruns of Monday including the same result. Thursday we decide to prepare everything for leaving for Flamingo after dark Friday evening. In the back of the pickup is our new water transportation, a deflated, eighteen foot Zodiac with a 150 horsepower outboard. We estimate a top speed of fifty miles per hour will cut our travel time to the cabin to three hours and will be relatively easy to push through the sawgrass to the cabin. The Zodiac can carry at least four times the weight the john boat can. With food, clothes and other items along with a folding bed for our newest resident, we couldn't make it in the john boat.

After seven Friday evening we finish dinner with Carla, say our farewells, and head south following the exact same route we had before. Three drivers make the trip much less stressful.

✳ Saturday, May 24, 2014 8:00 am ✳

About eight Saturday morning, we again pull into the Pilot Travel Center at the Tamiami Trail. We fill the gas tank and enter the restaurant for a leisurely breakfast. While waiting for our breakfast, we discuss what the day will bring.

"When we are ready to leave, I'll call Charley and tell him about the Zodiac and that we won't need the john boat. We should be there around ten-thirty. I'm anticipating the fastest trip I ever made to the cabin. With all the stuff we are carrying, it should be interesting."

Lydia says to Ralph. "At the end of the trip we'll enjoy poling this big Zodiac through tons of reeds. Brooks, I don't understand how you can possibly think it is going to be easier than the john boat."

I grin. "There is a secret I won't tell until we are there. Wait and find out how our new Zodiac handles that little problem."

"You're not going to clue us in?" Lydia asks.

"Nope!"

✳ *Calder Voss II* ✳

Chapter 31 - Who is This Andrea Mitchell?
✳ Monday, May 19, 2014 ✳

As I walk into the offices of the power company in KC at about eight in the morning, who is talking to the receptionist but that old government complainer, Mao zu Chin. *What the hell is he doing here?* I wonder as I wait for him to leave the desk. I am not about to speak with him and I do not want him to find out I am here. After he walks out of the lobby I saunter up to the desk and introduce myself.

"Hi there. I'm Calder Voss to see Mr. Richfield," I say as I hand the receptionist my card.

"Yes, Mr. Voss, I'm pleased to meet you," she says, shaking my hand. "I'm Andrea Mitchell. I'll be working with you on the project."

"You will?" I was curious.

"Oh, I'm the KCP&L engineer for the well project. I happened to be here when the receptionist needed a break so since I was waiting, I volunteered to sit in for her."

This is an unexpected pleasant surprise. "I'm pleased to meet you as well," I reply. When our eyes meet there is immediate electricity. Andrea is thirty ish, a pleasant, Midwesterner. She is no raving beauty, but I feel an unusual and potent sexual attraction.

"We've been expecting you," she says, pauses, and then reaches down and picks up a large, tan envelope and hands it to me. "Mr. Richfield will be with you in a few minutes. There's a small conference room on the left side of the hall," she says, pointing. "Mr. Richfield asked me to suggest you go through the information in this envelope while waiting. It's the latest plans for the project on which we will be working."

"Thank you, I will."

"I'll be joining you and Mr. Richfield when the receptionist returns from her break." she says.

I am strongly and warmly attracted to Andrea. This comes as a complete surprise, actually startling. I rarely react like this to any woman. Oh, I show the normal male reactions to attractive females, but this is much more than that, and she is little more than ordinary at first glance. I walk to the conference room, wondering why she affects me so strongly.

I am about half way through the information in the envelope when my new employer comes in. "Fletcher Richfield, Mr. Voss. I'm pleased you are on this project with us."

"Likewise," I assure him. "Just call me Calder. I'm not much on formality."

"I feel the same, Calder. Call me Fletch."

We talk in generalities for several minutes, two men who will be working closely together and are sizing each other up. We do not need long to decide we will probably work well together.

"How about we start to work? You went over the papers I had Andrea give you, right? They are a bit more detailed than the preliminary designs we sent you."

"Yes, it was obvious immediately. I also realized most of the details are like GTW2. I take it that is no coincidence."

Fletch laughs. "There is not much we could improve on. Your designs will work on our project. No sense in reinventing the wheel."

"Except we will be drilling eight wells rather than two, and they will be much larger in capacity. This will entail some new engineering."

"You and Andrea will be handling that. She did tell you she would be working with you didn't she?"

"Yes, she did, a bit of a surprise. I anticipated working with your engineer who spent time at GTW2. Rick Peckinpaugh wasn't it. What happened to him?"

"Rick was promoted to chief engineer of our entire organization a few weeks after he finished at GTW2. Don't be disappointed."

"I thought Rick was sharp, a real professional."

"We'll have another real professional working with us. Andrea Mitchell is another sharp engineer. She's an honors grad from Penn and has a masters in power plant design from Wisconsin. She's a good one."

"Is she married? Does she have a family, or plan one?"

"Come on, Calder. You're not a male chauvinist are you? You can't be one of those with qualms about working with women?"

"No, not at all. I was curious, that's all. She struck me as a pleasant person. I have no qualms about females in what used to be traditional male roles. In fact, I rather like it."

"She's worked for us since she received her MS, worked with my group for about four years. Funny, She shared almost nothing about her private life. She's a private person, at least to my knowledge. She's not married. I have never even heard her refer to a boyfriend or any of her family. I never thought about how little I heard of her private life until our conversation. Of course, this will be the first time we've worked closely together on the same project."

At this point Andrea walks in. "Sorry I'm late. What did I miss?"

"Not a thing, Andrea. Calder and I were getting acquainted. You know, sorting things out. We've not started on the project yet."

Andrea turns to me. "I understand you had quite a problem in Nevada, your own private war, wasn't it? And you won. I hope things are much more peaceful on this project."

"So do I," I say emphatically. "I was lucky at GTW2, incredibly lucky."

"How about telling us about your escapade over a beer or two after work," Fletch says. "Right now we should be working."

"Right on, boss. I was curious. Sorry about that," Andrea says.

We spend the next three hours going through the project and developing a tentative schedule which will be fine tuned in the next week or so.

"It's nearly noon, guys, let's break for lunch," Fletch says. "After lunch we'll go out to the site so you can check out where we are and learn the lay of the land."

While we are still sitting at the table, I ask Andrea about Mr. Mao. "If you don't mind my asking, remember that Chinese guy you were talking to you when I came in this morning? What's he doing here?"

"Mr. Mao?" Andrea asks. "He's from the Federal Government. Why do you ask?"

"Only because he can be a real pest. He made several unreasonable demands when he visited GTW2. Wrote us a nasty letter because we didn't drop everything and squire him around. We were far too busy to spend time with him, at least for his demands on short notice."

Fletch says, "He is from the Commerce Department in Washington and has interests in power generation. There's no secret about that."

"I thought it a bit unusual, him being here after his act in Nevada. I avoided him this morning, but he wouldn't recognize me. We never met face to face."

"Interesting. He asked about you, knew you would be working on our power project. He was quite interested in your being aboard."

"Our government at work," I say sarcastically. "He's probably trying to figure out how to screw things up."

"Why would you say that?" Fletch asks.

"Frankly, I don't much trust government bureaucrats—or politicians. I particularly don't trust Mao. He knows how to muck things up, to slow down or even stop progress. He'd have cost us several days and kept us from meeting our deadline if we hadn't ignored him, and all for nothing except them being nosy. He was probably trying to find a way to syphon off some public money into his own pocket."

"My, you are suspicious of our government," Andrea says with a grin.

"Only government people. Don't start me on those idiots. I get angry thinking about them. Let's return to our project and hope Mao goes back to Washington."

❊　　　❊　　　❊

The site for the wells is about half a mile long and a quarter mile wide. It was graded and compacted. There are four places marked off where the wells will be drilled, each one about 500 feet from the next. There's a warehouse building with a large door at one end near the graded area.

Fletch explains, "That doorway leads to what will be the shop. Some of the tools and equipment are already there and most of those for the first phase are to be delivered next week. Everything is on or ahead of schedule. We hope to be able to start drilling around the first of October."

"I assume the drilling rigs will be here and set up long before then," I say.

"Supposed to arrive around mid September. There will be two rigs. We figure the optimum cost in both time and money will be best served with two rigs. That way we will only need four crews working twelve hour shifts to do all of the drilling."

"I assume you're talking twelve-man crews with one supervisor. We used three eight-man crews working eight hour shifts at GTW2 and some times Chuck and I had to help out. Of course there were times when half of the men were not needed. Many of them slept when they were not needed. Those arrangements worked out quite well."

"We worked out a similar plan here," Andrea says. "With so many men idle for much of the time, we arranged for sleeping quarters on the site. Then the twelve hour shifts would not be so hard on them. The crews all liked our proposal."

During the rest of our time on the site, Fletch and Andrea explain the detailed site plans for me. All are well considered and meticulously spelled out in the plans. I am impressed when Fletch tells me he gave Andrea a rough draft and she worked out and drew up the details and work schedule. I realize now she is a talented engineer. We'll find out how good she is when her plans are put into action.

✻ Monday, June 9, 2014 ✻

With drilling not scheduled to start for nearly four months, I spend many hours working with Andrea, designing the manifold systems that will connect the wells with the steam turbine section of the power plant. We also spend many hours designing and redesigning the large coupling for connecting each pair of wells. We work well together, mostly because she catches on quickly and contributes her own good ideas to the project. She is not shy about suggesting improvements and revisions for my previous work. I like that. Our design meetings and the drawing of each piece take gobs of time. Each part must be constructed, tested and approved. The detail work takes many hours.

At the end of our work day about three weeks into the design phase, we are leaving work when she says, "Calder, Can I ask you a favor."

"Oh, sure, what's that."

"My dad is visiting me for a few weeks and I want you to tell him and me the story of your little private war at GTW2. Some time back, you promised to do that, remember?"

"Hey, I did, didn't I?"

"Could you come for dinner Saturday night? My dad is a retired Marine and I think you two would get on famously. Besides, I'm dying to hear the story. I heard rumors, but would love to hear about it from the central character himself."

"Delighted! Do you really want to hear war stories from an old warrior?"

Andrea laughs. "I've been listening to war stories from an old warrior all my life. I think I can handle a few more."

"Wonderful, and I will enjoy meeting your dad. He sounds like my kind of man."

"How about four Saturday afternoon? We can enjoy cocktails by the pool while you weave your story and then a leisurely dinner after."

"I'll be there if you'll tell me where you live. I can punch your address into the GPS in my rental car."

"Oh, and bring a bathing suit. It's going to be another scorching weekend and you might want to take a dip in my pool."

Chapter 32 - War Stories and More

✳ Saturday, June 14, 2014, 4:00 pm ✳

Andrea's home is a neat three bedroom ranch nestled among the trees on a large wooded lot in Raytown. There is a small stream, almost a river, running along the rear of her property. The road crosses the stream before turning south and becoming her street. There's a HumVee II with Pennsylvania plates parked in her drive. I pull up behind it.

"Welcome!" shouts Andrea from her open door as I step out of my car. "Come on in and meet my dad."

As I walk in, I meet a man who could have been my brother about twenty years older. Like me, he is about six feet, around 200 pounds with curly black hair with patches of white. I'm still waiting to earn those patches of white in my hair.

"Sag Mitchell, Calder. I'm pleased to meet you," he says sticking out his hand.

"And I'm happy to meet you—Sag is it? That's an unusual name, a nickname?"

"Short for Sagamore and it's the name my parents hung on me. It's an old name. Early in my life I shortened Sagamore to Sag."

I take an immediate liking to this friendly man with the warm, relaxed manner. "You're lucky. I never found a good nickname for Calder."

Andrea calls out, "Hey you two. Don't stand there talking. Let's head for the pool side and some refreshment."

Sag and I each grab a beer before we sit on lounge chairs by the pool and relax.

"All those fancy wines and cocktail fixings I set out and you each grab a beer."

Sag grins and puts his arm around his daughter. "Andrea you remember I enjoy my favorite drink. It's the oldest and most popular beverage the world has ever known. Calder here likes it too."

"Okay, dad. I know. Calder, how about it? I'm dying to hear the original version of the story that preceded your arrival and had everyone talking about you."

Sag laughs. "Been telling war stories for years. I like the idea of listening to one for a change. My gal here says this should be quite a tale, coming from the horse's mouth so to speak."

✳   ✳   ✳

A six-pack later I finish my story and answer their questions. Sag shakes his head.

"What a tale, a small intense war right here on American soil. I wonder why the media people didn't play it up. I never heard a hint of what went on until Andrea told me about it. Seems strange, unusual."

"I'm as happy as can be about that. The less said, the better I like it. It keeps me from having to explain things I don't want to explain."

"I can certainly identify with those sentiments. This old Marine understands."

"Now if you two can avoid exchanging any more war stories, we can all hop in the pool. It's above 90 and I for one am going in the pool to cool off before starting dinner. Dad's on for grilling the lamb chops, and I can find something for you to do, Calder. I hope you brought your swim suit. I don't allow skinny dipping during daylight hours."

"Where can I change?"

"Go with Dad. He can show you. Last one in is a rotten egg!" Andrea says as she bolts inside.

I end up being the rotten egg.

✳   ✳   ✳

After an hour or so in the pool, we climb out, shower, and dress for a casual dinner. Andrea assigns me table setting and a few other duties. Sag handles the grill and Andrea does the rest. The meal is fantastic. After dinner we sit around the pool and relax. Sag talks of the difficulty a career Marine and his wife had raising three daughters. There were many stories, mostly quite funny. The saddest is Andrea telling of her mother's bout with cancer and eventual demise. She was 45 when she died. Between Sag and Andrea, I mostly listen. Obviously the pain of her loss is still considerable.

Around ten, Sag stands up, yawns and says, "I'm hitting the sack, kids. It's getting past my bed time. You think you two are okay without me?"

Andrea jumps up and hugs her dad. "Good night Dad. We may stay up for a while and talk, you know—business?"

"Yeah, I'll bet," Sag says with a broad grin as he heads inside.

I wonder about his *I'll bet* comment but don't mention it. "Your dad's quite a guy," I say when Andrea sits down across the table. "He sounds like he is a wonderful father for you girls."

"Yep, Dad has always been a jewel. We three girls positively adore him. Too bad he set such a high standard for men in our eyes, Our oldest sister, Renee is the only one ever found a man to marry. Have you ever been married?"

"Not even close. I enlisted in the Army when I was seventeen, right after the love of my life decided she liked my best friend better than me. Once I joined Special Forces I had little time for much else. We moved around a lot, so there were few chances to meet many young women."

"Whatever happened to your best friend and your ex girlfriend? Are they still together?"

"Hell no. That lasted about three years. Kermit got in touch with me afterwards and said I was the lucky one. I guess she made his life a concentrated hell. He didn't tell me how. Go figure. I thought she was a nice person. I was obviously quite wrong."

"How about I turn on some music? What do you like?"

"About anything but the crap the kids listen to these days. I'm good with anything from soft jazz to a big band to the classics. I'm a bit old fashioned where music is concerned. I don't enjoy most pop music since the weird name groups and rap came on the scene."

"In that case, you wouldn't enjoy any of my music. All my recordings are rap and heavy metal."

"I find that extremely hard to believe. You must be kidding."

Andrea doubles over laughing. "Gotcha!"

"I thought you were full of it. We've been working together every work day for what is it, three weeks? I'll bet a month's pay you hate rap and all the other crap today's kids call music, no hard knowledge, just a feeling."

"You will enjoy most of the music in my collection. I'll have my system play random selections from my hard drive. Tell me if you don't like it. One word spoken and it will be changed to a different selection."

"Pretty fancy."

"Any time I hear something I like, I add the title to my hard drive. I can't tell what's coming up when it's on random search. I love surprises. It's simple, if I want to listen to something specific, I ask for it by name. It's voice activated."

"Who would ever guess you were a gadget loving engineer?"

"Not really. I like practical gadgets and what could be more practical than a music system you can ask to play any one of several thousand pieces and it will instantly start playing. I call that practical."

We listen to Ferde Grofe's Grand Canyon Suite, a smattering of things from Stan Kenton, Eddie Rabbit and Shearing.

"That's a dance able one. Do you dance?"

"Not for years, but of course I'll try. Shall we?"

I am quite surprised when I take her in my arms. Andrea Mitchell is a substantial woman, not slim, but not stout either. She feels quite muscular yet still feminine. Holding her to dance is an exhilarating experience, at least for me. I realized she has an attractive body when she was in her bathing suit, but holding her is several orders higher in appreciation. This woman is turning me on like no woman ever did before. Then she surprises me. She stops dancing and takes a step back from me.

"Calder, I must tell you something that has bothered me since we first met and is wild tonight. I hope you won't be upset with me. I even wonder if I should tell you."

"My God, Andrea, tell me. It can't be that drastic."

"Remember when we first met, in the conference room?"

"Yes, I do. I remember being impressed."

"I had an unexpected, electric reaction when our eyes met. The best way I can describe it is a deep, primordial, animal attraction. My whole body sort of lit up. That look turned me on. I had never experienced such a high level reaction before. It startled me and I don't scare easily. There were numerous similar, but less intense reactions working with you ever since."

My mind and body are reeling. I can hardly believe what I am hearing. All I can say is, "Wow!"

"Since you walked in the door, all this time, the same reaction has been happening. Then when you held me dancing, those feelings became unbelievably intense. I hope it doesn't bother you, but I had to let you know. I hope this doesn't affect our working together."

I struggle desperately for words, but none come. There is a tense silence.

"I'm sorry. I upset you, didn't I?" She says quietly.

Finally my brain starts functioning. "No Andrea, you did not upset me, not at all. But you certainly surprised me. You described in detail, precisely what's been happening to me. Your initial reaction when our eyes met at our introduction is precisely what I experienced. I could not describe it any differently. Right now I am turned on like never before and it's all your doing."

"My God, Calder, that's scary. I never considered you might experience the same type of reactions."

"Those primordial reactions can be dangerous."

"I don't know, to me they are magical, even mystical experiences. They're quite beautiful, at least in my opinion."

"That depends on what they lead to and right this moment I have no idea where we're headed."

"I'll be brave and tell you my instincts want me to abandon all restraints and drag you into my bedroom. This may be a sudden, powerful, and real thing, but my common sense wants me to take some time, to move slowly and not be carried away. I can be quite cautious about personal, romantic relationships and this could be a big one."

"Andrea, it's been a long time since I was involved in a relationship. It's hard for me to know what to say or how to act. This is a big surprise to me, your reaction I mean. I feel like a kid with his first big crush. Let's go easy and not rush into anything. One thing though."

"What's that?"

I throw my arms around her and we are in a passionate embrace. Her lips are positively devastating. I'm thinking keeping things under control will be difficult. We stand there in each other's arms for a long time. Then she breaks away and heads inside.

"I'm getting into my bathing suit for another swim. Care to join me?"

"Sure do," I shout, jump up, and go put on my suit.

✳   ✳   ✳

We spend the next hour at least, alternating between chasing each other around the pool and pausing for lingering kisses. I feel like a teenager again. We both do. We then jump up on the edge of the pool and sit next to each other.

"Calder, I think you are a special man. Few men would show the kind of restraint as you, and we are each turned on by the other."

"The thought this could turn into something long lasting is a big factor. I tend to lean toward long-lasting things. You are a special woman yourself. We should do some planning about getting together other than at work. Been working 24-7 for so long, I forgot what it's like to simply relax and enjoy life and some fun."

"And what do you suggest?"

"What do you say we plan a weekend together to learn about each other?"

"That could be dangerous you know."

"Yep, definitely. The interim will give us time to think things over and learn if the feelings last. Who knows? We might decide it was all a mistake."

"I seriously doubt that, but I can only speak for myself. If we feel the same two weeks from now, we will both realize it's not a passing thing. I doubt anything can change that."

"That still leaves us with a few problems."

"Oh?"

"How are we going to keep a lid on this at work?"

"Good question . . . we'll tough it out . . . act like the professionals we've been up until now. Surely we can do that."

"I hope so. I don't think an office romance would sit well with the others at work. It could cause considerable disruption, even some serious conflicts. That will require us to be discreet and careful."

"Do you think we can hide this from everyone at least until the project is finished? That'll be almost a year."

"We can do it okay. Come on Andrea, we're mature adults, not two moon-eyed kids. We can act as if nothing is going on. Remember how you lit into me the time I gave you the wrong setting for the base coupling and you caught it?"

"I'm sorry about that."

"Well, don't be sorry again. What did Fletch say?"

"Something about my being tougher on colleagues than any male engineer. I didn't appreciate that comment. You don't think it's true, do you?"

"Whether it's true or not doesn't matter. What does matter is you maintaining that reputation with me at work. That should go a long way toward keeping our relationship away from gossip."

"Yeah. That could work."

We talk until two. When I stand up to leave, Andrea asks, "Why don't you crash in the spare bedroom? It's a long way back to your place and it's late. Besides, I love the idea of breakfast with you and my dad."

"Don't mind if I do. I have nothing scheduled anyway."

✳ Sunday, June 15, 2014 ✳

I'm glad I stayed. Sag and I spend the whole morning telling each other stories of our experiences. A lot of his were about his wife and their three daughters. He is obviously quite proud of his family.

We are sitting at the table after lunch when Sag says, "Calder and I hit it off, right Calder?"

"I'll say we have. We became kindred souls in a few hours."

"Why didn't you tell me about this man of yours, Andrea? I'm surprised you haven't been bragging to me about him."

Andrea and I exchange quick glances and Andrea says, "Did we ever say anything about us being other than fellow workers, Dad? How did you come to say that?"

"I'm sorry, I assumed . . . well, if you aren't, you ought to be. You two look at each other like . . . well . . . like something's going on, something exciting. Last night, I couldn't help hearing all the commotion in the pool so I got up and went to the window. Something serious was happening and it had nothing do with wells, or engineering."

Andrea looks at me, then her dad. "Dad, it started last night and we have no idea where it will take us. It's brand new."

"I'll be damned. I hope it works out. Calder, my daughter is quite something, has been since she was little. I hope I don't jinx anything, but I'd grab her and hold on tightly if I were you. She's a keeper."

"Sag, it's much too early for either of us to have any kind of a handle on where or even if we're going anywhere together. We'll play it out to learn what happens. I will agree with you on one thing. She is absolutely something special. No matter what, that's for sure."

I didn't go home until Sunday evening. Andrea launders my clothes while Sag and I sit by the pool in our bathing suits and talk. This turned out to be quite a weekend. Monday we will be tested.

Chapter 33 - Mao Creates Some Problems
✳ Monday, June 16, 2014 ✳

I walk into the office Monday at eight sharp and Corrine, our receptionist, calls me over.

"Mr. Mao from the Department of Commerce is waiting for you in the small conference room. Just a warning, he was not very pleasant when I told him you were not in yet. He said he expected you to be here by 7:30."

"That miserable bastard. I had no idea he would be here. He didn't make an appointment. Tell him I am running some tests and won't be available until noon."

"I'm sorry, Mr. Voss, but I told him you had an open morning. There are no tests scheduled for you today on the schedule I have."

"Damn. Damn. Damn. Not your fault at all Corrine. Let me think. I hate letting him demand meetings with no previous arrangements. I crossed swords with him a few months ago at GTW2. He's probably angry at me since I ignored him when he did the same thing there. I know, I'll go into my office, check the schedule, learn how the drilling is going, and check on some other stuff while I let him stew for half an hour or so. Tell him I'll be with him the minute I finish getting the day's work started in about 30 minutes."

"He's not going to like that. He'll yell at me."

"You tell me if he does. No stupid bureaucrat is going to yell at our people without repercussions."

"I hope you know what you're doing."

"Believe me. I do."

I am still steaming when I sit down at my desk. Andrea and Fletch are out at the site and I am to be there by early afternoon. Except for a few minor duties and a little catching up on paperwork, my time is quite open. I seriously resent Mao's demanding, unreasonable intrusions. I spend the next ten minutes trying to work out a way to get back at him and put an end to his demanding crap. I am in the midst of formulating my plan when Mao bursts into my office with Corrine right on his heels.

"Mr. Voss, I will not stand for you avoiding me."

Corrine interrupts. "I'm sorry, Mr. Voss, I couldn't stop him."

"Chin, I'll be damned if I'll let you push our people around. Get out of my office now and stay out. I'll talk to you when I'm ready."

"I have no intention of leaving until I give you my orders."

With that, I stand, walk around my desk, face him, and say in a calm, firm voice, "Orders! You are going to give me orders? Not if I have a say about it you won't. I doubt you have any authority over me, but if you do, I'll kick your ass and walk away from this job in an instant."

Mao is a big, muscular man. He could be an expert at martial arts as well. At least he looks the part. I am prepared to do battle. Then he backs down. Unexpectedly he reverses course. I do not believe it is rational or even know what to make of it.

"My purpose might be better served if I returned to the conference room and waited for you. Please come when you can," he says in a calm voice.

I am dumbfounded—speechless. Corrine stands there in shocked amazement as Mao walks calmly past her and out into the lobby.

"Can you believe what happened?" I ask Corrine.

"Never been through anything like it in all my years of working. That's unbelievable."

"I am totally confused and wonder what to do at this point. I'll go talk with him to find out."

"I'm going back to my duties. I hope things work out."

I call Fletch, tell him what happened, and ask what kind of authority Mao has over the project.

"Probably none," is the reply.

"Is there any federal government money being used?"

"None at all. This is a combined state and private operation. The state has a minority interest, mostly to satisfy permit requirements and environmental compliance."

"How about federal licensing, environmental impact, permits, any type of federal governmental controls or involvement?"

"Only minimal and all those have already been met or exceeded. We had to meet more state requirements than federal. Our legal department took care of all of those many months ago."

"Thanks, Fletch. I'll tell you how it went when I am out there this afternoon."

About ten minutes later I walk into the conference room.

"Ah, Mr. Voss, I have a few simple requests of you and your team."

The hair on the back of my neck stands up. "Oh, and what might those requests be?"

"Your government would like copies of all of the progress reports on the project, weekly if possible."

"And what would the Department of Commerce want with those reports?"

"We like to have the details of any project having commercial impact, for our statistical records of course. This project will certainly impact commercial activity here in Kansas."

"Who's going pay for the time required to prepare those reports, The Department of Commerce?"

"All we want are copies of the reports you are already making. There should be no additional expense."

"To the contrary, there will be the costs of copying and sending those reports, and of keeping track of them. We'll send you a billing each month."

"I suppose that will be acceptable. We will also require a log of all time spent on the project by everyone who works on it."

"Hold on. Those records are already submitted to the labor department, are they not?"

"Only for hourly employees. We will need the records for everyone who does any work on the project, yourself, other engineering, and management personnel included."

"Only if we are paid for all additional record keeping. My guess is we will need one full time office clerk. You pay."

"I don't think that would be possible."

"What if I decline?"

"Your government would be displeased and might create problems for the project."

"I don't yield to threats, ever, especially threats from government types. Also, I need to correct your last statement. Faceless *Government* is never pleased or displeased. *Government* is absolutely emotionless—an unfeeling entity. What you should say is, *some government bureaucrats would be displeased,* most likely you and your cohorts whoever they may be. Frankly, nothing would make me happier than to displease any government bureaucrats."

"You're not being cooperative."

"Why in the devil should I be cooperative? You government geeks certainly aren't. I still don't understand why you need all those details. I want you to tell me the real reason but I'll bet you won't. Is the government planning on nationalizing all means of energy production, or only geothermal?"

"Neither, of course. Those records are for our statistical studies on energy production."

"Are all other energy plants getting the same treatment or is geothermal the only one?"

"We monitor the building of all energy facilities for the same information. The information collected is used to help plan the best solutions and design for the grid."

"Bull crap. The DOE already does all of that and they show no concerns for the details you are asking for, mostly completion dates and expected capacities. The Department of Labor gets our employment reports now so what does the Commerce Department want with all these fine details?"

"I'm not at liberty to divulge that information."

"In that case, I'm not at liberty to provide the information you are asking for without compensation. Here are our terms for the request you made. Submit the request including all of the specific details in writing to my office. I will go through them, make editorial changes, estimate the costs you will pay, and return them to you. You can accept them or make changes. If you make changes, we will go through the process again until we create a proposal acceptable to all parties. Then and only then will we supply the information you request. That's it."

"That is unacceptable."

"I don't care. Take it or leave it. I am now going back to work."

I turn and walk out of the conference room and go to my office. I do not care what Mao does or where he goes.

Corrine reports to me later, "Mr. Mao was greatly displeased by whatever you told him. He stormed up to my desk and said you would be receiving a detailed request for information and I should make sure you comply with all of his requests. I told him I would do what I could, but you were my boss and not the other way around. He left in a huff saying he would be back. Should I have done something else?"

"No, Corrine, what you did was perfect. I want you to log any and all time spent due to Mao's efforts, yours, mine, and anyone else's including clear back to his arrival. I have no clue what his game is. As much as I want to know, I refuse to spend time trying to find out. If there are any statisticians available find out what their time costs are. The damned government is going to pay dearly for all these ridiculous demands."

"You don't like government bureaucrats, do you, Mr. Voss?"

"Not when all they do is waste time and money on questionable statistics duplicated by other bureaucrats, and hinder progress on important projects like this one. In my opinion, most bureaucrats are empire builders increasing the cost to taxpayers with no real reason other than to feather their own nests. It infuriates me. Our government has become a self-serving, self-perpetuating monster serving only politicians and bureaucrats. They neglect serving the real interests of the public."

"You actually believe that?"

"With every fiber of my mind and body. Please don't start me. I get all riled up and I need to attend to the real problems of the world, the ones out there where those wells are going to be drilled. That's the real world."

"Okay, boss. I'm not into politics, but I do understand your frustration. I'll make up the log you requested and estimate the time thus far."

"Good girl. Best I go back to work—and calm my frustration."

Chapter 34 - A Quiet, Intense Weekend

✻ Friday, June 27, 2014 ✻

Andrea and I plan our *get acquainted* weekend at the KC Hyatt Regency Crown Center Hotel. We of course tell no one about it but Sag who is still at Andrea's.

His parting words as we drive off in her car are, "Don't do anything I wouldn't do." His words tumble out with an enormous grin and a wink.

As we drive away I tell Andrea, "I like your father. He's a straight-up, tell-it-like-it-is guy."

"And he likes you. You two are so much alike, real men, honest and fair, nothing put on. In addition, you have this mutual admiration society going. If it wasn't genuine, it would be sickening."

"I guess that's a complimentary remark, right?"

Andrea's face is like the one on the proverbial cat that swallowed the canary. "Of course."

"Just checking."

"What do you suppose is going on right now?"

"Why? What is happening outside of this car?"

"I'll give you ten to one odds my father is calling both of my sisters to report our little tryst if he hasn't done so yet."

"Really?"

"Really!"

"Does it bother you?"

Andrea grins broadly. "Not in the least. He saves me the trouble and I won't be asked a million personal questions."

"Tell me about your sisters. Sag says you three are all a lot alike but also quite different. How can that be? He says you are all definitely your mother's daughters."

"Genetics provides us with many similarities. We look a lot like our mother—family resemblance you know. In many ways we sound and act like her as well. We all recognized these things in each other. But—and there is a big but—there was one thing drummed into us from early ages, and from both parents. If I heard it once I heard it a thousand times as did my sisters. 'Don't be a second edition, be an original, be your own person.' That instruction we followed faithfully. Still do.

"I imagine that when we were young, we fought at least as often as any siblings. Our parents neither discouraged nor encouraged that activity. What they did do was insist we fought fairly and cleanly, and that no serious damage was incurred. One overpowering demand our parents made was that we always made up and apologized, right away. That had more to do with preventing arguments and fights than any other factor. Knowing we would be required to make up kept many a conflict from ever even starting. We were forced to find peaceful ways of settling our differences. Serious conflicts ceased during our early teen years, or even earlier. We grew extremely close, a tight knit, loving family."

"Knowing you and your dad that doesn't surprise me. But tell me about your sisters. What are they like? Where do they live? You told me a little about Renee, she's the one who got married, but that's all. I don't even know your younger sister's name."

"It's Carol, Carol Ann Mitchell. She lives in St. Augustine, Florida where she owns a travel agency, Travels by Carol. She's owned and operated it for four years. She calls it a travel arrangements company, much more than a travel agency. She has eight employees and is quite successful financially. She is by far the best looking of the three of us, a real doll baby—resembles our mom when she and Dad were married."

"She sounds fantastic. Hey, maybe I should meet this sister of yours."

"Careful, big boy, or this flight will be history before it ever gets off the ground."

I laugh. "Did I pull your chain, or didn't I?"

"Are you certain whose chain was being pulled?"

We both laugh over the exchange, then Andrea gets serious.

"Carol is still recovering from a major tragedy. A few months ago, in October, she lost the man she was deeply in love with. He was murdered by terrorists. She lived with him in his house for just six months in an unusual relationship. Our family understood it, but many people didn't."

"Why is that?"

"I visited Carol about three months after she moved in with him. Jack was quite a man, an unusual, charming, ageless man. He was seventy-two, forty-four years older than Carol, actually older than our grandmother. Carol told me they discussed this seriously early in their relationship and decided they could deal with it. According to Carol, 'It was a non issue.' They were so much in love and happy in their relationship. I think they were a terrific match. Carol was as happy as I can remember, and she has always been a happy, up person."

"You say he was murdered by terrorists?"

"Yes. It's all hush-hush. Jack was involved in helping the government antiterrorism effort. He had a lot of experience in this area where he made some bad enemies. His work was and still is top secret. Carol couldn't tell us much about it. She did say he killed five of the terrorists that came to assassinate him only succumbing to overpowering numbers of assassins. Although she can't talk about it, she is now working undercover for the same government agency Jack had been helping. Please don't ever repeat any of this."

"Don't worry. As an ex-Ranger, there are things I can't talk about. I can keep secrets secret."

"Of course, I momentarily forgot that. I shouldn't ever."

"Don't sweat it. I remember who you are. Now . . . what do you want to do at the Hyatt? There are shows and other entertainment and a sumptuous brunch on Sunday."

"You don't expect me to answer that, do you?"

"I guess we'll have to play it by ear when we are there."

"Yeah, something like that. I wonder what will happen?" Andrea says as she snuggles up to me.

There is a long silence lasting till we turn in at the Hyatt driveway. There may be silence, but our primordial body language speaks volumes. We don't need to say anything to turn each other on big time.

Andrea breaks the meaningful, silent spell. "Here we are."

✳   ✳   ✳

A half hour later we are checked into a room on the eighth floor. It's seven o'clock. I order a bottle of the least expensive champagne and a tray of appetizers. After putting our clothes in drawers and on hangers, I open my portable bar and show Andrea the three bottles of special champagne I brought with me.

"I saved these for a special occasion, and this is certainly one special occasion. If I bought these here, they would cost nearly a thousand bucks. We can throw the champagne I ordered away and put one of these in the ice bucket and save nearly six hundred bucks. How's that for being frugal?"

"Cheap, you mean."

"You don't mince words, do you?"

"I try not to."

"Well, you're wrong. Cheap would be if I hadn't brought the good champagne and gave you the cheap stuff."

Andrea laughed. "Okay, so you are frugal. I guess you thought you didn't need to impress me by buying expensive champagne here."

"Eau contraire mademoiselle. I thought to impress you by doing what I did. My point is to show you I display classic frugality."

Just then the appetizers, champagne and ice bucket arrive.

After setting up the appetizers and ice bucket, the bellman asks "Would you like me to open the champagne for you?"

"No thanks. I rather like doing that myself. Here you go," I say, handing him his tip.

"Thank you, sir," he says as he turns and goes out the door.

I grab one of my bottles of champagne and move to place it in the ice bucket. Andrea stops me, takes the bottle out of my hand and places it on the table with the appetizers. Then she reaches up and puts her arms around my neck.

"If you don't kiss me right now you're going to be wearing some of these appetizers."

I need no coaxing. It is a good five minutes before we break and Andrea steps back and grabs the cold, house champagne.

"How about a glass for a toast now. Why don't we open this bottle? It's cold and Hyatt doesn't serve any cheap stuff. I don't want to wait for a warm bottle to cool. Your special wine can be cooling while we are drinking a toast with Hyatt's offering."

"I like the way you think. Grab those glasses while I open the bottle."

Bottle open, two glasses poured, and Andrea makes a toast. "To a fantastic weekend for two crazy people. May it never end."

"I'll drink to that."

When she finishes her glass, she places it on the table. Then she reaches up and starts slowly unbuttoning my shirt.

"Now, lover, let's take it slow and make it last. We both want this to be special."

I do and she does and we do, and it is special. Funny, we never do eat the appetizers, or drink another bottle of champagne. I don't say a single word after she starts unbuttoning my shirt. We both speak softly and slowly with our eyes, our lips, our hands and finally our entire bodies. The fourth of July may be a couple of days away, but we both experience sky rockets in flight on Friday night, actually, several flights.

✴   ✴   ✴

I awake entangled with Andrea's warm, soft body. It's daylight out. I start to sit up, but two soft arms pull me back down.

"You're not going anywhere yet, are you?"

"Not when there's a much better alternative."

It is another hour before Andrea sits up and then hops out of bed. "I'm taking a hot shower. Come and join me?"

I don't need a second invitation. There's something sensual about two soapy bodies moving against each other in a hot shower. It is at least half an hour before we step out of the large shower stall and into dry towels. As she dries herself, Andrea is all smiles and giggles. We finish toweling and sit on the edge of the bed.

With a serious face, Andrea says, "I was thinking, three weeks ago I would not imagine spending a weekend with a man, any man. You certainly altered my life, turned it on in more ways than one. It's terribly exciting. My big question is, where do we go from here?"

"Specifically, I have but a sketchy idea. Generally I can only think of us together. I too find this hard to believe. Dear lady, you caused a major change in my life. I love it and I love you. Loved you since that first night by your pool. Never felt this way before, ever."

"I'm the female side of that equation, and I love it. I'm going to say what I never said to a man before in my entire life. I love you, Calder. Like you, I felt this way since that same night. I'm as giddy as ever. I can hardly handle it."

"Thus far I think you handled it quite well—fantastic in fact. To answer your question, I have many thoughts about where we go from here. All are positive. If we can do anything else as well as we make love, our life together will be a blast."

"Oh, Calder, I do love you. I do, I do, I do."

"I love hearing you say that. Now, shall we dress?"

She giggles. "You mean actually put on clothes?"

"We could have breakfast sent to our room. Even then we would need to at least put on our robes for when the food arrives."

"There's a whole day together ahead of us. Let's decide what we're going to do. Are you as ravenous as I am? We've eaten nothing since yesterday's lunch."

"Which is it? Shall we eat in our room or dress and go down to the restaurant?"

"As much I love being naked with you, maybe we should take a break and go down for breakfast. How about it?"

"Now you're getting sensible. Is that good or bad?"

"Last one dressed is a rotten egg," Andrea says as she jumps up and heads for her clothes.

It is close to a tie. We are two kids in love for the first time when we trip down the walkway to the elevator. We are without a care in the world.

✳   ✳   ✳

As our waitress clears the table, Andrea becomes serious. "Why don't we sit here and do some planning? I'm afraid if we go to our room we'll be distracted."

"Ah, the engineer—always the engineer, planning and calculating."

"Calder, it takes one to know one. Similar thoughts are surely flashing through your brain. It's the nature of the beast."

"Guilty! What plans do you have in mind?"

"Nothing major, just for the next few months. For one, I plan to visit to my sister Carol in St. Augustine. Why don't you come along with me? She is dying to meet you. She will hear about you from Dad."

"How can we possibly be away from our project for several days?"

"If you remember, our work schedule leaves a one week hole in the middle of September when we will be waiting for the drilling rigs to arrive from Texas. All of our work will be up to date by at least a week before those rigs are scheduled to arrive. I made arrangements to visit both Carol and Renee during that down time. I'm sure there are seats available on the flights I have. Why don't you make reservations on the same flights?"

"Sounds like a plan. Will do."

"There's one more thing that's been on my mind all morning."

"Oh, what's that?"

"Your living arrangements."

"What about them?"

"You can't be comfortable living in a hotel room, all alone."

"Do I detect a possible invitation?"

"You bet. Why don't you move in with me?"

"And give up my free and wild lifestyle?"

"Ha!"

"Do you really want me to clutter up your little home? I can be messy, you know."

"I doubt that. You forget, I'm in your *messy* workplace every day."

"What about your dad? He might not approve."

"Ha! He'll say what took you so long. That's my dad. Besides, he'll be leaving for his own home in two weeks."

"What about the folks at work? How will we keep our new relationship from them? They're bound to eventually find out."

"Frankly, I don't give a damn. Let them think and talk about what they will. If we don't make an issue of it and it doesn't interfere with our work, they might never be aware of the change. I don't intend talking about it—or hiding it for that matter. We can continue cooling it like we did for the last few weeks. Besides, the company won't pay for your hotel room, and you could return the rental car as well. You won't need it. Maybe your firm will stick that money onto your paycheck"

"You didn't know, of course, Berne and Associates, the group, or I should say the full partners, are part owners of the company. Of course, no one gains full partnership status automatically. New engineer hires must prove themselves first. If they do well, we decide together to make them a junior partner, few perks, and regular pay. After three to five years, if they continue to do well, they are offered a full partnership with all it entails. We are paid well, high standard pay for proven professional engineers. Then, at the end of the year, we split up the firm's profits according to our partnership agreement. In good years it can equal a year's pay. In bad years it can be nothing. As a result, we each are quite careful about expenses. We've not had a bad year since I joined the firm eight years ago."

"I didn't know any of that, never thought about it. I assumed you were hired like I was."

"We don't talk much about it outside the group, and never with clients. It's not a rule, just a good policy. All of our group will talk with their spouses or significant others about it. It's no secret."

"Gee, and I thought I was getting special treatment."

"Dear heart, you will always receive special treatment, count on it."

"So it's decided. When do you want to move in?"

"Yesterday."

"I like the way you think. We can work out the details after we are home from our weekend."

"Maybe I should keep the rental car in case we both need wheels on occasion."

"You've never seen it, but there's a little bright red Miata in my garage. I use the jeep for all normal transportation. I take the roadster out on special occasions. We can use it when we need two cars."

"You seem to have thought of everything."

"You noticed."

"I'll say one thing."

"What's that?"

"It's going to be difficult if not impossible to stay ahead of you on anything."

"You noticed."

"You said that before."

"I meant it both times."

"I believed it both times."

At that we both start laughing and are soon nearly out of control. For some time we are kids who burst out laughing contagiously and uncontrollably whenever we look at each other or try to speak. I'm quite sure everyone around us thought we were crazy or drunk. This nonsense took at least fifteen minutes to subside.

Andrea managed to say, "I hope no one we know is in this room."

I try to control my laughter. "I don't care. All we are doing is being gloriously joyful. Anyone who can't appreciate that is a stuffy old stick-in-the-mud."

"My God Calder. From what old relic did you dig up that one? What the devil is a stick-in-the-mud?"

I chuckle. "A stick-in-the-mud is someone who is dull and unwilling to change, an old fogey. I'm surprised you never heard of the phrase. I guess it isn't used much any longer. It's quite old. It is a favorite saying of my grandmother."

"I guess you learn something new every day. That's a new one on me, stick-in-the-mud. I'll remember that, and use it on you whenever you drag out any of those old ideas."

"I don't drag out old ideas."

"Stick-in-the-mud is not an old idea?"

"Come on Andrea."

"Gotcha!"

"Damn, you're good at that, zinging me I mean."

"You need to be zinged once in awhile. Keeps you on your toes. Should I stop?"

"Oh for God's sake. If you ever do, I'll be certain the magic between us is gone."

"Never happen. The magic between us is permanent and forever."

"That I'll agree with. What other little surprises are you going to spring on me?"

"How about we go shopping? There are some interesting shops in Crown Center. No telling what we might find to match our new life style."

"I'm not much of a shopper."

"Ordinarily I'm not much for shopping either, but I'd like to find something for my house, for our home, to commemorate this weekend. Will you help?"

"Lead on a dear lady. I'll be available whenever needed."

As we head out into Crown Center, Andrea stops. "I just thought of something about you I don't know."

"What's that?"

"Where's your home? I mean, where do you live when you're not working on a project out in the field. Do you have a home, a house, an apartment, what? You never mentioned where you were from."

"That's because I don't have a real home any where. I left home at seventeen and joined the army to be away from an unhappy place with a father who was abusive and a mother who was a drunk. That place was in Lorain, Ohio where I grew up. I am a fugitive from Catholic schools where I learned a lot about life and got a good basic education. I never graduated, but escaped into the army. I never saw my parents again. They both died within two years of when I left. I qualified for Ranger training and took enough engineering courses for my degree in 1991. Whatever you have heard about the Rangers, the reality is we were moved around a lot and quickly. We rarely stayed in the same place for long. Our specialty was move in fast, perform our mission, and move out fast. I had time in between missions for my degrees. I earned my masters in geology in 1995.

"I might as well tell you now. I was involved in ten missions between 1989 and 1994. Two in Panama, four in the gulf war, one in Granada, two in Bosnia, and one in Haiti. I retired from the Rangers in 1996. I was getting too old. I skipped several promotions because I didn't want the duties of command. I certainly did not want a desk job so I left the army and went to work at Berne and Associates in 1996. I was made full partner in 1999. I worked on a number of diverse projects, here and abroad ever since. The first geothermal well was GTW2 in Nevada. Now I'm working on my second. Could you imagine any possibility of my having a real home at any time during the last twenty years?"

"That's quite a story. Let me catch my breath. So you don't have any kind of a home, anywhere."

"That's not exactly true. In 1990, between Panama and the Gulf War I was stationed at Fort Bragg near Fayetteville, North Carolina. I had a weak moment and bought a mountain cabin near a reservoir about twenty miles west of Asheville, North Carolina as the crow flies. By road it's at least twice that distance on curvy mountain roads, mostly gravel. There was a captain on the base who had to sell it for some reason. I got a real bargain. I spend time there every chance I get. I love the place, especially the quiet. There is no sign of civilization that can be seen from the cabin other than the dirt road used to go there. It's quite a comfortable place, two bedrooms and a bath upstairs. One large room downstairs with a kitchen across the back and windows clear across the front facing out on the valley below and part of the reservoir. I spent the six weeks before coming to KC there in the woods, isolated. I guess you could say that's my home. I went there when I could for the last fourteen years, always alone. I'd love to take you there some time."

"It sounds enchanting."

"That's a good word for it, enchanting, a rather magical, no, mystical place. A drive of more than sixteen miles of gravel mountain roads from the nearest pavement where there is civilization and stores takes quite a time to get there. Whenever I do go there, I try to take enough supplies to last for my entire stay."

"What about electricity and water? How about refrigeration? If you are there for long you would soon run out of fresh food. And what about communication? There are no cell phone towers so far from civilization."

"For electricity there's a diesel generator and a hundred-gallon fuel tank. It costs a fortune to call a truck up the narrow dirt road to fill the tank, but one tank lasts a couple of months in the winter, and several months when it's warmer. That's fuel for heat and to run the generator. I planned for a long time to install a solar array to provide electricity during the day, but didn't do it yet. There's also a solar water heater that works when the sun shines. Sometimes you rough it. Oh yes, communications. I use an ancient short wave radio to contact radio friends all over the country or for emergency. If ever I need to send a message out, those friendly helpers can do it for me."

"When can we go there?"

"Not until this project is completed and signed off. Of course, I'll be free until I start a new project, but you won't. Therein lies a problem."

"I'll need to work on that."

"Now, are we going shopping or are we going to stand here gabbing all day?"

"I thought you did not like shopping?"

"It's just that I want to do it and be done with it. We've got better things to do than shop, or had you forgotten?"

"Okay, Scrooge. Let's go shopping."

✳   ✳   ✳

We ate a late lunch in a small restaurant in Crown Center. Andrea purchased several pieces of furniture for our room in her house, two chairs and a chest of drawers to match her other furniture. They will be delivered next week. We spend most of the day searching for the right pieces. I think we were in every furniture store in and around Crown Center. At five o'clock we return to our room.

Saturday night is a near repeat of Friday except we opened a chilled bottle of the good champagne. We finally succumbed to watching TV for a late movie and fell asleep wrapped in each other's arms when it was about half over. Someone once said, "The second and third best things in life are a drink before and a nap after." We couldn't agree more.

✳   ✳   ✳

Sunday morning we finally struggle out of bed in time to catch the tail end of the Hyatt Sunday Brunch. Most of the good stuff is gone, but we find lots to eat. After a late check out around four we head for home. An hour later we are seated with Sag at the kitchen table explaining our decision and plans for me to move in.

"I thought you were a smart man, Calder. This proves it. How about we drink a toast to the success of your new arrangement?"

"Hon, isn't there half a bottle of good champagne we didn't drink? I'll bet it's still cold. Grab it will you?"

I retrieve the bottle. "It's not very cold."

Sag grinned. "Hell, I'll drink this toast with warm champagne if necessary. Let me pour. . . . A toast. . . . Here's to a wonderful young couple. May this arrangement flower into a fantastic relationship and last forever."

In unplanned unison Andrea and I say, "I'll drink to that," turn toward each other, and laugh.

After our laughter and Sag's congratulations, we sit and talk about our situation for some time. When Andrea mentions she will call Renee and Carol and tell them, Sag coughs.

"I was talking to each of them yesterday and told them about your weekend together. I also told them I wouldn't be surprised if Calder soon moved in."

Andrea almost shouted, "I told you he'd be on the phone with them. Didn't I say so on our way to the hotel? Didn't I? Dad, you are so predictable."

"Are you angry with me for telling?"

"Of course not, Dad. I told Calder your calling them would save me from a thousand questions if I had to call and tell them. Boy, was I on the mark. I know you like a book, Dad."

Chapter 35 - Calder Meets Andrea's Sisters

By Wednesday, September tenth we are caught up with what we can do and waiting for the drilling rigs to arrive in about ten days. As a result we change our flights from Saturday to Thursday. Our first flight goes to Atlanta and leaves at 8:15 in the morning. We leave Atlanta after noon and arrive in Jacksonville at 1:24 in the afternoon, rent a car, and head south for St. Augustine. Andrea is driving since she knows where we are going.

"Have you ever been to St. Augustine?" Andrea asks as we head south on I-95.

"Been many places, but never St. Augustine."

"You're in for a treat. St Augustine is one of the greatest little cities in the country and is included on more top ten and top twenty lists than any other American city. Did you know St Augustine is the oldest city in the US?"

"Nope. Don't even know much about the state of Florida. The only time I spent in Florida was when we were staging for Panama and when we were doing the same for Granada. Both were short intense stays at Tyndall Air Force Base. We never got off the base. I am looking forward not only to meeting your sisters, but to enjoying new places."

"I didn't tell you, but Carol inherited Jack's fantastic house on the beach on Anastasia Island after he died. The house is about a mile south of one of the best restaurants in St. Augustine. At first she didn't want to live in the house because of the tragedy. Then she realized that among the things she could do to defy the power of his killers was to live in the house. She said within a week of moving back into the house she had a feeling of well being and relief."

"I understand. She's right. That's how you keep those terrorists from winning and making you live in fear. Your sister is one sharp cookie."

"Still, I worry about her safety."

"And for good reason. Those pigs murder people for enjoyment. I came up against them several times. They are less than human. They are also irrational. That makes them difficult to catch and virtually impossible to predict. On one of our missions in Kuwait we were working with a group we thought were on our side because they killed a number of our enemy. Those bastards actually killed a dozen of their own people to gain our confidence. Over several days, they worked their way in toward our headquarters. If not for the suspicions of our captain, they would have blown up our headquarters killing a hundred or more of our top personnel. We ended up in a fire fight inside our protected compound. They wounded three of our team before we killed all six of them. They were wearing enough explosives to flatten the entire headquarters and kill everyone in the compound, themselves included, of course. Fortunately, they had not armed the explosives when the captain ordered them to freeze. They immediately turned their guns on us and started the fire fight. At such close range the battle was over in two minutes. I like to think our Ranger training kept us alive. When the captain told them to freeze, we automatically brought up our weapons--standard procedure. They only managed to fire a few rounds wounding three of us before we cut them down."

"Question, why didn't their explosives go off? Didn't you risk being blown apart by firing at them?"

"The explosives they wore do not explode from bullet impacts, but must be exploded by primers. In addition, Rangers are trained to use head shots in this type of situation. That's to avoid explosive or armored vests. We shot all six of them before they could arm the primers. Of course, we were unaware of what explosives they were wearing or even if they had explosives. All of us would have died if their explosives went off. Everyone in the compound was lucky--except the terrorists of course."

"That's terrible. How can a human be so filled with hate they murder their own to further their cause?"

"Because they are slaves to a primitive, violent, evil ideology. I imagine Carol thinks a lot like I do about Islamic terrorists since her experience, but don't start me on that. I want this to be a pleasant visit without the intrusion of sick, evil monsters."

"I understand. One more question and I'll drop the subject. Didn't you tell me you had reason to believe that guy Mao could somehow be involved with al-Qaeda? Considering her new work with OSI, you should share that with Carol sometime during our visit."

"Don't worry, Hon. I will. Right now my blood is about to boil so let's switch to more pleasant subject matter, okay?"

"Absolutely! Want to stop for lunch? We've not eaten since breakfast and right now it's past one our time. Or how about waiting 'till we arrive an hour from now."

"Makes little difference to me. Did you talk to your sister about eating? Did she make any plans?"

"Probably not. I'll call her and check."

Hearing but one side of nearly ten minutes of some mostly unintelligible communication I learn we are to meet Carol for a late lunch.

"She'll call and reserve a table for us at the South Beach Grille about three. They serve fine seafood about a mile from her house," Andrea reports.

"Think you can survive without eating for that long?"

"I can if you can."

At ten to three we turn off I-95 onto Florida 206 and pull into the restaurant parking lot fifteen minutes later. Andrea leads me upstairs where we meet Carol. She is a slightly younger, slightly slimmer version of Andrea and quite pretty. After introductions and hugs all around, we sit. Our waitress takes our order and disappears.

I gaze intently out the front window at the surf breaking on the beach. "That is a breathtaking view. What a beautiful beach."

Carol follows my gaze and says, "I never tire of seeing the waves break on the shore. I see virtually the same view from my main room. It's always changing, sometimes full of fury and excitement, others, calm and peaceful."

"Sounds a bit like a description of our relationship, Right Andrea. Never a dull moment," I say with a smile.

"We've had no conflicts yet," Andrea responds. "But I'll bet it will be a donnybrook if and when it happens."

Carol changes the subject. "Dad had kind things to say about you, Calder."

"And I say the same about him too."

Andrea shakes her head. "Ha! Those two developed a mutual admiration society of two. You should hear them trading stories."

"I can imagine. Love to hear what happened. How did you two come together? Calder, my sis is not enamored of the opposite sex, with a few exceptions. How the devil did you move past that?"

"Two can play that game, dear sister. Most men leave you quite cold as I recall. I can answer your question for him. Out of the blue, sudden and immediately, we were involved, Calder and I, isn't that so. Calder, you tell her."

"Hey, don't put me in the middle of your sisterly warfare. I'm an innocent bystander. Besides, Andrea most likely gave you all the gory details already. Your dad filled me in on how you two share virtually everything."

"You weren't so innocent. You chased me around my pool the first time you were at my house."

"If I remember correctly, you were trying hard not to keep away from me, and in fact, you did your own share of chasing."

"I told you about how he affected me the first time we met. Tell her what happened from your viewpoint, Calder. I never said anything about that."

"The strange thing is how we revealed our first impressions to each other. The first moment, when we met, was more of a primordial animal reaction. When our eyes met, I turned on like never happened before. We discovered we both had similar reactions to each other the first time I was at her house. During a quiet moment when we were alone, she told me how her whole body sort of lit up when our eyes met, said so apologetically. I was flabbergasted. She described my initial reaction exactly."

Carol lowers her eyes and saddens when she says, "That's about what happened between Jack and me. Not immediately, but soon after we got to know each other."

A silent pause interrupts us as we all react to a painful moment. Both Carol and Andrea are near tears as they glance back and forth at each other. A powerfully sad moment overcomes us and then fades away.

Andrea breaks the spell. "When are we going to see Renee? That hadn't been decided the last time we spoke."

"She wants to come here for the weekend and bring the kids. Mack can't be away so we'll go to their place with her on Monday, if that works for you of course."

Andrea turns to me. I shrug. "Whatever you two want do is okey with me. I'm at your mercy."

"I must be back at the office Thursday for a meeting with an important client. You two will be on your own for most of the day. In the evening I will surprise you."

Andrea sits up and stares at her sis intently. "Oh? Are you going to tell us or must we wait?"

"I want you to meet a young man I've been seeing so I invited him for a visit."

Andrea's eyebrows peak in a stunned appearance of surprise, almost shock. "That is a surprise. How long has this been going on and why didn't you tell me about him?"

"I met him last November at Jack's funeral. We were strongly attracted to each other, but were so cautious about the situation we waited nearly six months before deciding to see each other."

"Why? A problem?" Andrea leans forward, eyes wide with curiosity.

"No. . . . he's Jack's grandson, Eric. We were both fearful of what his family might think."

"I understand why you were concerned," Andrea says as she leans back. "What changed?"

"We went out a few times--things would begin to be serious and we would stop seeing each other. We did this three times. Eric then spoke to his mother and told her. She called me and urged me to come to their home as fast as I could. I made the trip in about half an hour. She sat us down and gave us a short, pointed lecture. 'If you two don't stop this silly business, I'm going to light into you, both of you. Eric, nothing could possibly please your grandfather more than for you to take up with his lady, his widow truly. I'll be cheering for him, and for you two as well. Although I doubt any negative comment will come from any family member, I'll come down on any perpetrator of such nonsense with the proverbial ton of bricks. So will you two please park the guilt and find out if you are special. If not, nothing will happen. Your grandfather saw something special about this lady. Since you and he were as alike as two peas in a pod, I'll bet you will too. I shouldn't be so outspoken with you, but damn! I had to stop all your nonsense.' She laid everything out for us. Since that lecture we tried once more without any guilt. I came to admire the lady. She turned us around."

I can't resist a little appropriate jab. "So another Mitchell girl bites the dust. Has your father heard about this yet?"

"Not yet, but after today he will," Carol says looking directly at Andrea.

"What makes you think I'll tell him before you do?"

"You mean you won't say anything to him? We'd like to be sure we're a go before telling everyone."

"Sister dear, If you're not sure by now you never will be. Calder and I knew within a couple of weeks, and we were cautious. Right, Calder?"

"What can I say but yes? Being with the two of you at the same time is an intimidating experience. I can only imagine being around all three Mitchell girls at one time."

"Wrong word, Calder. I don't see you as being in the least intimidated. You seem to be enjoying yourself immensely, doesn't he Carol?"

This banter continues unabated through the meal and during the short drive to Carol's house in Crescent Beach. Her house faces and sits right on the Atlantic shore. The beach is spectacular. Across A1A in the back, the Intercoastal Waterway comes up to the road. She is half an hour from her office in downtown St. Augustine.

✳   ✳   ✳

Thursday, with Carol as our guide, we tour St. Augustine. We walk down St. George Street where I buy a pair of sunglasses. The girls pick up several things as we shop our way down the street. Right by the old city gate we stop at Al's Pizza for pizza and beer. We walk across A1A and visit the Spanish fort. Then we walked to and across the Bridge of Lions. After doing the typical tourist things we drive to the Salt Water Cowboys for dinner. I enjoy rock shrimp which I never even heard of before. Shelling and eating them is quite messy, but they are fantastic.

After dinner we are sitting in Carol's great room talking. Andrea turns to me and says, "Tell Carol about Mr. Mao."

Carol sits up straight. "Who's Mr. Mao and why should you be telling me about him?"

"You heard about our mini war in Nevada, where a bunch of terrorists tried to destroy the entire compound? Or did you?"

"Dad mentioned you had a terrorist attack where you were working, but didn't provide any details. He was too busy telling me about you and Andrea."

"I can give you the details if you want, but Andrea thinks the business about Mao could be of interest to you. One of the terrorists we were interrogating did not fit the terrorist mold. In fact, he told us how he got conned into working in their cell and became fearful for his life if he tried to escape being part of their group. He became fearful when he learned something of what they were doing. I believed him because of what others in the group did and said. He told us he was working on a PhD in mathematics at the University of New Mexico. He did check out. He also told us their up line al-Qaeda leader was a US government official named Mao zu Chin.

"I quote his exact words, 'He works for the American government, in the Department of Commerce, but he is a member of the Chinese Communist party. He is the one who organized the attack on GTW2, and provided all the money and equipment.'"

"A Chinese is an unlikely al-Qaeda leader. I didn't think much about him until a few days later when who shows up at GTW2 but a federal government official named Mao zu Chin. This clown was an egotistical ass. He expected us to drop everything and do his bidding. Chuck and I basically told him to go to hell. He did not like what we did or said one bit. Then, on the day I started on the job in KC, who shows up but Mao, just as nasty and demanding as he had been in Nevada. He checks out to be a high level bureaucrat in the Commerce Department. No way can we confirm or deny his connection with the terrorists, but he was nasty enough be one. He's a big bruiser. more than six feet and 220 pounds."

"What's the name of your informant and how can we contact him?" Carol asks.

"His name is Abdur Zaman and he was in a government safe house for a while after the attack. He seemed to be a fairly decent human being to me. You'll need to contact the rescue group . . . Their name is Relocations Anonymous, or Relocators Anonymous. The University of New Mexico could possibly help. He was a PhD candidate and most likely went back to pursue his PhD."

"Sounds quite far-fetched, but do you think what the guy said could be true?"

"How could I? Wouldn't have any idea where to start to find out."

"I can check Jack's list of al-Qaeda members for his name. My boss at OSI can check their records as well. He would like the information and would check it out. He might even tell us what he finds. I am going to call him as soon as I check Jack's lists."

Carol disappears and returns with a large, well-worn notebook. "I should check these files with my computer. Most of the information that's in this notebook is in digital format on the hard drive. I'll do a search on his name and see what comes up."

After half an hour Carol found but one reference to Mao by name. "All I found in a search is his full name, but no other information. Here's a page reference for the notebook. That must be for this notebook. Let's check out his book."

Before long she found the page in Jack's notebook. "Wow. Several paragraphs are in here about Mr. Mao. He escaped from China through Hong Kong and asked for asylum in the US claiming he feared for his life. He ended up in Seattle where he provided the government with quite a bit of economic information about China. Then he moved to Washington, D.C., and went to work in the Commerce department as a reward for his help. His specialty in China was alternative forms of energy so that's where he ended up. Within two years he was made head of the department section on alternative energy."

I am amazed. "That certainly jibes with part of what Zaman told us."

Carol flips several pages. "Here's more. He is not Chinese at all. He's Korean, and his real name is Hwang Jang Lee. Jack describes him as a high level North Korean agent and wrote quite a bit about his activities, four long paragraphs. He worked with al-Qaeda in Yemen where he traveled several times. I wonder where Jack got this information? Wait, here's a note labeled simply, source. Another name, probably Korean or sounds Korean anyway, Lee Sung Yong. He left no reference to more information. Mr. Lee must be one of Jack's contacts.

I say, "Look his name up on your computer like you did Mao's."

"That's what I'm doing now . . . He's in here with a page reference."

Carol again looks the reference up in the notebook. "Jack recorded a lot of information about Mr. Lee. He grew up in North Korea, left with his family when they escaped to the south, and rose to the rank of major in the South Korean Army. He was in intelligence. He became an undercover agent posing as Hwang Jang Hwan, a North Korean after he supposedly defected to the north. Jack says here he had family in the north and was probably a double agent. As Hwan he traveled extensively spending several months in Teheran working with the Iranian military and in Somalia and Yemen. He only notes that he spent time in Somalia and Yemen, not what he did. Next he disappeared for almost a year before showing up in Hong Kong as Mao zu Chin. We are quite familiar with Mao's history."

"Wow! He gets around," I comment. "I would say his loyalties are impossible to understand. Didn't Jack's notes you read earlier say he was working with al-Qaeda in Yemen? He could be on almost any side. My bet is his loyalty goes to the highest bidder."

"Yeah, but who is he working for now? I wonder if OSI has any information on him, real information that is? I'll check with our data specialists when I get the chance."

The rest of the week goes well including our trip to Mt. Dora to visit Renee's family and meet Mack. I enjoy being with the rest of Andrea's delightful family. Wednesday late afternoon we leave to return to St. Augustine so Carol can make her appointment the next morning. Thursday afternoon, Renee, Mack and the children will drive down so they can be here for Eric's visit.

✳ Thursday, September 18, 2014 ✳

Carol returns from her all-day meeting around four. Renee and Mack show up shortly after. We all are soon busy preparing for dinner. Carol is on a noticeable emotional high. At five the doorbell rings and Carol goes to the door expecting Eric.

"Dad! What a surprise. How did you know?" Carol was overcome with emotion.

Sag says, "A little bird named Renee called me and suggested I come down here pronto, so here I am. Don't just stand like statues. How about a hug?"

Hugs all around and the entire Mitchell clan is gathered in Carol's house. Tears of joy, smiles, laughter and hurried conversation continue for some time.

"I will need a couch where I can crash or is every place to sleep taken?"

Renee says, "Of course we'll find a place for you to stay. We brought the kids' sleeping bags. If all else fails, we brought two air mattresses in our van."

While all are still standing talking, the door opens and a cheery, "Hi everyone," comes from the tall, slender young man in the doorway.

"Eric," Carol calls out as she rushes to the door and grabs Eric's arm.

After twenty minutes of introductions, more hugs, smiles, laughter and conversations, Eric holds up his hands.

"I must say this is the most genuinely exciting, exhilarating, warm and friendly introduction I ever experienced with any group, family included. I am extremely pleased to meet all of you. You are an impressive bunch. You made me feel at home and welcome. Thank you. Now, how can I help?"

The Mitchell girls are all smiles and obviously charmed. I look at Andrea and think, *Calder, you are indeed a lucky man. You are now part of a warm and delightful family, something you never knew before. Enjoy! You must share these thoughts with Andrea as soon as you can.*

Carol finally takes charge. "Okay guys, We three girls will handle the dinner preparations. If you gentlemen will help by adding leaves to the table and setting up the chairs, please. Coolers of beer are in the store room. Eric and Mack, you know where the rest of the drink stuff is stored. Will you gents kindly take all the accessories out on the deck, and place them on the table for drink fixings? The coolers can sit on the floor. Several trays of appetizers are in the fridge. Take them out too. Soon as dinner is under control, we'll join you on the deck for a party."

✳   ✳   ✳

The party, dinner, and after dinner party as well went wonderfully. About eight, and out of the blue, Eric asks Carol, "How are you coming on finishing the book Granddad was writing?"

A stony silence comes over the room. Carol appears to be stunned.

"Did I say something I shouldn't?" Eric says softly, looking at Carol. "You never told me not to talk about your finishing his book. Were you keeping your work secret from your family?"

"If I was, the secret's out now, but no, I wasn't. I just never got around to mentioning what I am doing mostly because I'm just beginning to understand what he wrote. The information is extremely complicated. I only started seriously working on his book two weeks ago. The subject just never came up until this moment when you mentioned it. I would appreciate you all keeping this within the family. Some extremely nasty and violent people are around who would do anything to keep his book from being published. They are most likely the same kind of terrorists as the ones who murdered Jack. Thus far I don't think any of them learned anything about his book. I hope they don't until the job is finished."

I am intrigued. "Can we talk about this? I had some first hand experience with some of those idiots. Where are you on this project?"

"I read his manuscript through twice. Much of the information about those he wrote about is not in the book, but is in his notebooks and CD records. He did not plan on entering the actual names and places in the book until the last thing. That is in case someone managed to steal his manuscript. His manuscript contains nothing but code names and page references. I am doing the same thing. The actual names, places, incidents and procedures will not be placed in the book until near publication. Some of those names will blow your minds, even after you read the irrefutable evidence he provides."

"Granddad talked with me a lot about them," Eric says. "Said several of them are among the keys to some dangerous events coming in the near future. He did not yet know exactly what they are or when they will occur, but was quite certain they add up to a major threat. He also told me he was certain a number of double agents are using several aliases to hide or mask their activities. Some of these double agents are quite high up in the federal government. He identified many in his notebooks and digital records."

"Bingo! Carol," I say. "Mao zu Chin and his aliases are in those notebooks because we found him in them last week. Now I'm thinking a fairly good reason for part of his motivation is becoming obvious."

Carol says, "Let's hear those reasons. So far what you told me makes little sense."

"He went to considerable effort to completely destroy GTW2 and failed. Then he shows up in KC, the second geothermal power plant of the new closed cycle type. I now think he was scoping out the site for another major attack, hoping this one would be successful. All those acts of arrogance were nothing but a smoke screen designed to hide his true purpose. The major oil exporting nations, mostly in the middle east, must view geothermal as a serious threat to their domination of the energy markets. Actually, the coal and nuclear energy companies must see the same handwriting on the wall. That could make for some strange bedfellows."

Eric asks, "Can geothermal compete cost-wise with those other energy systems? If so you are probably correct."

"Figures from these first two plants should answer that question. Our projections currently point to a much lower final cost then any current power generation system. Add to that the expected cost of a geothermal power plant is about the same as for a coal fired plant of the same capacity. Once the plant is in operation, the only costs are for maintenance. Costs for fuel and the transport of fuel are zero, and maintenance costs should be no more than for a coal plant, probably less. The plant has no carbon footprint or pollution from the closed loop geothermal generator system. Those factors should make for much lower costs than any other system. In addition, environmentalist's will love the lack of carbon dioxide exhaust or of pollution. Think how that would affect the mix of power generation. Once that bandwagon is rolling, few would be foolhardy enough to use any other system. Those wealthy Arab oil sheiks would not be very happy, nor would the oil and coal companies in this country."

This discussion continues until finally Carol calls a halt. "Enough of the serious worrisome stuff already. Let's come back to enjoying ourselves." From this point on the evening takes on a much more pleasant party atmosphere. The revelry continues until the wee hours when the last revelers crash and all becomes silent.

✳ Sunday, September 21, 2014 ✳

Sunday is filled with often teary good byes as the visitors depart. No doubt, a great time was enjoyed by all. I thought Eric fit in well. So did the rest. He was certainly in sync with everyone, and a real gentleman.

Chapter 36 - Getting to the Cabin - A Change in Plan
✳ Saturday, May 24, 2014, 9:00 am ✳

After we finish breakfast at the Pilot Travel Center, I call Charley. He does not give me good news.

"Those people you were trying to avoid showed up here Wednesday. My guess is the State recorded the license number of your RV and that is how they found it. Flamingo is a state RV park. They asked lots of questions about your whereabouts. I plead complete ignorance. I don't think they believed me."

"That's not good. We've got a new boat to use, a Zodiac not yet inflated. The only access to Coot Bay is by boat and the only launch ramps are in Flamingo."

"They park their SUV on the highway right over the canal. Every twelve hours another SUV comes and relieves the previous ones. Where are you now?"

"We're at the Pilot station on the Tamiami Trail, about an hour and a half from you."

"Here's an idea."

"A good one I hope."

"You know where Coot Bay Pond is?"

"Yep!"

"A narrow channel leads from that pond to Coot Bay. Do you think you could navigate this channel in that Zodiac? It was about twenty feet wide when they first cut through. I went through to Coot bay a few times over the years in a john boat."

"Little chance. The last time I remember seeing it, the channel was nearly closed with mangroves."

"You might be able to cut your way through."

"An 18-foot Zodiac is far too wide to go through that channel without a lot of brush clearing. A mile from the pond to the bay is far too much to cut through. We are heavily loaded. I'll only try to go that way as a last resort. Can you think of any way we could move past the watchdog without being caught?"

"How about you meet me at the parking lot at Nine-Mile Pond? Another idea is flitting around in my head, but not gelled yet. I'll be ready with it by the time we meet. I'm guessing you will take about an hour and a quarter to drive to the spot."

"Can't you give me some idea?"

"Not yet. My plan is quite complicated and involves several people transfers and hiding you to go past the watchdog without being seen. A risk is also involved, and everything must be timed perfectly. I'll work on the time table while you are on the road and right now you should be on your way. You don't want to be in the lot when either of their SUVs pass Nine Mile Pond. They switched at noon while I stood nearby. The other switch is probably at midnight."

"Okay, Charley. I'll trust your instincts. We'll be with you as quickly as we can."

"Good, Bye."

✳ Saturday, May 24, 2014, 10:30 ✳

We pull into the Nine Mile Pond parking lot. Charley is parked with one of his guys in their truck with a large boat on a trailer. We introduce Ralph as soon as we are out of the truck.

"Hi Charley. What's with the trailer?"

"We left without a boat and will return with this one. I had to pick this one up at the West Lake ramp for some work. Today being Saturday, a parade of boats will come to put in at our ramps. Your Zodiac will be just one of quite a few on a typical Saturday morning."

"That's all well and good, but did they stop anyone coming or going?"

"Not so far. They must be looking for you in every vehicle that passes. They use binoculars probably checking their visual sighting against photos of each of you."

"So how are we going to move past them unseen?"

"Lift the cover on the back of our pickup."

I lift the cover and see a mattress filling the entire bed and a folded blue tarp.

"I assume you will close the cover and hide us inside. You think that will let us go past them? Then what?"

"First, we'll pull the truck and boat into our storage building. We'll open the back so you can sit up and breathe some fresh air. While you're doing that, we'll unload your Zodiac out by the channel, inflate it, and load all your stuff. Then we'll fill your fuel tanks, put the boat into the water, and my guy Ray will motor north up the canal, right past their noses."

"How will you move us into our boat without being seen?"

"That's the slick part. You three climb back under the cover in the back of the pickup. I'll drive north on Bear Lake Road past the bend in the canal. Once you are past the bend we'll be out of sight of the watchdogs. Ray will pull your Zodiac ashore to the side right by the road. You hop out of the truck, jump in your boat, and be on your way."

"Won't they be alerted when the motor on the Zodiac stops half a mile up the canal? They probably use listening devices. I'm sure this will not escape their attention. Besides, won't they be suspicious of a truck going up that road? The road goes less than two miles and stops."

"Marci, our office gal will take care of that. She'll use the PA to tell me the guy in the Zodiac called. His motor quit and won't start. I'll hop in the pickup and go to his rescue. Our PA can be heard clearly from much further away than the SUV. Just another boat problem for marina personnel. What do you think?"

"Sounds like a plan. I hope Murphy's law doesn't shoot us down."

"Several boat trailers will soon come past headed for our boat ramp. I'll pull in behind them with your Zodiac and Ray will follow with our boat and with you hidden in the bed of the pickup. With luck several others will follow. A number already passed while we've been here. If you'll climb in, I'll close the lid. I hope you are not too uncomfortable. We should be in the storage building in about twenty minutes."

"Okay, let's board our limousine."

We are closed in and on our way in a few minutes. Fortunately, everything with the pickup goes well. The watchdogs never blink and Mr. Murphy's laws never happen.

✳   ✳   ✳

Again, everything goes as planned with the Zodiac. We wave goodby to Charley as we take off down the channel. Charley takes the pickup back to the marina right past the watchdogs. We fly through the channel, Coot bay and out into Whitewater Bay. Once we are on Whitewater Bay we slow down. Going wide open we are taking quite a pounding. The last mile or so we are in relatively small waves so we go flat out. When we approach the channel where we usually pole, I open the throttle and aim for the tiny channel filled with reeds.

"Hang on!" I shout.

I cut the engine just as we hit the reeds. Up and over the growth we fly bursting onto the pond still on a plane. We coast clear across the pond before slowing to drift speed.

"Didn't I tell you not to worry?"

"Brooks, you scared the crap outta me when you gunned the motor at those reeds. I had no idea what was coming," Ralph says as he calms down.

"Now all we do is pull the Zodiac up by the shack, pull the cover over, and no one can see the damned thing from the air. I'll say one thing though, the Zodiac is a lot bigger and heavier than the john boat. We should cut some rollers. I don't think even the three of us can drag it."

Ralph laughs. "You don't know much about this particular Zodiac, do you?"

"What do you mean?"

"Pay attention!"

Ralph reaches inside and unzips a long pocket in the floor right next to the tube. He extracts several long pieces of rubberized fabric material like the material the boat tube is made of.

"I was reading the manual for the Zodiac while riding along. Inflate these. They provided three rollers to use to pull it up on the beach. Pretty slick, eh?"

"I was unaware of that. I bought this on reputation and what the dealer told me in the short time I had. What other useful information did you find?"

"This Zodiac is amazing," Ralph says as he starts the air pump and inflates the rollers. "This baby has two marine batteries and a reversible air pump. Knock down the console, remove the floor and motor and you can power deflate the air chambers in about ten minutes. The pieces would be much easier to hide than the whole boat. One man is supposed to be able to reassemble the whole thing ready for the water in no more than twenty minutes."

"I think we had better not do that in case we must leave in a hurry. We can pull the boat up right next to the shack and use the tarp for camouflage---perfect and out of sight."

The rollers enable us to pull it all the way up. Then we remove all the stuff we brought including Ralph's bed. With everything out, we pull the rollers out and place them in the boat. We take but a moment to pull up the dark green tarp. Then we take an hour or more to rearrange the place for the three of us. Purely by accident we discover Ralph's bed, folded up, can be used as a table or desk. A week passes while we sort out how to live together in such cramped quarters. A month is required for us to develop our interacting work routines and minimize space conflicts. With only two computers between the three of us, we take turns at the screens. The odd man will go through the printouts of what our search algorithms give us.

"A damned good thing we are all flexible," I remark one trying day.

Ralph responds, "Blessed are the flexible, for they shall not be bent out of shape."

We all laugh at that old truism. Laughing provides a welcome break from the continuous tension of virtually fruitless searching through pages of often irrational communications from all the sources we are examining. I do manage to sneak a worm into the fake Homeland Security computer at Ft., Lauderdale. The worm will silently search for any name used repeatedly and save it along with any other phrase the algorithms single out. Months pass by before we find anything of significance.

Chapter 37 - Misleading Intelligence Reports
✳ Wednesday, March 11, 2015 ✳

Lydia, Ralph, and I are sitting at the table in the cabin going through the intelligence reports I deciphered out of the Pentagon reports. A year passed since our hasty trip to and from Atlanta when we picked up Ralph.

"I can't believe the intelligence reports out of Washington," I say, shaking my head in disbelief. "Don't those idiots understand this whole anthrax balloon thing is a red herring? I keep sneaking that info into their internal reports and they keep on ignoring the messages. What's with those people anyway?"

"Some people in high places don't want anyone to know," Ralph says. "I keep telling you, Brooks, I ran across lots of Muslims in Homeland Security, some in fairly high places. I can't imagine our government permitting them to be in those critical positions, but they are."

I say in disgust, "All those PC do-gooders and anti profiling people in our government and in the media are responsible. They're either too stupid to realize they are our enemies, or are in league with them."

Lydia adds her two-cents worth. "Or they're getting paid off. A lot of Americans would sell out their mothers for a few bucks. I'll bet government departments are loaded with those types."

"That describes some of the people in the part of Homeland Security where I worked. Of course, you don't need a high percentage of bad guys to mess up an entire department. Four or five out of a hundred could do the job, especially if they are high in the hierarchy. You got me out just in time Brooks. When my boss asked if I was related to you and I said, yes, everyone in my section heard. Instantly I put in a coded call to Carla. I was lucky you were able to pick me up like you did. If I started my car while I was far away and the explosion did not get me, I would have been a sitting duck with no escape. I would have had some sort of an accident."

"We might all now be dead by an accident if we had not gone into hiding," I say.

Ralph looks at me. "Yes, probably. I wonder about the people in my department who either had an accident or never showed up at work without an explanation from anyone. Only a few of them disappeared that way, but enough did to raise my suspicions. Some of them could have gone into hiding like I did."

"Did you ever receive any kind of threats or warnings?" Lydia asks.

"None that were overt or obvious. The place was loaded with a lot of propaganda promoting loyalty to the government and to the department, mostly strict political correctness. You could consider some of that to be warnings not to step over the line, or else. Quite a bit of office gossip suggested employees who did not conform to the department's unwritten code would suffer because of their actions. I walked that line carefully, keeping my opinions to myself. The PC police were out in force at Homeland Security. Employees were encouraged to report any gossip detrimental to the department. It was vicious."

I recall some similar happenings from history. "How can anyone explain any American group behaving in such a manner. If I'm not mistaken, that's exactly how the NAZIs operated in Germany in the thirties. They set neighbor against neighbor. Ordinary people lived in fear an angry neighbor would lie about them to the Gestapo or SS and they would be hauled off and never heard from again. That's what your Homeland Security office sounds like to me. Makes me wonder what our present Fascist enemies are up to."

"Fascist, I never thought of them that way, but that's what they are, Fascists," Ralph says adamantly, "Islam is the purest form of Fascism, right down to the genocide of non Muslims, especially Jews and Christians. Anthrax to kill millions could be coming right out of Hitler's play book."

Lydia says, "I personally don't think this anthrax scare is real. They must be cooking up something different and touting the balloons with anthrax to hide their real plans. We see no mention of anthrax in any of their SS communications. If true, we would expect countless references. Any plot requiring the participation of thousands of their agents would be referred to frequently if only by some code name. The big news about anthrax in government and media circles makes no sense. Pure propaganda designed to focus our attention away from any other possible threat must be the intent. Something else is up their sleeves, something big and dangerous."

"Yeah, but what?" I ask. "We've gone through all the SSC messages our algorithms picked out and they provided no clues. The only one to catch our attention was that exchange with North Korea where the Arabic term for arrow was used several times. I set up the system to pick out any messages using that term in both new and old messages. The term for arrow was never mentioned until quite recently. Among old messages we found one where the term was used in the Arabic phrase, Sahm'Allah, the Arrow of Allah in English. That must be significant."

"How about doing a plain Internet search on that phrase and see what comes up," Ralph suggests. "You never know what might turn up."

Lydia responds, "Ralph, that's a great idea, simple and direct. I'll check out the phrase immediately."

About ten minutes later Lydia rushes back. "The Arrow of Allah is a small cargo ship used in coastal trade which flies the flag of Yemen. The present location of The Arrow is unknown, or kept secret."

Brooks is elated. "That gives me ammunition for SSC searches. I'll plug this information into our search algorithms and see what we get. Considerable time is required to search back a few months, but with this information we may learn something new. I hope so anyway."

✳ Friday, March 13, 2015 ✳

The search algorithms take several days to go through all of the messages saved from the last year. Two new messages were found involving a cargo vessel matching the description of the Arrow of Allah and flying the flag of Yemen. One had the vessel docking at the port of Nampo on the west coast of North Korea in November of last year. The other placed the ship in their naval shipyard in the same port a few weeks later. They undoubtedly moved it for some purpose.

Lydia says, "I wonder when the last satellite photo of that area was posted to Google Earth? Let's check and see if we can find a view of that ship."

Within twenty minutes they have their answer. Lydia reports what she found.

"The last Google satellite photo was on December 16, after the ship was moved to the shipyard. It took me some time to find the shipyard which held several possible ships. One of them is surrounded by a number of trucks and shows what we believe are modifications to the part of the ship forward of the cabin or wheelhouse. I wish we had someone familiar with making detailed analysis of these photographs. I'm no expert, but something major is being done to the ship. No activity of any kind is going on near any of the other ones about the same size. I think that one is The Arrow of Allah, or Sahm' Allah in Arabic."

Brooks says, "We are lucky to have that photo. Too bad we don't have the option of a real time look. That photo doesn't tell us much. No way can we access any other satellite photos of the area. I'll try to find any related satellite transmissions, but that kind of data is virtually impossible to access even with our technology. The hope would be to intercept SSC transmission of that particular photo. The likelihood of that happening is virtually nil. No one would make such a transmission. I'll try to set up an algorithm to check, but I doubt any good info will be obtained. Our best bet is to continue checking any SSC transmissions with the name of the vessel in several languages. Also important would be any key name for the project or dates associated with any possible names. I'll try to find any record of ship departures from the shipyard. Even the North Koreans keep track of ships going in or out of their harbors. Their report of the arrival of Sahm' Allah gave us that information."

Ralph is not convinced. "I'll bet if they are mounting any kind of operation against the US they won't ever report the ship leaving. I'm surprised they didn't cover the ship like they do most of their military stuff. They know our satellites are watching them."

"All we can do is keep listening," Lydia says. "Hopefully they will communicate something to help us learn what is going on. They must need to communicate when whatever action they are planning starts. Hopefully we will intercept that communication."

Chapter 38 - Mao Shows up With a New Alias
✳ Tuesday, March 18, 2015 ✳

Around ten Tuesday morning, Sylvia, my receptionist, calls me on the phone. "Carol, we're holding a call for you from a Jerry Cash from Operations United. He says it's quite important, an answer to a request you made some time ago. Do you want to talk to him?"

Recognizing Operations United as the code name for OSI, I immediately say, "yes, put him through."

"Carol. This is Jerry Cash from OSI central data. Several months back you requested notification of any unusual activity involving any of three names."

I am instantly very interested. "Yes, Jerry, I assume you are calling because you have something for me on one of those names."

"Well, yes and no. We found some interesting activity involving all three. In an intercept of a coded North Korean government transmission, all three names were mentioned along with a fourth, Charles Chang. Thus far we are unable to decipher the rest of the communication, but the names were not in code. The North Koreans often do not code names of persons for some unknown reason."

"I wonder what that means, a listing of those three names are aliases of the same man together with a fourth. Do you have any idea?"

"Yes, we believe all four names refer to the same individual. That's four aliases for one person. If and when we decipher any of the rest of the message, I will call to tell you."

"Thanks, Jerry, that's strange. You think Charles Chang as another alias for the same person. That gives us another name to search on. I assume you will be doing your standard searches on Charles Chang now."

"Right you are. If any thing more comes up, I'll call."

"Thanks, Jerry, I'll call you if we find anything on Charles Chang at this end. Good bye."

I immediately set my local Internet search to look for any instances of Charles Chang. Nothing comes up other than a reference to Charles Chang's Cantonese Restaurant in Jacksonville. This establishment has been in Jacksonville for many years so I don't think he's the same person. I decide to pursue other search methods when I am home in the evening.

After searching by several methods with zero success I set up an automatic search system on my PC. A search of the Internet will be made every twelve hours. The search will activate a pop up and sound signal should any reference to Charles Chang be found. This automatic search will continue repeating until I shut down.

Months pass before Charles Chang appears in any of our searches.

✳ Monday, July 20, 2015 ✳

Monday morning I check my home PC before leaving for work. My searches found a reference to Charles Chang in the local real estate notices. Charles Chang rented a house on Porpoise Point for a month starting August 23, 2015.

I wonder what that's all about, I think as I drive to the office. Maybe it's not the Charles Chang with four aliases. I wonder how I can find that out?

I call OSI and tell Jerry Cash about the rental.

"Thanks, Carol. Right away. I'll see if we can find any trail from your info. He either paid the rent or made a deposit. I'll see if that gets us anywhere."

Two hours later Jerry calls me at my office. "Chang paid a deposit with a credit card. That gave us access to a lot of information including an apartment in Jacksonville, a bank account, a telephone number and a post office box in Jacksonville. He's had all of them for four years. Also his bank account is a joint account with guess who, Mao zu Chin."

"That is interesting. I wonder why they made no effort to hide the connection to Mao?"

"We're trying to get a warrant to search his apartment, but I doubt we will since we cannot show sufficient cause and using an alias is legal. We are setting up a surveillance camera to see who comes and goes. We'll try to monitor his financial activity, but there are limits to what we can do as well. I'll keep you posted."

"Thanks, Jerry. Nothing new from my end as yet. Bye."

✳ Tue July 21, 2015, 8:30 am ✳

Jerry calls me at my office. "Chang made another big purchase, paid for with a cashier's check on the Bank of Dubai. He chartered a Qatar Airline Boeing 777-300 out of Jacksonville to fly to Prague and then Qatar. The flight is to leave on September 5. That's a huge private expenditure, especially for a government bureaucrat. What do you make of that?"

"Sounds to me as if a lot of their people are leaving the US at one time and don't want to fly by regular airlines. I believe that plane can carry around 350 passengers. That's a lot of people to be leaving at once. My guess is that they are using a charter so as not to reveal the number leaving, and keep their identities secret."

"This gave us another bank account to check and a destination. The 777 is flying empty to Jacksonville one day before its return flight to Qatar. That's all we've learned thus far. I doubt we can obtain much information from the Bank of Dubai, but I'll keep digging."

"Thanks, Jerry. I can do some research with our systems and call you if anything else shows up."

My mind is in a flurry of wonderment. This is significant, I'm sure, but why exactly would so many people associated with Chang and his aliases plan to leave at that particular time. I also wonder who and how many. Are they expecting a catastrophe, a financial melt down? We've been suspecting some kind of financial coup for some time. And where does that ship fit in?

✳ Sunday, August 9, 2015, 7:00 am ✳

Tony Rawls and I are parked in an OSI surveillance van near an intersection on Porpoise Point near the Matanzas inlet. Early Sunday morning we are watching the house rented by Charles Chang out a back window .

Tony says, "Carol, I'm sorry to drag you out so early on a Sunday morning, but when that surveillance camera quit working we had no other choice. They should fix the camera by the end of the day."

"That's okay, Tony. I know how important this could be. Maybe we'll be lucky and he will show up soon. The alternate camera's all set up and ready to roll. All we need now is some action."

✳   ✳   ✳

At almost three in the afternoon a small SUV pulls into the driveway of the house. Two men in delivery service uniforms step out and stand by the vehicle. They are obviously waiting for someone. We take photos of the men being sure to capture their faces We also take one of the SUV license plate. Half an hour later a woman in a small sedan shows up and pulls in the driveway beside the SUV. She gets out and talks with the men, then unlocks the door and goes inside. The men open the rear hatch of the SUV and remove a large metal box with ventilating louvers on three sides and an odd configuration of wires and metal rods on the fourth. They carry the box by handles onto the porch by the front door. It is obviously quite heavy.

"What do you make of that?" I ask.

"I have no idea what that is but did take several good photos. My guess is that box is a piece of heavy duty electronic equipment with a strange looking antenna fastened to one side and a heavy power cable."

Another car drives up and a large man in a dark blue suit gets out and goes to inspect the metal box. The delivery men pick up the box and go into the house. In about half an hour they all come out and enter their vehicles. The man in the blue suit backs his car up and waits in the street until the other two back out and leave. Then he pulls back into the driveway and walks back into the house. Everything we can see is photographed, recorded by our TV cameras, and sent off by secure transmission to our office in Jacksonville.

Within half an hour we receive the following message from OSI analysts: "The SUV is from a delivery service in Jacksonville. Since it's Sunday, they can't be contacted until tomorrow. The woman is from the real estate company who rented the place for the owners and the man is . . .

who else, Mao zu Chin, Alias Huan, Lee, and Chang, his car is a rental. The metal box is still being investigated."

I look at Tony and shake my head. "Not much we couldn't figure out on our own."

Just past five o'clock the man in blue comes out, hops into his car and drives away.

"Instinct tells me he won't be back. What do you think?" I ask.

"He carried no luggage or anything. If he was going to stay, he would surely have been carrying something."

A mobile Cherry Picker drives up and parks across the street under the faulty TV camera.

"At last," Tony says. "I was afraid we might need to stay here all night. Shall we go?"

"We should stay here until we know the new camera is working. If we went home now we might need to come back later."

"Of course. What was I thinking?" Tony says with a grin.

In another hour the camera is checked out and we can leave. During this time OSI reports they do not yet have any information about the box. They are hoping to obtain a court order to enter the house and examine the box. Tony drops me off at my house.

✷ Wednesday, August 10, 2015, 6:30 pm ✷

I just arrived home at 6:30 when my iphone vibrates. "Carol. We got that court order. Can you meet me on Porpoise Point in half an hour?" Tony sounds excited as he tells me.

"How are you going to enter the house?"

"The real estate lady and a Sheriff's deputy will make it official. I'll bring an electronics expert from UNF with me. All we will be able to do is examine the box to determine exactly what it is."

"Terrific! I'll be with you."

I drive through downtown and over the Mary Usina Bridge about as fast as I ever have. I beat the rest of them. A minute after I arrive, a Sheriff's car and Tony's SUV both roll up. We all step out.

"This is Deputy Max Rolf, Carol, Max, my colleague, Carol Mitchell, and this is Terrence Overton from UNF technology."

We shake hands. "Nice to meet your Miss Mitchell. Mr. Overton," Max says not sounding too official.

"Likewise, Max. Just call me Carol. Where's our lady with the key? She's the one closest and she's not here yet."

"She said she'd be here by now," Tony says. "She's late."

About ten minutes later she arrives.

"I'm Madie McDonald, the rental agent for this house. Am I to understand you have a court order to examine a piece of equipment inside this house?"

Deputy Rolf answers, "Yes, but only the one piece of equipment shown in this photo."

After introductions all around, Ms. McDonald opens the door and we walk inside.

Deputy Rolf says, "Let me first find the item, then we can all examine the box. Ms. McDonald, will you please come with me?"

"Certainly."

The rest of us stay near the entrance while they search. Half an hour later Deputy Rolf calls out from the second floor, "The device is up on the third floor, in front. Come on up."

"This way," Deputy Rolf directs when we reach the third floor. "It's clear out in front by the door to the porch."

The box with its electric cord plugged into an outlet, stands upright on top of a chair with the antenna centered on the door facing almost due east. The screen was removed from the door. In its place is a sheet of thin, clear vinyl taped to the frame of the screen door. The inside main door is propped open. The box is humming and warm to the touch.

"Okay, Mr. Overton, what is that" I ask.

"Damned if I know," Overton says. "Never seen anything even similar. It's definitely a custom piece. There's an access plate on the back. I'll remove the plate and see if I can find anything."

He removes the access plate and looks inside.

"A wiring diagram and some oriental characters are printed on the inside of the cover plate. The wiring diagram is in universal electrical symbols. I may be able to understand them, but without being able to read the characters, deciphering the schematic may be impossible."

This annoys Tony. "Well, Terry, tell us what you can from the symbols. Anything is better than a complete unknown."

"First, here on the bottom is a large power supply. That I can tell just by looking. The top of the box is held on with screws. I'll try to remove the top to see what's inside. I must do that carefully since you don't want me to turn the power off. I hope no high voltage is inside."

Just as he starts removing the screws, the hum suddenly becomes much louder and the light inside the box dims noticeably.

Terry jumps back. "That was a huge power draw."

After about thirty seconds, the sound and light intensity returns to the previous state. Terry resumes removing the cover, taking out lots of screws. Finally he lifts the top cover completely off and looks inside.

"Those are certainly big coils. Now I can tell you It's a powerful radio transmitter, most likely short wave by the size and shape of those coils. The antenna is highly directional and aimed east. The transmitter sends a powerful 30 second burst of radio waves to the east every once in a while. I'll time the next transmission to determine how often those signals are sent."

"Can you say what its purpose is? Why would anyone set up such a device?" I ask.

"A radio beacon like this is an electronic lighthouse, to guide someone coming from the east. It gives them a pinpoint location for their navigation system to use as a guide to almost any location, north or south of St. Augustine. Of that I am certain. I'll tell you something else. Whoever set this up modified the main fuse box to carry a lot more current, one, two hundred amps for a short time, thirty seconds at most. Much longer and the number twelve wiring to the box would melt and burn up."

"Are you sure?" I ask.

"Positively. My guess is the beacon is to guide a ship from a thousand, or as far as two thousand miles from this spot. All the ship would need is a very ordinary radio direction finder tuned to the same frequency as this transmitter."

"Are you certain this is a fact?"

"Absolutely. My guess is the transmission sends at five to fifteen megahertz. That signal could go half way around the earth. To check, take a receiver out east of here and search for a signal between those frequencies I mentioned. Because of the power of the system, the signal may slop over into a number of frequencies. I would try 10.7 MHz first and then move up and down. the system is so powerful the signal shouldn't be hard to find. Since it's probably also on a single audio frequency, you will know when you hear the beep."

Tony says, "If you do not need further examination, replace the top and panels so we can be out of here. We don't want the guy who put this here to find us. Wait until we take our photos before you start closing the openings. Should we turn the damned thing off and silence their beacon?"

I think for a moment and then say, "Let's not. We're certain of what they are doing here. We can always come and pull the plug if we decide we must."

Tony and I talk with Terry for quite some time before we go our separate ways home. I fix a quick late supper and go to bed, thinking about the beacon. That definitely confirms that the Sahm' Allah is headed for our east coast. The device could be used as a guide to almost any place on the east coast as the destination for the ship. Should we turn the switch off and mess up their plans for the ship, or should we not so the ship will come to where we can most likely deal with it? After I agonize over the decision for a long time, I decide to leave the machine on. Once I do, I go right to sleep.

Chapter 39 - At Last, Confirming Information
✳ Wednesday, July 22, 2015 ✳

Lydia breaks the news. "Finally movement of the ship is reported. The North Koreans report a ship of Yemen registration left the harbor of Nampo on July 21. No destination was listed. The only ship of Yemen registration we know to be in North Korea is Sahm'Allah, The Arrow of Allah, and it is in Nampo. Now what, Brooks?"

"Looks like Sahm' Allah is the key. Their planned attack is based around the Sahm' Allah. The sudden increase in the frequency of SSC messages using its name helps confirm that. My guess is a nuclear bomb supplied by North Korea is aboard. A bomb which they plan to explode in an American harbor. Which harbor, is the question. If we knew, would anyone in our government believe us, or even pay attention to our warnings?"

"I didn't realize the North Koreans had a nuclear bomb. Are you positive?"

"Lydia, they have been working on the design of one for years. They might have one now that they are playing Footsie with the Iranians, those two renegade states may be cooperating to produce a bomb. We've been worried about each of them having a missile and bomb combination that could reach our coasts for years. The media reported they equipped several submarines with missile launch tubes. They doubt that would work because of our effective sub surveillance system. Perhaps they decided to forgo an unpredictable missile or submarine attack in favor of a far more dependable surface ship. They would not need a large one. A small ship like Sahm' Allah would do nicely and be less likely to be challenged. They could sneak a small ship into almost any major US harbor, most likely New York, and set off their bomb. That's the scary part."

"Shouldn't we warn the government?"

"I doubt anyone in the government will listen," Ralph says. "They never paid any attention to your earlier warnings and I don't see that as changing. Besides, I don't trust anyone federal I don't know personally, and few of those I do. Someone with extremely high authority thwarted all of your efforts to warn the proper federal agencies of any of the growing menaces."

Lydia replies, "Aren't any intelligence agencies willing to listen? Did you contact any? Perhaps we should do a search for all intelligence gathering organizations, government and private. Have you ever tried to find a private one? Surely some big company has an effective intelligence section."

"All the contacts made with intelligence went no where. We provided a security system for one several years ago. I can't remember the name or who the operators are. This agency was authorized by the federal government to access many of their secure data files. That's why they needed a special kind of security. I'll call Carla right now to find out their name and how to contact them."

Ralph warns, "If they are federal, I wouldn't trust them."

"Wait until I talk with Carla."

Brooks takes until ten to reach Carla. She hunts for the name and details of their work. "Their name is the Office of Strategic Intelligence, the OSI. They are a unique agency, a combination federal government and private consortium intelligence gathering and policing agency wherein the private section hires all employees under their rules. They insist on absolute proof of an applicant being born in this country of US citizen parents, no exceptions. Several groups including the ACLU tried to have that rule thrown out, but somehow the Supreme Court ruled in their favor. They operate one office in Florida in Gainesville. For some unknown reason their office is associated with the University of Florida and here's their number."

"Thanks, Carla."

Carla is adamant. "Will you please keep me posted on what's going on? This is the first I heard from you in several weeks."

"Until today no new information was received since our last phone conversation. I promise to call you when I talk to someone at OSI and decide if I can trust them or not."

"How about calling me every few days even if nothing is new. Then I'll be sure you're okay."

"Okay, worry wart, I'll do that. Bye."

I turn to Lydia. "Will you call this number for me? I want to hear what you think about this group, OSI. You are much better at sizing people up than I am. Tell them we have some significant information about an imminent attack on the US by a foreign power. Ask them how we can meet with them to explain. Also, tell them we are in fear for our lives from foreign agents who infiltrated our government and cannot divulge our location. We will come to them. I'll be listening in."

"Okay, boss. Here goes."

"This is OSI, southern division. How may I direct your call?"

"Our sources gave us information about a planned attack on our country, a major attack in the near future. To whom can I speak concerning this?"

"One moment please. I will transfer you to Mr. Allan Griffith. He will help you."

"Thank you."

"This is Allan Griffith. How can I help you?"

"We discovered a plan for a major attack on the US. We believe a possible nuclear attack is imminent. How can we send this information to you and what will you do?"

"What is your name and the name of your organization?"

"I am Lydia d'Ober, an associate of Brooks McKibben of BMK systems. We designed and built your security systems a few years ago."

"I am familiar with our security system but not with your company. Did you contact the CIA or any other federal agency?"

"No."

"Why not?"

"Frankly, we don't trust them. We have good reason to believe the same enemy who is mounting this attack infiltrated a number of federal agencies including the CIA. Because of this, we fear for our lives if we divulge our location. We were once attacked with automatic weapons, but escaped. How can we safely meet with you to share our information?"

"Please wait while I check out your information. We cannot take or give any sensitive information over the phone. This will take several minutes. Please be patient."

Lydia turns to Ralph and Brooks. "This should be interesting."

In ten minutes he returns to the phone. "Miss d'Ober, your ID checks out, but of course we cannot confirm what you told us. Can you tell me why your call has no origination number?"

"As one of the foremost organizations in the world on digital technology, we are able to mask our origination number as a protective measure for our people, legally. Now, how can we secretly and safely meet with you or someone in your organization to share with you what information we have."

"Can you come to Gainesville safely?"

"I believe we can."

"How long will you take? When could you be here?"

"The earliest would be this evening about seven, or possibly a day later. Things are difficult at this location. We will call you when we know. We would need a secure and secret meeting place."

"One will be arranged before you reach Gainesville. Call and ask for me when you know. Safe travels by the way."

"Thank you. Bye."

"What do you think, Lydia? Can we trust them?"

"I am quite certain we can. He had all the right reactions. How are we going to go past our friends in those SUVs?"

"First I better call Charley to see if we can borrow his pickup again."

An hour later I finally contact Charley by phone. He has more bad news. "Your friends moved a large motor home into the front row in the campground where they can see the canal and the bridge in well hidden comfort. Two of them are in the RV at all times. Their shift changes are now five days, regular as clockwork. The SUV shows up with two guys. They exchange places with the other two who then drive away. I don't know where they go, but several times we passed them on the road near Homestead. My guess is they come all the way from Miami."

"Do you have Pete's phone number? I'm going to ask him if we can bum a ride in his chopper. Could you meet us somewhere and let us use your pickup again?"

"How about the Nine Mile Pond parking lot? If you connect and we can move, tell Pete to call and let me know. I hope this phone is not tapped or you are duck soup."

"Yeah, I wondered about that. Too late to worry anyway. I'll try to contact Pete right away. Bye"

"Good bye and good luck. I'll see you at Nine Mile."

Pete answers on the first ring. "Hey, Brooks. Got your problem solved yet? Cindy and I were talking about you this morning and wondering how you and Lydia were doing."

"We're doing fine, but need your help. Any chance you could pick three of us up in your chopper and take us to the Nine Mile Pond parking lot? I'll gladly reimburse the county for the costs. This is important."

"Hell, Brooks, I need to make a run out near your way anyhow. You say three people? How about luggage? I'll need to take the boat. The boat and four people comes close to my weight limit."

"The three of us total at most, 500 pounds, without luggage."

"That means no more than fifty pounds additional."

"No problem. We'll be under that. All we must take is my computer, a change of clothes and toothbrushes for each of us. How soon can you come?"

"I can make your place in an hour so be ready by noon. I assume you are in a hurry."

"Right you are. We are driving to Gainesville, about 400 miles. An eight-hour trip if all goes well."

✳ Wednesday, July 22, 2015, 5:00 pm ✳

Everything goes as planned. Lydia calls OSI when we are two hours out of Gainesville.

"Mr. Griffith please. Lydia d'Ober calling."

"Hello Ms. d'Ober. Where are you?"

"We're two hours away. Where should we go?"

"We operate a safe house on the south side near I-75 and US 24. Turn off I-75 at US 24 and go east. I'll be driving a red Toyota Rav4. What are you driving?"

"A battered, ten year old, red and gray Ford F150 crew-cab pickup you can't miss."

"When I see you, I'll flash my lights. Follow me and I'll lead you to the house about half a mile away. Okay?"

"You bet. We should arrive within two hours. See you."

✳   ✳   ✳

At seven thirty we all walk into the safe house. After introductions, we sit down in the living room. Griffith has another agent with him, Danny Holcomb. After we tell them what we know about the situation, Griffith is curious.

"How did you obtain this information and how can we get confirmation"

I am adamant. "We cannot divulge how we obtained this information. Let's say that is a trade secret. If we divulged our source, it would no longer exist, so we must use strict confidentiality. You understand of course."

Griffith says, "Yeah, we understand, we don't like it though. It may be impossible for us to act on your information without knowing how you acquired the information. If we can confirm anything you tell us, we could possibly act."

Danny adds, "That would require finding and examining the ship. Without any way to do this, our hands are tied. Can you support any of your claims with confirmable info?"

I keep trying. "The military satellite photos would confirm the existence of the ship in the shipyard and could even show what they did to the ship. I doubt you can obtain those photos. I'll give you the dates that are most significant. Surely the military would like to know about this."

Griffith shook his head. "I believe you, and I'm quite certain Danny believes you. Your credibility is excellent because of your business reputation. Unfortunately you offer no valid confirmation. I'll try to obtain those satellite photos, but that may be difficult, even for us. You can stay here in this safe house while we try to confirm your information. We will run down everything you give us regarding those questionable Homeland Security people. That will take some time. If you want, you can stay here until we run this down. Any information we find we will share with you. Right now we had better return to our office so we can start the process of confirmation. Should you think of anything you missed, please call us. The phone here is a secure direct line to our office. No need to dial, just pick up and we will answer. Oh yes, all records of this visit will remain within OSI. None will be shared with any other agency. We are certain moles are hiding within many federal agencies. One of the things we are working on is the apprehension of those moles. Your information may help us with that."

We end up staying for five days. On Monday Danny comes over to give us an update.

"Everything we tried led to a dead end. The military satellite people couldn't or wouldn't provide us the photos you suggested. The thing we were able to confirm is the existence of a ship named The Arrow of Allah operating under the Yemen flag. We could not find its whereabouts or even its last port of call. That confirms part of your story. We're working on the information you gave us on the Ft., Lauderdale branch of Homeland Security. Mr. Chandra is in jail in Atlanta awaiting trial on charges of impersonating a federal officer. He refuses to cooperate and will provide no proof of citizenship, or even his real name. He is considered an illegal alien. All of his

ID is fraudulent including his driver's license. No one has been able to identify him from photographs or fingerprints. He remains a complete mystery. We are continuing to work on the names you provided of questionable people in the Atlanta office of Homeland Security."

Ralph asks him, "Did you find any information about my car exploding in the HS parking lot?"

"Yes. The media reported a leak in the gas tank of a car parked in their lot led to a fire and explosion destroying the car. No injuries were reported and the owner of the car was not identified."

I turn toward Ralph. "That's precisely what you told us the news reports would say. It's good enough for me. The facts about that explosion are being hidden from the public."

Danny smiled. "Don't give up. Two of our agents are trying to locate the remains of your car. If they are found, we can determine the actual cause of the explosion, even after going in the crusher. They will also test the spot where the car blew up for explosive residue. We will release our findings to good, loyal news sources."

"That's encouraging," Ralph says.

"We've been in touch with the contractor who repaired your house. Mr. Young is sharp. He saved a number of pieces of your house containing the bullets from the attack. If we're extremely lucky, those bullets can lead us to your attackers."

"That's certainly good news," I say. "Your people have been busy. I'm impressed and delighted we found OSI. You are part of an agency I now trust completely. That is extremely comforting. We will not hesitate to provide you any additional information we come across."

"Thank you. We take our responsibilities and loyalty to America and Americans quite seriously. We are a relatively small agency, but our people are clever, resourceful, and dedicated. We don't quit. We'll get to the bottom of this if possible."

"I don't doubt that at all," Lydia says. "And thank you for keeping us informed."

"One question, how soon do you plan to leave and return to wherever you came from? I understand you wish to keep the location a secret. I also understand you provided us a way to keep in secure contact. We need to know when the safe house will be vacant. We may not need the house for some time, but that could quickly change at any time."

I reply, "Now that a secure way of contact between us is available, nothing is holding us here. We should be able to leave by tomorrow morning, or even today depending on some people I will call. I'll let you know when we do."

"Thank you. I now need to return to our office and go after the bad guys," Danny says with a grin. "Good luck in your travels, and good bye. Working with you has been enlightening."

After we say our goodbyes, I call Pete to make arrangements for our return to the cabin. He will contact Charley. We will be in the parking lot this afternoon if we hurry. Then Pete can make the trip out and back in daylight. We call Danny and are able to leave by eleven. With little to pack, we are all back in the cabin and working by seven.

Chapter 40 - Information Comes in Dribbles

A week since our return brought up nothing new about the ship. Then we have a break. In one message the date, September 7, appears along with the name of the ship and the word rocket. We can only guess the meaning as no mention is made of its significance.

Lydia notes the date. "September 7 is Labor Day in America. I wonder what cooks?"

"I just realized the attack will be carried out on Labor day, a big holiday with many parades and gatherings all over the country. Labor Day is the ideal day for an attack when people are most vulnerable. I better put in a call to OSI to let them know."

Before I can make the call Ralph shouts, "Hey, here's another one from North Korea. The words, Arrow, Unha-3 rocket, and the same date, September 7, are linked. What kind of rocket is their Unha-3?"

"OSI is on the phone. I'm waiting for Griffith."

"Hello Brooks. Do you have something new?"

"Yes, we found two communications linking the ship name, the word rocket, and the date September 7, 2015. That's this coming Labor Day, just five weeks from now. In one the rocket is identified as a North Korean Unha-3. I hope this helps."

"We'll start working right away. I'll call you back if and when we find anything."

"Allan, please use the secure method I explained to you. I don't want any snoopers picking up your call."

"Don't worry. I will. Bye."

Lydia is shocked. "My God, Brooks, that doesn't give us much time to act. Labor day is five weeks away and we don't ave any idea where the ship is going. They may be able to fire their rocket from far out at sea."

About an hour later, Allan from OSI is on the phone.

"Brooks, the Unha-3 rocket is a medium to long range rocket the North Koreans only tested twice. One was a complete failure. The other landed in the Philippine Sea about 2,200 miles from their launch site. This rocket can carry a substantial payload. An atomic bomb is well within its capability."

"That means they could reach much of our country from far out at sea, right?"

"No. The Unha-3 rocket is land-based requiring a solid, stable platform for launch. It could not possibly be launched from a ship at sea."

"That means they would need to unload . . . no, wait. Could the Unha-3 be fired from the ship if the ship were run aground and firmly positioned on the bottom?"

"Your observation is clever and on the mark. We obtained the plans of the ship from the builder of the hull. This ship is a small, shallow draft vessel requiring only two meters to clear the bottom when fully loaded, even less if lightly loaded. It would not only need to be aground, but the launch platform must be quite solid and level or the rocket's trajectory would suffer. A lean of as much as eight degrees from vertical during launch, and it would not rise off the platform. We determined the ship could be grounded and the hull flooded to provide a stable enough platform for a launch. That's only on a solid sea bottom. Many suitable locations are near the Atlantic coast. Some are close enough to the mainland in and around the Bahama Islands. We warned Bahamian authorities to watch for the ship and detain it if possible in water six or more meters deep."

"Allan, are any harbors on the East coast suitable, or places near shore where they could run the ship aground firmly enough for a launch?"

"Countless of those are all along the coast, but every major harbor has security. I don't think they would try a harbor. All of the shoreline places would give them the problem of wave action. Many hidden coves exist also, far too many to even consider protecting. That is one place where we are vulnerable. Very few places exist where a ship, even a small one, could enter without being observed and reported by someone. Several hours will be required for them to run aground, flood the ship and level the launch platform. That will give us time to attack the ship and destroy the rocket. Many U.S. bases are in operation all up and down the coast. Of course, we would need to convince the military of the seriousness of the situation. At this point we do not have enough provable data to convince them. We couldn't even convince them to search for the ship. Too little hard evidence and far too many guesses are available for the military to act. We may be convinced an attack is imminent, but proving so to those who need to act is another matter entirely."

Brooks is fearful. "Another factor in play. We know from experience many enemies of our country are hiding in our government, many of them in high places. They will do what they can to thwart our efforts including blocking our warnings and using the media to ridicule our conclusions. All they need to do is delay action for a few hours, a relatively short time. They always promote 'Let's wait and see before doing something rash.' That alone could easily scuttle all of our efforts. And there is the ridiculous red herring of balloon born anthrax. That is still an active and constantly touted false purveyor of fear in the news daily."

"I don't know about the enemies in high places, but I agree on the anthrax. I cannot believe the media continues promoting a major diversion and distraction being used by our enemies to hide the real menace. I hope greed and ignorance is causing that reaction in the media and not subversion. I hate to think our media might be a willing partner with our enemies."

"A few bad apples among the members of the media can emotionally sway many to think and act in a wrong way. The vast majority of media people care about the country. It only takes a few clever manipulators to move the majority onto the wrong track. Any suggestions as to what we can do?"

"Brooks, you obviously can access information we cannot. Continue your search. Call and tell us of any new developments. We will do the same. Given confirmation, you might even be able to convince me about enemies in high places. I'll keep an open mind on that. Bye for now."

✱ Thursday, August 13, 2015, 10:15 am ✱

Another ten days pass before we find some new information which is solid gold. Lydia shouts from her seat at the computer.

"Here's a copy of some new communication with the ship. A lot of numbers are included with no significant text. When organized on a page, the numbers form a table of some sort."

"Let me take a look," Brooks says as he comes over to examine the numbers.

"Wait a sec," Lydia says. "I think I know what those numbers are. The first numbers mark a physical location, longitude and latitude. The rest . . . It's a tide table for that location."

Lydia brings up a map of the location. "My God, . . . That tells us where they are taking the ship. . . . St. Augustine."

"Why do you think that?"

"Those numbers are a tide table for the Matanzas inlet. The ship is being provided information on the tides in Matanzas inlet. That's the inlet to the harbor at St. Augustine. The date they provided the tidal data for is September 7. Call OSI and tell them, Brooks."

Within minutes, Brooks is talking to Allan at OSI.

Allan questions, "I wonder why St Augustine? No major metro area is nearby other than Jacksonville."

"With a 2,200 mile range a rocket fired from St. Augustine could reach most of the country. Lots of suitable shallow areas near the inlet could provide a stable place to launch a rocket. On Labor day many small ships will be going in and out of the harbor with virtually no security. The Arrow could cruise in and do her dirty work with little interference."

"I'll put you in touch with our local agent in St. Augustine," Allan says. "Her name is Carol Mitchell and she lives on the coast not far from the inlet. I suggest you call her and give her all the information you have. I'll call her immediately and fill her in. Hold off calling for fifteen minutes while I talk with her. Here's her number."

At ten thirty I call Carol. She answers with a cheery hello.

"Carol, this is Brooks McKibben. I assume Allan Griffith filled you in."

"Yes, Brooks, I just finished talking to him. I can't believe St. Augustine is their destination. That is confirmed by the beacon we found on Porpoise Point. That beacon will lead them directly to the Matanzas Inlet. Labor Day is the perfect time for them to arrive. Not only will Labor Day in Matanzas harbor be extremely busy, but it's right at the height of St. Augustine's 450th anniversary celebration. The harbor will be full of boats and small ships coming and going. The city will be full of celebrants. The harbor is an ideal place and Labor Day is a perfect time to come here and not be noticed. Allan is contacting all the necessary authorities of course. He will be calling me back when he knows. He will let me know what they are going to do. A good thing you were able to inform OSI. We're quite familiar with these murderers and their methods, but this is something quite new and unexpected. Of course, 9-11 was new and unexpected as well. This is much bigger than 9-11. The lives of millions are at stake."

"I hope we can stop them. They put together a rather elaborate scheme to drop an atomic bomb somewhere in America. My guess is the plan is to hit somewhere in the northeast, probably New York in the area of maximum destruction."

"You're right. I'm wondering if our New York office noticed any movement of known terrorists out of the area? We'll need to check that as soon as we can. All we've been able to do is research the anthrax from balloons threat. We've dismissed that completely as a red herring. The coordination of such an attack would be huge and we've seen no evidence of any kind. It's a complete hoax. No other explanation is possible. How did you come by all this information?"

"Carol, as I explained to Allan, if we divulged our source or method, our source would cease to exist. In fact, we cannot even act directly on our information. We must carefully plan and find ways to act that will conceal the actual information we have. That's the only way we can keep those channels open. That is especially true now. Unfortunately this makes for extreme difficulty to prompt anyone, and especially government people, to act on the information we provide. They want positive confirmation of any threat before they act. Some times this is not possible. I hope such is not the case with this dangerous situation. If not acted on, an inconceivable tragedy will occur, one of immense proportions with possibly millions of Americans dead and injured. This could even mean the end of America which is exactly what our enemies are planning for."

Carol is incredulous. "You would not even divulge your secret if doing so would prevent the tragedy?"

"Unfortunately, doing so would only delay the tragedy, for we would lose our access to information that could avert another even larger calamity. I will do one thing to prevent this bomb from being exploded. I will meet anyone who the authority to order a strike and tell the individual how we obtained the information if I have the assurance he or she will not divulge our secret to anyone else. This must be done in time so the necessary action can be taken."

"Brooks, do you mean you would require this of even the President? That's who would be needed to make such a decision."

"Yes, especially the President."

"Do you trust him to keep silent? A great deal of pressure would be used on him to divulge the source and method used to obtain such information."

Brooks is quite positive."I can guarantee he will remain silent."

"Impressive. I hope you are right."

"We have 25 days to develop an effective response. We see the solution as simple, destroy the ship before the rocket can be fired. The difficulty will be in convincing those with the power, to do so. Once the rocket is launched, any action will be too late."

"I hope your OSI people can do some powerful convincing. I don't see anyone else even trying."

"I agree. How distressing, but I think you're right."

"Now I must go back to work to see what if anything we can learn and use. Keep me informed."

"Don't worry. I will. Good bye for now."

Chapter 41 - Some Startling New Revelations

Lydia is listening to the news on Al Jazeera while the other two are busy looking at SSC data. Suddenly she cries out, "Brooks, come over here, now. They're showing some radical Islamist from ISIS on the TV. He's ranting about something. I need you to translate what he is saying."

By the time Brooks is near the TV, the rant is finished. The network then proceeds to show a rerun of his rant with English subtitles.

They say, "Death to America. In a few days the Arrow of Allah will rain death and destruction down on the great Satan. Her planes will fall from the skies. Her military will be unable to function. Her trains, busses, cars and trucks will stop running. Her factories and offices will shut down. All means of communication will cease. Her power grid will collapse and darkness will spread throughout their nation. Allah will triumph as our soldiers take over their military bases."

"What do you make of that?" Lydia asks. "I never heard of any claims like this before. It's scary."

"They made a fair translation of his words," Brooks says. "Just another rant of a fanatic or is some truth in his words more than that? I wonder?"

Lydia jumps up and shrieks. "He just told us what the Arrow of Allah is going to do. It's going launch an atomic bomb designed to produce a monstrous EMP surge. Such a bomb would do exactly what he said, fry all solid state electronics for a thousand, even two thousand miles from the explosion. That's what's aboard their rocket, an atomic bomb designed to produce a powerful EMP blast miles above the earth. They don't need accuracy. All they need to do is lob the damned thing out over the middle of the US and explode it high up. We have but ten days to stop this unbelievable catastrophe."

Brooks jumps up. "I'll call OSI right away."

Soon Allan is on the phone. "Allan, I have some bad news. The bomb the rocket is carrying is not an ordinary atomic bomb but is a much more devastating EMP bomb. If and when an EMP bomb explodes, every solid state device within a couple of thousand miles will be fried---completely destroyed. That includes the US, and most of Canada and Mexico, all of North America. Our ability to function as nations will be completely destroyed, wiped out."

"Brooks, I am familiar with what an atomic EMP bomb would do. Are you positive about this?"

"I can give you the source on this one. Try to find a rerun of the latest Al Jazeera news. Some crazy ISIS bastard on TV described the effects of an EMP bomb precisely. He even described launching it from Sahm' Allah, The Arrow of Allah. That's what's aboard the rocket on that ship. We must stop it at all costs. That broadcast should provide all the ammunition you need to convince whomever you need convinced that our information is accurate. We know where the ship is headed, the arrival time, and what their mission is. Our mission . . . stop the damned thing."

"I'll start on this right away."

"I'll call your agent in St. Augustine. She should be told about this immediately."

Call placed.

"Hello. This is Carol Mitchell of the OSI office in St. Augustine. I am not available at present. Please leave your name, call back number, and any message. I will return your call as soon as I am back. 'Beep.'"

"Carol, this is Brooks McKibben. Here's startling news. An EMP bomb is on the rocket. You cannot call me back so call Allan in Gainesville. He has all the details. You might also view a rerun of a short part of an ISIS report on Al Jazeera. I'll call you later."

About an hour later the phone rings. It must be Allan, I think. "Hello?"

"Hello, Brooks. This is Carol Mitchell. I just got off the phone with Allan. Did he tell you what happened yet?"

"No, and how did you find this number?"

"Tell one OSI agent something important and we all know. What you don't know is we are unable to start any action, even with that Al Jazeera piece. Someone high up in the administration is blocking everything. Allan is hoping to find out who is doing this and go around them. So far without success."

"Damn it, Carol. What can we do now? We must come up with some sort of contingency plan."

"After hearing the bad news from Allan, I contacted my father and my sisters. My dad is an ex Marine who might come up with some ideas. And Calder Voss, my sister Andrea's guy, is ex Special Forces. I'm hoping they can conjure up something. All of them are extremely resourceful and capable of getting difficult things done. If anyone can come up with a solution, they can."

"I hope they can. I am so frustrated with our government. Why can't they check things out? I can't think of a thing we could do short of storming the Whitehouse and that would be a fruitless effort. Somehow we must scuttle that ship and the best place would be in the Matanzas Inlet close to shore."

"That's exactly what I said to my dad. He's going to talk to Calder. I'll bet between the two of them they will come up with something."

"Let me know if they do. In the meantime, I'll keep trying. Bye for now."

✳ Tuesday, September 1, 2015 ✳

Once again the satellite phone in the Everglades cabin rings.

"Brooks, this is Carol. We have a terribly risky plan but one that makes sense and might work. While talking with Calder, my dad discovered Calder's friend owns this powerful and accurate sniper rifle. If we could put him and his gun close enough to the ship, he thinks he could sink the ship or blow up the rocket. Our problem would be getting the guy and his sniper rifle from Battle Mountain, Nevada to St. Augustine. His name is Emory Boozer and he is an ex Navy Seal. His rifle is illegal in the hands of any civilian so you can't take it on an airplane. Right now Emory is in Alaska on a hunting trip and won't be back home to Nevada until the second of September at the earliest. We were lucky we caught him in range of a cell tower before he went out into the wilds on a hunt. He cancelled the hunt and is presently trying to find the quickest way to fly home."

"That sounds good. Perhaps I could help. I can arrange for the BMK jet to pick him and his equipment up in, did you say Battle Mountain, Nevada? Where's that?"

"West of Elko."

"Do you know if Elko's airport can handle a Lear Jet?"

"No, I don't, but I will find out"

"Don't bother. My pilot will find out. The land around most of those small towns in the high desert is so flat long runways are on every airport. If he can't land at Battle Mountain, other suitable places are nearby where he can land to pick up our man. Randy may want to fly in the day before and leave early the next morning. Night landings at those remote airports can sometimes be tricky. Give me Emory's phone number. I'll give it to Randy and he can make pickup arrangements directly."

"Okay. Now I'll ask my dad where would be a suitable sniper location. I'd ask Emory, but we may not be able to ask him anything until he gets here. I think we should find and arrange for several suitable locations before then."

✳ Thursday, September 3, 2015 ✳

By Thursday we go into full crisis mode when Emory calls Calder.

"Hey buddy, I'm stuck at the hunting camp. Bad weather with high winds is preventing my pickup plane from getting to me. That plane is the only way I can reach Anchorage to catch a flight home. If the wind doesn't settle down in the next two days, I will not make Juneau in time. I can give you some instructions and you can pick up my gun and do the job. I can't think of another way. Can you go to my house okay?"

"Yes, if necessary, but I never fired anything like your gun."

"If you can go to my house, Shellie can bring the gun out for you. I built a range I marked out about a mile north of my house where you can take some practice shots. If I don't leave here by Saturday, I'll never be home in time. I'll instruct you by phone. That's the best we can do."

"I'll make arrangements for Brooks to tell his pilot to fly me out and back. Boy, will that be cutting it close."

"Buddy, I can even make Juneau in time if I'm out of here by early Sunday. That's three more days here. I would fly into Elko and be home on Sunday evening. Brooks's pilot could fly me to St. Augustine early Monday morning and hopefully we could be set up and ready to fire by say eleven o'clock."

"My God, Emory, that will be cutting things far too close. One little glitch and all will be over. We can't take that chance. If you're not on your way home by Saturday morning, I'm coming out to get your gun. Even that is a bit too close for comfort. You must fly out by tomorrow."

"Hey, if the pickup plane can get me I'll have a shot. If not, well it's not up to me. Old mother nature will decide this one. I'll call soon as I know whichever way things turn out."

"Everything is out of your hands. I'm going make arrangements with Brooks anyway, just in case."

"Have you found any good sniper locations yet? I must be prone for a shot that far away."

"We examined three possible locations so far. The bridge we decided against. Too open to the public. The top of the tallest building downtown is a possibility, but we would need to figure out how to place you and the gun up top without a big fuss from a number of people. So far that's not possible. The Lighthouse is by far the best, with a clear view of the inlet, and being up quite high. We devised a way to get us up on the platform while keeping everyone else down on the ground. The platform may be a bit tight for a comfortable prone firing position, but we are sure it can work."

"Sounds like a winner. I hope I can make your party."

"So do I. Good bye Emory. I must do tons of things with little time to do them in. Pray that plane can get you here by tomorrow."

"Will do. Bye."

✳ The Coming Together ✳

Chapter 42 - OSI and a Plane Full of Enemies
✳ Saturday, September 5, 2015, 9:00 am ✳

OSI agents Allan Griffith and Tony Rawls watch from the control tower at Jacksonville International Airport. They are observing a chartered Qatar Boeing 777-300 loading passengers. Two other agents are standing near the gate filming those boarding with a hidden TV camera. On the ground are six more OSI agents moving unobtrusively among the many airport and security personnel loading luggage and watching the aircraft. The crowd waiting is large enough to fill most of the 360 seats in the plane.

✳ Saturday, September 5, 2015, 11:00 am ✳

After the last few stragglers enter the plane, the ground crew prepares the plane for push back. As the entrance stairway is moved away and before the ground crew can disconnect the ground power, half a dozen dark SUVs pull up around the landing gear, blocking the plane and preventing its departure.

In the tower, agent Allan Griffith speaks with the pilot.

"This is agent Allen Griffith of the OSI. I am in command of a number of both OSI and US Immigration officers with orders to detain Qatar flight CJ101 until all occupants are cleared for leaving the country. Shut down your engines and await further instructions. The ground crew will keep the power connected for the comfort of your passengers. Do you understand?"

The pilot replies, "This is Captain Omar Dejan. I understand but question your authority to do so. I ask that you remove the vehicles, disconnect the power, and permit us to leave. All of our exit requirements are met. A rather long, tight and demanding flight schedule lies ahead of us and we need to depart immediately."

He does not shut down the engines.

"Sir, under US law, we do have the authority to detain your flight by any means at our disposal. If you do not shut down your engines immediately, we will shut them down for you. The damage to the aircraft resulting from a forced shut down will not be easily repaired. We will give you ten minutes to shut down your engines before we take action. Please respond."

"I protest, but under your threat of violence, I will shut down the engines. We demand immediate release under International Law. The highest legal authorities will be notified."

"Sir, in a few minutes, our agents will be at the top of the entrance stairway. Please open the door so they can provide the documentation for our action. We will then proceed to process a number of your passengers who are traveling on forged or illegitimate papers. Once our examination of all exit papers is complete, we will withdraw and permit you to leave. The more cooperation from you and your passengers, the quicker this will be over and the sooner you will be able to leave."

"Why did you not do this during our pre boarding? All of our papers were checked at that time and found to be in order."

"As long as your plane remained with the stairway attached, the plane was considered as open for exit by anyone on board. No laws were broken even though we know a number of passengers on board are holding forged passports and other illegal documents. Once the stairs were removed, the plane was legally considered as having departed and laws were broken by some passengers, major laws. This gave us the right to detain the plane and reexamine the passengers and their papers. We consider this to be a matter of serious disregard of many laws, US and International. In the interests of quickly getting through this process, I am certain you and your crew understand and will cooperate fully."

"We will comply, but will still file a complaint with all of the proper authorities."

"If every person on board carries legal and proper papers, you should be on your way in about three hours. That's the best I can promise. Thank you for your cooperation."

At this point a number of large vans pull up near the stairs. One van, OSI's mobile lab and remote communication system, pulls up right by the stairs. The others, small busses with barred windows, park in a line nearby. The agent in charge enters the plane and explains the procedure to all on board.

"Each passenger and crew member will exit the plane and stop at the vehicle at the bottom of the stairs. Please have all your papers with you including passports, exit visas, drivers licenses, and/or student IDs. These will be examined closely for authenticity and current status. Anyone with proper and current papers will be permitted to leave in the plane. Those with improper or fraudulent papers will be detained. Wait at the bottom of the stairs until you are called to the van. The next passenger will wait at the top of the stairs until the one at the bottom goes to the van, then descend to the bottom and wait. Follow the directions of the agents posted at all positions. They will direct you to your next place. The more orderly manner in which this progresses, the quicker it will be over and those who are legal will be able to leave."

One of the agents steps into the plane and begins directing passengers to leave by rows.

The first passenger asks, "Should we take our carry-ons with us?"

"If you are certain your papers are in order, you will be permitted to leave on the plane and will not need them while waiting, leave them. If you are unsure of your status or will need anything, take those things with you," the agent replies.

The first man to exit takes his carry-on as he walks down the stairs. The minute he reaches the bottom he bolts and is quickly collared by two of the waiting agents. They handcuff him and put him into one of the waiting buses for transport to a detention lockup.

In the OSI mobile lab are two stations with a computer and wireless access to the Internet. The agent at each station takes the papers from each passenger and checks them directly with the issuing agencies for being authentic. Any discrepancy found identifies the holder as illegal. Each of the illegal passengers is handcuffed and ushered to one of the secured buses to be moved to federal prison.

By the time about half of the passengers walked down the steps, the rest refuse to leave the plane. When this happens, twenty agents entered the plane and begin handcuffing the remaining passengers. All but about two dozen are taken into custody by the agents. Those that remain are all young men who link arms and threaten the agents. When this happens, the agents move quietly to the door and leave, all but one.

This agent announces to the resisting passengers, "When I leave, tear gas will be circulated through the air-conditioning system of the plane. I don't think any of you will be able to resist or even breathe. I suggest you come to the door and go down the stairs while you can still breathe. Any that remain will be rendered unconscious with nitrous oxide and carried unconscious from the plane."

As soon as he leaves, a small amount of tear gas is sent through the AC. Immediately most of the young men come to the door and descend the stairs. The remaining six doggedly refuse to leave. Enough nitrous oxide is then sent through the AC to render those remaining unconscious. Agents wearing gas masks then enter and half carry, half drag the remaining semiconscious young men from the plane. The gas will safely disperse and the plane will be safe for entry in about twenty minutes.

Of the 348 passengers and crew, only the eight crew and 95 passengers are not detained. A dozen of these elect to stay with family members or friends who are being detained. Shortly after 2:30 the plane takes off with 83 passengers and the eight crew members.

Among those detained was one Charles Chang who identified himself as Mao zu Chin, a high official of the US Commerce department. When asked why he was carrying a forged passport and driver's license in the name of Charles Chang, he did not have an answer. He was singled out for special treatment. OSI wants to know why he is on that plane with forged documents, trying to leave the country without anyone knowing. They also ask him why he had placed the transmitter in the house on Porpoise Point. He pled complete ignorance even when shown the video of him entering the house with the transmitter. He doesn't know of the charges he will be facing.

Several dozen similar incidents were reported at airports throughout the country. Nationwide. Nearly three thousand individuals with forged or otherwise illegal documentation were detained. There were so many that several federal and military prisons that had been closed were reopened and restaffed to handle the load.

Chapter 43 - The Conspirators Gather
✴ Friday, September 4, 2015, 3:00 pm ✴

About three o'clock Friday afternoon, the BMK jet lands at the Northeast Florida Regional Airport north of St. Augustine. Six passengers along with the pilot, Randy Melbourne are aboard. Starting off in the morning he stopped at Pittsburgh to pick up Sag Mitchell, Kansas City, for Calder and Andrea, and finally he stopped at Homestead, Florida and picked up Lydia, Brooks and Ralph. Brooks arranged for a large rental SUV, a Lincoln Navigator, to handle all of them and their luggage. The SUV is waiting near the general aviation gate when the plane pulls up and parks. After moving their luggage from the plane to the SUV and saying good bye to Randy, they head south for Carol's. Brooks is driving.

✴   ✴   ✴

Around four they pull into Carol's driveway. A pickup and fifth wheel RV are parked off the side of the driveway. A white hose and orange power cable snake from the RV to the garage. Carol, Renee, and two children are standing by the door of the RV. After introductions and a bit of small talk, Calder, Andrea, and Sag grab their luggage and go inside the house. Carol, Renee, and the children go with them. The other three climb back into the SUV and head downtown for the Casa Monica Hotel. Once they are checked in and refreshed, they will come back to Carol's.

We all gather in the main room for instructions.

My house is going be a bit crowded here this weekend," Carol announces. "Calder, you and Andrea can use the master bedroom. Sag, You can sleep in the guest room. You'll be sharing with Eric after tonight. You saw that Renee brought their RV for her family. Mack will be here tomorrow."

"Where will you sleep?" I ask.

"See those two couches? They open up into comfortable beds. I will use one and the other will serve any unexpected guests that might show up. Why don't you take your things to your rooms and freshen up? We can meet out here and talk about the weekend together. Renee will help me fix a little spread, some snacks and drinks. You must be hungry."

✴   ✴   ✴

Calder has been trying to contact Emory for most of the day. No luck. He isn't answering his phone. He hopes it means he is on his way home. At ten that night his phone rings when he is in his bedroom. Emory is on the phone.

"Good news old buddy. I'm in Elko about to pick up my car and head for home. Had to leave the camp in a hurry when the plane showed up trying to make up for lost time. The pilot had four others to pick up for the flight to Anchorage. We barely made the Delta flight here from

Anchorage. This is the first time I could use my phone. I'll call Randy soon as I hang up and make arrangements for my trip."

"That is good news. I'll be on hand to pick you up at the regional airport whenever you arrive. Be sure to call and tell me when."

"Okay, Calder. Now I better hurry. I'll let you know when I know. See ya."

Calder walks into the main room, smiling.

"Hey folks, that was Emory. He's almost home so that's one big worry off our chests. He's going to call with the details when he and Randy work out the flight here."

Everyone cheers.

✳   ✳   ✳

Late Saturday Calder receives the call from Emory.

"We won't get to St Augustine until about six Monday morning. Randy is flying all day Saturday and Sunday and will end up here at about six Sunday evening. He plans on sleeping till about midnight when we will head for Florida. He told me we will arrive at exactly six Monday morning."

"Damn, Emory, that's cutting it close. From the latest information available, we should have enough time. My guess is we can be at the lighthouse long before eight when they open the museum. We may stop back here. I hope we don't run into any delays."

Chapter 44 - Sahm' Allah Strikes
✳ Monday, September 7, 2015 6:00am ✳

Out of the west a small swept wing jet on approach banks sharply over the Atlantic, flashes golden briefly in the early morning sun, levels off, and then touches down at St Augustine Regional Airport. The BMK private jet taxis to a place at the terminal, turns and parks sending a rush of dusty air that ruffles the hair and clothes of a couple standing and waiting near a dark-blue Lincoln Navigator. The pilot powers down the engines, lowers the staircase, exits the cabin, and walks to greet the couple.

Andrea and I are at the airport to pick up Emory Boozer and his equipment arriving from Battle Mountain, Nevada. The pilot extends his hand. "I'm Randy Melbourne. You two are Calder and Andrea, right?"

We shake hands and I say,"You remember. It's nice to meet you. How was the flight?"

"Other than a bit of turbulence coming over the Rockies, the flight was perfect and on time.

"We just got here. We're in a bit of a hurry. Where's your passenger?"

Randy shook his head. "That's a real problem you folks face, a serious problem. I didn't realize the passenger is an alcoholic in spite of his name. He's passed out on the couch in the cabin. I couldn't wake him. He's blotto."

Both of us are visibly shaken. "That's catastrophic. It was a huge mistake, not telling you he was an alcoholic?"

"No one said a word. If I knew, the liquor cabinet would be locked."

I couldn't believe it. "This is a major disaster. I wonder what we can do?"

Randy was at a loss. "I'm stumped. When he got in the plane at Battle Mountain, he was fine. He helped me load his gear, acted really congenial. Then I made the mistake of pointing out the liquor cabinet along with all the other beverages and told him to help himself, just as a courtesy. He did that. I thought it a bit strange when he didn't come up and join me in the front seat. I figured he was tired and wanted to sleep. About an hour ago, I put the plane on autopilot and went to the john. I found him passed out, empty Jack Daniels and Makers Mark bottles lay on the floor. That's one and a half liters of 80 proof whisky. How can anyone drink that much booze and live?"

Both Andrea and I are dumbfounded—shaken."Damn! Damn! Damn!" is all I can think of to say.

Andrea, equally disturbed said, "One of us should have made you aware of his problem. Neglecting to tell you was a disastrous error. Now, can the three of us put him into our car? He's a large man."

Randy says, "We can try. The hardest part will be getting him down those stairs. Come take a look."

We enter the cabin and survey the situation.

"First let's try to lift him, to find out if we can. Andrea and I will take his upper body. You grab his feet and we'll take him out feet first."

As we struggled and finally managed to lift him off the couch Randy says, "Okay, we can lift him. Getting him down those steps and into the car is going to be another matter. Set him back down while one of you brings your car right up to the staircase? Open the door so we won't need to do that while carrying him."

Andrea moves the Navigator close to the plane and opens the big side door.

Randy opens a storage compartment in the rear of the plane and brings out a roll of carpet. He rolls about half of the carpet out and covers the staircase. "This will help us slide him down and into the SUV. Andrea, pull the SUV door right up close to the staircase, as close as you can get it."

This maneuver took about ten minutes. Randy and I then rolled the bottom part of the carpet into the door opening.

"Now, if we can slide him down the carpet it should help us move him into the back seat."

Randy agreed with me so we climbed into the plane to move Emory.

We struggle a bit getting him to the stairs. Emory groans when we move him. Then he opens his eyes and tries to get up.

I yell in his ear, "Emory, can you help us take you down into the SUV?"

Andrea says, "He can't understand. Try to get him to stay still. You two use his arms and I'll guide his legs. Let me get in the SUV first. God, what a mess."

With Andrea standing in the SUV, the two of us manage to slide him onto the carpet and start him down the stairs. He doesn't help by again trying to stand. By holding his arms we manage to slide him down into the back seat. Andrea must pull herself out from beneath his legs before he is all the way down. Unfortunately he ends up half on the seat and half on the floor. By now we are all sweating profusely in the warm weather. The next struggle is removing the carpet. Somehow Emory manages to move himself onto the seat and off the carpet. Randy rolls it up quickly before he can move again.

Andrea looks at me. "Well, we did it. We're a mess, but we got him into the seat without breaking anything. Now what?"

"I'll get his luggage when I store the carpet," Randy says.

When he picks up the gun case Randy says, "What the devil is in the case? It weighs a ton."

I roll my eyes. "You don't want to know. That way you won't worry."

"I'll take your word and not ask. Next I'm off to Boston to pick up a possible new client for BMK and take him to Atlanta. Brooks told me to hurry as I positively must park the jet at our airport by 1:00 p.m."

"Enjoy a safe trip. You may be ferrying our friend here back home. I'd lock up the liquor cabinet if you do."

"No, I'll remove all the booze from the plane. That's the safest thing to do. Ironic his name being Boozer. He certainly is."

"You don't know what happened to him, do you?"

"No one said a thing to me except I was to pick him up at Battle Mountain, Nevada and deliver him and his equipment here. All I knew was his name."

"Let me take a moment to explain Emory for you. He was a Navy Seal, one of their best. He has seven successful missions to his credit, all dangerous. His many citations include four Purple Hearts and a Navy Cross. His last action was in the ill-fated Somalia action where, wounded seriously, he dragged two wounded comrades to safety under heavy fire. They ended up in the wreckage of a stone building right at the shore with seven Marines. They were under attack by a sizeable enemy force using heavy machine guns and mortars and they were low on ammunition. They had a radio and called for air support. They were told to use laser pointers to guide the aircraft fire.

"At great personal risk the men took turns laser marking both the mortars and the machine guns. Someone up the hierarchy ordered the air support to stand down even after they were on their way. In fact, one was only minutes away. They could hear all the orders and counter orders on their radio. The pilot of the closest plane reported he had the target in sight and begged for permission to complete the mission. He cursed when permission was denied.

"When they realized no air support was coming, they decided to make a dash for a Zodiac inflatable boat with a large outboard motor pulled up on the beach. Of the ten men in the building, only five made it to the Zodiac and two of them were hit as they headed out to sea. Miraculously, one of the Marines was only slightly wounded. He took the Zodiac out to an American ship about five miles offshore. All five eventually recovered. Emory was the only one of the Seal team to survive. He swore if he ever found out who issued the stand down order to the aircraft he would kill him.

"He refused to report for duty when he recovered. He said he was through with the US Military no matter what they did to him. They gave him the Navy Cross and an honorable discharge. He never got over the betrayal as he called it, never forgave the Navy. He accuses the Navy of murdering five men including two of his team. That's why he drinks, to forget that betrayal. Sober, he's a loyal friend and a model citizen, but still haunted by the ghosts of those comrades who died around him. That betrayal will always haunt him."

"Wow! That's some story. I now think of him in an entirely different light. Take good care of him. I hope I get the chance to ferry him home. I will consider it an honor. Now, safe travels and good luck in whatever you are doing."

"We will, thanks, and have a safe flight," I say through gritted teeth. Emory's story always makes my blood boil. At quarter after seven we leave.

"Let's stop at the first place where we can buy some coffee. Will you try to put some down his throat while I drive? Should we take him to a hospital Emergency room? What do you think?"

"I think both. We're half an hour from Flagler Hospital east off of US 1 south of town. There may be a coffee shop in the airport. Pull right over and I'll run in and try to buy some coffee."

In about ten minutes Andrea comes out with a large plastic container of coffee. She climbs into the back seat while I turn onto US 1 and head for St. Augustine. (7:25)

"I don't want to drown him so I'm trying to sit him up. Can you stop and help ? . . No, he's trying to sit up on his own. Emory! Can you understand me? I'm trying to give you some coffee. Please drink this. Here's a straw."

"Wha? Who you? Burp!"

"I'm Andrea. I'm with Calder Voss. Remember him? We're on our way to St. Augustine. Drink, drink this coffee,"

"Calder? From the geo well? Calder needs my help."

"Yes he does, but right now you are in no condition to help anyone. Drink this coffee which may help. Please, Emory, drink this coffee, NOW!"

I ask, "Is he drinking any at all? Should we gag him to throw up."

"Yes, that's it, Emory, drink! . . . He's drinking some. . . . Come on Emory, down the hatch. That's it. Drink . . . it . . . all . . . I can't believe him. Calder, he drank the whole quart of coffee right down."

"He's probably been this route before. Let's stop and buy some more coffee."

"Stop. Let me out. Gotta pee!"

"Okay, Emory. Hold on until I find a place to stop."

"Gotta pee! Gotta pee!"

"Okay, here are some bushes. I'll go out and help him."

Emory is out almost before the car stops. By the time I reach him, he is already going and not even close to the bushes. I stand between him and oncoming traffic to shield their view the best I can. When finished, Emory staggers back to the car. He is still drunk.

"I'll stop at the first place we can and buy some more coffee. He's . . . what's he doing now. I can't see him in the mirror."

"He crashed again, Calder. He went sound asleep as soon as he lay down. I'm calling Carol's. I need to warn them and find out if they can come up with any idea of what to do. Can anyone else fire that weapon of his?"

"I suppose I could in a pinch. I saw him fire it several times. It's a simple bolt action rifle with a monstrous kick. Trouble will be firing at a long range. I don't know how to compensate for range, windage or anything else. We must somehow sober him up enough so he can aim and fire. When you talk to Carol, ask if she knows a doctor she could call to find the best way to sober him up. It can be done, but I don't know how. Maybe she could look it up on the Internet."

"Hey, a place for coffee. You nearly passed the driveway. I'll call while you buy the coffee."

I brake hard and still struggle turning in the driveway. The biggest to go cups are 16 ounces so I buy two of them. The coffee is hot so I dump in a bunch of ice from the soda dispenser and hurry back to the car. When I reach the SUV, Emory is outside with Andrea, barfing. I hand her the coffees and take over holding him.

"Did you reach Carol?"

"Hardly! No sooner had you walked away when he starts heaving. Luckily I got him out of the car before he upchucked. He's a mess. I'll call them right now. You'll be occupied for a while."

"Call me right away when you find out anything."

✳   Monday, September 7, 2015, 8:00 am   ✳

Emory keeps stopping and wiping his mouth with a rag Andrea gave him. He seems to be through barfing. We start for the car, and he starts in again. This goes on for several cycles before Andrea steps out of the car, phone in hand.

She explains, "Brooks is furious. He called the BMK emergency care center to ask if they had any suggestions. No one called back yet. Carol left a message for her doctor to call back saying she has an unusual, non life-threatening emergency and all she needs are instructions. In the meantime, she is looking on the Internet. . . . Found no good information yet. How's he doing, still barfing?"

"I don't know. He stops and seems to be through, then starts up again after a few minutes. Could be he's done now. He's been calm for a while. Let's give him some of that coffee before he gets back in the car."

Andrea brings one of the cups out of the car. "Emory. Can you understand me? Here's some coffee for you. You must drink."

"Drink? Oh yes, I'm thirsty."

"Between the booze and the barfing he must be dehydrated, maybe even dangerously so. While I'm giving him the coffee, why don't you go in and bring some water, as much as you can carry."

"Okay, will do."

When I come out with a case of bottled water, Emory is sitting in the open car door drinking coffee.

"Man, I am dying of thirst. Can you give me one of those bottles of water?" Emory seems quite lucid at the moment. "I am so sorry, Calder. And your name again, ma'am?"

"Andrea, Andrea Mitchell."

"I'm sorry I let you down. I don't know what gets into me. No, that's not true. I'm quite familiar with those devils in my head. I start thinking about things, remembering, and the booze is the only thing takes them away."

"Emory, we understand, both of us. So does everyone else that hears your story. However, you must be completely operational in a few hours in order to try and stop this pending disaster. This menace will destroy our nation totally if not stopped. Right now you and your rifle are our only hope. Any suggestions to help sober you?"

"Sleep seems to be the only thing. Usually I sleep for twenty or thirty hours after one of these benders. I drink a couple of gallons of water and in a day or two, I'm back to normal."

"Unfortunately, there is nowhere near that kind of time available. We need to place you and your rifle up at the top of the lighthouse in a few hours. They plan to fire the rocket between two and three this after noon. They could fire at any time once they run their ship aground and stabilize it. That ship may already be in the harbor. Absolutely no one else can or will try to stop this. Every government official we contacted about the danger refused to believe what we tried to explain to them, let alone act. Idiots!"

✳ 8:10 am ✳

Calder gets a call from Brooks. He speaks rapidly.

"Meet us at Flagler Hospital, ASAP."

"Barring an accident, we should arrive by 8:40. What's cooking?"

"Carol convinced her doctor to help us. Come to the ER and ask for Dr. Rawlings. Everything will be ready and waiting. Now go. We can talk later."

"We're gone," I say as I hang up.

I yell, "Climb in. We're headed for Flagler Hospital ASAP." I pull back onto US1 and head south as fast I can safely maneuver.

"We're to go to the Flagler Hospital ER. Should arrive in about half an hour if I hurry. Brooks and Lydia will meet us in the emergency room. The others will join us at the lighthouse and be ready to go up top when we arrive. Remember, we are photographers taking special photos of the 450th celebration. Emory's case holds our camera equipment. No one other than our crew will be permitted on the lighthouse while we are on the platform."

Emory says, "My mind's quite fuzzy, but beginning to come around. I need some sleep. May I sleep till we are there, please?"

"Stretch out on the back seat, but first, did you finish the coffee?"

"Drank the last drop a few minutes ago, before those two bottles of water. I think it's going to stay down. Now, may I sleep?"

"Just till we arrive at the hospital."

We drive in silence the rest of the way, through town and past the 312 intersection to the Flagler Hospital ER. We have quite a hassle getting him out of the car and into the chair.

"So that's Emory." Brooks says as we wheel him in. "An IV will be ready for him. A nurse will insert the needle and hook up the IV. She's an expert."

"What are they giving him? Is it dangerous?" Andrea asks the nurse.

"A regular IV solution, water, a bit of glucose and some salt. We'll give him as much as we dare. We'll also give him an injection of vitamin B with a fairly strong stimulant. In half an hour or a bit more, this should provide as near to sobriety as you can hope for. Time is the only thing that will remove the alcohol from his system. His liver is what does the job. He should be somewhat close to normal for most of the time. He should drink as much water as he can. All this will dilute the alcohol in his blood. It won't sober him up completely, but should help a lot. It's a lot less dangerous than all the alcohol he's ingested. He will get a big time headache if he doesn't keep drinking lots of water. A good meal will help, if he can keep it down, protein. A plate of scrambled eggs would help."

"Emory, I'm Brooks and this is Lydia. You're getting an IV and will receive a shot to help counteract the alcohol. The nurse needs to know how much you weigh in order determine the amount to use. Emory, wake up. Now!"

I ask, "Andrea, will you hand me one of those water bottles?"

I take the cold water and pour the entire bottle over his head. That wakes him up.

"Emory, This is Roberta, a nurse. She needs to know how much you weigh in order to determine how much of this IV you can handle."

"Uh, okay, about two sixty, two hundred and sixty Pounds, okay?"

Roberta steps up, rubber tubing and syringe in hand. "Give me your hand, palm up and make a fist. This will sting a bit."

She wraps the tubing around his upper arm and feels for a vein. "Your veins are nice and fat. That makes this easier."

Soon the IV is in place and the bag is hanging on its holder. The injection in his other arm goes fast and smoothly. Roberta places a band aid with a bit of cotton over the injection site and makes him close his elbow by raising his forearm.

Roberta explains, "Half an hour from now you should be feeling much better. That should last about four hours. Drink lots of water or you will be hit with a monstrous headache lasting several hours. A couple of Aleve will diminish but not stop the headache. I suggest that when we are through with the IV you lie down and try to go to sleep."

The IV and shot done, Emory goes back in the SUV and lies down. He immediately falls asleep.

Lydia smiles. "Roberta told me in about thirty minutes he will wake up feeling much more sober. I hope the job is done in less than five hours. After then he won't be worth a plugged nickel for the rest of the day."

Brooks urges them to hurry. "Let's run his equipment up to the top of the lighthouse as fast as possible. We must be ready by the time they run their ship aground. My spotter called to advise me the ship, Arrow of Allah, has already passed through the inlet and is maneuvering toward the shallows. We're guessing they will take a couple of hours to run the ship aground and flood the hull to the point where the launch platform can be stabilized enough for a launch. I don't know how long it will take to level the launch platform. Lydia will stay with Emory to make sure he is okay. The rest of you are needed to help take the stuff up the staircase to the platform. The time is almost ten. If my guessing is close, we had better be ready to fire that weapon by no later than ten-forty-five, in case they are ready ahead of schedule. Let's move, people."

After a fifteen minute delay by the guards who wanted to examine our photographic equipment, we climb up the spiral staircase to the platform. By the time we reach the platform, Emory joins us and is in much improved condition. The platform surrounding the light is hard and smooth and surrounded by a guard railing. We place some furniture pads on the platform to provide a comfortable place for Emory to lay prone, aim, and shoot. He might be waiting for a long time. He is soon sitting on the pads assembling his *shootin' arn* as he calls it. Unfortunately, a gathering crowd of onlookers is on the ground below. We do not need that. At the first shot, they will be a surprised group of people.

Brooks mounts a large pair of binoculars to the railing and watches the activities on the ship.

He says, "We are lucky as the ship is pointed directly at the lighthouse. The missile will be fully visible from here. Oh, oh. They seem be having some problems leveling the platform. The ship is slowly continuing to sink further into the bottom. The rocket is forward of the cabin and covered with tarps for protection and to hide it until the last minute"

Andrea says, "They might not be able stabilize it. Will you shoot even if they are unable to fire their rocket?"

"Don't worry," I say. "They came this far and with no return. They'll fire the rocket and hope, even if the platform is unstable."

Brooks says, "They seem to have stabilized the rocket. You don't suppose they'll fire without removing the tarp covering, do you?"

"Not if they want any degree of accuracy they won't," Emory says. "Leaving a tarp on the nose could cause the rocket to wander off course, even turn over and crash. Don't worry. They will remove the tarp before they fire."

Andrea asks, "Emory, how can you possibly climb down with your rifle after firing? Everyone will be looking for you and your loud gun. Both will be hard to hide."

Emory laughs. "That's one thing I worked out in detail. I used Google Earth to inspect the lighthouse and grounds. I worked out a way to take my gun and me off the lighthouse and away while no one is looking. My gun and I will be off the lighthouse and gone within five minutes of my firing the shot that blows the rocket. When the SUV drives calmly out of the parking lot, my gun and I will be gone. While all the spectators are occupied looking the other way, I'll be gone like a will-o'-the-wisp. All you'll need to do is deny everything and act ignorant of what happened."

Andrea smiled. "I don't suppose you are going to tell us?"

"Nope! You will be amazed if you do see me go."

"Emory, that's interesting, but how close are you to being ready to fire?" Carol asks.

"The range settings are in and locked. The Coriolis and gravity variables are calculated and entered. I even compensated for a slight mirage effect. I will be aiming for the lowest part of the rocket I can see. That should be the fuel section and will destroy the rocket without hitting the EMP bomb, That's one thing I don't want to hit with a high impact round. Windage is the only real problem. Without wind instruments it's a seat-of-the-pants setting. Brooks, will you use those binoculars to tell me how close my first shot is. I can then adjust for my second shot."

"Can do, Emory. How will I know where the shot goes, and how do you want me to tell you where your shot hits?"

"Don't worry, you'll see where. Even if it misses the boat, you will see a large dark spot in the water followed by a big splash. Try to estimate how far the shell passed from the center of the rocket. The adjustment will take five or six seconds. The second shot should take out the rocket. If I miss again, another adjustment will need to be made. Brooks will tell me where the shot hits and I will once again adjust accordingly. If we need a fourth shot, I'll know something is wrong and begin shooting a pattern. Don't worry, one way or another we'll blow the damned rocket."

✷ Monday, September 7, 2015, 1:00 pm ✷

More than two hours later, Brooks says. "Emory, wake up and do your thing. They are removing the tarps."

"I'm wide awake and ready," comes from the prostrate form behind the gun.

The wait is over. At quarter to one they are ready, slightly ahead of schedule.

As soon as the tarps are gone, Emory, using the telescopic sight, reports, "A strong offshore breeze makes for windage problems. I'm guessing between 30 and 45 miles per hour. I'll aim upwind, but since I don't know the wind speed, I will be guessing. Brooks, look to the right of the rocket for the hit. Show time. Here goes nothing."

BLAM!

The gun fires off with a powerful report. The people on the open ground in front of the lighthouse react by huddling down and looking around like frightened sheep.

Brooks says, "Your shot went to the right, missed the rocket and hit the rear of the ship. It took out a large chunk of the gunwale. The crew reacted by running around looking. They are wondering what happened. Then they heard the report and started looking this way."

Emory makes some adjustments and fires again. People on the lighthouse grounds begin running away. The two security guards run toward the lighthouse, looking up and shouting.

Again Brooks reports what he sees. "This time you barely missed to the left, hit the cabin behind the rocket and left a hole. The crew is running around frantically."

Emory makes another small adjustment. A blast of fire comes up from around the rocket which starts to rise. Someone shouts, "They fired it!" Emory's rifle roars again. A long second or so passes as the depleted uranium round flies toward its target. Spinning to maintain its attitude, the heavy shell maintains a perfect trajectory even when buffeted by the strong air movement near its target. It strikes the fuel section of the rocket dead center. For a tiny fraction of a second a white ball of splattering fuel appears before the flames ignite the expanding cloud of fuel. The resulting fireball erupts and rises high over the water. It makes no loud explosive boom, just a huge, earth shaking *WHUMP* as the fireball expands rapidly, rises, and then turns into a giant black cloud sprinkled with orange flames which rises rapidly. The flash of heat is felt for miles, especially on the lighthouse. The Arrow of Allah is a huge mass of flames out on the water. The rocket is gone and the EMP bomb remains unexploded where it falls, somewhere among the wreckage of the boat. Everyone on the platform is jumping and shouting for joy. Those on the ground wonder what happened. They heard or felt the *whump* and maybe even saw parts of the fireball through the trees. The screaming shouts of joy from those on the lighthouse platform merely confuses them. The guards have no idea what to do.

"We did it!" the conspirators on the platform shout over and over hugging each other.

Emory alone does not join in. He is busy. Sitting on the platform and working rapidly, he disassembles his gun and packs it in its case. Packed with the gun are the three spent casings and several intact shells. When all is packed, he picks up the case, slips the case strap over his shoulder, and walks to the rear of the lighthouse platform. Out of sight of those on the ground and using climbers rope and equipment, he quickly rappels down with his rifle to the ground amidst the trees and shrubs behind the lighthouse. Once down, he calmly pulls down and rolls up the rope, packs it and all of the climbing hardware in the case with the rifle, picks up the case and once more slings it over his shoulder. Stealthily he moves around the museum and out to their rented SUV. He places the case in the space under the folded-down third seat, climbs in, and drives off casually toward Carol's house, all according to plan.

Everyone on the grounds including the guards are so absorbed with the lighthouse and the occupants of the platform, they don't notice Emory or the SUV quietly leaving the parking lot. When the five on the platform see the SUV leave, they unfasten the binoculars, pick up the furniture pads and proceed down the staircase, a camera hanging around each of their necks.

As they near half way down, one of the security guards shouts up to them, "What the hell were those explosions?"

With a questioning voice Brooks replies, "That's what we would like to know. They about blew out our eardrums. Could you see that huge fireball from the ground? We even felt its heat."

One of the onlookers says, "You mean you don't know what made those loud bangs? We thought they came from the platform."

Brooks answers, "They came from close nearby. We all covered our ears. Mine are still ringing. They messed up our picture taking big time. I almost dropped my camera when that first explosion came."

Another of the people on the ground says, "You must be kidding. Those explosions all seemed to come from the top of the lighthouse."

Brooks, now near the bottom of the spiral staircase, turns and looks up at us. "Where did those explosions come from? Do any of you know?"

Carol answers. "Sounds, sharp sounds like explosions, can echo and reverberate so much they seem to come from many directions, isn't that right people."

A chorus of yeahs and rights come from us as we descend the staircase. This is followed by a few confirming comments from the crowd gathered near the door. Soon many in the crowd are muttering in agreement. As we five conspirators walk slowly through the crowd and to our cars, numerous comments come from the growing crowd.

"What did you see from up top?"

"Did you see where those explosions came from?"

"Were you the photographers who were up on the lighthouse when those bombs went off?"

As we walk to our cars, I look at Andrea and burst out laughing.

"Can you believe the impossible luck? We couldn't have pulled it off any better if we planned it."

"How did that happen? Did Brooks say anything to you, Lydia?"

"Not a word. He used a spur of the moment stroke of genius. The rest of us picked up on his lead immediately."

I say, "I couldn't believe when, the crowd joined in. Then the security guards joined right in with the crowd. That was unbelievable."

Andrea says, "Yes, and did you see how Emory snuck away? I never even saw him go. One minute he was on the platform with his gun, and a few minutes later, he drives away in the SUV. I saw the SUV leave without a single person around him."

I told them. "I saw. He used a rope at the back of the lighthouse. He rappelled down with his gun case slung over his shoulder. He pulled his rope down to him in less than a minute. Special forces training taught him how to do that. He's an expert at that kind of action."

Carol urges everyone, "Let's move quickly, but without seeming to be running away. The sooner we leave and head for my house the better. Some official authorities will be here looking for answers. The longer we've been gone, the better for us."

Within a few minutes we all drove away, heading for Carol's.

Chapter 45 - Aftermath at Carol's

A s Andrea and I drive, we listen to the radio. News is breaking with all kinds of speculation on the part of the news media.

"We interrupt this program for a breaking news story. Here's Cindy Newman from St. Augustine."

"A huge fireball erupted in Matanzas Bay within a mile of the St. Augustine Bridge of Lions a short time ago. A small ship blew up in flames in the shallow water inside the entrance to the bay. As yet we don't know about injuries or what happened. We are trying to find out the name of the ship and will tell you when the information is available. Fire rescue is rushing to the scene. We heard reports of several explosions near the lighthouse. Witnesses say they seemed to come from the lighthouse, but no sign of any kind of damage is visible. It might have been some very loud fireworks, aerial bombs celebrating the 450th. That's merely a guess on our part. We don't know as yet. What an unusual coincidence that the explosion of the ship and the explosions at the lighthouse occurred at the same exact time. One of our reporters is on his way to the lighthouse to interview witnesses. We do know nearly a hundred people were on the grounds near the lighthouse. As soon as we receive any new, confirmed information, we will come on and report to you. This is Cindy Newman reporting from Sky Witness News."

"There are a lot more surprises coming. I wonder how the media will react when the full impact of what happened hits?" I comment.

"Calder, this is going to be a spectacular few days of news. Especially if Brooks succeeds in sending out the information he plans to. I can't wait to learn what he is sending and to whom."

"We'll be at Carol's in a few minutes, then you can ask."

As we drive in the driveway, Carol, Lydia, and Brooks are stepping out of Carol's car.

Lydia calls out, "Hurry inside. Emory turned the TV on and Brooks wants to compose his message and send it ASAP."

Soon all of our eyes are glued to the TV news break Emory found. The scene is the smoldering hulk of The Arrow of Allah obviously taken from a news helicopter. The name in arabic, Sahm'Allah, is clearly visible on the relatively undamaged stern of the ship. The media has yet to translate the name. Brooks, who is fluent in Arabic, reads it for us. Now several police and rescue boats are on the scene.

The commentator says, "They pulled a number of badly burned crew members from the water. So far none of them are alive. The explosion was forward of the center of the ship. That is where it burned completely down almost to the waterline. Nothing is left of the cabin or crew quarters. The hull of the ship appears be steel, but the decks, the gunwales, and cabin were all of wood and burned. We spoke to the marine fire chief who described the explosion and fire as quite unusual. He told me the fuel tanks of the ship could never cause such a large, hot fire. 'They must have been carrying a large quantity of extremely flammable liquid to cause such a fire,' were his words."

The scene shifts to the lighthouse and another reporter. "This is the St. Augustine lighthouse where a number of explosions were heard, but no damage or evidence of any explosions is visible. Several people suggested they were aerial fireworks, but they would leave considerable smoke. No one reported seeing any smoke anywhere near the lighthouse. The explosions remain a complete mystery. It's an unusual and suspicious coincidence that three explosions near the lighthouse would happen at precisely the same time as the explosion on the ship. You can count on it. Those kinds of coincidences don't happen. Your Sky Witness News team will keep digging until we get some answers. This is Mel Bertram, reporting for Sky Witness News."

✳   ✳   ✳

An hour later, Brooks has everyone checking for news of his message. Something interesting is happening near the still smoldering hulk as they wait. Four military helicopters with pontoons arrive from the Navy base at Mayport. Immediately after landing they launch four Zodiac boats with two Marines on each one. The Marines immediately begin chasing all occupied boats away from the wreck, clearing a larger and larger circle. Another helicopter, a large one, flies in and hovers over the wreck. They quickly lower a group of six divers in scuba gear. At this point the camera shot disappears, replaced with a studio shot of a reporter.

"This is Tim Dalton of Sky Witness News. I'm sorry folks, the Marines ordered us to stop filming and take our news helicopters away from the area. They gave no reason."

He is handed a note which he reads. "I was just informed that we received a frightening and detailed message from an unknown source telling us what happened to the ship, and why. We were requested, no, ordered by federal authorities to refrain from divulging the content to the public as a matter of national security."

At this point, Brooks laughs and tells us, "Wait for what happens next. This will blow their minds, and all their security."

Lydia says, "Some of you don't know Brooks can send messages almost anywhere by coded satellite, impossible to trace. He's far ahead of anyone else in digital communication and security expertise. He can also put messages and worms in virtually any computer that uses the Internet. He's been making digital magic since he was a kid."

Tim is joined on the TV program by another man who speaks privately to him for several moments, then takes over the mic. He says, "I don't think the efforts of our government to stop the dissemination of that message is going to work. Apparently every news service, radio and TV network, many private stations, the Internet, and all of the social media received copies of the message. It has been posted everywhere and is available to the entire world. Let me read the text to you as we received it. I quote, word for word."

'This is a message from a concerned free citizen of the United States of America. The explosion and fire in the harbor of St. Augustine, Florida were caused by the destruction of a powerful rocket made in North Korea and transported to the Matanzas inlet at St. Augustine. It was carried by a ship named The Arrow of Allah. Its mission was the complete destruction of the United States and its origin is obvious. The rocket was destroyed by the courageous effort of a retired US Navy Seal who at great personal risk, managed to destroy the rocket just as it was being fired from the ship. The payload of the rocket was an atomic bomb designed to create an intense Electro Magnetic Pulse high in the sky above the center of the country. That powerful EMP blast would destroy every piece of solid state electronics in mainland America, southern Canada and northern Mexico. Planes would no longer fly, their control, navigation and communication equipment destroyed. Most would have crashed killing everyone on board. Cars, trucks, and buses would cease operating, except old ones without electronic systems. Our manufacturing, distribution, and transportation systems, even our electric power systems would shut down, their control systems burnt to a crisp. People would die and many would starve to death as the food supply could not reach those needing food.

'At this instant, that bomb lies somewhere in the shallow water in or near the remains of the Arrow of Allah. Our hope is that the bomb is now inoperable, destroyed along with the rocket that carried it. Unfortunately we will not be truly safe until the entire bomb is found and disarmed or is known to be inoperative and cannot explode. My understanding is that our military is trying to find the bomb and if necessary, disarm it. I certainly hope they succeed. Sadly, many in foreign lands and even inside the borders of our nation hope they fail and the bomb explodes. They are the enemies of America both foreign and home-grown. They include those who devised this diabolical scheme of destruction.

'With the help of a network of like minded patriotic citizens, I discovered the recent and long discussed anthrax by balloon threat to be a complete hoax, a red herring designed to hide the real menace being prepared in total secrecy. I am sorry to report this hoax continues to be promoted and advanced by individuals in our own government and news media, inadvertently by most, but deliberately by enough to keep the false rumor going. As an American who loves his country, I contacted various members of both our government and the media and warned them about the hoax. My warnings were ignored even though I provided confirmable proof. One commentator, the one who acknowledged receipt of some of my messages, referred to them as 'pathetic rants of a crackpot with no credibility.' He did not divulge their content. This shows how effective our enemies are in manipulating the media, guiding public opinion, and stopping these warnings.

'Three weeks ago some of my numerous informants found out the details about the Arrow of Allah, the EMP bomb, and where and when it was to be fired. Once again I sent warnings which were ignored. All real Americans are fortunate we were able put together a team of patriots and find a way to destroy that rocket. No longer can any person or organization deny the efficacy of our information. Once the bomb is found, disarmed, and the parts examined, the truth will be known, if no one hides it. After this confirmation we will provide known loyal Americans in our government the names and details of most of the enemy agents and their organizations who infiltrated our government and our news media. Some in the media will label this a witch hunt. Those who do this will identify themselves as enemy agents masquerading as journalists within our own news media. We will call it what it truly is, a traitor hunt. I will let the American public decide which it is. I wish and pray for good fortune for all loyal Americans.'

"That is the entire message. Nothing deleted or edited. As yet there is no word on the bomb, or if it was found. We will let you know when we receive any word. I will return you to Tim Dalton, your news reporter. Tim?"

Brooks turns off the TV and grins. "How do you like them apples? I hope they soon find the bomb and make certain it is harmless. There's not much we can do but wait and pray."

Lydia says, "Why'd you turn off the TV? I want to watch what's happening."

"I'm sorry, Lydia. Until the Marines let the cameras roll, all TV will show is the studio. I doubt they will allow any filming until they locate the bomb and it is disarmed. Radio news will likely be the first to announce the finding and handling of the actual bomb. Why don't we turn on both and mute the TV? That will give us the best of both."

Calder shouts, "My God, most of the population will be trying to run away from the bomb. Highways and bridges will be jammed with frightened people. It could become a major disaster. Quick turn on the radio and TV."

The radio comes on with local news. "This is Cindy Newman reporting some important news from Sky Witness News. The Navy divers found the bomb and report it is disarmed. Apparently the explosion that destroyed the rocket and the ship also destroyed the firing mechanism of the bomb. The remains of the rocket and bomb are being taken to an undisclosed destination to be dismantled and examined.

"I am pleased to report the mass exodus from the area stopped almost as soon as it started. Bridges and other traffic bottlenecks are still jammed, but thankful drivers are calmly sorting the jam out. Traffic should be back to normal within an hour or so. The police reported a few minor accidents because of the rush, but no serious injuries.

"Here's news from the Navy. They report the markings on the bomb are in Arabic and the rocket is of North Korean origin. This positively confirms what the message read earlier said. The person who sent the message was dubbed The Minuteman by news reporters. We would like to know who it is, but no one is admitting to being The Minuteman yet."

"And I hope they never find out," Brooks says emphatically. "Remember that everyone. For the safety of Lydia, Ralph, and myself, no one must ever divulge this secret. The Minuteman will be number one on every Islamic terrorist's hit list because of this action. None of us should ever tell anyone what we did. Public knowledge would be a potential death warrant for any of us. We were all extremely fortunate. My guess is no one will be able to tie any of us to the lighthouse. As long as we never show up again, or are never seen by security or any of those visitors we walked through, we'll be safe."

"Fortunately, I'm the only one who lives here," Carol says. "I'll need to be careful about getting my picture in the news for a year or so. I also wonder why the Navy released that information so quickly? Such a release is quite unusual. They usually hold that kind of information for a long time."

"The government is undoubtedly smarting big time for not releasing the information in Brooks's message," Andrea says. "They have a long way to go to win back the confidence of the public. I wonder how long that will take?"

Lydia adds, "I wonder what they will do with all the information about those enemy agents, the spies and saboteurs that will show up on the list we send them from Brooks's and Jack's information?"

I reply, "The ACLU will surely jump in to protect all those bastards. The stupids will join our enemies and denounce any effort to deport any of the illegal or seditious aliens on the list. The only thing that will stop it is a huge public clamor. Americans may have finally had enough because of the bomb and the revelations about our enemies. They could wake up to the reality that there are many enemies among us masquerading as citizens."

Emory adds his comments. "I'll be pleasantly surprised if any of those traitors in high places are ever touched. After what happened to my team, I doubt we will ever clean out our house, even the military. All thanks to all those do-gooders and multiculturalists cramming their destructive agenda down the throats of so many people, and with the aid of the media to boot. As a result, we have too many enemies in high places. I hope to God I'm wrong, but fear I'm right."

"You are right on the mark, Emory," Lydia says. "All those sick so-called Americans who are obfuscating the Constitution are truly destroying the America that lead the world for so long and in so many ways, especially personal freedom. I often wonder if enough Americans are left who still believe in our exceptionalism to counter the nanny state idiots?"

"Wait, what's on the TV? Listen."

"A terrorist force flying the ISIS flag estimated at about 200 attacked the naval base at Mayport with automatic weapons including three heavy machine guns mounted on pickups. They were repulsed with heavy losses by Marines guarding the base. Apparently the Marines had been forewarned of the attack and were well prepared. Here's another late release from the same Navy spokesperson: Marines surrounded and killed or captured the entire attacking force soon after they stormed onto the base. It's unbelievable, but there was not a single Marine fatality. Using hidden tanks and armored weapon carriers, the Marines waited until the entire attacking force was inside the perimeter of the base before letting loose a withering crossfire. The battle was over in a few minutes when the remaining terrorists threw down their weapons and surrendered. About a third of them were killed or wounded before they surrendered.

"After the battle, Marines spread out through the neighborhood searching for other terrorists. They captured about forty who were found hiding in a number of small busses and SUVs that were used to transport the force to the area for the attack. None of them offered resistance. A number of weapons and boxes of ammunition were found in the busses. Marines are now going house to house through the entire area searching for any terrorists who might take refuge in houses or threatened the occupants. They also reassured the occupants, most of whom wondered what all the gunfire was about. Few had any inkling of the attack coming from the area where they lived."

Carol says, "Finally, somebody paid attention to your messages, Brooks. I wonder if there were any other attacks? Those murdering thugs were counting on all communications and transportation to be down. I'll bet there are lots of military people scurrying around trying to find your previous messages, read them, and take them seriously."

"I did send messages to a lot of the US Military warning of attacks on bases as soon as the bomb went off. That's one thing I learned from listening, that many groups of terrorists were to gather today and be prepared to attack US Military bases. I'll bet all of our military were alerted soon after the rocket exploded around the time I said it would. We're lucky they reacted so quickly. Now that I think about it, some individuals in our military took my warnings somewhat seriously and set up contingency plans just in case. I am surprised at how quickly they reacted after the rocket blew up. They must have been somewhat alerted. I'm still surprised that not one Navy or Coast Guard vessel challenged the boat carrying the missile and bomb."

Epilog

What will happen in America during the months and years to follow? Will we root out, punish and expel the enemies in our government, media, and elsewhere? Will we reawaken the diligence, patriotism, independence and loyalty that made us the most free and exceptional nation on the planet with the most even distribution of wealth for its people, or will we sink back into the anti patriotic, complacent, self-serving stupidity and rancor that marked America in recent years? Will we become the America described in the last part of the quote sometimes attributed to eighteenth century Scottish historian, Alexander Tyler, and recounted in a memorable speech by Henning Webb Prentiss, Jr. President of the Armstrong Cork Company in 1943?

Here is the quote: "The historical cycle of democracy seems to be: from bondage to spiritual faith; from spiritual faith to courage; from courage to liberty; from liberty to abundance; from abundance to selfishness; from selfishness to apathy; from apathy to dependency, and from dependency back to bondage once more."

www.ingramcontent.com/pod-product-compliance
Lightning Source LLC
Chambersburg PA
CBHW080838250626
47161CB00009B/3110